PRAISE FOR THE MAEVE CHRONICLES

"From the beginning we are caught up in a cocky irreverence that is captivating. Wrestling with destiny as all true heroines must, Maeve searches for the land of Mona and its famous Druid university. Once she is there, prophesies begin to fulfill themselves and we are swept into an adventure that tugs at our hearts and minds. This amazing book could well become a classic of women's literature."

-Booklist, Starred Review
(*Magdalen Rising*)

"Magdalene fans are in for more surprises in Cunningham's classy, sexy novel... this will be snapped up by Magdelene fans as well as Celtophiles, feminists and lovers of a good yarn—controversial."

-Booklist, Starred Review
(*The Passion of Mary Magdalen*)

"[*The Passion of Mary Magdalen*] gives readers what [*The Da Vinci Code*] does not... freedom from a false claim that historical elements in the book are factual....there is engaging language, too, such as her intriguing description of Jesus as "a man who broke Sabbath rules like fingernails."

-Kansas City Star

"[*The Passion*] offers a digestive to Mel Gibson's film, *The Passion of the Christ*, and a fascination way beyond Dan Brown's exploitation in *The Da Vinci Code*."

-Pages Magazine

"As you might imagine, *The Passion of Mary Magdalen* is hardly traditional—and is all the better for it. Sassy, salty, sexy—all three words aptly describe Cunningham's prose, her heroine, and *The Passion of Mary Magdalen* as a whole. Those without an irreverent sense of humor will likely balk, but that just leaves more copies for the rest of us to pass around."

-LesbianNation.com

"Amazing story!"

-Historical Novels Review
(*The Passion of Mary Magdalen*)

"This year's must-have summer reading."

-Kink Radio
(*The Passion of Mary Magdalen*)

"*The Passion of Mary Magdalen* is certain to appeal to fans of historical fiction, to Celtophiles, to those who love fantasy, to feminists, and to anyone who loves a great story. Unconventional? Controversial? You bet. It kept me up all night, and I loved it!"

-MyShelf.com

"I now see *The Passion* is a Pagan book.... I am sitting on the edge of my seat waiting for the sequel."

-Pagan News and Links

"High adventure, magic, a detailed look at the world of the ancient Druids, and the most engaging heroine of recent goddess fiction come together to make *Magdalen Rising* a must-have for any lover of historical or goddess-oriented fantasy."

-SageWoman Magazine
(*Magdalen Rising*)

"Cunningham weaves Hebrew Scripture, Celtic and Egyptian mythology, and early Christian legend into a nearly seamless whole, creating an unforgettable fifth gospel story in which the women most involved in Jesus's ministry are given far more representation...."

-Library Journal
(*The Passion of Mary Magdalen*)

"If you're a *Mists of Avalon* type, you'll be thrilled with this sexy, women-centric take on life."

-Hot Picks, The Advocate
(*The Passion of Mary Magdalen*)

"Gleefully iconoclastic!"

-Kirkus
(*Bright Dark Madonna*)

Red-Robed Priestess

Other Novels by Elizabeth Cunningham

The Return of the Goddess, A Divine Comedy
The Wild Mother
How To Spin Gold, A Woman's Tale

THE MAEVE CHRONICLES
Magdalen Rising
The Passion of Mary Magdalen
Bright Dark Madonna

Poetry
Small Bird
Wild Mercy

Musical Work
MaevenSong: A Musical Odyssey through The Maeve Chronicles

THE MAEVE CHRONICLES

RED-ROBED PRIESTESS

~ *A Novel* ~

ELIZABETH CUNNINGHAM

MONKFISH BOOK PUBLISHING COMPANY
RHINEBECK, NEW YORK

Printed in the United States of America

Cover illustration: Leonardo da Vinci (attributed), Mary Magdalene, c. 1515. Private collection, in trust of The Rossana and Carlo Pedretti Foundation, Los Angeles, California.

Book and cover design by Georgia Dent

Library of Congress Cataloging-in-Publication Data

Cunningham, Elizabeth, 1953-
Red-robed priestess / Elizabeth Cunningham.
p. cm. -- (The Maeve chronicles ; 4)
ISBN 978-0-9823246-9-1 (hard cover : alk. paper)
1. Mary Magdalene, Saint--Fiction. 2. Women priests--Fiction. 3. Women, Celtic--Fiction. I. Title.
PS3553.U473R43 2011
813'.54--dc23

2011026199

ISBN: 978-0982324691

Monkfish Book Publishing Company
22 East Market Street
Suite 304
Rhinebeck, New York 12572
www.monkfishpublishing.com
USA 845-876-4861

for Hawksbrother

PREFACE
WELCOME TO MAEVE'S WORLD

WELCOME to the fourth and final volume of The Maeve Chronicles. Be assured that you can read the last book first and the first, last—or in any order you please. Each novel is designed to stand alone as well as to continue the account of Maeve's adventures from birth to, well, you'll see. Occasionally passages from other volumes of The Maeve Chronicles are woven into this story. These quotations appear in *italics*.

When I began to write Maeve's story in 1991 I did not expect to write more than one book. Early in the writing, I decided I would have to write three, a good Celtic number. In *Magdalen Rising*, I planted the seed for the story you are about to read, hinting that Maeve had a connection with the rebel Queen Boudica. Partway through the writing of *Bright Dark Madonna*, I realized that the story of Maeve's return to Britain required its own volume.

Red-Robed Priestess surprised me by being the most compelling and challenging book I have yet written. There were times when I sorely wished I had not entwined Maeve's life with Boudica's, for this story has demanded that I stretch my imagination and my heart beyond where I thought I could. That said, I also found it deeply satisfying to revisit places and people Maeve knew in her youth as she comes full circle. Longtime readers, I hope you will, too.

Readers new to Maeve: her resumé follows, everything you need to know about her to begin reading *Red-Robed Priestess*. Welcome to Maeve's world.

Maeve's updated curriculum vitae

She was born on the Isle of Women in the Celtic Otherworld and raised by eight warrior-witch mothers.

She attended druid school where she studied to be a bard—until she got kicked out, which is to say exiled, for saving the life of a certain young foreign exchange student.

She left behind an infant daughter stolen from her arms by the druids.

She was sold into prostitution in Rome and worked at a brothel named The Vine and Fig Tree.

She eventually founded her own holy whorehouse in Magdala, Galilee.

She is a healer with "the fire of the stars" in her hands.

She loved and loves Jesus from "before and beyond time in all the worlds."

She never became his disciple—or anyone else's, for that matter. She is not disciple material.

She has a daughter by Jesus named Sarah.

She gave the Early Church a run for its money and had a particularly fraught relationship with Paul of Tarsus.

She is incapable of staying out of trouble.

She is telling her story to you. Now. In the twenty-first century.

Historical Note

Boudica (also spelled Boudicca and Boadicea) Queen of the Iceni tribe is an historic figure. Other historic figures appearing in this novel include Boudica's husband Prasutagus, her two daughters, Governor Gaius Suetonius Paulinus, and the Roman procurator of Britain, Catus Decianus. Accounts of Suetonius's attack on the druid Isle of Mona and of Boudica's uprising, the last significant rebellion against Roman rule in the British Isles, can be found in the writings of Roman historians Tacitus and Dio Cassius. For more information on my research, see source acknowledgments.

I followed historic fact as closely as possible in depicting the battles as well as the events and conditions that led to them. *Red-Robed Priestess,* like all The Maeve Chronicles, is a work of fiction. My interpretation of the characters and their relationships to each other and to Maeve is entirely imaginative.

PROLOGUE
OUT OF RETIREMENT INTO THE CELTIC KNOT

I AM SUPPOSED TO BE OLD NOW, though age is not as fixed or reliable as it seems. I am not as wise as I might wish, but I feel I have earned the right to make cryptic prophecies impossible to interpret till after the fact—just as old women did over me all my life. I would like to hum and sing maddening songs like Miriam of Nazareth, my eternal mother-in-law. I wouldn't mind my own well of eels like Dwynwyn of Mona and young girls coming to me for love divination so that I can console and ridicule them in equal measure. Or a valley with a sacred spring and nine hazelnut trees, like the Cailleach on Tir na mBan. At the very least, I should have doves flocking to me like Anna the Prophetess of Jerusalem and flying where I bid them from my outstretched hands.

In fact, for awhile I had a pretty good arrangement in a cave in southern Gaul where the local populace revered me for no particular reason and brought me offerings, kegs of wine, wheels of cheese, fruit and flowers in season. They said my presence in the cave filled the valley with the smell of roses.

That's what I had in mind for my retirement.

Here is a word of advice: If that's what you want, too, don't leave any unfinished business. Or have a daughter who won't let you rest till you face a past that is really none of her business, no matter what she thinks. Don't adore her so much that you'll do anything she says: leave your comfortable cave, travel across the whole of Gaul on horseback (when you've hardly even ridden a donkey) to return to a people who exiled you long ago for meddling in high mysteries, exiled you so thoroughly that they did not expect you to survive, or they would not have sent you out with the tide, beyond the ninth wave, in a tiny boat without sail or oar.

Above all, do not ever leave behind a child, your first-born, forcibly taken from your arms, a child whose name you don't even know, a child you can never forget no matter how old you've grown. No matter how much or little she might welcome your return—if you can ever find her.

These circumstances, mine, pretty much rule out a peaceful, permanent retirement and pretty much dictate a last quest, foolish, heroic or both.

A story must begin (or begin again) somewhere, though this story, I must warn you, is a story mostly of endings. I will forego adjectives for now. You might argue that the story really began long ago, when I conceived this child by rape, or before that, with what drove that man, my own father, to such madness. The end of a story is in its beginning, the beginning in the end, as a seed lies at the heart of the fruit.

But there are many strands to a story. I have already told many of the tales that will weave their way into this story. But there is one new strand, one new twist that binds all the stories into an impossible Celtic knot, one that with all my blinding flashes of second sight I never saw coming.

And so I begin again.

Here. On the northern coast of Gaul on a full moon night in Spring.

PART ONE

Water
Back From Beyond The Ninth Wave

CHAPTER ONE
CLIFF HANGER

I WAS WALKING on a cliff path looking across the narrows of the sea to the answering cliffs I could just see on the other side. It was clear as the moonlight that some catastrophic flood had torn these shores apart, and they still looked stark and startled at the sudden separation.

I had, perhaps foolishly, slipped away from our camp, leaving my daughter Sarah and her companions sleeping, exhausted from a hard day's ride. Despite my own fatigue, I was wakeful, restless. I wanted some time alone. Tomorrow we would go to Portus Itius to seek passage across the channel. Though we had traveled for weeks over land, for me the short voyage over water would mark a point of no return in my return to what my people called the Holy Isles, as if my life would come full circle and then close over my head—like a noose. Well, not quite a full circle. I had been set adrift from the Isle of Mona far to the west of here. And I would set foot again in the Holy Isles in the southeast, at the very site of the recent Roman invasion, the fortress settlement at Rutupiae.

I had to wonder: did the druids still blame me for the Romans' success? Did they still think the human sacrifice I had stolen from under their noses would have saved the Holy Isles from Roman occupation?

"Well," I stopped and spoke aloud to them, as if they were even now arrayed in judgment against me in their full-feathered druid regalia. "If it makes any difference to you, it didn't save him, either. Esus, the one you called the Stranger. Not in the end. Not from the god-making death."

I stopped and gazed at the water. More than sunlight, moonlight appeared to make a path, illuminated the cross-hatch and ripples of the waves, a bright way across the darkness. My vision skimmed along it to the shining cliffs and the dark land beyond. I had been punished thoroughly for my crime. Not only by exile. The druids had stolen my daughter from my arms only hours after her birth and sent her to foster among the Iceni in the east, territory now under Roman rule.

Who was lost, who was saved? Who was wrong and who wronged? And how do you tell the difference?

I closed my eyes and listened to the sound of the pebbles on the shingle beach below being raked and rolled over and over by the waves. Even at this height, I could smell the seaweed; the tide must be going out.

"Beloved," I whispered; for he had said he was always with me, although I did not always believe it. "I am going to find her at last, the misbegotten child of a misbegotten child. Do you remember the druids called her that? I am going with our own Sarah. It was her idea, really. But *cariad*, what if I am making a terrible mistake? Before Sarah came to find me, I had such terrifying dreams. Maybe they were meant to warn us away. What if I am taking Sarah into danger? What if—"

I cannot say that he laughed. It was more that I felt his laughter. *Sarah*, I heard him say, *Sarah, our pirate daughter. You can't protect her any more than you could protect me. She is what she will be.*

And all at once, I felt so light that a breath of wind could have carried me over the cliff. I stretched out my arms to steady myself and opened my eyes. Then I saw him some distance away, standing perilously close to the edge. Or not perilously, since he was a vision. I began to walk toward him, delirious with joy; he so rarely appeared to me. Then he turned toward me—

A Roman soldier with worn chain mail glinting in the moonlight beneath his cloak, his hand on the hilt of his short sword.

Behold, whispered my beloved, *one of these, the least of my brethren.*

Then he was gone (typical), leaving me alone to face an armed man, one, moreover, who looked as though he were seeing a ghost. All my instincts went on the alert, and I began to fear for the man more than fear him. He was awfully close to the edge, and if he lost his balance, even for a moment, he could easily pitch over. I wondered what dreadful apparition he saw in me. Roman soldiers, I knew from long experience as a whore-priestess, could be very superstitious, easily spooked, especially if separated from their rank and file. When on the march, they set up camp each night in perfect formation, each man to his task, each man in his place. What was this one doing off by himself on a cliff edge? I decided to stay very still and do nothing to alarm him.

"How do you come to be here?" he spoke at last in a low voice, his Latin distinctly of the senatorial class, though he was dressed as a common foot soldier.

Something was definitely amiss here.

"It is a beautiful night for a walk," I answered carefully in my own best Latin.

"How do you come to be here?" he asked again. "This night of all nights."

As he took a step towards me, I got a better look at his face and almost cried out. He looked so like the boy Esus, and yet how could he? His face was lined and his short-cropped hair almost as grey as mine. It was the eyes, something about the eyes, the pleading, the intensity.

"Tell me, how do you come to be here?" He stopped too far away for me to touch him or I might have reached out to steady him, to steady myself.

I don't know why I didn't just say: I walked. I came here for the view. Or why I didn't just back away from this man who was, quite possibly, mad. But there was something about his bearing that drew my attention and held it.

"Long ago," I heard myself answer, "I left behind a child. I wanted to look out across the water—"

My voice caught in my throat. And he looked at me, his face opening in wonder. How had I thought him old a moment ago? He was just a boy.

"That is why I am here, too, beloved."

Beloved, he called me beloved, and in that voice, that deep voice, so like Jesus's, that carried without effort. What was happening here?

"I should never have left you," he went on. "I should never have left you alone with them."

I did not even have to close my eyes to see Esus racing on horseback across the Menai Straits with the druids in pursuit and me, about to give birth, remaining behind on the shore. It was as if no time had passed. No time at all.

"I made you go," I spoke to the boy who had blamed himself for years. "They would have killed you. I made you go. I commanded you in the name of the god of your forefathers."

The soldier hung on my every word, as if he was starving and only my words could nourish him.

"I should have defied you," he accused himself again. "I could have fought them all, killed them one by one. Instead, I killed you. It was my child you died of. Tell me the truth. It was *my* child."

As I stared at his anguished face, I felt my own story recede. It came to me: I had a choice to make, a terrible, beautiful choice to make. And I must make it now.

"I never blamed you, beloved," I said slowly.

"But you died believing I had abandoned you. How could you not?"

I gazed at his eyes, eyes darker than the moon-flooded night; eyes shimmering like scrying pools. I let my ordinary vision blur. I looked. I saw.

"You were meant to be a warrior, beloved, it was all you had, all that was left of the old ways, the only way you had to restore honor and fortune to your family. I knew that, beloved. No one knew it better than I did. I knew you would never abandon me. I knew you would come back."

His tears caught the moonlight, tiny oceans with their own tides. I wanted to touch them, but he knuckled them away with his fist like a small boy, and then his anguish gave way to something else.

"Then how could you—"

He choked on the words; I could taste their bitterness in my own mouth.

"Go on," I urged him. "Say it."

"How could you marry my enemy? How could you let him raise our child to his knee, claim our child for *that* family, *that* lineage."

This time, I did not look into his eyes. I closed mine and prayed to Isis, the compassionate, and Mithras, the soldiers' god. And yes, to Jesus, too, in whose name I had received countless men. Show me what he needs to know. Give me the words to speak.

"They blackmailed my father," I said, opening my eyes and looking directly into his. "Claimed they had evidence that my father was part of the conspiracy to kill Germanicus. Tiberius was looking for people to punish to deflect guilt from himself. I was the price they demanded for silence. Even so, I might have risked everything, run away, left my family to ruin. Then word came that you were dead. Dead in Germania."

He let out a wordless sound, not a cry or a sob, something more elemental like the groan of a tree before it breaks. I did not know the rules of this strange engagement. Maybe there weren't any. Maybe it didn't matter. A wind sprang up, and blew back my hood. Out of the corner of my eye, I saw my hair streaming out in the moonlight. Red hair. And the man before me was a beautiful, heartbroken boy.

I held out my arms to him, and he ran into my embrace.

Now here is where it gets a little dicey. Now we aren't just talking about a trick of moonlight, his apparition of me or mine of him, as a long-lost (long dead) love. Two warm-blooded bodies are pressed together here.

"How can this be?" he whispered, holding me tight. "No one returns from the dead, alive again."

That's what *you* think, I did not say. Perhaps I ought to have said: Listen, I'm not who you think I am. I should go now. But I didn't. Even with his armor cutting into my flesh, I wanted to stay right where I was, pressed against this man who was at once so strange and familiar.

"Love is as strong as death," I said at last.

There, at least, I spoke the truth, and after that there were no more words. We needed our mouths, our tongues for other things. And it was sweet, I tell you, sweet. We let go of each other only to strip off armor and clothes. We made a bed with my cloak, and a shelter with his cloak and spear, and we drew each other down and made love for hours as the moon sped west and the night chill turned to mist. It was not like learning a new lover at all. It was as if I had known him all my life. We fell asleep entwined.

* * *

In the night, I had a dream, so vivid, I still wonder if it was a dream. I am standing with my beloved on the tower at Temple Magdalen on a full moon night, just as I stood with him long ago before he left, feeling his warmth become insubstantial, as if he was a patch of sunlight.

"Stay this time," I whisper.

When I turn to him, he is the soldier, not warm but cool as moonlight. And we are not at Temple Magdalen but on the edge of the cliff. I reach to pull him away from the edge, but he backs away from me.

"Don't," I cry, "you'll fall!"

Then he disappears, and all at once a hawk lifts from the cliffs, moonlight bright on its underwings.

My heart trembles in my small dove's breast.

CHAPTER TWO
THE MORNING AFTER

HE WOKE FIRST, sitting up abruptly and almost dislocating my arm as he flung it off him. I opened my eyes and saw him staring about wildly—looking everywhere but at me.

"I'm in a fog," he said.

"Well, yes," I agreed. "We both are. It must have rolled in while we were sleeping."

Dawn had broken, but the fog was so dense, it would not be safe to go anywhere until it thinned—not with the cliffs close by and the ground slippery with damp.

"Who are you?" he said, his voice so low in his throat it was almost a growl.

(It is not so unusual, really, what happened to us. Don't most people fall in love with their own longings? Then wake up months or years later to wonder who *is* that person lying next to me? The true lovers stay to find out.)

I propped myself up on my elbow and glanced at the hair tumbling over my shoulder. Grey again. I looked at my arms and my hands, quite muscular from weeks of riding, but with a few age spots that might have been more noticeable if not for my freckles. Continuing my survey of myself, I lifted up one of the breasts that the druid Nissyen had once told me men would die for. My breasts were still beautiful, I decided, round with perfectly shaped nipples. No need to hide away in shame, though I might want to cover myself against the chill. I began to feel around for my tunic.

"Why did you deceive me?"

(Another common question of disillusioned lovers.)

He was on his feet now, his back turned to me, though I couldn't see much in the fog, pulling his tunic over his head, and fretting that his chain mail, beaded with dew, would have to be dried and oiled. In my earlier career as a whore, I had seen many men dress in a hurry. Sometimes it was a relief, but after a night like the one we'd just spent, his haste was depressing—and insulting.

"If you want me to answer you, look at me," I insisted.

I knew he must be avoiding the sight of me. He had no doubt woken in horror to discover that his lost love returned from the dead was in fact an old woman he'd never laid eyes on before. If I hadn't been the one he was reviling, I might have felt some sympathy for him. *Some*. As it was, I felt increasingly irritated as he fussed with his chain mail shirt and tried to get it over his head. He probably had slaves who dressed and armed him. I got up, still fully naked, and helped him pull down the shirt. Even with me standing in front of him, he still looked away, staring out blindly into the fog. I studied his profile. His nose was prominent but not overly beak-like. The lines around his eyes and his mouth had taken some time to get so pronounced. I did not think they came from smiling. His hair still had some black underlying the grey, but I doubted he was any younger than me, or not much.

"What's the matter?" I said, as I bent down and picked up my tunic, a bit damp but not as nasty as his chain mail. "Don't the Romans have stories of maidens disguised as hags and hags disguised as maidens? Heroes are supposed to be able to look on both with equanimity and not be taken in by appearances. But then maybe you're not."

I slipped the tunic over my head.

"Not what?"

"A hero."

"Etruscan," he muttered, still not looking at me.

"What?"

"My family is of old Etruscan stock, not Roman. But among all peoples, there are plenty of stories of sorcery. Of women, old and young, true or treacherous, who use magic for their own purposes."

I supposed that might be an accusation, but it was too veiled to bother with.

"Why did you take her form?" he pressed when I remained silent. "What did you hope to gain?"

"Man," I said, taking a step closer to him. "I don't know who your gods are, but beware lest they take note of your ingratitude."

"Ingratitude!"

He finally turned to face me, and I felt the full effect of his eyes, dark, angry, with just a hint of gold that made them seem raptor-like, the eyes of someone accustomed to scanning for enemy or prey. For a moment, they took my breath away, but I was not about to let him intimidate me.

"Ingratitude," I repeated. "All the gods I've ever known are touchy about spoiled mortals scorning their gifts, whining about timing or presentation."

The fog swirled around us as the temperature began to shift. We almost appeared to be floating. But our eyes were locked.

"Woman," he addressed me, and I felt unreasonably grateful that he did not call me old woman. "Is that what you call yourself? A gift from the gods?"

I think I might have slugged him, if I hadn't seen the tiniest of smiles fighting with the grim set of his mouth.

"It makes no difference what I call myself. That is what I am—or was to you last night. The moonlight, your guilty conscience, or your own eyes might have deceived you, but what I saw of your past, the words I spoke to you in her voice, were all true. The gods merely used me as a way to get through to you." I paused for a beat. "Maybe they shouldn't have bothered."

My indignation warmed me more than the cloak I retrieved and wrapped around me, the cloak that had been our bed.

"And who did you see in me?" he asked.

His question took me by surprise. He seemed so completely absorbed in himself. I wasn't sure I wanted to answer.

"Was it the father of the child you left behind?" he persisted. "You were not only speaking of my child."

I looked at him again. His eyes were intent, his whole body still, patient. Predators were patient, I reminded myself. What did he want from me?

"I saw someone I loved as he looked when he was young and tormented, just as you must have been." I decided I could say that much. "He was not the father of the child I left behind. Your story and mine are not identical. When I realized what was happening to us both, I chose to let go of my story and step into yours. The gods did the rest."

He made no response other than an almost imperceptible shrug. Though he had previously accused me of deceiving him, I sensed that he did not like the implication that I had been more aware than he had—and therefore more in control. Yet, for all I had glimpsed of his past last night, I knew nothing of his present or why his standing on the cliffs had unleashed memories that had overtaken both of us.

"Last night when I told you why I wanted to look across the water, you said 'that's why I'm here, too.' " I took up the role of interrogator. "What did you mean by that? And why were you away from your camp disguised as a foot soldier?"

He gave me a severe look, or tried to. Again, I could see him fighting a smile. That's why the lines around his mouth were so deep; he had to force himself to frown.

"Those are too many questions from someone who has still not answered the question I asked first."

"I've forgotten what it was," I told him.

"Who are you?" he said and then again, "who are you?"

Now I shrugged and turned my face away. The fog was still thick and swirling.

"Who I am would mean nothing to you."

I did not intend to lie, but as soon as the words were out, I knew I had. That I was the daughter (however unacknowledged) of the late famous druid tactician Lovernios and the foster-daughter of Bran, the late king of the Silures, a tribe that still resisted Roman rule, might very well mean something to an officer (for I was sure he was) in the Roman army. But then I had seldom identified myself by my patrilineage. My mothers (all eight of them) did not think it was nice. I saw no reason to begin now.

"I am descended from a goddess," I answered, truthfully so far as I knew. He need not know which goddess. That might give him too much information.

He snorted. It was almost a laugh, albeit a derisive one.

"So am I. Venus or, as the Etruscans call her, Turan."

"Right, you and Julius Caesar." I am afraid I sneered.

"As a matter of fact, yes," he said. "And that's your answer to why I was looking over the water last night. I wanted to see what Caesar saw the night of his first invasion. It was a full moon then, too."

I did not believe him. He might be some scion of the illustrious Caesar's family, but that was not why he had come out last night.

"You mean the cliffs his fleet was dashed against when a storm came out of nowhere on that full moon night?"

My opponent, as I had come to think of him, gave me a sharp look.

"You seem to know a lot about it."

"Common knowledge." I waved it away; I did not want him making any connections between me and the druids, who had likely orchestrated the storm. "Also, when I was a whore at The Vine and Fig Tree in Rome, my tutor made me read *The Conquest of Gaul*," I added to throw him off further.

He looked so amazed, I felt irritated.

"You've never heard of a literate whore? I'm sure the Etruscans had them."

"You were a whore at The Vine and Fig Tree?" he said.

"For a short time. Why?"

"My mother's family owned Priapus Court." He named a rival house that also catered to the senatorial class run by down-at-heel aristocrats, who had been on the wrong side of some conspiracy or another.

Goddess, Rome, the heart of the Empire, was such a small town.

"So you're a whore. A literate whore," he amended.

"Was a whore," I said. "I'm still literate." Though I won't tell you in how many languages, I added silently, or that I still consider writing the ruin of civilization.

"Well, that explains some things."

Such as why I opened my legs without a second thought? I decided not to ask.

"And you're a whoreson soldier," I countered, "who abandoned his post to indulge in raptures about Julius Caesar on a moonlight night."

His face darkened. For a moment, I thought he might hit me.

"My mother wasn't, she didn't–"

He could not bring himself to say the word mother and whore in the same sentence. I caught a glimpse of the boy who had no doubt endured the taunts of senators' brats who ran in packs and had nothing better to do than torment other people. No wonder he had joined the army. The only way to restore his family's honor and fortune, as I–or whoever she was–had said to him last night.

"I meant no disrespect to your mother," I spoke to the boy. "Not that there is any shame in being a whore."

But the boy had vanished again. The man looked away from me, glowering at the fog, which still had not lifted.

"I have to get back," he said almost angrily, as if he held me responsible for the fog and everything else that had gone wrong in his life.

"Not a problem," I said.

I knew I could do it. I had spent seven years of my life as a wind whistler bartering passage on ships for fair weather. But I wasn't thinking now of all those bustling Mediterranean ports. Maybe it was being so near to the Holy Isles, my mothers' island Tir na mBan, the holiest one of all. I closed my eyes and was back inside my earliest memory: my womb mother, Grainne of the golden hair, standing by the sea in the midst of one of my other mother's miasmic fogs, waiting till the light filled the chalice she made with her arms, till warmth spilled over the world again.

When I opened my eyes, I was standing with my own arms catching the sun, and the last of the mist melting into light. The soldier stood perfectly still, looking at me, not with awe or amazement but with something else, I still can't quite name. Knowledge comes closest.

"Who are you?" he asked again, but it didn't sound like a question.

My arms lowered themselves into a gesture of bewilderment.

"Never mind," he said. "Someday, I will find out."

"And someday I will find out who you are," I answered, just for effect.

Then, with a sudden chill the spring sun could not touch, I knew I had spoken the truth.

"Ma!"

It was my daughter Sarah calling from somewhere down the hill, her voice more frantic than I had ever heard it. "Where are you! Ma!"

"Coming!" I called.

I gave my opponent, my lover, one more look, and then I turned and ran.

CHAPTER THREE
ON GUARD

LET ME PAUSE for a moment before I run pell-mell into Sarah. Let me give myself the time I did not have then to take in what has just happened.

For all its ups and downs, my life has at least had a coherent plotline. One of the simplest there is: the great love, the one love that transcends time and death. Granted I have lived as a widow much longer than I would have chosen (a condition resurrection complicates) but there's a kind of poetry in that, too. As lovers, Jesus and I will never grow old. We are still standing together under the tree in the resurrection garden, the tree with the golden leaves that shed their own light.

That's in eternal time, of course.

In ordinary time I have been with two other men since Jesus. My encounter with the first man was the most disastrous mistake (to date) of my life, though you could say it worked out in the end. My affair with the second man was a deep comfort, a healing balm I thought was meant to last me the rest of my life. (If you are itching with curiosity, I am talking about Paul of Tarsus and John the beloved disciple in that order, but that is another of the stories I've already told.)

If you are disconcerted or even affronted that I have had a night of soul-shaking love-making with a man who is not Jesus, so am I. It was not supposed to happen, never mind what I said last night about the terrible, beautiful choice I had to make. Do I regret that choice? I don't know yet. Right now I only know two things for sure:

My body feels incredibly young and happy.

I am not going to tell Sarah a thing.

We collided midway down (or in her case up) the hill, having sighted and lost sight of each other on the zigzag paths. She was out of breath from climbing, and I was out of breath for other reasons. She hugged me hard, then held me away from her, her hair so dark the sunlight made rainbows in it, her eyes gold and at the moment, fierce.

"Where *were* you?" she demanded. "We were worried sick."

I tried not to laugh. I suppose I really had behaved irresponsibly, but here was my daughter who had run away from home when she was twelve now in a tizzy because her old mother had spent the night out. There was a sweet irony to this reversal of roles I couldn't help but savor.

"I went for a walk on the cliffs. I suppose I should have let you know."

"You could have *fallen*!" she protested.

You could argue I *had* fallen, but let's leave that metaphor alone.

"It was bright moonlight," I pointed out. "Anyway, I guess I must have dozed off."

"You *guess*?" she eyed me balefully.

"And when I woke it was foggy, so of course I waited—"

"Waited," she repeated skeptically.

"All right. So I cleared the fog when I saw it wouldn't lift. You could have done it yourself, if you were so worried."

"I'm not as practiced at weather-witching as you are. And I couldn't concentrate. I was too upset."

She looked away. This was a huge admission for Sarah. I touched her cheek lightly and turned her face back to me.

"I'm sorry," I said.

She looked at me for a long moment. I wondered what she saw and if her fear had been for more than my footing on the cliffs.

"Come on, let's go," she said, turning to lead the way. "Alyssa and Bele are breaking camp."

"Is there breakfast?" I called after her, suddenly aware of how hungry I was.

"The usual."

Oatcakes. Celtic comfort food. The taste of home. I had to admit that the food of my long exile had been a lot tastier. And I felt a hunger pang of homesickness for ripe olives and figs, dark red wine from the vineyards of Temple Magdalen.

Alyssa and Bele (short for Cybele)—two of the sometime pirates who had kidnapped and/or rescued my daughter, depending on who was telling the story—had the horses saddled up and ready to go by the time we got back. After I had sprung the pirate cohort from prison in Ephesus, the whole crew had retired from terrorizing the seas and taken up horse breeding and trading in the Camargue, a suitable occupation for neo-amazons and a profitable one in any horse-crazed Celtic territory. All three of them were determined to take the horses with us across the Channel.

On horseback—or off, come to that—we were quite a sight. The three younger women wore *bricae* (the derivation of the word britches) and short tunics. Alyssa, tall and slim, had long blond braids and might have had a lot of trouble with men pursuing her, except for the formidable scar on her cheek and her lightning speed with a sword. Bele was short and round, built like a Hittite fertility goddess with dreadlocks piled high like a beehive. Sarah's black hair always came unbraided to make a dark halo around her head. I have already mentioned her eyes, golden as the leaves on that dawn tree in the garden. Then, there was me, the grey one (once called Red) a game old woman (of sixty something, if you must know) doing her best to keep up. We were all armed with short swords and daggers, though Alyssa insisted we keep our weapons concealed under our cloaks to give us the advantage of surprise should any fools think us easy targets.

"Let's go by the beach," said Alyssa, already mounted on her mare Seafairy, dainty and silvery white, who did indeed look as if she had risen from the surf. "The tide's on its way out. It'll be quicker than going inland to pick up the road again."

"And maybe we'll avoid being interrogated at the city gate," Bele added. Her horse, a Celtic pony, was small, brown and extremely sturdy. She was named Hippolyta for the legendary Amazon queen, but we called her Hippo for short.

"What are the odds?" shrugged Alyssa. "The port is controlled by Romans."

"What port isn't?" Sarah put in, as she gave me a leg up onto Macha, yes, an older grey mare indigenous to the Camargue, well-matched with my age and speed. I was fond of her, and she tolerated me.

"And of course we have your lovely many-tongued mother to smooth our way," added Bele. "You've been awfully subdued this morning, Mother of Sarah." That had been their title for me ever since I came to their rescue in Ephesus. "I hope you didn't get a chill, out all night on the heath."

I could feel myself blush from the roots of my hair to my toes, but no one noticed. Sarah was busy mounting her own horse, Blackfire, a young mare of Arabian stock bred with wild pony that only Sarah could handle, a lethal weapon on legs.

(Note: It's true we all did resemble our mounts and, yes, it was a deliberate choice on the part of my companions, centaur wannabees to a woman.)

"I'm fine," I assured her. "Just a little tired."

"And maybe you're just a tad nervous now you're almost back," said Alyssa. "You never told us, what will the druids do if they figure out you're that traitorous wench they thought they were rid of?"

She led the way at a leisurely pace down a slope toward a shingled beach.

"I don't know," I answered. "There aren't any stories that I ever heard about anyone returning from beyond the ninth wave."

"I guess we'll find out, then," called Bele cheerfully. "They could always ship you off again. Or maybe execute you in some grisly way. I never did understand why they didn't sacrifice you before."

"These matters are very delicate, Bele," I said, trying to sound serious but feeling giddy. "You have to get the timing right. I threw it off."

"And besides," put in Sarah, "a sacrificial victim has to be without fault. That's why they wanted my father. It's an honor to be sacrificed, not a punishment, and my mother had a *bad* attitude."

Sarah had certainly grasped the theological subtleties. Somehow she managed to sound equally proud of her father's suitability as a candidate for sacrifice and her mother's lack of it. I decided to be pleased.

"I hate to disappoint you all," I called out; as always I was falling a bit behind. "But we're going to be landing on the other side of the country in a Roman-controlled port. I doubt the druids of Mona will trouble themselves to meet me. It's unlikely we'll see any druids at all."

"Mother of Sarah," said Alyssa over the clatter of hooves. "Don't be so modest. It doesn't become you."

When we all arrived on the beach, we stopped and looked out over the channel. The land on the other side was nowhere to be seen. It was not just haze obscuring the view; it was a bank of fog. We stood in full sunlight under a blue sky with blue water sparkling before us until everything suddenly disappeared.

"I thought you dispersed the fog," Sarah said. "It's only moved out to sea."

"I thought I had, too." I agreed, trying to remember that moment.

When I'd opened my eyes that morning, I had only looked at the soldier, not out over the water, and then I had run to meet Sarah.

"Don't worry about it," said Bele. "It's still early. It'll be gone by the time we get to Portus Itius."

"We've got a clear stretch of beach here," Alyssa gestured. "Let's race."

Alyssa and Bele took off, but Sarah waited for a moment, still staring out at the strange fog bank. At last she turned and looked at me. I nodded, a wordless acknowledgment.

Something is wrong.

Then Sarah took off after the others, easily making up the distance, and then passing them both.

"Come on, old lady," I said to Macha. "Let's show them what we can do."

And we managed a respectable gallop under the cliffs where only last night my hair had gleamed red in the moonlight.

* * *

We arrived at Portus Itius in good spirits after our race. But no sooner had we dismounted and entered the gates than we were surrounded by soldiers.

"That must be one," said the chief guard, pointing to me.

I don't know if they actually intended to seize me without further ado or if there might have been some niceties that were cut short when my companions drew their swords.

"On guard already, Mother of Sarah," barked Bele.

A little clumsily, I drew mine, too, and the next thing I knew I was in the midst of my first sword fight.

Not my first practice fight, by any means. In my early youth, I had been trained in all the warrior arts by my mothers, and in my old age, my daughter had been giving me a refresher course. But this was for real. I had an armored, helmeted, shield-bearing man thrusting at me with a gladius. And though Sarah had drilled me in Roman parrying techniques, I remembered very little and clanged away with no finesse and with one object only—to keep that sharp piece of metal away from me.

"Ma, don't look at the sword. Wide-angle vision," Sarah called out calmly, as if this were just another drill.

As soon as my vision widened, I noticed blood spurting from somewhere, heard a few groans and curses, distinctly male.

"Hey!" I shouted. "Easy does it, girls." I am sorry, but I still thought of them as girls. "Someone could get hurt."

"That's the idea!" said Alyssa.

"But we can't win!" I shouted, as much to my astonishment, I twirled and kicked my opponent's wrist, knocking his sword from his hand.

"Why not!" cried Bele, landing a blow on her opponent's helmet that sent him reeling.

"Use your wide angle vision," I said. "They've got *backup*!"

That's the last thing I remember before my opponent charged me with his shield, coming up under my chin and knocking me backwards.

When I came to, I had no idea where I was or what had happened. The fact that I was lying in the dark didn't help. All I knew was that my jaw hurt, and so did the back of my head, and the small of my back. A lot. I took a deep breath, which also hurt but helped me focus. With my healer's sense, I took a quick inventory of my injuries. Serious bruises, mild concussion, strained lower back, but no broken bones or internal bleeding.

I must have been in a hell of a fight. Wait, yes, that was it. Images flooded in. I *had* been in a fight. We all had. With some Roman soldiers. I couldn't remember where we had been or why, but that much was clear.

"Sarah?" I called out, suddenly panicked. "Alyssa? Bele? Are you all right? Are you there?"

No one answered, but I heard footsteps scurrying away. A moment later, someone came back, a different someone, I thought, my senses heightened even in the midst of my confusion.

"Can you sit up?"

Jesus speaking Latin? Odd. But his voice was so comforting, and so were his arms as he lifted me up and supported me.

"Drink this."

Warm wine, laced with some kind of pain drug, skullcap maybe.

"Why are you here, *cariad*?" I murmured in Aramaic. "I'm not...I'm not dead, am I? It hurts too much. And where's Sarah?"

There was a moment's silence.

"Aramaic?" he guessed. "I don't speak that language, although my father knew a little. Only Latin, Greek, a smattering of Carthaginian, the odd Germanic and Celtic dialects, and of course Etruscan."

"Shit," I said in Latin, and then in all languages I knew. "Shit. It's *you*."

"Who did you think I was?" he answered.

"None of your business," I snapped.

I winced as he opened a shutter and let in a shaft of light, clearing up any doubts about his identity.

"Does the light hurt your head?"

Why did he have to be so damn solicitous? It confused me.

"I'd rather be able to see my enemy," I told him. "Where's my daughter?"

I instantly regretted my words. It is always a mistake to let an enemy know you have children. He could hold Sarah hostage.

"Which one of the hellcats was she?" he asked.

Insults were much better. I kept my face expressionless.

"Never mind," he said. "I can guess. The dark one with the unusual eyes."

"Where are they?" I persisted.

"They are in comfortable confinement nearby. The horses, too. All of them unharmed, which is more than I can say for my men."

I will admit it, I smirked. But only for an instant. It occurred to me that if the girls had killed any soldiers it would go very badly for us.

"I knew you were an officer," I turned to look at him. No longer dressed a foot soldier, he wore a cloak of excellent quality with emblems of high rank on the shoulders. With a prickle of alarm, I noticed that the clasp of his cloak was shaped like a hawk in flight. His personal insignia? "In fact, you're a general. You ordered your men to attack us. Why?"

"I am a general," he acknowledged. "But I did not order my men to attack you. I have it on good authority that you and your companions drew your swords first."

That was probably true. No, I knew it was true. The girls definitely had itchy hilt fingers.

"What were your orders then?" I demanded.

"Simply to have anyone who matched your description brought to me."

I wondered how he had described me and decided it was better not to know.

"I knew you were traveling with at least one younger woman," he added, answering my thoughts. "And don't worry that you just now let slip that she is your daughter. I already knew that."

I frowned but managed to refrain from asking him how he knew. He told me anyway.

"The woman searching for you through the fog called for Ma, and you answered. I gather she is not the child you left behind long ago."

No, I thought, this one left me behind. But then I found her. And where had it led me? To a brief inglorious career as a swordswoman and interrogation by a Roman general.

"Listen, I thought we had a perfectly decent one night stand," I changed tack. "I'm flattered, but I'm not sure it's such a great idea for us to see each other again."

He looked at me uncomprehendingly for a moment. Then he rolled his eyes.

"Don't be flattered on my account. That's not why I detained you."

"Oh, now it's detained, is it?" I said. "By what authority? For what purpose?"

"Now that you've attacked the guard of a Roman port city, as a general in the Roman imperial army I can detain you indefinitely—or worse."

I decided it was my turn to roll my eyes.

"You are, to put it bluntly, at my mercy," he informed me. "So you and I are going to have a little talk."

"Talk?" I was wary. Were we going to delve into our deep dark pasts again? Was he worried that I knew too much? "Talk about what?"

"The weather."

"Very well," I said. "Lovely weather we're having, isn't it?"

"You tell me," he countered. "Are you steady enough to walk?"

I nodded, then shook my head, but he already had his arm around me and was helping me to my feet. Maybe my old nemesis Paul of Tarsus had a point about the weakness of the flesh. My body, despite its sprains and bruises, was altogether too happy. And damn it, I liked how he smelled.

"Come on," he said. "I want to show you something."

He led me out of the room into a courtyard where I shielded my eyes against the light, afternoon light I guessed by its slant. He kept his arm around me and guided me to a staircase that climbed to a watchtower. My eyes now better adapted to the light, I saw that we were in a Roman military fort, laid out on a grid pattern like all Roman forts and towns. I scanned the complex to see if I could figure out where prisoners might be kept, but my opponent hadn't brought me up here to gather intelligence about my immediate surroundings.

"Look," he said, keeping a firm grip on me with one hand, pointing with his other across the channel.

The same bank of fog was still there, maybe halfway across the channel, even thicker if possible. Now it also swirled and billowed as if it were not a low-lying fog but a huge tumbling thunder cloud that had come down too low and gotten caught in the narrows.

"Looks like nasty weather on the other side," I observed, keeping my tone light and conversational.

He *said* he wanted to talk about the weather. If he wanted anything else he'd have come out with it. He remained silent. I sensed he was having some inner debate with himself.

"What do you know about it?" he said at length.

I didn't look at him, but I could feel his tension.

"Why should I know anything more about it than you?"

"You're a weather witch," he stated.

I stopped myself from saying, how do *you* know. I knew very well how he knew. It was my own fault. I had been showing off that morning. Shamelessly.

"I know enough about weather magic myself," he added, "to know that there's something strange about that fog bank."

"Maybe there is," I said noncommittally. "But just because I cleared a little morning fog so you could get back to your post doesn't mean I have anything to do with what's going on across the water."

"I didn't say you did," he said. "I thought you might be interested in clearing it."

"Why would you think that?"

"Don't play games with me," he dismissed my evasion. "It's a waste of time, yours and mine. You want to cross the channel. Don't bother asking me how I know that. No one travels to Portus Itius for any other reason. You've clearly come a long way and on some very fine horse flesh. Last night you were out gazing across the water. You're going back to find that long-lost child. You're going back to where you came from—and I'll lay odds you're druid-trained."

There was no point in denying any of that, but I wasn't going to confirm it either.

"You must want to cross the channel yourself and in a hurry," I observed. "Or else you could wait until the weather clears and not beleaguer innocent travelers."

"Not innocent anymore," he reminded me. "But yes, I need to cross the channel. I have an appointment in Pretannia."

"And a son you've never seen before," I added.

"How do you know it's a son?" His grip tightened and he turned me to face him.

"Who was it that just said it's a waste of time to play games?" I demanded, struggling not to lose myself in his eyes. "What do you want from me?"

"I want you to see," he said fiercely. "I want you to look into that fog and *see*."

I knew, whether he did or not, that he wanted more than weather magic.

"If I agree, what will you do for me?" I stayed cool. "None of my services has ever come cheap."

He looked at me disbelievingly. He clearly was not accustomed to being challenged.

"Did you forget that you're at a disadvantage?"

"Just answer my question," I said.

"I'll let you and your women go without the punishment your crime merits."

My women. His men. Amusing to think of myself as a fellow commanding officer—especially as nothing could be farther from the truth. But if I could bring off the deal I had in mind, my women would be immensely pleased with me.

"Not good enough," I said.

"State your terms and be done with it."

"I want safe passage across the channel for us and our mounts, no matter what I see or don't see, no matter what I can do or not do about that fog. And your pledge that any troops under your command will not trouble us further in any way."

He just stared at me.

"Take it or leave it," I said for good measure.

"I could take or leave you," he retorted. "Leave you to rot in prison."

I shrugged and turned back to the view.

"As you will."

Now it was a waiting game. I kept my head down, to prevent any inadvertent visions. In fact, I was not at all confident that I could see anything. But he didn't need to know that. I wondered why it hadn't occurred to him that I could just make something up.

"I agree to your terms," he finally spoke. "Just tell me the truth, and don't think I won't know if you are lying. I have something of the sight myself."

"Then why do you need me?"

"I don't know," he admitted, sounding honestly perplexed.

In that moment I couldn't help but like him.

"All right," I said. "I'll do my best."

CHAPTER FOUR
THE VIEW THROUGH THE FOG

PART OF ME remained standing on the tower, close enough that I could feel the heat of his arm that almost touched mine. The rest of me flew out over the water, feeling the low sun graze the underside of my wings, hearing the cries of other birds, catching the prevailing wind from the west until, all at once, I found myself flying blind, swirled and tumbled in a knot of winds. I was inside the storm, and there was nothing to do but surrender to it, follow its chaotic pattern, its wild logic.

I don't know how much time passed. For awhile I lost all sense of myself even in my bird form. There was only the sound of the wind, and then not even that. When I came to myself again—if I did actually take form—I was on a tiny tidal island, gazing out at a stretch of sand and a body of water much narrower than the channel I had just left.

"About time you showed up," someone spoke from behind me.

I turned and saw Dwynwyn, the old woman with whom I had changed shapes when I rescued my beloved so long ago. The old woman who had spoken a prophecy neither of us had ever forgotten. *You are the lovers of the world.* She was still wearing her blood-red robe, her necklace of small skulls stark in contrast. Her white hair still floated on the wind.

"Not that either of us is really here," she added. "I just thought it would be as good a place as any to talk."

"You don't live on your island, anymore, Dwynwyn?"

For, of course, now I recognized it; it hadn't changed in all the years I had been gone. The sheep still grazed. The wind still blew over the wild grasses of what was little more than a tidal dune. No doubt the oracular eels still swam in their well waiting for foolish young girls to come feed them.

"Only in the way you will always inhabit that swanky cave they're going to name after you."

"Are you dead, then?" I asked uncertainly.

"That's a crude way to describe the comings and goings between the worlds, lamb chop." Dead or alive, terms for food and endearment were still one to her. "Haven't you learned anything in all your years of wandering to and fro, loving and losing, losing and loving? Are you still as young and brash as ever?"

Considering recent events, I thought the answer might very probably be yes.

"Dwynwyn," I said remembering my errand. "Did you brew that storm?"

"What storm would that be, cabbage?"

"The one," I said with effort, as if speaking aloud in a dream, "the one, well, it's far from here, that is, if we're here, away to the southeast."

"Away, far away," she sang, "far away, along the hard stone road that leads from here to there. That leads from there to here."

I was starting to feel cross. What was the point of coming and going between worlds, shape-shifting your way through magical storms, only to feel young and helpless again in the face of an old woman's maddening wisdom?

"Let's have a look in the well," she said.

"I have no interest in love luck," I protested.

"If only that were true, sweet pie," she sighed. "But there are other things to see. You know that better than most."

It was true, and I felt afraid. The last time she had dragged me to the well, I saw my own begetting—or misbegetting, as the druids had called it. That well was bottomless, a repository of things people could not bear to know.

"You can bear it," she spoke to my thoughts. "That's why you're here. And that's why you will be here on this island, taking my place, when the terrible things happen."

Oh, jolly, I thought. Then why did I need to bother foreseeing anything?

"I'll leave you my red robe and my skull necklace," she added. "You'll have to make do with your own hair. Come along. I don't have much time."

Who needed time when they had timelessness?

The well was still there in its cleft between rocks, almost in a cave. For a while I could see nothing but the curving swish of an eel tail lashing the surface. And then the tail turned into a road, that hard road, a rock vein or spine crossing a green body of land, for the land seemed so like flesh, hills rising and falling, like breasts, like breath. Something moved over the hard road. At first I thought it must be a plague of insects, some life form with a relentless path, like the ants that would pass through Temple Magdalen each spring.

Then I lost the wide view and plunged headlong into the vision. And for a time I saw nothing, but I could hear the sound of a horse's hooves pounding, of someone's heart pounding. Mine. I was on that road. I was riding for dear life, but not just my life, I had to bring a message; I had to warn someone.

Then I saw her.

How could I not know her in all the worlds, even though I had last seen her when she was a tiny newborn with a red, puckered face, sleeping in the crook of my arm? I tried to cry out to her, to call her by the name no one knew but me, but no sound came out. And then a terrifying thing happened: her eyes changed, her eyes became just like the eyes that had haunted and terrified me all my life, my father's eyes full of hatred, my father's face twisted with rage. I called to her again, but she couldn't see me, she couldn't hear me, and then everything went dark.

I waited but nothing happened. Was I trapped in the well, stuck in some lightless passageway between the worlds, with no sight, no self, no voice? Then I sensed I was not alone in this dark, nor was the darkness complete. Close by, someone held an oil lantern he was trying to keep hidden. He was giving furtive orders to several other men. In Latin. Now I could smell brackish water. I could hear the sound of a boat being rowed, then pulled onto a shingle beach. The men loaded some heavy casks into the boat. For just a moment the man with the lantern turned towards me, and I glimpsed his face. He looked familiar, but I didn't know why. Before I could get a closer look, he was gone.

Or I was gone. Or not gone but in several places at once: galloping over the green land, the soft land, flying over it, the hard road like a weapon, a scar. I was inside the storm, tossed by forces that hurled themselves at each other without mercy. And I was surfacing from the well, meeting Dwynwyn's blind and sighted eyes.

"Warn him," she said. "Warn him."

"Warn him?" I felt utterly confused.

"Warn who?" Someone gripped my arm.

I turned and there was the general whose name I still didn't know.

"Don't go," I heard myself saying. "Don't go over the water. Don't go."

"What do you mean, don't go?" he said, moving to stand behind me and placing a hand on each shoulder. "Look!"

The fog had gone, and the cliffs on the other side of the channel caught the last light.

"Wherever you went, whatever you did, you opened the way for us."

"No," I said. "You have to understand, I did no weather magic. That fog, that storm...." The words I wanted wouldn't come. It was as if that fog had not dispersed at all but merely changed location: inside my skull, which still ached. I didn't know how to say something I had barely intuited. It wasn't druids, it wasn't weather witches, it was the very land that made that strange, tumultuous fog, the land with its soft flesh, its hard bone, its terrible knowing. If only the Holy Isles could stay shrouded in mist forever.

"No matter, it's over now."

"It's not over," I insisted. "It hasn't even begun."

But he wasn't listening. Putting his arm around me, he led me back to the stairs.

"You will eat something and then rest," he informed me.

"I am not resting until I see my women."

"Of course," he said, going ahead of me on the stairs in case I fell. Such a gentleman.

"Are you planning to keep us confined, as you so delicately put it?" I asked.

"Should I?"

"I wouldn't, if I were you." I hoped I sounded both mysterious and menacing.

"All right," he said, taking my elbow and leading me across a courtyard. "Then you will be treated as guests and given the use of the baths and a private suite. But if they—or you—try anything, our deal is off. Make sure they understand that. Be ready to sail at first light."

My women were not as pleased or impressed with me as I might have hoped. Their noses were still out of joint from being outnumbered and forced to surrender.

"We could have fought to the death, Mother of Sarah," sighed Bele, easing herself into the caldarium. "And we would have, if they'd killed you. But when we saw you were alive, and that the general was most insistent on your staying that way, we figured we'd have a better chance of rescuing you if we pretended to surrender."

I decided it would be tactless to state the obvious, that it was, in fact, I who had saved them.

"Well, I say once we've had our baths and a good meal to hell with safe passage. Let's go commandeer one of those ships," said Alyssa, stretching out full length in the bath. "It'll be like old times. Besides, I reckon they owe us a ship after stealing the *Penthesilea*."

"Which we stole from the Romans in the first place," Sarah reminded her. "Anyway, the channel's too narrow here, and we don't know all the hidden coves or where the tide would work for us or against us."

I looked at Sarah. Was she seriously weighing the pros and cons of stealing a Roman vessel? I couldn't read her face, and she seemed to be avoiding looking my way. I gave up trying to make sense of anything and lay back and closed my eyes, almost falling into a doze.

"What did you trade for it?" Sarah's voice, low and quiet as it was, startled me awake.

"For what?"

"For our release, for our so-called safe passage."

Now she was looking straight at me, but I still couldn't fathom her expression.

"The general believes I cleared that strange fog."

Sarah said nothing for a moment, and the other two fell silent, watching us the way you might watch two cats lashing their tails.

"And you didn't?"

"No," I said without elaboration.

"You mean you hoodwinked him?" Bele kindly tried to relieve the mounting tension. "Nice work, Mother of Sarah."

"No," I said. "I didn't have to. He believes what he wants to believe."

"And he believes you did." Sarah was relentless. "Tell me, mother, how did he know you were a weather witch? He clearly had the watch on the lookout for you. Why?"

My daughter was interrogating me. Would I ever have any maternal dignity or authority? Somehow I didn't think it would help my standing to confess I'd met him on the cliffs and spent the night screwing his brains out, or my brains, whichever.

"That is not important," I said, and before she could say I'll be the judge of that, which would have really pissed me off, I threw everyone a curve. "What matters is this: I told him he shouldn't go to Pretannia. Come to that, we shouldn't either."

"What do you mean, not go?" Bele and Alyssa were speaking at once. "We've just crossed the whole of Gaul. We've got a Roman general escorting us, for Artemis's sake."

Sarah just looked at me, and I looked back, lost for a moment in her eyes, their light like the morning in the garden with my beloved.

"Tell me what you saw."

I don't even know if she spoke aloud but I could hear her. I tried to speak to her, mind to mind, send her images of the woman's rage, of the furtive man, of my own mad heart-racing ride along the hard road, of the way the storm winds writhed and twisted and flung themselves one against the other with such fury. Then I heard Dwynwyn's voice again, "You will be here on this island, taking my place when the terrible things happen."

"You can't stop it, can you?" Sarah spoke, aloud this time.

"No," I said softly. "No, I don't think so."

"I hate it when they do that, don't you?" said Bele to Alyssa.

"You mean have these deep conversations where they leave nearly everything out, so that we can't possibly understand what's going on?"

"Exactly."

"I'm sorry, Alyssa, Bele," I turned to include them. "I will say this to you, too. Go back, go back to the lives you have made for yourselves. Go back!" I felt a terrible knowledge overtake me. "Or you may never see your homes again."

"Homes?" said Alyssa. "What are you talking about, Mother of Sarah? Our wheeled tents? We can make those anywhere. We are each other's home, isn't that so, Black Sarah?"

Sarah nodded.

"You can't make this choice for us, Mother. But you could be a little more forthcoming. Who is that man? Who is that man to you?"

I met her gaze as coolly as I could and willed the blood not to rush to my face.

"I don't know who he is, or who he is to me, Sarah. I will tell you this much. I feel as though I have known him for a very long time, but I don't know why."

"I don't like him," Sarah almost growled, and if she had been a wolf her hair would have stood up along her back. "I don't trust him. You told me yourself you warned him not to go to Pretannia. Whatever dreadful thing is coming, he's part of it."

"You are very likely right," I acknowledged. "That is why I am urging you three to turn back."

"Fat chance," said Sarah. "I'm going with you, and I'm not letting you out of my sight."

"I didn't rescue you from prison—twice now," I rubbed it in, "so that you could be my jailer."

"Oh, stop it, you two," Alyssa intervened. "As far as I'm concerned, the matter is settled. If no one is willing to steal a ship with me, let's take the safe passage. Once we're on the other side, we ride off into the sunset or the sunrise, whichever (by the way, do we even know where we're going?) and we will have nothing further to do with the general."

"Hear, hear!" cried Bele.

I threw up my hands and let them fall back with a splash into the bathwater.

"It's settled then. And Mother, don't try anything tonight," Sarah admonished, sounding exactly like the general she despised. "You've done enough."

"Then try being grateful," I said between gritted teeth.

"Oh, she is, Mother of Sarah, we all are," Bele assured me. "Oh, look, there are servants coming with clean tunics for us. There is something to be said for Roman amenities. I hope they give us a good spread. I, for one, am sick of oatcakes."

CHAPTER FIVE
HOME

AT LONG LAST I was returning from beyond the ninth wave, though in fact there were no waves worthy of the name. The channel was placid, and the weather as unremarkable today as yesterday's had been ominous. As promised (or ordered) we did indeed set sail at first light on a large merchant vessel, I was relieved to note, rather than a warship. The general had a sizable escort of high ranking officers, but whatever troops he was to command must already be stationed in Pretannia.

I stood with my women on deck, watching the huge chalk cliffs go by, as we headed east along the channel to Rutupiae. Now we were near enough to watch nesting sea birds dart in and out of the folds of the cliffs, diving for food and returning. Their cries filled the air with comforting, familiar sound. I had never walked this shore, but islands, large or small, were holy, were home.

This fleeting sense of rightness and peace was interrupted by the approach of the general. I could feel Sarah's hackles rising, and Bele and Alyssa's curiosity. As for me, I was flustered and annoyed to be reminded again that I was returning from exile courtesy of the enemy.

"Will you walk apart with me," he said abruptly. He had a way of making a request sound like a command.

"You don't have to," hissed Sarah in the dialect of the mountain Galatians that only I could understand.

"There's no reason for me to be rude," I answered her. "He's kept his word."

"So far," said Sarah, turning back to the view. "He might keep us as hostages on the other side."

"For what purpose?" I reasoned. "No one knows who we are or cares."

"Yet," she added ominously.

Oh, let her have the last word, I thought, and I turned to the general who was waiting more patiently than I would have imagined he could.

We walked from one end of the ship to the other while he held forth on the difference between Celtic and Roman maritime techniques in the Gallic wars. In our short acquaintance, I had already learned that he loved to talk about his relative, or ancestor, Caesar. I didn't bother to tell him that I knew all about the flat-bottomed boats and heavy-leather sails of the Celts that gave them advantage in storms and helped them hide out in shallow coves. I also knew that the Romans had oar power, because of their endless supply of slaves. Nor did I mention that my knowledge came not only from my cursory Latin lessons but from druids, like my father, who studied and taught military strategy.

At length we stopped and stood together in the ship's prow as it pointed past the cliffs to a low, green, marshy landscape. Neither of us spoke for a time. In the absence of words, I became intensely aware of his body, not quite touching mine, but close enough so that there was heat lightning in the air between us. Though he probably hadn't, he smelled as if he had slept outside and eaten something cooked over a peat fire.

"Your daughter dislikes me," he said without preamble.

"You didn't make a good first impression," I admitted, "what with your standing orders to have her mother seized and brought to you for questioning."

I suspected there might be more to her hostility than that, but it did not seem wise to speculate.

"No matter. Her defense of you was admirable, if mistaken. Someone must have trained her well."

"Not me," I said.

"That much is obvious."

I bridled a bit. "I did disarm one of your men, you know. That's why he attacked me so viciously with his shield."

"If he'd attacked you viciously, you'd be dead."

No one had taught this man tact, let alone how to flatter.

"What language were you and your daughter speaking just now?" He changed the subject. "It sounded like a Gallic dialect, but I couldn't quite place it. I'm just curious," he added, as if anticipating my resistance to imparting any information. "If I'd had the leisure, I would have done nothing but study languages."

"You're right," I said, cautiously. "It's a dialect spoken by the Galatians in the Taurus Mountains. The Keltoi, as the Greeks call them, live in many places."

"Yes, I know."

Of course he knew. He knew everything, or thought he did.

"I wouldn't say they ever ran the world, but in their time, they overran it," he went on, clearly implying that their time was past. "And of course they once made the mistake of sacking Rome. They've been paying for it ever since. Still, I can't help but admire their spirit. Great warriors, none braver, but not much strategy. That's why Rome always wins in the end."

Instead of sounding smug and complacent, he seemed curiously regretful, as if he identified with the conquered more than with the Empire he served. That was his precious Etruscan blood, I supposed. Part of me wanted to argue that the Celtic warriors did have strategy, or at least strategists, the druids, the unifying force among the tribes. The reason Gaul fell to Caesar, or so we had been taught at school, was the weakness of the druid presence there. Still, however drawn to this man I might be, I could not ignore Sarah's intense distrust of him or Dwynwyn's prophecy about the terrible times to come.

"Have you ever faced Celts in battle?" I tried to sound merely curious.

"No, but I have fought Germanic tribes. They are similar in their fierceness, and like the Gallic tribes, easy to play against one another. My first campaign was in Germania. I served under Germanicus."

"I remember," I said. "That was where you were rumored to have died."

"Yes, well," he said after a moment, clearly uncomfortable, "as to that, I am afraid I distinguished myself instead, which had been my intention, but it didn't mean what I thought it would; it didn't lead to the life I thought I'd wanted."

You mean the woman you wanted, I did not say aloud.

"So why do you keep doing it?

"Doing what?"

"Defending the Empire, distinguishing yourself further."

I could feel him shrug.

"It's the life I'm suited for now. I once held the office of *praetor* in Rome. That made me eligible to serve as *legatus legionis* in the campaign against the Mauritanian uprising. I never went back to civilian life after that. I can't stomach the sycophants and the backstabbers, the conspiracies, the betrayals, everyone out for himself. Nothing ever changes in Rome." I could hear the boy again, the one who had been taunted and excluded. "In battle, at least you know who the enemy is."

Who was his enemy now? My skin suddenly felt damp and clammy, as if the fog had not lifted.

"You never told me," I ventured. "Why are you going to Pretannia? It's not just to see your son, is it?"

"No. No one knows about my son." He paused for a beat. "I don't care to have it known."

"You are asking me not to tell anyone," I spelled it out.

"I am," he admitted, clearly uncomfortable to be a suppliant, to be, as he might have put it, at my mercy.

"I have no reason to tell anyone," I assured him, without, as I'm sure he noticed, making any promises. "But you didn't answer my question.

There is no war in Pretannia that I have heard of. Isn't the invasion long since over?"

"It's never that simple," he said. "Or maybe it is. I am sure you've heard of the Pax Romana."

All my life, I thought, refraining from the long-ingrained urge to spit.

"It requires a military presence. I will be presiding over the Fourteenth Legion, primarily. It will be my job to keep the peace and to ensure the safety of Roman settlements. In the south and east, the natives have largely accepted, even welcomed, Roman rule. But there is still resistance to the north and west."

Mona, I thought, and the territory of the Silures where my late foster father King Bran had been a key part of that resistance.

Despite the calm waters and the fresh sea breeze, I began to feel queasy. It was not as if I'd never slept with a Roman general before. I'd had one as my first client at The Vine and Fig Tree, and at Temple Magdalen we made a point of not discriminating. All our god-bearing strangers, as we called them, came to us stripped of rank—just as this man had come to me on the cliffs. Yet to know now that I had slept with a commander of the Roman forces occupying Pretannia made me break out in a cold sweat.

"Are you all right?"

He turned towards me and touched my shoulder lightly. Damn the man. Why couldn't he just be an insensitive boor, easy to hate and dismiss as a mindless imperialist?

"I'm fine," I said, not looking at him.

"No, you're not," he informed me, confident that he knew more about me than I did.

"Why didn't you tell me your rank that night?" I asked.

"Would it have made a difference?"

But hadn't I known, even then? Known at least that he wasn't a foot soldier, that something didn't add up? And it hadn't mattered. I had opened my arms to a boy, a heartbroken boy.

"No," I answered. "I don't know. It doesn't matter now."

"Apparently, it does," he said.

And neither of us spoke for a time. The silence was loud.

"You spoke to me in Aramaic yesterday," he said at length. "Where did you learn it?"

The same place I learned Greek and Latin, I did not say. In a cave on an island in the Otherworld, with an ancient shape-shifting human goddess as my tutor.

"I lived in the Galilee for a long time." That seemed an innocuous answer, but there I was wrong.

"In the Galilee? My father was stationed there around the time when I was born. In a town called Sepphoris. Do you know it?"

I knew about Sepphoris, all right. It's where all the bad boys from sleepy, pious little Nazareth went to booze it up. Jesus had done his share of that in his younger days, distressing his mother and outraging his brothers by disappearing for weeks at a time.

"Sepphoris is in the hills," I said carefully. "I lived in Magdala, right on the shore of the Gennesaret."

"I don't know the country," he said, "though I've always wanted to see it. My father died there of an illness. I never knew him."

I turned to look at him. But I wasn't seeing him; I was remembering a cliff at the outskirts of Nazareth, where the boy Jesus had gone to be alone. He had been taunted by the other children, called "son of Miriam," sometimes "son of crazy Miriam," who might have been pitched over that cliff herself, if it hadn't been for Joseph's protection. When I was there with him in that desolate place, I had suddenly known that Miriam had met Jesus's father there, the father she would never name, the father that merged in her mind with the god she called the Terrible One.

"You're staring," the general said. "Are you seeing ghosts again?"

I nodded, then shook my head. It couldn't be. It was absurd even to think it. They did not look alike, and yet he was so familiar, his voice, his touch, his acute powers of observation.

One of these the least of my brethren, my beloved had said, just before he left me on the cliffs. Damn.

"I think I am going to faint or be sick," I said as calmly as possible.

It was all too much. I turned and heaved over the side.

To his credit, the general was unperturbed and showed no signs of distaste. He even held my hair out of the way and kept a hand on my shoulder until I was done.

"I will escort you back to your women," he announced.

"No need. I am perfectly capable of walking."

But he paid no attention and kept his arm around me as we walked, an arrangement that would not endear me to Sarah, I knew.

"The *domina* has a touch of seasickness," he said, as if he sensed he better explain why he dared to touch me.

Sarah ignored him and gave me one of those eloquent looks that I could translate all too easily. Right, seasick on a flat sea, my mother, who has spent seven years on ships in all weathers. I don't think so.

"I will leave you then," he said awkwardly. "We will be landing soon. I have much to attend to on shore, but if you need anything, send word to me."

Out of the corner of my eye, I could see Alyssa and Bele exchanging glances that involved raised eyebrows. Sarah continued to glare.

"Wait," I said as he turned away. "I don't know your name."

He turned back.

"Gaius Suetonius Paulinus," he said, "the newly appointed Governor of Pretannia, at your service." He paused for a beat. "Who are you?"

"Don't you tell him anything, not anything," muttered Sarah.

I felt suddenly rebellious. This was between me and Gaius.

"Maeve," I answered. "My name is Maeve Rhuad."

"Maeve the Red?" he translated.

I nodded. Inadvertently, I touched my hair. He looked at me curiously, as if trying to remember something, then smiled (a rare smile) and walked away.

"Are you going to tell me what that was all about?" said Sarah.

How nice of her to ask instead of order. I considered. Let's see. Tell Sarah that the man who has so aroused her animosity, the Roman Governor of Pretannia, just might be her uncle?

"No."

"I didn't think so," she sighed. "But let's get one thing straight, Mother." (How harsh that title could sound.) "He is not at our service. We are not asking him for any more favors."

"I doubt we will have any need to," I answered, noting with both admiration at myself and alarm that I had become as adept as any druid or pharisee at evasion.

I should have been more prepared than I was for the sight that greeted us on shore. I knew the Romans had invaded Pretannia almost fifteen years ago. I had lived in Rome itself and visited Romanized cities all over the Empire, but it was still a shock to see a see a busy Roman port town, no different from any other, encroaching on land that had once no doubt been wild marsh with a few homesteads here and there. I stopped myself from saying to the others: It wasn't like this when I was a girl. And I reminded myself that I had never been to this part of the Holy Isles anyway. No need to get sentimental or indignant. So I just stood with the others, watching as our ship found its berth at the end of what appeared to be the main street of the city.

"This ship has been expected," said Alyssa. "Look up the street. There's a parade of officials coming towards us."

"Not towards us," corrected Bele. "They're here for Mother of Sarah's boyfriend, the newly-appointed Governor of Pretannia, my dears. Always good to have friends in high places."

Sarah said nothing, but I swear I could hear her grinding her teeth. I thought it wisest not to protest too much.

"We'll probably have to wait until the damn ceremonial greeting is over before we disembark," grumbled Alyssa. "I hope there aren't going to be any orations."

I watched as the dignitaries approached, flanked by soldiers, but headed by a civilian in a formal gold and purple-trimmed toga. He appeared to be in his thirties and was already beginning to run to fat or maybe it was just that he hadn't lost his baby fat yet. He wasn't young, but there was something petulant about his expression that made him appear so.

"Who is that?" wondered Bele. "Do you think our general is his replacement? He doesn't look very pleased."

"He's not military," I said. "He's probably the procurator."

Like Pontius Pilate, I thought with distaste, a petty official put in charge of an outpost of the Empire. Maybe that's why he seemed familiar to me. He was a type.

"Look," said Alyssa," I think our general's about to strut down the gangway."

"He's not our general," objected Sarah, teeth definitely still clenched.

"Ease up, Black Sarah," said Bele, "and enjoy the show. I always love to watch men in a pissing contest. My money's on the general."

There could be no contest, I thought. The man waiting on the shore, despite all his signs of rank, was a child compared to the general. His presence had no command; his was the kind of authority you inherit or buy. The general, in contrast, couldn't disguise his authority even when he had tried. Jesus had been like that, too. But I decided not to follow that train of thought. It led nowhere I wanted to go.

I was diverted by watching the meeting of these two men, heads of the civil and military occupation of the Holy Isles. They saluted, right arms outstretched in the Roman fashion, which put the procurator at an automatic disadvantage, as he was shorter. The general, wearing his dress helmet, had his back to me, so I could not see his face. The procurator had replaced his look of petulance with one of bland politeness, which I found unconvincing. Then he began to speak—or orate, as Alyssa had feared. I couldn't make out the words, but there was something about the procurator's voice that bothered me. I tried to think what it was, but it was like searching for a familiar word that is for a time utterly lost to you. So I gave up and listened instead to the sound of the water lapping against the ship and the dock workers further down the harbor loading or unloading other vessels.

Then, all at once, it came to me where I knew his voice. It had been night in my vision, and the boat had been a small one pulled onto a shingle beach. But it was the same voice, raised now in formal speech, that had given those hushed commands, and it was the same face that I had glimpsed in the lamp light.

"Warn him," Dwynwyn had urged.

The stranger who was so familiar to me, I had to warn him. I had to warn him about this man.

Now the new governor was making a speech in return. I caught a word here and there. Great joy. Honor. Happiness. There was something wrong with his voice. It almost broke here and there. Then the speech was over, far more quickly than the procurator's had been. For a moment, the assembled dignitaries seemed at a loss. Then the two men saluted again, and the parade began to re-form with the procurator and the governor at the head. Just before they began to march, Gaius turned and looked towards the ship, scanning it till he caught my eye. He smiled and nodded his head almost imperceptibly towards the procurator. And all at once, I understood.

The procurator of Pretannia was his son, his beloved son in whom he was determined to be well-pleased—no matter what.

I had to warn him.

But when at last I set foot on the ground of the Holy Isles—or the Roman pavement that overlay it—I forgot all about Governor Gaius Suetonius Paulinus and his secret son. A woman in a black cloak and tunic approached me. A breeze sprang up and her garments flapped in the wind. She might have been any one of the priestesses on Mona, the ones we called the Crow ladies. She could have shape-shifted and blown here on a storm wind. Though I was as old as she was now, my hair as grey as her long grey braids, I felt young again, confronted with a female authority figure so obviously in charge.

"Maeve Rhuad," she addressed me solemnly in the Celtic of the Isles. "You will come with me to a place where we can speak. Your women, too."

And she strode on ahead.

"Uh oh, looks like you're in trouble, Mother of Sarah," whispered Alyssa.

"I thought you said the druid college was on the other side of the country," said Bele. "That no one would bother to meet you."

"I told you Mother of Sarah was being too modest. She is a major bad-ass," insisted Alyssa.

I began to wonder if she was right. Could the druids possibly have sent someone all the way from Mona to enforce my exile?

"Don't worry, Ma," said Sarah. "Whatever it is, we'll handle it."

It did not occur to any of us to refuse to go with the woman or to demand more information first. We followed her, our horses on lead, away from the wharves, through the streets of shops and houses, past a military barracks and out of the town. We stayed on the Roman road only a little way; then our guide turned and disappeared (or so it seemed) into the marsh. Sarah, Bele, and Alyssa, marsh dwellers for years, kept on unperturbed and soon picked up the path our guide had taken through tall grasses loud with invisible birds.

We found the black-robed woman waiting for us beneath a huge white swamp oak just coming into spring leaf. She had a campfire over which she'd hung a small cauldron. While we tethered our horses, she ladled something steaming into a round wooden cup, something that smelled sweet and earthy at once. We each took a drink, honey ale, I guessed, brewed with marsh herbs. After one sip, I felt I had taken the spring sun inside me. Bees hummed over early blossoms. The Roman town, the whole Roman Empire, seemed far, far away, far-fetched even, nothing more than a dream.

I was home.

"Maeve Rhuad," the priestess, for so she must be, spoke again at last. "My name is Aoife. Joseph of Arimathea sent me for you."

"Joseph!" I cried out.

Joseph, who had taken my beloved back to Galilee when he escaped from Mona. Joseph, who had found me and taught me to read when I was a whore at The Vine and Fig Tree. Joseph, who had secured Jesus's body and laid it in his own tomb. Joseph, who had wanted to marry me and bring me back to the Holy Isles. Joseph, who had rescued all of us in Ephesus. Sarah and I had tried to send him word when we began our journey, but none of us had heard from him for more than a year.

"Where is he?" I asked the priestess. "Why didn't he come himself?"

"He is dying," she said simply, "in Avalon. Will you come?"

I did not have to translate or confer with the others. There was no question. It was only when we were miles away that I spared a backward glance or thought for Gaius Suetonius Paulinus and the warning I had failed to deliver to him.

CHAPTER SIX
TOO LATE

BY NOW YOU are probably not surprised that a priestess from the other side of the country, who had never met me, should know of the time and place of my arrival and be there to meet me. That is the way things were in the Holy Isles. It is not that other peoples did not have seers and soothsayers. (My mother-in-law set herself up as an oracle in her last years; she had gossipy angels giving her inside information.) But in those days, the island Celts did not rely on the written word, and so they found messages everywhere: the pattern of birds' wings, the way a stick fell or a leaf rode the current of a stream. They gazed into wells and skies. And because they were paying attention, the earth, the water, and skies, animals and birds yielded secrets.

Though the Roman settlers were busy building roads and towns in the south and the east and though there were plenty of Celtic tribes happy to share in the wealth and to enjoy imported luxuries, that other wilder world of marsh and wood still existed. Aoife, our guide, clearly preferred it, choosing sometimes barely visible paths even when a Roman road was near. We skirted the towns, sleeping in makeshift lean-tos and catching our own game, something all of us were used to. What we weren't so accustomed to was a companion who was mostly silent, who emanated silence. Have you ever heard wind roaring in the next field, tossing the trees, but it hasn't reached you yet, and where you are the air is still? Being with Aoife was like that. Her silence was neither restful nor awkward; it was a force, a living thing, a fifth element.

Sarah took to this silence, absorbed it, as if it were her second nature, which no doubt it was. She had grown up a solitary mountain child. But Bele and Alyssa were clearly spooked. By our third day of travel, they'd had enough and confronted me while we were out gathering firewood.

"Mother of Sarah," said Bele, "you're the only one who speaks Aoife's dialect. Why don't you talk to her, ask her some questions at least?"

"What do you want me to ask her?" I wondered, and I realized Aoife's silence had infected me, too.

"Oh, just little things," put in Alyssa, "like where are we going and when are we going to get there?"

"We know where we're going," I pointed out.

"All I know is we're going west," said Bele. "Wasn't our original plan to go east to find that tribe that fostered your daughter?"

But we are in Holy Isles now, I did not say, going west to go east makes a kind of sense, like Celtic knot work.

"We're going because of Joseph," I reminded them. "We have to see him first."

"I know," acknowledged Alyssa, "but could you at least ask how far it is? Could you try making some conversation? I don't want to spend another evening listening to everyone chewing. I thought your people were famous for talking, battle challenges that go on for hours, stories that go on for days. Get her to tell a story for Artemis's sake—or tell one yourself."

"All right," I sighed, thinking it might be easier to ask a boulder to regale us with tales. "I'll give it a go."

That night we had fresh rabbit stewed in the honey ale with wild spring onions. We were camped in a grove of old growth hardwood trees. I couldn't help but notice that the further west we traveled, the more abundant were the trees. Romans were famous deforesters, hungry for wood to heat their houses and baths and for grain to feed city dwellers on the dole, not to mention their huge armies. Would they do in Pretannia what they had already done in Ostia, Ravenna, Ephesus, strip the hills of trees so that erosion inexorably filled the harbors with silt?

A light rain began to fall, but the canopy of the forest was so thick that even with the trees still in early leaf, we hardly needed more shelter. We just pulled our cloaks over our heads and moved a little closer to the fire. The sound of the rain pattering on the leaves and hissing as it hit the coals lulled me into a half trance, and I forgot my promise to Alyssa and Bele till I felt their knees pressing against mine on either side.

"Aoife," I began, feeling awkward. "Do you mind if I speak?"

She turned her large, mild eyes on me, not startled exactly, more bovine in expression, curious, as if my request was an oddity to her but not frightening. Sarah, sitting next to Aoife, regarded me more warily.

"Speak," said Aoife when I hesitated.

What was it Alyssa and Bele had wanted me to ask? Words felt like unfamiliar objects now, heavy compared to silence, and clumsy on my tongue.

"Will we reach Avalon soon?" I asked.

"If nothing impedes us, by tomorrow sundown," she answered.

I felt the silence settle on me again, fine as the rain.

"Did she say we would arrive tomorrow?" Alyssa prompted softly, and I realized I had forgotten to translate.

"Yes."

"Ask her something more," urged Bele.

Sarah frowned at all three of us, but Aoife almost smiled.

"You have nothing to fear from me, Maeve Rhuad, or from anyone at Avalon. Say what you will. Ask what you most want to know."

She said it as if she already knew what it was. Then suddenly I knew, too. Alyssa and Bele had wanted a story. I would ask Aoife to tell it, if she could.

"Were you there," I began, "I mean in Avalon, when Joseph of Arimathea first came to that place? Do you remember who he brought with him?"

She took such a long time answering, I wondered if she had thought better of her offer or simply not heard me as the wind picked up and the rain fell harder.

"Let's move under the lean-to where we can be dryer," she spoke at last. "I will tell you what I remember."

So we all re-arranged ourselves, Aoife at the center, Bele and I on one side, Sarah and Alyssa on the other, all of us close enough to feel each other's warmth, hear each other's breathing.

"I was only a young girl then, barely fourteen," she began. "I had just come to Avalon. My parents and siblings had been taken in a raid when I was out in the marshes. The priestesses found me, half-starving and half-crazed and took me in. But my story is of no matter here, except as a witness.

"On a night like this one, of mist and rain, three women on horseback came to our shores. They were strangers and didn't know the waterways through the marshes. But one woman, with a Hibernian accent, sang out in a loud voice that carried across the water.

"'We need succor and asylum. And you might as well know at outset we're desperate outlaws who've committed any number of outrages, not least the stealing of a human sacrifice from under the long snouts of the druids of Mona, though it was the Hag of Beara herself put us up to it, melting our shackles with her bare hands, so she did, but in exchange foisting upon us a young stranger, who has been raving in a barbarous tongue all the way over the Cambrian mountains. And I won't lie to you. In Nidum we tried to foist him off on a merchant who speaks the same gabble. But in Brigid's name the lad needs a healer, so we've brought the pair of them here. Send us away or take us in, but do not leave us standing in the muck."

Aoife paused to catch her breath. As I translated, Sarah caught my eye and nodded. She knew who had melted the shackles in the guise of the hag. She knew the name of the boy they'd reluctantly rescued.

"The priestesses could not resist the Hibernian woman's frank and spirited appeal," Aoife went on, "so they came in several boats and took the whole party to the island where we house guests. When the women went off to bathe and eat and tell their own stories, the merchant refused to be parted from the boy.

"I remember when I first saw the two strangers," she resumed after another pause for translation. We heard the shift in her tone, the shift from *the* story to her story. "The healers had tended to the boy and given him a sleeping draught. They sent me to watch over him, with orders to fetch a priestess if there was any change or if he woke.

"I sat down on a low stool beside him. I remember thinking that he could not be much older than me. His hair was so dark and springy. I wanted to touch it, but I didn't dare. Even though he was asleep, his face looked sad, old and young at the same time. The merchant, who sat on his other side, looked sad, too, sad and full of yearning as if the boy were his own son. Though I felt shy of these strangers, I summoned the courage to speak.

"'He will be all right,' I told the man. 'The priestesses will heal him.'

"He looked at me, startled, as if he had not realized I was there.

"'What is your name, child?' he asked in my language.

"When I told him, he spoke to me in words I did not fully understand.

"'He is so like him, he is so like him. This one I will not lose. This one I can save. We will save him, Aoife, won't we?'

"'Yes,' I told him, 'yes.' And I wondered if I should fetch a priestess for him, he seemed so distraught. At last he accepted some of the ale I offered him and ate a little bread.

"'You are weary,' I said to the merchant. 'Sleep. I will stay awake with him. I will stay with you both.'

"And I did."

Aoife fell silent and remained silent long after I translated. None of us spoke or stirred. It was as if we were all sharing that long ago night vigil, listening to the sound of rain, the fire, the tides of breath. I wondered if Aoife's deep silence began that night, watching over the sleep of a beautiful lost boy.

"I had red hair then."

Her words surfaced from the silence, bright and strange.

"When he opened his eyes that is what he saw first. My hair. He reached for one of my braids and wound it around his fingers. I knew I was supposed to get the priestess, but I couldn't move; I couldn't speak. Then he looked at me."

I knew better than anyone there what it was like to look into those eyes. You could set sail in them and never return or return to find everything utterly changed.

"'Maeve.' That was the first word he spoke, and then he said, 'You are not Maeve.'"

Sarah looked at me again. I didn't have to translate this part. She understood everything Aoife had said—and not said.

"I ran to get the priestesses then. By the time I got back, the merchant was awake and vainly trying to restrain the boy from getting dressed and charging off. The only words I caught were Maeve and Mona, which he shouted again and again. At last Madrone, the chief priestess, slapped him hard across the face, and he fell silent.

"'You will not go back to Mona,' she told him. 'From what the Hibernian women have told me, that would be certain death for you, and no help at all to the one you call Maeve, who as I understand it is about to have a child. Now you will sit down and when you have had something to eat, you will tell us the whole story, from the beginning.'

"And the young stranger did just that," said Aoife, "spinning us a tale to rival any a bard could tell."

Except, I reflected, he didn't know the whole story then. He didn't know that I had been the old woman who loosed his bonds. He didn't know that I raised the tidal bore that prevented the druids from pursuing him or that Lovernios, my father, the one who had rigged his sacrifice, had walked into the wave and disappeared. He didn't know that I was to stand trial not only for meddling in high mysteries but for murder.

"He went on spinning his tale all night, till the dawn crept into the hut.

"'So you must see now,' he said, 'I have to go back for Maeve. I should never have left her.'

"No one answered him for awhile," said Aoife. "As for me, I think they had forgotten I was there or they might have sent me away. I was the only one who thought he was right. I was young, too, and had lost so much myself. I did not understand or care then about the predicament the priestesses found themselves in.

"'Young stranger,' Madrone spoke at last, 'Esus, as you say the druids call you after a sacrificial god. It is our ancient right to offer asylum to fugitives. To interfere with the rites or sacrifices of the druids of Mona or any justice they might see fit to administer, that is another matter.'

"Weak as he was from his fever, the boy stood up again. There was a calm about him that made him seem older than he was, as if he would have us all know the strength of his will, the certainty of his intent.

"'Thank you, all of you, for your kindness to a stranger. I will go alone.'

"All of us were touched by his determination. No one wanted to say the stark truth: you could not find your way out of this marsh alone, let alone across the wild mountains. We all watched, speechless, as he walked towards the door.

"'Don't go, my son, don't go,' the merchant cried out in such anguish that the boy turned around. 'There must be another way.'

"The boy's weakness began to overtake him against his will. He hadn't eaten anything but a bit of broth. His legs began to shake. I didn't wait for instruction from the priestesses, I went to him and slipped my arm around him.

"'Eat something. At least eat something before you go.'

"I saw the priestesses exchange glances. I learned later that it was then they decided to train me, instead of just keeping me as a servant. I only tell you, because it was a gift that came to me from his presence among us."

"Don't be so humble, Aoife," I interrupted for the first time. "We all love you for loving him."

She nodded and bent her head, while I translated again, and then she went on.

"He sat down and accepted food, and while he ate, Madrone spoke to him again.

"'Think, Esus, think carefully. You have been gone some days. You don't know what has happened since then. It may be there is no danger to your Maeve, no danger unless you return. You were the one they wanted for sacrifice, not her. She is also carrying a child who was foretold. By now she may have given birth.'

"'The misbegotten child of a misbegotten child,' Esus quoted the druid prophecy.

"'From whose line will spring the last one of us to stand against the Romans,' Madrone completed the druid prophecy; she had paid close attention to his story. 'The druids of Mona will not allow harm to come to this child, however it was begotten.'

"'But Maeve.' The boy's voice broke. 'Once the child is born....Maeve. What will happen to her then? She was afraid of what the druids might do. She asked me to run away with her before, to take her home with me, and I wouldn't, I wouldn't.'

"He broke down then and wept silently, and such was the force of his grief that everyone else wept, too.

"'It may be that you can take her to safety yet,' said the merchant, coming and putting his arm around the boy. 'I have a ship at Nidum, loaded and ready to sail.'

I smiled to hear these words, Joseph ready to rescue me, sight unseen, not knowing how many chances he would have in the future.

"'But we must find out first what has happened and where she is,' Madrone insisted, 'not have you rushing off into danger and endangering her.'

"I understood better than the older people how hard it was for him to wait, to be patient, how desperately he wanted to be like a hero in tales told by the bards.

"'How?' he asked at last. 'Is there someone trustworthy you can send to Mona to look for her, someone the druids will answer to?'

"No one spoke right away. He had raised a sticky point. The priestesses of Avalon were the poor relations, the ones who did not live on the gold route, hold arbitrations among the tribes, maneuver and manipulate kings.

"'There may be a better way,' said Madrone, 'a quicker way. It's worth a try.'

"'What way?' asked Esus, suddenly uneasy.

"'We have seers here as well as healers. Surely as a student at the college, you studied the arts of divination.'

"'I have studied them,' he said after a moment, 'but I have never practiced them. It is forbidden.'

"The priestesses were taken aback.

"'Forbidden for students, you mean?' Madrone asked. 'I don't see how else you can learn except by practice, but that's druids for you. Anyway, you wouldn't be doing it, we would.'

"'Not forbidden by the druids, forbidden by Yahweh, my God.'"

Aoife did not add this detail, but I could imagine the looks passing among the priestesses. He was a stranger, so it figured that he had a strange god. And he was called by the name of one of the more peculiar Celtic gods. Too many gods in the mix.

"'Your god forbids the consulting of oracles?' Madrone asked, with a touch of exasperation. 'How does your god make himself understood?'

"'He doesn't,' said Esus, 'He doesn't expect to be understood; he is beyond our understanding. But he has given us many commandments to keep, so that we remember him always.'"

I could picture my beloved knitting his brow and chewing his cheek, becoming lost in thought, almost forgetting his heartbreak in pondering this quandary. It made me homesick for him, for all our debates under the yew trees on Mona.

"'How tedious of your god,' said Madrone.

"'Long ago his people, our people, had a king named Saul,' the merchant spoke up to ease the tension. 'He went to a sorceress to find out how he would fare in an important battle. After that Yahweh withdrew his favor from the king, and his reign and his life ended tragically. I expect the boy is thinking of that.'

"The priestesses were more mystified than ever. What king wouldn't consult an oracle before battle?

"'I am thinking of that,' the boy said after a silence. 'And I am thinking that Saul only cared about his own power. I care...I care about Maeve. I love Maeve and so,' he paused again. 'and so I will break the law. And I pray to my God, God of Abraham, Isaac, and Jacob, if I offend you, let the punishment for this offense fall on me alone.'"

Aoife fell silent, waiting for me to translate. I opened my mouth but found I couldn't speak. Long ago Joseph had told me something of what had happened at Avalon, but not like this, not so that I felt I was there in the room with my beloved when he defied his god. For me. The compression of time was dizzying, how strange to grieve for him after all that had happened, after I had lived the rest of this story and knew how it ended.

The sound of Sarah's voice brought me back to the present in this wood, where the rain had now stopped and the stars shone through wisps of mist. She had taken over the translation. She did not need to understand all Aoife's words to tell the story. She knew it in her bones.

"Do you want me to go on?" Aoife asked when Sarah had finished.

"I think I know the rest," I said. "You saw that I had been exiled, sent beyond the ninth wave. Joseph told me that he and Esus were going to try to find me at sea. And then the storm came."

Aoife nodded, almost bowed her head, and I could feel her relief at being released from the effort of words, as if she were a creature, like a silkie, forced to live out of her element and at last allowed to return to the sea.

"Thank you, Aoife." I wanted to acknowledge her gift. "No one could have answered me better."

But Sarah was not satisfied.

"There is more I want to know." Sarah spoke in Aoife's dialect now, which she must have picked up just from hearing the story. She was quick with languages. "If you are willing." She remembered her manners.

"Ask, daughter of Esus."

It occurred to me that I had not told Aoife who Sarah was. I suppose no second sight was needed to figure it out.

"What form of divination did you use? How did you see? How did you know?"

It startled me to realize that I did not know the answer to that question. Neither Joseph nor Jesus had ever told me.

"Madrone and a few other priestesses gifted in the sight walked the spiral path to the Otherworld where all things are revealed."

I noticed she spoke that phrase as if she had repeated it many times, as if the words could never be separated from each other.

"All?" said Sarah. Her voice was soft, but it had an edge. "All?"

"Say what you would say, daughter of Maeve."

She was my daughter now, I noticed, now that she was about to be difficult. No matter. Maybe I could retire and have my daughter be the one to upset everyone.

"If all is revealed, then why did you, or anyway the priestesses, let my father think my mother had died? Why did they let him suffer all those years, bearing the guilt of abandoning her, feeling as though he had as good as killed her? Why didn't they tell him she was alive? Why didn't they tell him where to find her? Do you know what it cost him to ask, to risk being forsaken by his god? What good is the sight if it can't spare people from suffering?"

I hadn't seen Sarah so angry since her rage at me had driven her to run away, away from my stories, to seek the truth for herself. I had been afraid of her anger then. It made me giddy to realize that I wasn't any more. Her anger was hers, fine, furious, a shining storm. I thought of the huge storm that had blown my boat hundreds of miles over mountainous billows. And I thought of her father, ranting against hypocrites, inciting riots in the Temple. It was a good thing there were no tables nearby to overturn.

There was only Aoife, sitting there, her silence deep as any votive well, ready to receive Sarah's rage as an offering.

"I don't know," Aoife said at length.

"Don't know what?" Sarah pressed.

"I don't know what good the sight is. I don't know why the priestesses didn't know your mother would survive or, if they did, why they did not tell your father."

I waited. We all waited to see if she would say something more, something like: they had to lose each other to find each other again. Or he had to know this guilt and grief to become who he was meant to be, and so did your mother.

But she said nothing.

I wondered if I would ever be that wise.

"It was more than ten years before they found each other again," Sarah added. "Then they had only a few years together. Do you know how he died?"

What was Sarah up to, I wondered. Alyssa and Bele shifted uneasily, and Alyssa mouthed something to me I couldn't catch. I shook my head as imperceptibly as I could, meaning, I don't know either.

"You mean the god-making death?" Aoife said matter-of-factly. "We know. We never lost sight of him. And Joseph always returned to us when he was in Pretannia. Long ago we hoped that Joseph would bring you and your mother back to Avalon with him. He wanted to protect you; we would have given you sanctuary. Now it is too late."

"Too late for what?" I blurted out, suddenly afraid that we would not get to Avalon in time to see Joseph.

"Too late," Aoife repeated. "Too late to be safe."

CHAPTER SEVEN
JOSEPH

AVALON, YNYS AFALON, the Isle of Apples, was and is a between-the-worlds place, between earth and water, between water and sky, between light and mist, between the human world and the other.

Not far from the marshy sanctuary, ports along the Sabrinae Aestuary received goods from all over the world and shipped out tin and lead from the Mendip Hills, as well as meat from abundant herds, and captives taken in raids to be sold as slaves. My foster-father's tribe, the Silures, lived to the north of the estuary and still fought other tribes who were more welcoming of the Roman merchants who wanted to settle there. So far there were no official Roman settlements, but there was scant doubt that the Romans wanted to gain control of the shipping routes. So the southwest of Pretannia was also between the worlds of skirmishing tribes, each with their own king and territory, however disputed, and the Roman occupation now firmly established in the east.

Still, Avalon itself, especially in Springtime a maze of waterways and islands with the mysterious Tor looming over the inland sea, remained set apart from commerce and conflict–a place you could vanish into if you were a fugitive, a place that could vanish, if threatened.

"What *is* that?" asked Bele, pointing to the singular uprising in the land, visible from miles away.

"We call it the Tor," Aoife answered; no one needed to translate Bele's question.

"Tor?" Bele repeated.

"It's a word that means high hill," I explained.

"I've never seen a hill like that," objected Alyssa. "It looks more like a finger, or, well, another kind of protuberance."

"I agree," said Bele. "It's too narrow and pointy to look like breasts the way hills should."

I had never pondered the metaphorical etiquette of landscape; I was amused, but also vaguely uneasy and not sure why. I decided not to translate for Aoife, but she must have gotten the gist. She smiled a small, private smile. She knew, as we could not, that the view from a distance was deceptive.

"Was it built?" Sarah spoke over her shoulder to Aoife, who rode pinion behind her.

A good question, I thought. There was something deliberate about the Tor, eloquent, as if this earth had risen up to speak, but to what? To the gods? To the people? To the stars? I did not know then that the whole landscape for miles around was encoded, alive with huge earthen figures. Only those who could shapeshift into flight could appreciate this eloquence.

"Some say yes, some say no," Aoife answered. "No one knows. No one remembers a time when the Tor was not."

We rode on, our silence matched by the silence of cloud shadow moving over the plains and the shadow of the Tor lengthening towards us. By sunset we were in a watery land, loud with bird song, and so full of reflection that it felt at times as though we were riding through the sky. At a signal from Aoife, Sarah halted her horse, and Aoife dismounted.

"From here we go by boat," Aoife said.

Alyssa and Bele got the gist and exchanged looks of alarm.

"What about our horses?" Alyssa wanted to know.

"We have no boats big enough, but we have a place nearby where they can be stabled and fed, as we do the horses of all our guests."

Sarah translated but Alyssa remained wary.

"Sarah and Mother of Sarah," she said, "you have a mission here to see your old friend, but I'd just as soon stay with the horses, if it's all the same to you."

"I'll keep you company," offered Bele.

I knew the two sometime pirates had transferred their passion for their lost ship to their horses, but I also sensed they were reluctant to go further into the water-land surrounding the protuberance. We were at some boundary here. The air felt charged with invisible currents that I suspected were intended to excite fear or even repulsion in anyone who approached.

"As you wish," said Aoife. "I will call someone to tend to you as well as the horses."

She turned her attention from us and made a series of calls, each distinct but all more bird-like than human. And through the now-dusky marsh came answering calls and women poling small boats, while other women appeared as if out of nowhere to welcome Alyssa, Bele and the horses.

After embracing our companions, human and equine, and assuring them we'd send word to them about Joseph's condition, Sarah and I got into a coracle with Aoife and another woman who maneuvered the boat with a pole. So deft were her movements that we glided through the water almost soundlessly. The wind had fallen with the dusk and the mists had risen, swirling over the waters, so thick sometimes that I could not see the other end of the boat, the torch set there a blurry and distant star. I understood better the intensity of Aoife's silence. There were other uses for hearing and for breath. Speech here would be a distraction, a disturbance to the air whose minute shifts of temperature and direction served in place of landmarks.

As the gloaming gave way to full night, I lost track of time as well as space. We might have been on the water only a few minutes or for years. There might never have been any other world than this one, and all that other life with its bright color and clamorous events just a series of strange dreams. At last, and with some effort, I recognized the rasp of reeds on the bottom of the boat and then felt it come to shore.

"Healers' island," said Aoife softly somewhere close to my ear. "I will take you straight to Joseph."

We followed Aoife's torch up and over a small hill. Sheltered and out of sight of the landing was a large wattle and daub round house.

"Is this where they brought my father?" Sarah wanted to know.

"Yes," answered Aoife, and she held aside the heavy plaid that covered the door and gestured for us to go inside.

I wondered if Sarah, too, half expected and longed to see a boy lying there with a young girl watching over him, and if she, too, found it strange to see instead an old man, much older than when we had last seen Joseph three years ago. He was lying on a raised pallet on his back, with his eyes closed, lids too dry and thin to keep out any light. His chest barely moved when he breathed.

The woman watching him was old, too, older than Aoife and me, ancient. The lines in her face did not seem the ordinary kind made by falling or shrinking flesh or exposure to time and elements. They swirled and intersected, like knot work, like currents in a river.

"Maeve Rhuad," she said. "We've been waiting for you."

Her voice was stronger and younger than I would have expected, and held a note of reproach that implied I'd kept them waiting, that I was late.

"Colomen Du." She addressed Sarah as Black Dove, her Celtic name that no one but me had ever used. "You are welcome here."

She gestured for us to approach. Sarah held back, letting me go first, and I knelt down next to Joseph and took his hand.

"Speak to him, Maeve Rhuad," said the old woman, "in whatever way you will. He's not gone yet. Come, Aoife. Help me up. We will leave him alone with his kinswomen."

Kinswomen. Surely she knew our lineage, and yet she rightly called us his kin.

"Yes, Madrone," said Aoife, slipping her arm around the woman who had sheltered my kinsmen here all those years ago.

Sarah came and knelt on the other side of Joseph and held his other hand.

"Joseph," I tried to speak aloud but my throat was too thick with tears.

I laid my head lightly on his chest, so that he didn't have to bear its weight, and I listened to his heart, beating so slowly, the last little wavelets before the tide is all the way out.

Joseph, I'm here.

Maeve.

Perhaps I fell asleep listening to his heart, perhaps I had a vision, or perhaps we dreamed together between the worlds.

We are standing together on the roof of the Temple Magdalen tower, looking out over the water just before dusk. The fishing boats are making for the harbor, and we can hear the sounds of their voices carrying over the water, singing in Greek, in Aramaic, and other languages, too. Flocks of birds lift from the water, circle, settle again. Behind us rise the voices of the priestess-whores, singing evening hymns to Isis.

"I was happy when I visited you here, Maeve," says Joseph, whether aloud or mind to mind I don't know; it doesn't matter, "especially that night...this night."

I do not need to ask which night he means. I remember it, too, the night he came to me as the god-bearing stranger and I received him as the goddess. For that brief time, all his sadness, that I would not be to him what he wanted me to be, went away along with all my regret.

"Not a brief time or not a brief time only," he speaks to my thought. "It's eternal. Plato was right," Joseph goes on, this renegade Temple priest turned philosopher and adventurer. "You remember, Maeve. I taught you about the Ideas, though I don't think you paid much attention. Temple Magdalen is an Idea. It will always exist, even when this place returns to dust and wild roses."

As he speaks, I remember when I first came there and heard the sound of the spring rising, flowing to the lake, and knew that I had found my home.

"But Plato didn't know everything."

Joseph turns me toward him and gathers me in his arms. I can hear his heart beating again, so slowly, so slowly, gentle as the lake water lapping at the shore.

"He didn't know how sweet it is, all of it, even the bitterness. You taught me that, Maeve. You."

Then night falls, so swiftly, the way it does in Galilee, and it is quiet, so quiet. Someone lays a hand on my head, steady, warm. Then gone.

* * *

When I sat up again, Sarah and I were alone in the room. She still held Joseph's hand in both her own.

"Should I call the priestesses?" she asked.

"Let's just sit with him for a while," I said.

She nodded, and after a time she spoke again.

"He was here, you know."

"Joseph?" I asked, not sure of what she meant.

She shook her head.

"My father."

And I hadn't known? I tried to hide my dismay. Sarah saw it anyway.

"He didn't want to disturb you and Joseph. He was waiting. He talked to me for awhile."

"What did he say?" I couldn't help my longing.

Sarah didn't answer right away, and I was afraid I had intruded.

"It's all right," I told her. "I don't need to know."

"It's not that," she said. "It's just when I say he talked, I don't mean he used words. It's hard to translate."

I nodded.

"He's glad we're here," she attempted. "He showed me a lot of pictures. Some of them were terrible, but at the same time I think he was trying to get me to see them from some other place, from his place, where things don't look quite the same. Am I making any sense?"

"As much as anyone could," I assured her.

"Good." She fell silent again, relieved.

And I fell into the silence, strangely comforted and at peace, sitting beside the body of my friend who had befriended both me and my beloved when we were so young and tormented and who had cared for us always as tenderly as he could.

"Here now is the center of the world."

I heard myself speaking the words of the old archdruid as I planted Joseph's walking staff on the fresh earth of his grave. We stood in a circle, the priestesses, Sarah, and I. Bele and Alyssa had joined us on this breast of a hill to the southeast of the mist-ringed Tor. People from the villages all along the aestuary had also gathered to honor Joseph. They seemed to know him not just as a trader, but also as someone who could tell a good story—the story of Maeve and Esus, though perhaps because of my grey hair and weathered face, they appeared to believe I was Jesus's mother and seemed inclined to venerate me. I decided to let the case of mistaken identity slide.

And so the church Joseph is supposed to have founded is dedicated to my mother-in-law.

We had all said or sung prayers in various tongues and traditions, with Sarah surprising me by offering one in Hebrew. Perhaps Miriam had taught it to her when she was a child or perhaps it came directly from her father. Now wordlessly we began to build a stone cairn over the grave to mark and protect it. Burial was not such a common practice in these watery parts, but however widely Joseph had ranged in his travels and convictions, he was still a Jew, and I felt his body needed to rest in the earth.

I walked back and forth carrying stones, my fingers numb with damp and cold, my eyes seeing only the ground. Where had the rest of Joseph gone? Had Jesus come, as Sarah said, to take Joseph to Tir nan Og where everything shone with its own light? Except that it was all here, really. *There is nowhere else,* Anna the prophetess had said. *It's all mirrors and shapeshifting. Now you see it, now you don't.* Mostly I didn't. I was grateful now to have a simple task to perform, to carry stones in my hands, not to have to think or see further than this moment.

"Look!" Sarah called out. "The staff."

I stopped and straightened up. Rising from the cairn was a thorn tree in full, fragrant flower. *Now you see it.* And there it still blooms. I cannot tell you if the Holy Grail is in the Chalice Well or if Joseph really carried a vial of Jesus's blood and sweat to this green and pleasant land. Nor do I know if he converted one person to Christianity, let alone the 18,000 of legend. But I can give you this much: his staff became a blossoming thorn tree, and some remnant or descendant blooms there still.

CHAPTER EIGHT
SPIRAL PATH

IN A BRIEF SPAN OF TIME, I have rashly embraced a new lover who could be a dangerous enemy, and I have lost an old friend and ally to death. I am a returned exile, still not sure of her official welcome to a divided land that shape-shifts in and out of time, between this world and the other, a place that has not yet made its reckoning with history. If I could have, I would have postponed that reckoning indefinitely, biding my timelessness in Avalon, drifting on the still waters in hidden marshes, letting both memory and foreknowledge become a forgotten dream.

"Now what?" asked Bele as we walked back to the boats. "Is there anything more you have to do in this place, Mother of Sarah?"

"I think it would be a good idea to ask directions," said Alyssa. "Something a little more specific than heading east."

"What about that path," put in Bele, "you know, the spiral path to the Otherworld where all things are revealed? Could be useful."

"You probably need to be initiated into their order or something like that," cautioned Alyssa. "I doubt they'd let us walk it. And I'm not sure I'd want to, thanks very much."

"What do you think we should do, Mother of Sarah?" Bele turned to me.

I didn't know what I thought, only what I felt, a sense of dread at the thought of pursuing this quest any further.

"No vision can direct us or protect us." Sarah did not wait for my response. "We need clear sight, not second sight. I say we leave as soon as possible."

I looked at Sarah, trying to read her face, which she seemed determined to keep unreadable. If Sarah had no premonitions, why this edge, this urgency?

"We have to say goodbye, at least," I said firmly. "The priestesses have given us hospitality. Aoife traveled for days to meet us and days to bring us back."

We had reached the water's edge, and it occurred to me that as we had no boat of our own, we were more or less at the mercy of the priestesses, like it or not. Priestesses all around us were stepping into boats, gliding away on the smooth water, seeming to take no notice of us. Then Aoife approached us. She stood beside Sarah for a moment without speaking, and I could almost see her silence envelop Sarah, ease her restlessness. Then Aoife turned to me.

"There are two druids here to see you, Maeve Rhuad. They have traveled all the way from Mona."

My stomach lurched and my hands began to shake. I reminded myself that I was full of years, and perhaps even wisdom, but it was useless. I was fifteen again and in deep shit.

"Will you come?"

She might as well have said: you will come. The question was only a formality.

"Of course," I said with as much calm and dignity as I could fake.

"You other three will go to the feasting," Aoife gestured towards a waiting boat.

"I go nowhere without my mother," said Sarah, and she took a step closer to me.

Bele and Alyssa couldn't follow the words, but they got the gist and they moved to flank us, hands on their sword hilts—which to their obvious horror were not there. Everyone who came to Avalon was required to disarm.

"No harm will come to your mother here," Aoife said softly. "This is a place of sanctuary. The druids asked to speak with your mother alone."

"They can ask all they like," countered Sarah. "The decision is not theirs."

"That's right," I agreed. "It's mine. I will go alone to meet them."

Sarah turned to me, ready to protest.

"It's all right," I told her. "I'm not afraid of any druids."

Never mind they had tried to make a human sacrifice of her father and sent me off to what might have been a watery doom after stealing my first-born child.

"Bullshit."

"Don't talk to me that way! I'm your mother."

I tried to sound severe, but I started to laugh, and suddenly we were all laughing, giddy and punch drunk. Even Aoife. And after a round of embraces, Sarah let me go. She and the others got into a larger boat and went one way. Aoife and I, in a smaller craft, went another. Soon we were lost to each other's sight.

I did not question Aoife further as we moved through the warrens of waterways. And after awhile, I forgot the confrontation awaiting me, forgot all fear. Again I had that strange sense that all of it was a dream, my whole life and all the other lives weaving in and out of mine. I closed my eyes and dozed a bit. When I opened them again, all I could see was green rising, rising. We had come ashore at the base of the protuberance.

"Do you see that path there?" Aoife asked when I had gotten out of the boat; she herself, I noticed, had not disembarked.

I looked where she pointed to a narrow strip, a worn green amidst the pasturage.

"Just follow it," she directed. "And you'll come to where you need to go."

No point in asking her when she'd be back, even if she hadn't already started skimming away in her little boat. I was a priestess myself, for Isis' sake, I knew an Otherworldly place when I saw one. I had little doubt that before me lay "the spiral path." Just like the druids to make you sweat just to have a word with them.

There was nothing for it. I began to walk. I walked and walked a path that wound seemingly endlessly around and around the hill. The protuberance was at one end of a wider, more gradual incline. After a time, though I kept my feet patiently on the earth, step after step, my vision rose and I saw with my dove's eye: I was walking on a great earthen vulva, fold on fold, lip on lip. The protuberance was the pleasure point, erect. This realization exhilarated me, and my walking became more like dancing as I approached the peak. There the path became steeper, a narrow terrace cut into the hill. I noticed sheep and cattle precariously grazing on the almost vertical sides and wondered if they had been bred to have two legs shorter than the others. Then I rose above the cattle line and into a wreath of cloud, cold and clammy as clouds can be, then higher still, into the welcome warmth of the sun, with cloud, land, waterways, river, sea spreading out below all the way to the curving rim of the earth. It was not hard to imagine that from the top, if I sent my dove vision flying, I could see anywhere in the world. But before I reached the summit, a doorway opened in the side of the hill, and the path took me inside.

I was less panicked than you might suppose. I was born and raised in the Otherworld; for my initiation I had followed a spiral path deep into the earth beneath Bride's breast on the Isle of Tir na mBan. So I just stood calmly as my eyes adjusted to the relative darkness. A fire burned, vented by some natural chimney, for the room was not smoky. The two druids, for so I supposed they were, sat facing the fire, their backs to me.

"All right, I'm here," I greeted them rather rudely. "What do you want?"

It seemed to me that the two backs shook a little, and I thought I heard a gasp or two. Good, I had unsettled them. Then they rose and turned to me, the silver bells on their poets' branches jingling, their feathered masks wild and inscrutable. At the sight of the masks, I broke a sweat. My father had worn a bird mask the night he had gone out of his head and raped me. But he was dead. Long dead. I took a deep breath, and sent down my roots, gathering the strength of this earth, sending my branches to gather light.

"My name is Maeve Rhuad, daughter of the warrior witches of Tir na mBan, daughters of the Cailleach, daughters all of Bride, as you well know if you are druids worth your salt. You have called me here. State your names, lineages, and business or I shall be on my way."

"She hasn't changed," said one druid to the other.

"Not one bit!"

And then they removed their masks.

But I didn't recognize them until they held out their arms.

The beach is crowded with Crows and Cranes. Further back, perched among the rocks and cliffs that rise on either side of the beach, the entire student body of the Druid College of Mona is assembled. No one is saying personal farewells; the occasion is too formal, but I am allowed a moment to scan the crowd. I find Viviane first. Her hair catches the light and glows. She and Branwen are standing together on a ledge partway up a cliff. Nissyen and the other first formers are clustered nearby. I try to catch everyone's eye, saving Branwen for last. When our eyes meet, Branwen lets go of Viviane's hand and stretches out her arms towards me. I lift my arms to her in return, and suddenly the cliffs come alive with upraised, outstretched arms as if some enormous flock of huge birds were about to take flight.

"Branwen? Viviane?"

I opened my arms and walked into theirs.

CHAPTER NINE
CLASS REUNION

After all the exclaiming and the holding each other at arm's length so that I could marvel at them and they at me, all of us now more than forty years older than the day I drifted away with the tide, we sat down together before the fire. Branwen handed me a cup of hot mead. Her hair, I noted without envy, was still mostly black, and her eyes as gentle as ever. Viviane, once a redhead like me (and how I had resented her for that) now had hair that was almost white, just a hint of yellowing. Mine was merely grey, and I admit my old rivalry with her instantly revived. She offered me a piece of barley cake.

"Not a burnt one, I hope," I quipped, referring to the way sacrificial victims were chosen.

"How *can* you make a joke like that?" Viviane shook her head. "After all that happened."

"You mean after Lovernios, my *father*, rigged the lot so it fell to Esus?"

"The *brehon* court never accepted that version of the events," Viviane said.

"I am no longer under its jurisdiction," I shot back. "What the druids choose to believe or not believe makes no difference to me. As to all that happened to Esus, and to me, after that, you don't know the half of it."

"We don't know any of it," Viviane pointed out. "But in point of fact, you are under our jurisdiction, now that you're back, and what we have chosen to believe may matter more than you know."

"*Your* jurisdiction?" I looked at my old friend and my old enemy.

"I am a *brehon* now, Maeve. And Branwen is a renowned bard, and a distinguished member of the faculty of the Druid College at Mona."

"Just as Dwynwyn predicted," I said softly. "And so you have become full-feathered druids. Cranes not Crows."

I wondered if they even remembered the irreverent names we cheeky first formers called the druids of Mona and the priestesses of Holy Island who came to the college to perform the thankless task of watching over the girl students.

"So have you come to enforce my exile?"

"Oh, Maeve, no!" Branwen was distressed. "We wanted to see you."

"Although," Viviane cautioned, "your presence in the Holy Isles could be considered controversial."

"I don't see why!" Branwen became unusually heated. "I know I am not a *brehon*, but you said it yourself, Viviane. The sea ruled in her favor. Therefore, she is innocent."

"No, Branwen," insisted Viviane. "What I said is, the case could be argued that way."

"Surely my case is long since closed," I said.

"There are some druids who still hold that the disrupted sacrifice and the subsequent Roman invasion in the southeast of the Holy Isles are directly linked."

Just as I had always feared. No matter that King Bran himself had exonerated me. No matter that I would have made the same choice over again. Part of me still wondered if the druids had been right.

"And there are also differing opinions about whether an exile, innocent or not, can return. You ought to know how long the druid memory is, Maeve. We may have lined faces and white, or grey, hair." Bitch, I thought. "But forty-five years is just a blink of an eye. And the Roman invasion and occupation are still a dire threat to the last of the free *combrogos* in the north and west."

"I see," I said, and I did or thought I did. "Then if you are not here to enforce my exile, why are you here? If you just wanted to see me, why did you insist that I go on an Otherworldly hike to find you? Why did you greet me in masks?"

Branwen looked pained, but as seemed to be her wont, Viviane answered first.

"It was my idea. Branwen didn't want to. Even though we were not sent in an official capacity, I felt it was important for you to understand what you may be up against. As for these masks, they do not conceal who we are; they reveal our true nature, our authority."

"Our authority, maybe." Branwen was a poet and not one to stand by when she felt words were being misused. "But no one mask can reveal someone's true nature. This one does not reveal mine. I am sorry, Maeve. I suppose you could say we were testing you, and that is not right among friends."

"Did I pass the test?" I immediately wanted to know.

"Yes."

"No."

Branwen and Viviane contradicted each other at once.

"Never mind," I said before Viviane could go on about my failure. "If the druids didn't send you as ambassadors, then who did? Who knows I'm here?"

"I should have thought that would be obvious," said Viviane. "Didn't she appear to you, too?"

"Dwynwyn," I guessed at once.

Dwynwyn, who had long ago prophesied over the three of us and predicted our fates with a fearsome degree of accuracy. Dwynwyn, who had told me I had chosen my true friend and my true enemy well. Dwynwyn who had just prophesied that I would take her place "when the terrible things happen."

"But isn't she...hasn't she," I began. Time and timelessness were so confusing.

"Died," finished Branwen.

"Or disappeared," said the precise *brehon*. "Gone but not done meddling. Dreams and visions, not my favorite mode of communication but necessary sometimes. She told us you were coming and where to find you. She more or less ordered us to come here and meet you."

"But Maeve, she didn't tell us anything else," Branwen said. "There is so much I want to know. Where have you been all these years? We didn't even dare to believe you had survived! Did you ever find Esus? I remember that day we first found Dwynwyn on the island, she said you would be a great lover. Do you know now what she meant, Maeve? Can you tell us?"

As Branwen spoke, Viviane opened a covered basket and laid out a feast of meats, dried fruits, and more barley cakes. She brought out a flagon of mead and poured us more to drink.

"We have all night," Branwen added.

I gazed at Branwen, my first friend in the world, and my vision began to blur with tears. I had just buried Joseph, the only friend who knew where I had come from and where I had gone, who had given his own tomb to my beloved. And I was very likely the only one in the Holy Isles who could tell Branwen how her own father's life had ended. Where to begin all these stories, how to be sure not to lose any thread?

"Begin at the beginning," Viviane commanded.

"Begin anywhere you like," countered Branwen, "and you will end up where you need to go."

And so I began with the story of the Rex Nemorensis, the brave escaped slave who became the King of the Wood and guarded the tree of the Golden Bough with his life. I told the story of how his foster-daughter, herself far from home, an exile and a slave, found him there.

"And these are the exact words he spoke to me, Branwen.

"'*And so I am a king again, Maeve. It is a strange fate, guarding a Holy Tree so far from the Holy Isles. Yet here in her embrace, I know I am not so far. When you see my Branwen again and my sons, tell them I am free and a king. Promise me, Maeve Rhuad.'*

"I never knew I would have a chance to keep my promise, Branwen," I said, holding her hands. "He would be so glad if he knew."

"He *is* glad," said Branwen fiercely. "He *does* know. And my brothers know, too, for they are with him in the Isles of the Blest."

"Oh, Branwen. Your brothers, too? Oh, Branwen!"

I hadn't known Branwen's brothers well. Bran had boasted only Branwen had the brains to become a druid. His sons were warriors, like him.

"They were with Caratacus in his last battle against the Romans."

"Caratacus, the son of the Catuvellauni king?" Lectures from school on the Roman question stirred in my memory. "I thought the Catuvellauni were pro-Roman."

"Cunobelin, the father, was friendly to the Romans, but when he died, his sons wanted to reclaim the southeastern territories for the old ways. They forced out the king of the Atrebates who fled to Gaul—and then went to Rome and pleaded for intervention on behalf of the Roman-friendly tribes. Not long after that, the Romans launched the invasion."

Then perhaps the invasion was not all my fault? I felt ashamed at the feeling of relief that came over me in the midst of a story that could only be tragic.

"Early in the fighting, the older son, Togodumnus, died at a terrible battle at the River Medway. That lost battle was the beginning of the end for the southeastern tribes. Caratacus fled west to the mountains to join forces with the Silures. My older brother, king after my father, welcomed him. My brothers also persuaded the Demetae, Ordovices and Deceangli to join the alliance. They knew the mountains and used the terrain to their advantage in ambushes and raids. They were so successful that the Roman general Scapula vowed to exterminate them, the Silures in particular," she said with bitter pride. "He almost succeeded."

All too easily, I could picture those wild mountains, the decimated villages, the stubborn, starving survivors.

"Caratacus made a terrible mistake when he decided to risk meeting the Romans in pitched battle," put in Viviane. "The druids of Mona advised against it, but Caratacus was tired of playing cat and mouse. He wanted to rout the Romans once and for all. His forces lured the enemy to a rock fortress. They thought they could slaughter them by raining down missiles. But the Romans, attacking from two sides, took shelter under their shields and kept climbing and climbing straight up the precipice like huge beetles. Our forces couldn't hold them back. They were shattered, and the ones who did not die, fled."

Viviane spoke with her jaw clenched.

"Caratacus escaped," Branwen took up the story again. "He fled to the Brigantes only to be betrayed to the Romans by their queen Cartimandua. They took him to Rome to be paraded there, just as they did my father. Only the emperor was so impressed by Caratacus, he spared his life and invited him to live in Rome. He lives there still, so we have heard."

And likely went to banquets as a celebrity noble savage, I did not say. I could hear all the judgment in Branwen's voice painstakingly reserved.

"But thanks to you, Maeve, now I know. My father died a king."

"And his sons after him," said Viviane, "and his sons after him."

We were all silent for a time, listening to the fire hiss and crackle, watching the changing patterns of light and shadow on the wall. I felt the weight of all that tragedy and turmoil settling into my bones, becoming inextricably linked with my own life.

"Now tell," said Viviane at length, "how you came to be enslaved, and if King Bran's prophesy about you and the Stranger ever came true. What did he mean about the living tree and the dead tree and you and Esus changing places?"

I looked at my friends and a wave of weariness stole over me. I felt as though I were drifting away from them again on that tide that had taken me beyond the ninth wave. I had words now to be my oar and sail, but they felt so heavy.

"I wish I could dream it to you," I said.

"You are tired." Branwen was immediately concerned. "Of course you are. How could you not be? And here we made you climb the Tor on top of everything else you've been through. You must rest now. There is no need to tell the whole story all at once."

"I'm afraid there is need," Viviane disagreed. "We can't stay in Avalon for long. We have to be getting back. The more we know, the more we can help, or advise her, anyway, always supposing she'll listen to us."

"Viviane has a point, Maeve," Branwen conceded. "But maybe you can dream to us. Let's lie down and curl up together, like we used to when we were first formers, and Nissyen would tell us stories to quiet us down, remember?"

"Of course I remember," I said. "I remember everything."

And at that moment, it was true. As soon as we lay down together on a pallet covered with soft, worn plaids, the words and memories flowed dreamlike, one turning into the other, and I took Branwen and Viviane on the long strange journey of my life. At times I think we did dream together, for when it was over, I felt refreshed, cleansed, as if my life had washed through me, carried me, and I had landed safely on this shore at last.

"Now," I said. "Your stories, your own stories. Tell."

"We are trained to tell the stories of the *combrogos*, Maeve, not our own," Branwen said, quickly, too quickly, I thought.

"Our stories were laid out for us long ago," agreed Viviane. "You lasted only a year at your studies. We stayed the full nineteen, and then went on to serve the *combrogos* according to our different abilities."

Viviane was certainly making the druid life sound awfully dull and dry. What about festivals, trials, sacrifice, scandal, intrigue?

"No lovers?" I pressed. "No children?"

Perhaps I shouldn't have mentioned children. I had been the one to find Viviane hemorrhaging from an abortion. She had been the first to guess my pregnancy and had helped me to hide it. We'd had a literal blood bond, since our first brawl when I smeared her with my menstrual blood.

"The druids are the mind of the *combrogos*," said Viviane. "Not the flesh."

The same metaphor my father had used when censuring me for arousing warriors to fight over me after I wantonly entered the caber-toss. Behavior unbecoming a druid-in-training.

"I like to think of us as worker bees," put in Branwen. "We don't have a life separate from the hive."

I sat up and looked from one to the other.

"I love you, but I have to say I think you are both full of shit. And more specifically, I think there is something you are not telling me."

That was it; that was what was bothering me.

"Just as there is something you are not telling us," countered Viviane, also sitting up and looking as cross as a cat that has had its fur rubbed the wrong way.

"What do you mean?" I protested. "I just told you the story of my whole life, and, unlike you, I didn't leave out the juicy bits."

"You didn't tell us why you've come back to the Holy Isles."

"I didn't?"

I thought back over my story and realized I had left out a few juicy bits, such as my escapade the night before I crossed the channel. Of course, I had told them about Sarah, from her Otherworldly conception to her running away and our reunion in a prison in Ephesus. They knew Sarah was here with me and had kept vigil with me over Joseph. But I had not told them that Sarah and I had come back to find *her*, the misbegotten child of the misbegotten child, stolen by the very authorities Branwen and Viviane now represented.

"I think we know why, Viviane," Branwen said.

"Maeve must say it," Viviane insisted. "We must talk of it."

"Her, you mean," I said. "My daughter. We must talk of her. Yes, I am here to find her, if I can."

I stopped myself from saying: my daughter Sarah insisted on this quest. It bothered me that it might be true.

"But I don't even know what name she is called."

As distinct from the name I had spoken into her ear for the few moments I had held her.

Viviane and Branwen exchanged a look. Then they turned to me.

"Boudica," they both spoke the name at the same time. "She is called Boudica."

Boudica? How could it be? Boudica, the name, the secret name I had given her.

It meant victory.

Boudica, my daughter, alive.

CHAPTER TEN
BOUDICA

"BOUDICA." I SPOKE HER NAME out loud for the first time since she was born.

Suddenly I felt dizzy, disoriented. Where was I? How many lifetimes had passed?

"Get her something to drink," said Viviane. "I think she's going to faint."

Branwen was already on her feet, and in a moment she knelt beside me, one arm around me, while she held a cup of honey wine to my lips. Viviane fetched a barley cake and a hunk of sheep's cheese.

"Eat," she ordered.

I obeyed and for a moment I thought of nothing else but the dryness of the crumbs, the sharpness of cheese, the warmth of the wine in my blood.

"I'm all right now," I said. "Tell me about her, about Boudica. The Crows told me she would be sent to foster with the Iceni in the east. That's the only thing I know."

"She did foster among the Iceni," began Branwen.

"And now she is their queen," said Viviane.

For the first time Branwen looked seriously peeved with Viviane. She, after all, was the bard. Viviane might be a brilliant *brehon*, but clearly she had no idea how to tell a story.

"Go on, Branwen," I pointedly took sides.

Viviane shrugged, then tossed her hair in that irritating way she always had.

"It was Beltane, as I am sure you remember. The visiting tribes hadn't dispersed yet. There was some concern that no one would want to take a misbegotten child of a misbegotten child. But the druids reminded the *combrogos* of the prophecy about the great hero to spring from this line who would make a stand against the Romans. Do you remember that, Maeve?"

How could I not? The memory was seared into my mind. It was my father who had made the prophecy on the very day he had tried to kill me and extinguish the misbegotten life I carried. He had broken from his predictable script and spoken in anguish and against his will.

"The child's lineage presented a problem, of course," Viviane couldn't help but point out. "Especially the maternal line."

"What about the paternal line. It wasn't considered a problem that a man raped his own daughter?" I demanded.

There was an awkward silence until Viviane took it upon herself to break it. Never one to shirk from an unpleasant task, our Viviane.

"Lovernios was an important druid who served the *combrogos* well. You came from, well, no one was ever really sure whether or not to believe your story, your claim of divine descent. You fell in love with the Stranger and defied the druids for his sake. Then you disappeared—"

"Most people do when they're sent out with the tide beyond the ninth wave. Are they—are you—denying that I was exiled?"

"That's neither here nor there," said Viviane. "The point is, they decided it was best to downplay your lineage."

Branwen took my hand and looked me in the eye, which was brave of her, considering what she had to say next.

"Maeve, in the story you are portrayed as a *beansidhe*, or, in some versions, a silkie, who seduced Lovernios with magic, bore a child, and then vanished. Lovernios went mad with grief and walked into that tidal bore hoping to find you in the Land under the Wave."

I looked at my friends, incredulous. What a stupid, hackneyed, unconvincing plot! Any bard should be ashamed to recite such a pack of tired lies. Why would anyone believe it at all?

"But people *knew*!" I burst out. "Maybe they didn't know everything. No one knew everything, except Dwynwyn. But people knew about Esus and me. They knew I was on trial for stopping the sacrifice."

"No, Maeve," countered Viviane. "Most people at the college knew something, but the visiting tribes can't have known much. Your trial was not public, as I am sure you remember."

"But the Iceni family who fostered my daughter took her away before my trial, before anything had been settled, before that ridiculous story could have been concocted."

"I don't know all the details of what they told the family at the time, Maeve," said Branwen. "We were only first formers. I believe that the foster mother had lost a daughter earlier that year, and only wanted to fill her arms with a child. It was the foster father and his *tuath* who had to be persuaded that they were not taking in some child born under a curse."

"And you must understand that Lovernios's reputation had to be preserved," insisted Viviane. "More than any other druid before or since, Lovernios commanded the respect of the warrior kings and rallied the tribes to unite against Rome."

"Oh, I understand, all right," I said. "Someone had to be sacrificed for the good of the *combrogos*, and I had stolen one sacrifice already. I owed them."

"Not just the *combrogos*, Maeve." Branwen sounded almost stern. "There was the child. What would you have wanted for her?"

What would I have wanted for her? What would I have *wanted* for her? No one had ever asked me.

"She means," Viviane jumped in, "would you have wanted your child to grow up knowing that she was the child of rape and incest, not to mention of a criminal and exile. Isn't the story better? Isn't it better to have a father who was revered by the *combrogos* for his leadership and wisdom?"

"Wisdom!" I snapped. "Falling in love with a sea mammal and drowning himself? And how about being the child of a wicked seducing mother who abandoned her? That's a pretty story. But I did not abandon her. I did *not* abandon her. How dare they, how dare *you*!"

Suddenly, I was on my feet, shaking with rage and wishing I had my sword, though I did not know who I would have turned it on. I wanted to smash at something, anything. Blindly.

"Maeve," Branwen said softly. Her voice seemed to come from a long way off, from a long time ago. "We are your friends."

"Possibly the only friends you have on Mona," added Viviane, "the only friends you have among the druids. So sit down and listen to us."

I looked from one to the other, and they kept their gaze on me, even Viviane, who had a nerve calling herself my friend, though true enemy might be the next best thing. But I did not sit down.

"No," I said. "If you call yourselves my friends, you listen. You listen to me. Do you want to know what I wanted for my daughter? I wanted her to have a mother. I wanted to keep her, just like I kept Sarah, even though I had to run away with her and leave my home and my friends behind. Both my daughters' fathers died before they were born. I never knew my father either. There was never anything I could do about that. But I could have kept Boudica, I could have loved her. I will never forgive the druids. First they steal her from me and then they lie to her. And if you have perpetuated that lie, I will never forgive you."

Oh, but you will forgive them, a voice inside me spoke.

"Shut up," I spoke aloud. "Who asked you?"

I am with you always.

"Maeve, are you all right?"

Branwen stood up and put her arm around me, and I could feel how badly I was still trembling.

"No, I am not all right," I said, but I sat down again and let Viviane give me another sip of wine.

For awhile none of us spoke.

"We're sorry," Viviane began, "but–"

"Don't," I cut her off. "Just tell me where she is now. Tell me how to find her."

"I am not sure that would be wise," cautioned Viviane. "I am not sure that would be in anyone's best interest."

"Viviane," said Branwen before I could protest. "I think we better tell her the whole story."

"What story?"

"When Boudica was fourteen," Branwen took the narrative reins, "her foster parents brought her back to Mona, and presented her as a candidate."

"Now you can see why her lineage mattered so much," put in Viviane.

"She studied to be a *druid*?"

"She was determined to follow in her father's footsteps, well, I mean not–"

"Not the footsteps that led to a tidal bore." I was starting to feel punch drunk and perhaps literally drunk after all the restorative sips of wine.

"Do you want to hear this story or not?" demanded Viviane, knowing that she had me by the short hairs (the ones I had left, anyway).

"Tell," I sighed. "All."

"Go ahead, Branwen," Viviane deferred. "You knew her best, as much as anyone did."

With continued interruption from Viviane, Branwen went on. The year Boudica arrived at college was the same year Branwen and Viviane were entering their last four of nineteen years of training. Of our form, they were the only two women remaining. They began to take on responsibilities in the college, especially mentoring younger women. Nissyen had long since been put out to pasture as a dorm head, and after the disasters that had occurred on his watch–me being chief among them–he was lucky to get bed and board. After my brief era, female students were housed separately and chaperoned far more vigorously. Along with one of the Crows, Branwen was junior dorm mother, so to speak, to the first form girls, among them my daughter.

"She looked so much like you, Maeve, when I first glimpsed her at admissions, I swear I thought I was seeing your ghost. Of course, she looked like Lovernios, too, but then, so do you...." Branwen trailed off for a moment, flustered; her narrative style was usually more confident. "But I could not see much of you in her as I got to know her."

"Except for her willfulness and arrogance," Viviane made sure to note.

"You are too harsh, Viviane," objected Branwen. "I think you mistook her seriousness for arrogance. It set her apart, made her seem a little aloof."

"You may be right, Branwen," Viviane conceded. "And she was not as willful as her mother. Strong-willed might be a better way to say it. Determined. And *she* actually studied."

"Unlike her mother, you mean," I said. "We all know that story. Stick to this one, would you."

"For her first dozen years or so at school there's not a lot to tell," Branwen went on. "She worked hard at all her studies, though what she wanted most was to be a *brehon* and military strategist like Lovernios. She did not make many close friends, and yet her classmates respected her and on those occasions when she let down her reserve to argue passionately on some point, everyone sat up and took notice, students and druids alike. She had great potential as a leader—"

"Which is why it was such a loss to the college when she had to leave just when she would have started studying law," Viviane broke in.

"Had to leave!" I repeated. "Was she...did she have a child?"

Like her mother before her. It was all I could think of. Her story, my story. A mother and daughter who shared the same father, all of it mixed up.

"No," said Viviane. "She wasn't stupid like you and me. No sneaking off into the moonlight for her. And remember you weren't exiled *because* you had a child. Boudica would not have been asked to leave, in any case. She was too devoted a student. The child would have been fostered. No, the druids would never have willingly interrupted her studies."

"Then why—"

"Does the name Claudius mean anything to you, Maeve?" said Viviane. "As in Emperor Claudius?"

"Of course. Do you mean she left because of the invasion? That doesn't make any sense. From what you tell me, she would have wanted to be in the thick of the resistance."

"Oh, she did want to," Branwen assured me. "More than anything. But her *tuath* withdrew support—"

"That wasn't the only reason she left," Viviane said before I could ask why again. "The druids would have kept her at college without tuition. I know. I was there when the matter was debated."

"So was I, Viviane," Branwen almost snapped "May I finish?"

"Please," I begged.

"Her *tuath* withdrew support because their tribe, the Iceni, well, they weren't conquered, Maeve. They were bought. It's a crude way to say it, but they made an alliance with the invading forces. As I am sure you know,

Romans have always feared and persecuted druids. After the invasion, Claudius outlawed the practice of druidry not just in Gaul but everywhere in the Empire, including, of course, the newly conquered territories. Boudica's *tuath* did not think it politic to have a daughter of a prominent family allied with one of the last druid strongholds."

"I see," I said. "But if she is as stubborn and determined as you say, it is hard to imagine that she went without a fight."

"Oh, she fought all right," Branwen acknowledged. "Her family sent a message ahead. The day it arrived she asked to speak with me alone. We walked away from the college, down to the straits and, oddly enough, Maeve, we ended up at the yew trees."

The yew trees where I had revealed my pregnancy to Esus, where I finally screamed the story of the rape. Where he and I had been lovers for the first time.

"I had known her for years by then," Branwen was saying. "She was about twenty-eight years old at the time, so she no longer reminded me so much of you. Most of the time, I was able to forget whose daughter she was. But that day in her anguish and defiance, there you were again. Her red hair had come loose and flew about her in the wind as she stood, and she looked fierce and frightened all at once."

"'I won't go back to live among traitors,'" she kept saying.

"'You will be going back to your family,'" I reasoned with her. "To ensure their safety. Don't judge your parents so harshly for the tribe's decisions."

"'They are not my blood,' she insisted. "They are not my lineage. My place is here where my father lived. I must go on with his work. It is more important now than ever with the eastern tribes conquered or colluding.'

"'Your place,' I said sternly, though I felt for her, 'is where you will do the most good, and the least harm.'

"She said nothing for a moment, and her face was still and expressionless. Horribly still like the air before a storm, like the stillness before an ambush.

"'Who decides?' she spoke at last, her voice low and caught in her throat like it was clawing to get out. 'Who can know another's place, another's fate? Who can know!'

"I almost felt frightened of her in that moment. She looked so haunted, her eyes staring as if she didn't see me or know me, as if she wasn't there with me."

Just like my father, just like her father.

"'The faculty will be holding a council,' I said. 'Signs and omens will be interpreted, auguries consulted. Everything will be taken into account.'

"'I want to be there,' said Boudica. 'Branwen, please, I have always trusted you, loved you like an older sister. Will you go intercede for me? I only want to be allowed to speak on my own behalf.'

"She was not a demonstrative person, but she reached out to me then and took both my hands and looked at me with such beseeching that it broke my heart. I gathered her into my arms, and she let me hold her, though she did not return my embrace.

"'*Cariad*, I will do what I can,' I said. 'But you must understand, the question under debate is not what would be best for you—'

"'I understand,' she cut me off and pulled away abruptly. 'What matters is the *combrogos*.'"

As Branwen went on with the story, I stopped hearing her voice, or Viviane's occasional outbursts. I was no longer in the timeless fire-lit dark inside the Tor. I was back on Mona. I knew those sacred groves, those solemn, perilous debates.

The old archdruid still lives. The same one who sent me beyond the ninth wave now presides over my daughter's fate. He has aged, stands less straight. Two younger druids support him on either side, but he still plants the staff, declares with a voice that refuses to relinquish authority: Here now is the center of the world.

It is night. Firelight fills the circle, laps at its edges, touching feet and faces, bark and branches, the underside of leaves, hushed now in the stilled wind. Now the words begin to move around the circle, from one druid to another, the way the breeze will liven this tree, then that. Through it all, my daughter stands silent, sinking her roots into this ground she means to hold, even as her leaves tremble and shiver with every shift in the argument.

Some say she is a dedicate to the college and cannot be turned away if she chooses to stay.

Others argue that the support of the *tuath* must be steadfast.

Some insist that her legendary patrilineage makes her an exception to any rule.

Others caution that keeping her against the will of her family and tribe may stir up trouble, draw unwanted attention from the Roman forces in the east.

A few say, bring it on. Let's use it as a cause for rallying the resisting tribes.

Many say a war over one person is a waste of resources; we must bide our time, plot.

"What say you?"

The archdruid's voice seems to come from everywhere, from the ground, from the trees, from the sky, from inside her own mind. Boudica looks around dazed. As attentively as she has listened, she feels someone has just shaken her awake.

"What say you, daughter of Lovernios?"

Boudica opens her mouth, but the speech she has prepared does not come out. She feels empty, has she always been empty, just a hollowness waiting to be filled, so that she can be poured out, poured out.

"What say you, Boudica?" the archdruid asks a third time.

"I say," she spoke at last, her voice seeming to come from far away, so that she heard it outside herself. "Like my father before me, the great Lovernios, I say: wherever I am, there is the enemy of Rome. And so it shall be until my death."

The archdruid raises his arms, and the wind lifts again.

"And so it shall be," his voice rises.

"And so it shall be," say the clattering branches, the dark oak leaves.

"And so it shall be," echo the human voices.

"And so it shall be," Boudica's voice rings out above them all.

CHAPTER ELEVEN
WHERE NOT ALL THINGS ARE REVEALED

"AND SO IT WAS DECIDED," Branwen was saying as I came out of my trance, "that Boudica should return without protest to her tribe, with the full cooperation and blessing of the druids, under secret instruction to be their eyes and ears in the occupied territory."

"You mean she is a spy?" I asked. "She's taken it pretty far, if she has married the collaborating King."

"Prasutagus," Viviane supplied his name. "Yes, that surprised even the druids when we heard of it. We are still not sure of all the details. Communication back and forth from conquered to free tribes is not easy. Bear in mind that none of us has seen Boudica since she left."

"But I bet every wandering bard has a story about that marriage," I said. "I bet there's more than one version going around. Which one is the best? Don't tell me you haven't heard rumors at least."

"You are right about that, Maeve," agreed Branwen.

"And I know which one you prefer to believe," put in Viviane.

"And I can guess which one you prefer," Branwen retorted.

"Tell both," I urged them.

"Mine is not poetic or long, but it's the most likely," asserted Viviane, ignoring my mother's maxim that a story is true if it's well told. "They are both using each other. Boudica gets the inside track on all the tribe's dealings with the Romans, and Prasutagus hedges his bets by marrying someone with connections to the druids, someone, moreover, from a prominent family with lots of horses and cattle. He also gets to spy on her and make it more difficult for her to send communications to Mona. It's simple really. The rest is sentimental nonsense for second rate bards."

I looked to Branwen and nodded for her to go ahead.

"This much we know," Branwen began her tale. "Boudica returned to her family, and since her hope of becoming a druid was lost to her, she took up where she had left off with her martial training. A bit late in life, but she had always been quite talented and her determination to go to druid school was considered a loss as well as an expense to the *tuath*. If it hadn't been for Lovernios's fame and her foster mother's gratitude to the druids, the tribe might never have sent her to college. Now that she was back, everyone hoped she would marry and have children before it was too late. But Boudica showed no interest in making a match, and despite her family's wealth, suitors were scarce on the ground. No one pushed her. I think they were all a little afraid of her.

"A full turn of the seasons after Boudica's return, Prasutagus came to pay a visit to the family. You might think he would have come sooner, but he had been in mourning for his young wife who died in childbed along with their only child. Now here is where the storytelling begins."

As Branwen spoke, I could see everything: Prasutagus and his entourage arriving on horseback to find Boudica racing a chariot up and down a fallow field. It's late autumn and the sky is full of low clouds, but Boudica is wearing only a tunic. Her braids unwind on the wind, a gash of color in the bleak landscape. She is as tall as most men, and in the chariot she towers against the sky. She sees the men but she does not slow her pace, and she makes one, two, three more circuits around the field. In one hand she holds the reins, in the other a *laigen*, which she casts as she completes her last circle, striking home into a moving target that hangs from a tree limb at the edge of the field. Only then does she slow her horse and come to a halt in front of the king, who is standing and staring, though by now her foster father's household has assembled to welcome him.

For a long moment she answers his stare from the chariot, both she and Prasutagus ignoring her foster father's attempt to at once introduce, excuse and dismiss this foster daughter who has become such an anomaly. Then Boudica steps down and comes to stand before him.

"I am Boudica," she says, "daughter of the druid Lovernios." And she recites her whole patrilineage and then, as an afterthought, recites the lineage of her foster family, both maternal and paternal. The only lineage left out is that of the mother who bore her (the less said the better). But she has surely demonstrated the prowess of her memory as well as of her spear arm. Then she concludes, "I am at the service of the *combrogos*."

The King of the Iceni is speechless for a moment. Does he notice that she has not affirmed her allegiance to him? Is he wondering whether to rebuke her or her foster father, perhaps have her punished in some way or kept under watch? Instead he blurts out,

"I remember you from when you were a girl. Do you remember me?"

And Boudica, who has been standing still and cool, reddens as only a red head can with bright, humiliating blotches. For she does remember a day she'd rather forget.

She had been with her family at a horse fair when a gang of children surrounded her and taunted her, calling her stuck-up and crazy, a changeling brat. She was swinging with both arms, but was hopelessly outnumbered. An older boy, old enough to carry a sword, came to her rescue, and chased the children away, beating them with the flat of the sword.

"One day, I'll be king, king of the Iceni," the boy said to the angry girl, who was still red with shame and fury. "When I am, there will be no bullying."

"I so don't believe this part," complained Viviane. "It makes the story of your being a seducing silkie look dazzlingly original."

"Shh," I said, totally caught up.

"And I will be your best warrior," the girl said, recovering her pride.

"We will not have wars, either," the boy informed her. "Too many people die or get captured and sold as slaves."

"That's silly," said the girl. "If you have enemies, you have to have wars. I already know how to fight. Let me use your sword. I'll show you."

And they spent an afternoon together, trading sword techniques and competing with their slingshots, the only weapon Boudica had at the age of seven, before they went back to their families and never saw each other except from a distance until the day they stand before each other, almost eye to eye, Boudica being slightly taller.

"I do remember," she says. "You told me you would be king, and so you are."

"And you told me you would be my best warrior."

He smiles at her, but Boudica remains unmoved.

"You have no need of warriors," she says. "You have made your peace."

She does not say, peace at a price or accuse him of having a price, but her words stir up the air around them, charge it, and everyone shifts nervously, as if they are cattle who sense a predator nearby.

"Boudica, come. Let's not keep our guest standing," her foster father attempts to intervene.

"Boudica, daughter of the great druid Lovernios, whose name is known to all the tribes," says Prasutagus, "I, too, serve the *combrogos*. A king always needs warriors to guard the peace."

Boudica bows her head, whether in deference or to mask her dissent, no one knows.

"But this we do know," Branwen concluded. "For whatever reason, Prasutagus began to court Boudica or to spend a great deal of time with her. No formal marriage negotiations. Not until the new governor decreed that all the tribes south and east of the rivers Severn and Trent must be disarmed, even the collaborating tribes."

"Publius Ostorius Scapula, the same general that defeated Caratacus," Viviane supplied. "The second governor, appointed about four years after the invasion. For all his victories or because of them, he died of exhaustion after a year in office. None of them seem to last long. I am proud to say that the Holy Isles are considered a hardship post. In fact, we have heard that the troops themselves rebelled on the eve of the invasion and had to be shamed into going through with it. So far, we've routed four governors, and a fifth one is just being installed. Gaius something or other."

Gaius Suetonius Paulinus, I did not say aloud. I did not want them to know I knew anything about him.

"Let's get back to Publius's decree," I said. "How did an imperial order to disarm persuade Boudica to marry?"

"There was an uprising, of course," said Viviane. "Led by the Iceni. We think Boudica instigated it."

"No one knows for certain why she agreed to marry," began Branwen.

"Or why he went through with it," said Viviane.

"But there's a story," I said. "Tell it."

Again, as I listened to Branwen, everything else fell away. I felt Boudica's rage at the decree, saw her fling herself onto her favorite horse, a silver-mane mare without bothering with reins or saddle. She rides hard to Prasutagus's compound, a Roman-style villa that Boudica has refused to enter till now. She strides barefoot over the warm tiles with their wasteful underfloor heating and confronts Prasutagus where he reclines with his retainers at the midday meal. She will not sit down or accept refreshment, and so he stands to meet her and tells the others to leave them alone.

"You once told me that when you were king there would be no bullying," she skips the preliminaries. "Do you remember that promise? Or do you dismiss it because a child made it to another child?"

"I do not dismiss that promise or any word that I have given."

"Then you will not cooperate with this decree."

He does not answer soon enough to satisfy Boudica.

"When an invading power insists on disarming the people," she presses, "what do you call that?"

"Protecting their interests, protecting their citizens who have settled here in peace."

"Wrong," she says flatly, "it's bullying. You are making yourself willfully blind. Or you would see: the Romans want to reduce us to slaves, and if you cooperate, though you call yourself king, you will be no better than a slave yourself. As for me, I will never be a slave. I will stand alone and fight if I have to, fight to the death, but I will resist."

And she turns and stalks away.

"Boudica!"

What is it about his voice that makes her pause? It is not anger; it is anguish, longing.

She turns; she gives him one more chance.

"You can't do it alone. Even the tribe can't do it alone. That will only lead to useless carnage. The tribes must agree, all of us, the ones who have made our peace with the Romans and the ones who have not. Be my queen, Boudica. We will go to the tribes together. We will show them that the old ways and the new ways can be one way for the good of the *combrogos*."

Boudica stands still, so still.

"Resistance," she says, "that is my bride price. Nothing less, nothing more."

"I will not see my people disarmed," he says. "I will go with you among the tribes."

She waits again. Can she be sure of what he has and hasn't promised?

"The marriage will take place tonight at my foster father's home," she says. "I will go now and tell them to prepare."

And with that she quits the villa.

"The point is," Viviane's voice brought me back to the present. "whichever version you believe, they both married for political advantage."

"We don't know that," Branwen countered. "Their intentions may have been honorable, even so. And they succeeded, don't forget. The Roman governor rescinded his decree. The tribes retain their weapons."

"That's just what makes me suspicious," said Viviane, "because, in fact, they didn't succeed. The uprising was put down. Why didn't the Romans disarm the tribes then? Instead of being punished for the rebellion, they were in effect rewarded."

"Maybe the governor realized disarming the tribes was impossible," argued Branwen. "He'd made his point by defeating them in battle. He could afford to be magnanimous."

Viviane shook her head vigorously.

"I think Prasutagus was playing both sides the whole time. He appeased the resisting tribes by marrying Boudica and lent her credibility among the compliant tribes. Very likely he also gave the Romans information that led to the rebels' defeat. I have no doubt he persuaded the governor that if the tribes were stripped of weapons, he would be deposed as a king friendly to Rome and the tribes would be re-armed by hostiles. And, as I said before, he may have agreed to spy on the druids through his wife, which could explain why we haven't heard much from her."

"We know that she has given birth to two daughters," put in Branwen.

Two daughters. My granddaughters!

"How old?" I asked. "What are their names?"

"The older one must be nearly thirteen. I am not sure about the younger one. Their names are Gwen and Lithben, or so we've heard," Branwen answered. "It's been a long time since Boudica left us. Prasutagus may be good to her; he may be good *for* her. She may have made peace with her life."

"Peace?" Viviane sounded skeptical. "It's not in her nature."

Branwen and Viviane continued to debate whether or not essential change was possible, Branwen's examples tending to the literary and Viviane's to the legal. I realized as I stopped listening, they had never left the druid groves from which I had so long ago been cast out to a life that had buffeted me about even as I stubbornly insisted on my purpose. Had my essential nature changed? Had I found or made any lasting peace?

"Maeve, what are you doing?"

Only when Branwen spoke did I notice that I had gotten to my feet. The other two also rose, but neither one reached out a restraining hand.

"I am going to find Boudica, of course. It's why I came back, not that I am not happy to see you again."

"And nothing we have said makes any difference to you?" asked Viviane. "You still mean to traipse off across country without a plan and without official sanction or help from the druids?"

"Like they'd give it!" I rolled my eyes at Viviane. It made me feel young again. Clearly my essential nature had not changed much. "More likely I'd end up out to sea again, if I was lucky, or pounded into a pit."

"It's hard to say," Viviane admitted. "But Branwen and I could make a case for clemency."

"Thank you for that, Viviane, and I may need your help one day. For now I'll try my luck on the open road. If you would tell me where the road is, I'd be grateful."

"There is only one main road," said Branwen. "Wyddelian, it's called. It runs all the way from Mona to Londinium and beyond to the Roman port. It's an old road, but the Romans have paved it with stone almost halfway."

As Branwen spoke, I remembered my vision of the hard road, my heart pounding louder than my horse's hooves.

"Travel east along it, and when you reach the territory of the Catuvellauni, ask the way. You'll be leaving the Roman road there and heading northeast," Viviane said. "Just remember, if you ever need or want to find Mona again, the Wyddelian road runs both ways."

"And if you find Boudica," added Branwen, "I mean when you find Boudica, for surely you will, give her our greetings. Tell her we remember her with love and that we know she has always kept faith with the druids of Mona."

"We don't know that," cautioned Viviane, her tone much gentler than her words. "But say it anyway."

"I will," I promised.

Then all three of us just stood and looked at each other, not wanting to say goodbye.

"Let's go to the top of the Tor before we go," I said. "You know, finish walking the spiral path to the place where all things are revealed."

"An absurdly exaggerated claim," grumbled Viviane. "That's priestesses for you. All visions, no traditions."

But she led the way out of the intimate darkness we had shared into the shock of light and cool, fresh air. At first I wondered how it could still be daylight. Had no time passed at all? Then I realized the light had shifted direction. It was the morning of a new day. It seemed like a good omen. Morning always does.

The rest of our spiral climb was not long, and soon we stood on the smooth, grassy top of the Tor in a strong wind that for some reason made us throw back our heads and laugh. In order to anchor ourselves, we took hands, facing out. Together we could see the round horizon of all that is, the green earth, veined with blue water, the homely smoke of cook fires, the herds of sheep and herds of clouds.

Slowly as if of one accord, we began to circle round and round. Maybe it was dizziness, maybe it was the long sleepless night, or maybe the priestesses' claim was true, but I found that I could see beyond the horizon to the hard road I would travel, and then when I turned to the west again, I saw something that stopped me in my tracks and nearly made us all lose our balance.

"What is it, Maeve?" asked Branwen. "What do you see?"

"Dwynwyn's Island."

"Well, at least you're looking in the right direction," said Viviane. "So what about it?"

I shook my head. I did not want to tell them the rest. That I had seen myself there, looking out over the straits that were as red as Dwynwyn's robe, the robe she had bequeathed to me.

"I will return to Mona one day," I said. "That's all I know."

I dropped their hands and we turned toward each other into a triple embrace.

PART TWO

Fire
Daughters Of Lovernios

CHAPTER TWELVE
PASSING THROUGH

FOR SO MANY YEARS she had been an ache, an absence, a hidden sorrow, a secret shame, not shame that I had borne her, but that I had lost her and never sought her till now. In my only memory of her, she was fierce, red, tiny, latching onto my breast as if she would never let go. I could still feel the small warm weight of her; I could still feel the emptiness when I woke to find her gone.

Now I had directions to the country where she was queen. I knew her name and the names of her husband and children. I knew her dream had been thwarted, just like her father's. I knew she looked like him, or like me, or like both of us.

I knew she believed I had abandoned her.

That knowledge propelled me forward and filled me equally with urgency and dread. Each day we travelled east, I also felt the pull of the west, despite the terrible things Dwynwyn insisted I would witness. It was like riding a breaking wave and being caught in an undertow all at once. Maybe I was simply homesick for my mountain cave. There was a smaller cave on Dwynwyn's Isle, and the well of eels, and the sheep that looked like no others with their strange markings and wildly twisted horns. And the sound of the waves and the tides coming and going in the straits and the wind whooshing over everything....

"Mother," Sarah had a way of knowing when I was drifting and pulled me back sharply sometimes. "Look. That must be a Roman fort. It's huge."

We had been riding for several days now on the Wyddelian Road since we parted with Branwen and Viviane in the country of the Silures. The going had been fairly easy, round hills (of perfect breast-like proportions) rising to the right, forming a ridge, and rolling land to the left that was now spreading out into a plain through which a river meandered. We all looked where Sarah was pointing to a vast walled complex with watch towers at regular intervals.

"Bloody Romans," said Alyssa, as she always did when we encountered anything that smacked of their influence, however convenient it might be, like the well-maintained road we were traveling right now. "They'll likely be thick on the ground from here on out. This is probably where they base themselves for campaigning against the western tribes."

"One of the places," put in Sarah. "There's more than one occupying legion."

"What do you say about a little detour into those hills?" Bele sounded nervous. "This road will probably take us right past the fort."

"Why should we?" Alyssa became belligerent. "We have as much right as anyone to travel these roads."

"The Romans might dispute that right," Sarah countered. "None of us are citizens. None of us belong to any tribute-paying tribe. We're on our way to visit a tribe that once led a rebellion, however docile they may have been since. You could make a case that we are outlaws. They might want to detain us for questioning–or other purposes."

Alyssa blew a raspberry at the idea of any soldier interfering with her, but she made no further objection to turning from the hard road to follow a stream up the fold of a hill to more sheltered terrain. I did notice that no one had asked my opinion, but it didn't bother me as much as perhaps it should have. Since we had turned east, I had become strangely passive.

As soon as we left the road, I again had that sense that we crossed through some portal into another world. Or rather that the Roman world was superimposed on this older one, older than the coming of the Celts, a world where water, soil, and rock ruled and trees led their deep-rooted, sheltering lives. We rode for awhile along a footpath that ran parallel to the ridge top and gradually climbed until we came to a narrow valley hidden in the fold between two swelling hills, backed by the ridge. We paused on the top of one of the hills and looked down the steep slope to the valley floor that was already in shadow.

"It might be good to make camp down there for the night," said Alyssa. "You probably can't even see it from the plain; it would blend right into the ridge from a distance, and there's most likely a stream somewhere."

"I want to be sure that we can make a quick getaway," cautioned Bele. "I wouldn't want to be backed against the ridge. The footing might be treacherous for the horses, if we had to make a run for it."

These were the kinds of things we considered whenever we made camp. Why did I suddenly feel panicked, almost sick to my stomach? Why did I feel that I did not so much want to set foot in that valley, let alone sleep there? Let's go on, I wanted to say, but something had happened to my voice, something was happening to my head. I couldn't hear anything over the din.

"Hush!" three voices demanded of me.

I must have cried out, but I hadn't even known it, hadn't even heard it over the strange clamor. Now suddenly everything was quiet. The birds had stopped singing. I could hear a trickle of water somewhere and the sound of horses' hooves on the other side of the valley. All of us tensed, and our horses did, too.

Then we saw them: five soldiers on horseback, directly facing us on the opposite hill. I caught the glint of a general's insignia on one man's chest, the one in the middle.

"I think they've seen us," Sarah spoke in a low voice. "But I don't think they're on military maneuvers or the general wouldn't be wearing that crested helmet. I'd say he's on a tour of inspection, getting the lay of the land."

"Well, I say we cease being part of the scenery," said Bele. "Let's disappear. Now."

"If we turn tail, they might pursue," objected Alyssa.

"We'd have a head start," Bele reasoned. "To follow us, they'd have to cross the valley or go around it."

"Let's wait a moment and see what they do," said Sarah. "We have no reason to run."

"We have no reason to face them, either," argued Bele.

"Yes, we do." I surprised us all. "I do."

For suddenly I knew, it had to be him, Gaius Suetonius Paulinus, the new governor, making the rounds of all the forts. Now I had another chance to deliver my warning to him, the one I had forgotten when we rushed off to find Joseph. Before anyone could stop me, I raised my hand and signaled to him in what I hoped was a nonthreatening gesture. He raised his arm in return.

"Now you've done it, Mother of Sarah!" Bele and Alyssa protested as one.

"I need to speak to the general," I said. "It's important. Trust me."

"You've given us no choice." Sarah was furious.

After days of trailing along after everyone else, I took the lead, urging my horse down a zigzagging path to the valley floor. On the other side of the valley, the general also began his descent. As I rode, the noise roared in my head again. There was a stench in my nostrils and bile in my throat; my eyes burned. But if I could just deliver the message, maybe I could stop it, whatever was coming. When I reached the bottom of the hill, I dismounted.

"I want to speak with him alone," I said handing the reins to Sarah. "Wait here."

Then everything was quiet again, as the general, too, dismounted, leaving his men behind. We walked towards each other at a deliberate pace, coming to stand face to face in the middle of the valley. There was no protocol for such a meeting, so we just stood for a moment, looking at each other, maybe both of us wondering how we kept straying into each other's story, as if some incoherent dream insisted on inhabiting waking hours.

"I have a message for you," I broke the silence.

"Speak," he said.

Just that one word, but his voice was so like my beloved's that it hurt, and I forgot everything else, just searching his face for a trace of the boy I had glimpsed on the moonlit cliffs.

"Are you all right?" he asked after a moment.

For an instant, the sounds rose around me again, closer, more distinct this time: clanging and screams. I saw him look around, wide-eyed, his hand on his sword hilt. Then the sounds subsided again, and he looked back at me, accusing.

"What are you doing?" he demanded.

"I am not doing anything," I told him. "But you heard it, too, didn't you?"

"What is it you want with me?" He refused to admit anything.

"I have a message for you," I repeated.

"So you said," he was curt. "Stop behaving like a mad prophetess and just give it to me."

"When you disembarked at Rutupiae," I began, "you were greeted by an official, the procurator," I paused so that he could hear the words I did not speak: your son. So that he could hear that I knew.

"Catus Decianus," he said, his voice neutral, but his face was closed; he was warning me off. "Well?"

I took a step closer to him, so that he would understand my words were only for him, close enough for my body to remember how much it liked his. His body seemed to remember, too, and he bent towards me. If only we could just be our warm bodies, without our haunted pasts and futures.

"You asked me to see for you the day before we sailed," I reminded him. "When I saw the man who greeted you, Catus Decianus, I recognized him. Here is my message for you: don't trust him. Keep a close watch on him. He is going to betray someone."

The general drew back from me abruptly and his hand went again to his sword. Well, fine then, let him kill me. I still had to warn him:

"It might be you."

I closed my eyes and waited for what he would do. I could hear the sounds again, but they were coming from a long way off. Or maybe I was a long way off. Far away, higher than the crows and vultures that circled.

At the same time, close by me, a man's breath came short as he struggled to regain control of himself.

"Is that all?"

Was that all? I opened my eyes and searched his face. It wasn't just his voice that was like my beloved's. There was something about the shape of his face, the mouth. But Jesus's mouth never lost its sweetness, even when he was angry or in pain. The general's mouth was resolutely grim as though to smile would be an affront to the rest of his face.

What manner of man is this? I asked my beloved silently.

The least of my brethren, I heard again, as I had that moonlit night.

Who is he to me then, why is he in my path?

You know, I thought I heard. *You will know.*

Then the general spoke again.

"Answer me," he commanded.

"If I did, would you listen?"

His face registered more surprise than anger. He was not used to being spoken to this way. Most people in his world were his subordinates and would not dare to question him.

"You didn't listen when I told you not to come to this country," I went on. "Will you listen now, if I tell you to leave?"

In the background, I could hear our horses stirring. My mare whinnied to me. By contrast, the soldiers' mounts held themselves as still as the riders, all of them in suspended animation for as long as this man willed.

"Did you follow me here?" he demanded.

If in doubt, answer a question with a question. A tactic Jesus had used, too.

"No, I just happened to be passing through."

It was the truth, but to my own ears I sounded evasive, like a bad liar.

"Then give me leave to wonder how urgent your message can be, or how much credence I should give it. By your own account you have made no effort to deliver your warning."

"I was called to an old friend's deathbed as soon as I disembarked."

Why did everything I say sound made up? The general kept his face expressionless, but I could tell he was skeptical.

"My condolences," he said perfunctorily. "Where are you going now?"

He didn't say: and just where do you think you're going? And by the way, it is within my power to stop you. But I could hear the implication.

"I am searching for my daughter."

I might as well try the truth again. It might throw him off track better than a lie

"The one you left behind," he said, "the reason you are here."

An unexpected gentleness in his tone brought back the night on the cliff, when neither of us knew the other, except as someone who had suffered terrible loss.

"Where are you searching?" he asked.

Don't tell him anything. Not anything. The voice in my head was not Jesus's this time but Sarah's. She was thinking to me from only a few feet away. I must remember to tell her, she didn't need to think so loud.

"Do you remember what you pledged?" It was my turn to answer a question with a question.

"Let us say for a moment that I don't remember."

"That if I agreed to use the sight for you, no troops under your command would ever interfere with me or my women."

He glanced over my shoulder at my companions and his lips twitched. Apparently their no doubt glaring countenances amused him. He better keep that smile to himself, if he didn't want to end up with an arrow in his back.

"I have never broken that pledge." He paused for a moment. "Will you think I am interfering if I offer you a night's hospitality at the fort?"

Sarah would have a cow was my first thought. And my second was why had he shifted so abruptly from curt to courteous? What did he hope to gain? But my third thought was strongest: Night was falling, and I wanted to get away from this valley. The silence was almost as bad as the din in my head had been, an absolute desperate silence that made my ears hurt.

"Will you give me your word of honor that this hospitality involves no lock and key and that we can leave at first light with our horses watered and fed?"

"I will," he said. "Follow my party. The fort is less than two miles from here. We have guest quarters suitable for women."

I did not bother to tell him that my women could rough it as well as any of his soldiers and far better than any Roman civilian.

"I have to consult my party," I told him.

Because I am no general, I did not add, but a long-suffering (and suffered) mother whose daughter is about to have a major snit. Or so I feared. Much to my surprise, I met with no resistance. The three of them had apparently anticipated this turn of events and come to an agreement.

"If they are foolish enough to let us inside, we might as well case the joint," Alyssa summed up their strategy.

"But you are not to tell him anything, Mother," added Sarah vehemently. "Not anything."

"I heard you the first time, Sarah."

"Swear!"

"Sarah!" Bele was shocked. "It is not nice to ask your own mother to swear an oath."

"Oh, I don't mind," I said. "I swear I won't tell him anything. I've already evaded him quite skillfully."

"That's probably why he wants to have another crack at you," said Alyssa.

"Let him, then," I shrugged. "You underestimate my talents, all of you. I am the only one of us who ever lived in Rome. And as a whore and a slave, I know how the information game is played."

Sarah, as unpredictably as the general, lightened up and actually grinned at me.

"In that case," she said. "Find out all you can."

Thus, I decided (in perhaps a very liberal interpretation) that I had my daughter's blessing for what I did that night.

CHAPTER THIRTEEN
LOVER OF THE WORLD

I AM IN the whores' bath at The Vine and Fig Tree with Dido and Berta, my sister whores. They look as young as they did when I first knew them, Berta all blonde and blowsy, Dido smooth, regal and black. But I am not young; I wear all my years of wandering and weather. I wonder if they even know I am there or if I am a ghost visible only to other ghosts. Then both turn and gaze at me, serenely without judgment or even curiosity.

"Once a whore always a whore," says Dido.

"Whore's deal," says Berta. "Do you remember how we seal it, Red?"

"Of course, I do," I say.

We all dip our fingers into our vulvas, then press the tips together. Then Berta and Dido turn to me and begin to run their fingertips over me. Wherever they touch me, roundness rises again, breasts, belly, and thighs. They touch me with light, deft, swirling motions. The mist of the bath becomes a sea mist; waves break on a shore, light turning the spray to gold. My mothers are here, too, all the women of my life are here, anointing me, mothers, whores and priestesses.

At last I stand alone in the center of this circle of women, and I look down at my naked body. All the patterns their fingers have made have turned blue. Woad, I think, they have painted me with woad. I look like Queen Maeve of Connacht before her battle with Cuchulain. Battle, it suddenly hits me. They have painted me for battle.

Then Queen Maeve herself steps into the circle to face me, my mirror image, both of us red-haired, woad-painted, in our prime.

"Sovereignty," she whispers. "Fuck for our sovereignty."

When I woke up I did not remember for a moment where I was. I was so used to sleeping outside, the thickness of the darkness surrounding me was disorienting as was the softness of the couch. Then my eyes adjusted, and I recognized Bele, keeping watch in the entryway of our chamber, as we had agreed to do in turns.

"Guests or no guests," Sarah had insisted. "We are in a Roman fortress. One of us will keep watch, and we'll all keep our weapons at hand."

The general had not insisted that we disarm or Sarah never would have accepted his hospitality. I felt for my dagger now, still in its place on my belt. The sword I had laid aside, and whatever Sarah would have said, I did not intend to take it with me to the latrines.

"Go back to sleep, Mother of Sarah," said Bele. "It's Alyssa's turn to relieve me."

"I'm just going out to relieve myself."

"Can't you do it in the piss bucket?" Bele whispered. "Your daughter would not want you wandering around the fort alone at night."

"My daughter doesn't want me to do anything without her supervision," I answered. "I want some air. Besides, the fort is practically empty except for the general and his staff."

He had explained to us at dinner that the fort was only used when a campaign was being waged. Otherwise, it just had a small defensive guard to keep the fort in readiness.

"That makes it less safe," grumbled Bele. "No one to help you if you get into trouble."

"I won't get into trouble," I assured her.

Despite a long life that included exile, capture, slavery, near crucifixion, not to mention witnessing the arrest and crucifixion of my beloved, I had never quite overcome my lack of fear or my perhaps unfounded assumption that I could handle anything or anyone.

After I had used the fairly sophisticated latrine (no mere ditch), I decided to take a turn around the perimeter of the fort before going back to our quarters. I could always justify my midnight ramble to my companions by saying I was taking the opportunity to gather information. But the truth was I felt restless, stirred up by the dream, so vivid that I could feel a sort of sensual echo of the women's touch.

It was a dark night, no moon, and the attention of the sentries on the watch towers was turned outward to the plain surrounding the fort. Barefoot and in a dark cloak, I passed unnoticed. Though there were sentries posted in every direction, I discerned that only every other tower was manned. Unlike most Romans, who lived in cities where the only landscapes they could see were stylized frescoes, I had never liked living behind walls. Temple Magdalen had been walled for safety, backed by a hill of caves, but I had spent many a night on our tower, gazing out over the Sea of Galilee, watching the reflection of moon and stars and the lanterns of the fishing boats going out before dawn. Out of homesickness and force of habit, I found myself scaling the ladder to stand on an empty tower. From there I could hear the river and just discern its dim gleaming. Across the plain rose the ridge, a black wave swallowing the stars, the ridge that hid the valley where something terrible had happened or would happen, unless someone stopped it.

Me.

The thought struck me like a blow, and I grabbed hold of the wall to steady myself.

Then I heard someone climbing the ladder. I turned and he was there before me dark as the ridge, with his own hidden places full of horror. As I faced him, I felt the woad swirling on my skin, cool and burning at once. I was painted for battle.

Once a whore always a whore.

Fuck for our sovereignty.

Neither of us spoke. I could not see his face clearly, but I could feel his presence, the unsettling familiarity of it. I knew what I had to do, what I wanted to do, what I might never have the chance do again. I unclasped my cloak and spread it out on the tower floor. Then I unbuckled my belt and stripped off my tunic, my flesh puckering in response to the cool air, my beautiful round woad-painted flesh, bright and dark as night.

"Who are you?" he demanded.

I drew him into my arms.

All mountains tumble to the sea.

Sometimes lovemaking takes you so deep inside the body that you fly out of it. It is like death. Your whole life unwinds. You can be in any time or place. You can become any animal or bird. You are the fire, the water, the earth, the wind. Only your lover is with you, only your lover holds the thread that can bring you back.

It was like that, and I cannot tell you more. If you have been there, then you know.

"Who are you?" he asked again when it was over and we lay back in our bodies, in the chill night, on the hard floor.

"I am the lover of the world."

It seemed to me that Dwynwyn's long ago prophecy still held, though my beloved had gone before me, and I had been alone for so long.

"What do you mean by that?"

We were lying on our sides facing each other, touching but no longer entwined. There was an edge to his voice; I knew he would not remain open to me much longer. What good did it do to fuck someone's brains out if you left a vacuum? All at once I knew what I had to do: tell the story of the lovers of the world, as I had when Mary of Bethany dragged me around southern Gaul until I ran away to my hermit cave. To put it crudely, I was going to proselytize.

Leaving out the location and circumstances of Dwynwyn's prophecy, I launched into my narrative, my gospel, if you will. You might think that telling your present lover about a past lover (and not just any lover but the one you love before and beyond time in all the worlds) would not go over well, but the general seemed fascinated by Jesus. I wonder if he somehow sensed what I suspected, that they were indeed brethren, that Jesus was somehow his other, his opposite, his long-lost mirror image. But when we got to the part about the feeding of the five thousand, and how Jesus fled the crowds refusing to be made king, the general interrupted.

"I am willing to suspend disbelief about the miracles, the multiplying loaves and fishes. I am not a stranger to sorcery. But why would this Jesus of yours refuse a chance to unify and lead his people, especially when his cousin had just been executed at the hands of a Roman puppet king?"

I had been doing my best to make this scene particularly compelling, this moment when Jesus turned his back forever on armed struggle. My momentum was broken, and I found myself unprepared to answer a logical and inevitable question.

"He probably knew he couldn't win," the general answered himself, regretful and scornful at once. "No rabble can win against a trained army. In the end, he would have lost face, or gotten himself killed along with a lot of other people. But what a chance he had. That would have been a real miracle, better than loaves and fishes, better than turning water into wine for a bunch of guests who were already soused."

He rudely dismissed our wedding miracle. But I decided to let it pass. No one who hadn't been there could know what that night had been like, especially not this man, this career soldier who not so secretly wished he'd had that same chance: to be a warrior king, a hero of a defiant people, worthy of a bard's song, instead of just a lackey for a bureaucratic empire. He was sitting up now. In a moment, he'd be on his feet and pacing. In a moment, I would lose him altogether.

"That is not why he refused," I countered, though many people at the time saw it just the way the general did, including some of the disciples, notably Judas. "Where he wanted to go, where he wanted to lead people, he could not go with an army."

"You said he wanted to restore the sovereignty of Israel. How could he hope to do that without an army?"

"He wanted more than that," I said. "He wanted to restore the sovereignty of his god, of what he called the kingdom of heaven."

I don't think the general actually spat, but he made a sound that could be a precursor to it.

"So he was nothing more than another religious fanatic, after all. Just like the druids, who refuse to bear arms themselves but incite other people to fight their losing battles."

"Is that really your view of the druids?" I ignored for a moment his insult to my beloved. I didn't want to be put on the defensive. I didn't want to keep backing up as he hacked away at me, so I side-stepped just enough to shift the direction and regain some control.

"Is there another?" he parried skillfully. "Yours perhaps?"

"Perhaps," I stalled, wondering where I could take the debate that would not reveal my first-hand knowledge of druid resistance to Roman rule. "Or maybe I just think your premise is faulty, not to mention arrogant. You assume that anyone who chooses not to bear arms is a fool or a coward, or, worse still, willing to exploit other people's bravery or skill."

"I don't assume," he said. "I know."

"What if someone willingly sacrificed the power of weapons for another kind of power?"

"I would say that proves what you just said: to sacrifice the right to self-defense makes someone a fool, a coward, or a knowing or unknowing exploiter of those who will fight. Power is power, however you wield it. Those who can make other people do their dirty work may be cleverer, but they are not morally superior. Quite the opposite."

I sighed. My proselytizing was not going well. I had never been good at it. I could keep track of a narrative but not of the moral points I was supposed to draw out. The moral of the story is or should be an oxymoron.

"You misunderstand," I tried again. "Jesus did not sacrifice military power for the kind of cynical power you imagine the druids have or for the kind of easy privilege Roman senators have, living off other people's labor and sacrifice. He did not have that kind of power at all. He did not want it. His power was in himself, the way he saw, the way he spoke, the way he touched people, the way he knew what to do in the moment. Not so different from what it must be like in the midst of a battle. But instead of killing people, he healed them."

The general was silent for a moment. Could I possibly have swayed him?

"Power is power," he said again. "It comes from the same place, the power to kill and the power to heal."

"Yes," I agreed, remembering my mothers saying the same thing long ago when the fire of the stars first came into my hands. I also remembered Peter using the power in his hands to strike two people dead in a moment of wrath.

"Killing, healing, one is not better than the other," he stated.

"I suppose you would think so," I said, "since killing is your job."

"It is my job, and it is a necessary job."

A heaviness settled on me like the night dew on my cloak. It would be time for my watch soon, or past time, and if I didn't show up Sarah and the women would be up in arms and searching for me. I looked around for my tunic, suddenly feeling old and absurd for imagining myself some Helen of Troy in reverse, able to stop a war with my irresistible charms.

"You didn't finish your story," he spoke gruffly, but I thought I heard a grudging gentleness underneath, almost as if he were making amends for being so dismissive. "What became of Jesus?"

Why had I started down this road? All his prejudices would be confirmed. Well, there was no help for it, no use in dressing it up.

"He was crucified," I said. "By Pontius Pilate, the Roman procurator of Judea."

"On what charges?"

"Sedition against Roman authority. In the end it didn't matter that Jesus had refused to lead an armed uprising. Pilate accused him of claiming to be king of the Jews. A trumped up charge, but Pilate didn't care. He saw Jesus as dangerous, because the crowds followed him."

"Those crowds can be violent and seditious," the general said, "whether or not Jesus believed in armed rebellion."

"That may be true," I conceded. "But that does not mean his death was just."

"Many aren't," the general conceded.

"So how can you say healing and killing are the same?" I demanded. "Healing is always by consent. You can't heal someone against their will. But you can kill them."

Yet as soon as I spoke I knew it was more complicated than that. Jesus had spent his whole life moving towards his death, foreseeing it, dreading it, courting it, and, as his apostles now proclaimed, triumphing over it (with help from me that no one knew about or would acknowledge if they did).

"And even if killing is necessary sometimes in self-defense or defense of your country," I went on, "even if someone accepts his death, it matters who you kill for—and why."

"And," he said, 'it matters who you die for—and why."

I waited for him to ask, who did Jesus die for? What did he die for? What difference did it make to anyone but me and his friends? What would I say? Don't think Rome got rid of him so easily. A movement is spreading in his name all over the Empire, a movement that you Romans are gearing up to persecute, a movement that will eventually conquer Rome and create a new empire. I didn't know that then. No one did. And if I had, frankly, I might have tried to stop it. But he didn't ask that question.

"Why are you here?" he asked instead.

"I've told you. I'm looking for my daughter."

"No," he said. "I mean why are you here with me, a Roman general, a Roman governor, part of the same power that killed your husband?"

Was he implying that I was a whore or a collaborator? Well, I was a whore, and I'd been accused of sleeping with the enemy before now. There was a reason, a compelling reason, a noble reason. What was it?

"Love is indiscriminate," I said.

"Love?" he repeated. I could hear his lip curling in disdain. "Indiscriminate?"

He was offended. I had wounded his vanity. I am afraid I was pleased.

"And it is as strong as death, love, that is, and passion as relentless as sheol."

"Sheol?"

"The realm of death," I explained.

Suddenly I remembered why I was with him. Love is as strong as death took on a new meaning.

"Something terrible is going to happen," I told him, "in that valley where we met. You sensed it, too, I know you did. But it doesn't have to happen. It doesn't. That is why I am with you; that is why I am here."

I stopped, confused. It had seemed so clear in the dream. Fuck for sovereignty. Make it so good for him that he'll want to pack up and go home, retire to a villa, take the rest of the Romans with him. But the Romans weren't going anywhere. They were building whole retirement communities here. And my general's job was to defend them.

"You are a mad prophetess," he told me. "You are as crazy as Jesus."

Then he turned to me and gathered me into his arms with a tenderness that utterly undid me.

"Who are you?" I asked.

"It doesn't matter," he said.

And then we didn't talk any more.

CHAPTER FOURTEEN
FILIAL WRATH

"OH, MOTHER OF SARAH!" Alyssa greeted me as I attempted to steal back to our quarters just before dawn. "You are in such deep shit."

"I'm late for my watch, I know" I said.

Of course I was. The general and I had made love exhaustively and exhaustingly till we fell asleep entwined, both of us starting like guilty things at the first cock crow. Our affair was not meant for daylight. Both of us had our reasons for clinging to the tattered cloak of night. No one would have thought twice if the general had taken one of the young women to bed, but consorting on the bare boards of the watchtower with an old crone? A general doesn't want to be viewed by his troops as too eccentric.

"Sorry, Alyssa, go get some rest."

Alyssa rolled her eyes at me.

"*I'm* not your problem, Mother of Sarah."

"Don't tell me," I said, looking past Alyssa into our quarters to Sarah's empty couch.

"I'm sure I don't have to. Didn't you know she'd ransack the fortress as soon as she knew you were missing?"

I didn't answer.

"Well," Alyssa stretched. "You don't have to tell me where you were or what you were doing with who-*ever*. But expect a thorough and ruthless interrogation when your daughter gets back, if she gets back. I wouldn't put it past her to get into a fight and get herself thrown into the brig. Bela's with her. I hope she'll have a restraining influence."

"I suppose I should go and look for her," I sighed.

"I wouldn't if I were you," said Alyssa. "Best to stay in one place, say you got lost and that's why you were late for your watch. Feign innocence."

Now I rolled my eyes. Feigned innocence was not becoming at any age, certainly not at mine.

"I'll go look for them," Alyssa offered. "Finish out your watch."

The filial interrogation that Alyssa had predicted never occurred, because Sarah had decided that she already knew everything. And she didn't like it.

"Get your things together," she said as she stalked past me without looking at me. "We're leaving. Now."

I should have said: who put you in charge? But it was a little late for that. Sarah had been in charge of this quest since before day one, and I had ceded authority to her. So, as usual, I said the wrong thing instead.

"What about breakfast?" I followed her inside.

"We're not having it," she snarled as she snatched up my sword and handed it to me; she was already fully armed. "We ate enough last night to keep us going for a week."

She spoke with such disgust that I thought she might heave up our decent but by no means extravagant dinner (by Roman standards) right then and there.

"Those horses better be goddamned saddled and ready to go," she said, and she strode out, clearly expecting us all to fall into line.

"I'm not going till I have a few of those olives," I declared; there were still some in a dish as well as some bread to soak up the oil. It might be my last taste of Mediterranean food for all I knew.

"Don't push it, Mother of Sarah," Bele pleaded. Alyssa was already out the door.

"Yes, I am the *Mother* of Sarah. Technically that means she is supposed to defer to *me*."

I spat an olive pit into an empty bowl. Bele sighed.

"We saw you and that Roman general climbing down from the watchtower."

My stomach gave a little lurch. I decided against more olives but I did put a hunk of bread in my pocket as I headed for door.

"If you saw me, then why were you still out looking for me?" I wondered.

"We weren't looking for you. I mean not after we saw you," Bele hesitated.

There was more, I could tell.

"Then what were you doing?" I demanded.

"I am not sure Sarah would want me to tell you," said Bele, glancing ahead at Sarah, though she was clearly too far away to hear.

"Let me guess. She accosted the general."

It sounded preposterous, but as soon as I said it, I knew it was true.

"We'd better catch up with them," Bele said as Sarah and Alyssa disappeared into the stable. "Sarah's in a bad, bad mood. Foul. Rotten. Stinking. Let's not make it worse."

The horses were fed and groomed, looking more respectable than they had in ages, and all ready to go. The general had come to the stable himself to see that everything was done properly, an honor Sarah clearly could have done without. She ignored him as she led her horse and mine out into the courtyard. He and I exchanged a glance, and, I confess, almost burst into laughter. I felt young again in a horrible, wonderful way and at the same time old and foolish. I was glad to have someone to share my predicament, if only for a moment.

Soon we were saying our farewells, or I was. Sarah took it on herself to refuse all offers of any further help in any form.

I was the last to mount, and the general helped me silently, his touch so much gentler than his face, which tended always toward the grim.

"It doesn't have to happen," I said to him quietly.

"You don't know that," he answered. "You don't know that at all. You may be a seer, but you are not the maker of fate."

"Who is then?"

"Let's go!" Sarah cut short our last-minute debate on fate and free will.

And we all followed her as she turned and galloped north across the open plain.

There was no way Macha, my staid and sturdy mare, could keep pace with the others, but I decided not to worry about it, even when I could barely see them. For us, we were going fast. Macha plunged forward, a warm-blooded ship, riding her own waves. And I felt something tightly coiled loosen in me, unravel and stream behind me on the wind, till it became a high cloud, not even mine anymore, just a part of a sky that was always changing.

After a few miles, I spied Bele walking out from a copse of trees to signal me. The others were waiting hidden there, watering their horses in a small stream. I dismounted, too, and Macha joined the other equines. Very soon it became apparent that the other humans had not benefited from their gallop on this summer morning. Sarah still refused to look at me, and the others seemed constrained by her attitude. Fine. I would take advantage of the quiet and rest.

"We're waiting here till we are sure no one has followed us," Bele relented, as I sat down with my back against a tree.

I just nodded, and closed my eyes.

"We've gone quite a bit out of our way," Alyssa added with a hint of reproach, "so that they won't know for sure which direction we're going."

Sarah still had not spoken. I glanced at her out of the corner of my eye. She stood arms folded across her chest, eyes narrowed, scanning the plain we'd just crossed, for signs of surreptitious pursuit. The message, however indirect, was not subtle. I was to blame for this detour. I had insisted on speaking to the general when we might have gotten away unnoticed or unrecognized. Because of me, we had spent the night in the fortress. And clearly they did not appreciate my efforts at reconnaissance.

"I am sure it's always wise to take precautions," I ventured. "But the general did give me his word that he would not interfere with us."

That did it. Sarah's icy silence shattered, and she turned on me in full molten fury.

"He is the *enemy*! His word is worth nothing."

Sarah was standing, but I decided to remain seated, my spine connected to the oak, for so it was. There were acorns on the ground. I picked one up and held it, an on-the-spot talisman. It wasn't a hazelnut or a mustard seed, but it gave me something to grasp as I wondered what to say to my daughter, who had so quickly adopted the enmities of her maternal line (at the same time as being appalled by her mother).

"The two don't necessarily follow," I said, looking up at her. "An enemy can be honorable." And your father said: love your enemy, I did not say aloud, which turned out to be just as well.

"If you acknowledge that he is the enemy, why were you consorting with him!"

Alyssa and Bele exchanged a glance and went to rub down the horses.

"Consorting?" I repeated.

"You fucked him," Sarah practically spat. Her golden eyes were fierce as a wild cat's and her dark skin looked purple. "Didn't you! I knew you were a whore, but I thought you had gotten over it. I thought you were sorry for what you did."

It was time for me to get to my feet, to face her, to have it out once and for all.

"But you haven't changed. You don't care about anything or anyone but yourself. You'll fuck anything that walks, and you'll ruin everything. Just like you did before."

With Paul of Tarsus. When she was twelve years old. Part of her was still twelve.

Suddenly I understood. Sarah needed something from me, something I'd never been able to give her. I dropped the acorn and slapped her across the face, so hard she staggered. And then before she could run away from me again, I took her in my arms and held her tight. She twisted and struggled to break my hold, but I was stronger than she thought. Stronger than I thought. I held her with all my might and held her still when she finally let go and wept.

"I am sorry," she said at last. "I should not have called you a whore."

"Ah, *cariad*, I am a whore," I said. "For better and worse. And I am sorrier than you will ever know for all the years I lost with you. But I am not ashamed of being a whore."

I loosed my hold, and Sarah drew apart from me but not away. She looked me in the face for the first time that day. I met her gaze, and then I bent and picked up the acorn.

"Here," I pressed it into her hand, unsure of what I meant by the gesture, but she accepted it, and held it quietly. For awhile neither of us spoke, just stood in the warming air, listening to the sound of the stream, the stir of leaves, the breath of the horses, the attentive silence of Bele and Alyssa, who were eavesdropping at a safe distance.

"I went after him, this morning, the general," she said at length.

"What did you say to him?" I asked.

She stared down at the acorn in her hand.

"I told him not to believe anything you said. I let him know you were quite mad, that we had come to Pretannia in the hope that returning to your native land would restore your wits."

"Why on earth did you tell him that?" I demanded.

"I was afraid you might have told him something or asked for his help finding Boudica."

"Sarah, I may be crazy, but I like to think that I'm not entirely stupid. I still don't understand why you went to him. Why didn't you just ask me what I'd told him? Did you think I would lie?"

She lifted her eyes to mine again.

"I was too angry with you," she said bluntly, "and too afraid of what I might do if I found out you had told him anything."

"Oh, Sarah."

I felt for us both, how hard it was to love each other and not understand each other.

"What did he say when you said I was crazy?" I asked after a moment.

"He sympathized," she said.

"What?"

"Yes, he agreed that you were demented. Said you had come to him babbling incoherently about some vision."

"Babbled, did he say babbled?" I felt insulted, and then I realized: he was covering for me.

"He did. I wanted to kill him on the spot, and I would have, but Bele grabbed my arm, and said we better not leave you unattended."

I started to laugh, and I couldn't stop. Sarah stared at me with mingled wonder and disgust.

"You *are* crazy," she said.

"So I've been told," I said, still gasping with laughter. "You and the general agree on that much."

And then I remembered why the general had called me crazy, and I sobered up.

"Listen, Sarah, I want to tell you something about why I, well, why I took the general as a lover."

"I *really* don't want to know," Sarah looked pained, "unless you did it to get information out of him. Did you? Find out anything?"

I shook my head.

"Nothing that we don't already know. Sarah, I saw something yesterday when we were in that valley. Maybe you sensed it, too. Something terrible. The general wasn't lying when he said I told him about a vision. I wanted to try to stop it happening. I wanted to him to *want* to stop it happening. I thought if I–"

It really did not make sense when I said it out loud.

"Anyway, I warned him," I concluded lamely.

"But he didn't believe you," Sarah stated. "He thought you were crazy."

I didn't answer. It might be worse than that. He had believed me; I swear he had shared my vision, but not my conclusion: that this horror could and must be prevented. By him. That's the part he thought was crazy.

"What's done is done," Sarah decided, and she reached for both my hands, the acorn pressed between her right and my left. "As far as I am concerned, we will never see that man again, we will never come to this place again."

Her voice was fierce, determined, as if by sheer will she could make it so. I wished she could, but I sensed some part of her knew that it wasn't over yet. But for now at least, she and I had come to some peace together.

"Alyssa, Bele. It's safe now," Sarah called over her shoulder, and then she turned to me. "Are you ready?"

It took me a moment to register. Sarah was deferring to me; she was waiting for me, waiting for me to claim my stake in this journey.

"Let's go, everyone," I said in a loud, clear voice. "We ride east!"

CHAPTER FIFTEEN
TRUTH?

After our confrontation, Sarah and I were at once more at ease and more careful of each other, as if the new peace between us had to be swaddled and held close. For someone who was the daughter of eight mothers, I confess I was finding it challenging to be the mother of two. Maybe that was it: the ratio was all wrong. My mothers could always pass the blame endlessly among them. Not to mention they had shipped me off to druid school when I was fourteen. And had never seen me again, I reminded myself. Did their hearts still ache for me as mine had ached for Sarah the long years she was missing, as mine still ached for the tiny red-headed baby who had grown up to be a queen? Had Boudica ever longed for her vanished mother? Would she welcome her sudden uninvited reappearance?

Each day we rode further east into more settled country, Roman towns cheek by jowl with the round wattle daub huts of native homesteads. Each day my doubts deepened. When Branwen and Viviane told me the story the druids had concocted about my disappearance, I had been incensed. At that moment, I would have rushed to Boudica's side, hell bent on setting the record straight: I never would have left you. I was forced into exile. I did not abandon you. Now I heard the implication of my self-exoneration. No, Boudica, it's the people you admired most and wanted to emulate who lied to you shamelessly for their own ends.

What about that truth would ever set her free? Free from what? And would I be telling the truth for her sake or for mine? *Cariad*, I spoke to my beloved silently. You never addressed that point, did you?

And he remained silent now.

At last it came time to leave the Wyddelian Road and ride northeast on smaller roads and cart tracks. Or, at least, Sarah had decided it was.

"We haven't asked directions of anyone," I pointed out.

We had paused for a midday break on a hill overlooking a valley. The road led across it to a large town with earth fortifications surrounding it.

"We don't need to," said Sarah. "You told us Branwen and Viviane said to leave the Roman road when we came into the territory of the Catuvellauni. We're right in the heart of it. By my calculations that town over there is Verulamium."

The Catuvellauni, the tribe who had spawned the resistance fighter Caratacus, had clearly returned to their Roman-loving ways. Though Verulamium looked like any other Roman settlement, it had been built by the Catuvellauni by themselves and for themselves, complete with Roman-style gymnasiums and baths. Flattered and encouraged by the imitation, Rome had granted the town status as a *municipium*, second only in status to a *colonia*. Local magistrates were rewarded with Roman citizenship at the end of their term. A model town from the Roman point of view.

"Why don't we stop there before we go north?' I suggested casually, aware that I wanted to stall the last leg of our journey for as long as I could. "We could go to the baths, eat something we haven't foraged or killed. Make ourselves presentable."

Sarah looked at me, almost sorrowfully I thought. Here was her mother, who had survived exile beyond the ninth wave, who had shared her father's open air ministry, who had toughed it out in the Taurus Mountains, lived aboard ships for seven years, inhabited a cave, here she was craving Roman-style luxuries at every turn.

"We bathed in the river this morning," Sarah said.

"So we did," I agreed. "I just like hot water now and again."

"Since you're usually in it, Mother of Sarah, that's just as well," remarked Alyssa.

"And you can hardly be hungry," Sarah went on. "We feasted last night on rabbit and greens."

"And ate cold leftovers this morning," Bele took my side, as she sometimes did. "Cold, just like the river water. No, sorry, the river was colder than the rabbit. Way colder. Try bone-numbing."

"We have precious few coins and nothing to barter," said Alyssa, who kept track of the purse.

"There's a more important reason not to go," Sarah stated. "We stand out. Four women traveling without men. People will be curious and the Catuvellauni are now an enemy tribe. We don't want them knowing our business."

I heard also what she wasn't saying, that if the general had sent out our description and wanted to keep track of our movements, we would be easily spotted there.

"All right, let's go on then, but before we do I want to say something." I took a breath and prepared to annoy my companions. "I am the one among us who was raised in the Holy Isles and trained by the druids. I was enslaved in Rome and saw my husband killed by Romans. So if anyone has reason to hate them and regard them all as enemies, it's me. Yes, I know you were arrested by the Romans and spent a night in a Roman jail, but let's face it, you were, in fact, pirates."

All three of them began to sputter.

"Wait," I held up my hand. "I'm not done. Do not imagine that all the natives here are blameless heroes or shameless collaborators or all Romans exploiting tyrants. The Romans invaded here, because they could. Because the tribes warred with each other and made and betrayed alliances as it suited them, Boudica's tribe among them."

There was a silence.

"Are you defending the Pax Romana?" Sarah asked, trying to keep her tone even and not quite succeeding. "Have you become an apologist for the Empire?"

Because of that man, she did not say, but I could hear her thinking it.

"No," I said, and I hoped it was true. "I only want to say, nothing is simple." I was old enough, why couldn't I speak wisdom instead of clichés. "Let me put it this way, Sarah. The Romans killed your father; the druids tried to. If it comes to choosing sides, I am on the side of truth." I startled myself by quoting my beloved. "Though I will admit I don't always know what it is."

That was the truth, all right, but it didn't have the same ring as: And all who are on the side of truth listen to my voice. No one was listening to me, as far as I could tell, or if they were, only reluctantly. Before anyone could answer or argue, I whistled for Macha, and led the way north.

I am glad now that I never saw Verulamium or any of its inhabitants.

When I think of Iceni country, always in my memory is the sound and smell of water. Streams everywhere, some running free, some cut as channels. In this flat country with just a hint of roll or hill, the sky is huge, yet often low with clouds and mists that swirl and shift. Because of the water, this is a country of birds—bitterns, larks, curlews, orioles—and their constant sound gives a brightness and lightness to a land of seamless green and grey. It was excellent grazing land for cattle, and I knew the Iceni exported lots of meat. They were also known for the horses they bred and trained. The pirates turned horse whisperers felt right at home, and our mounts as well. It was great country for galloping.

Late in the afternoon of our second day of riding north, we asked the way of a wizened cattle herder who'd brought his cows to drink in a shallow ford. Many Celts are tall and strapping, but he looked like he must be descended from the smaller peoples that the Celts (in their turn) had invaded.

"King Prasutagus and Queen Boudica?" the man repeated, seeming a bit wary. "Are you strangers here? Where do you come from?"

We had kept so much to ourselves on the road and been so suspicious of others, we had forgotten that we might encounter suspicion. We needed to offer credentials (that is to say, lineage) and I was the only one who had any that might be comprehensible.

"We've been living in Gaul," I said, truthfully enough. "I am the foster daughter of the late King Bran of the Silures. And I am kinswoman to Queen Boudica."

That sounded good, I thought. I was impressed with myself for quick thinking.

"Maybe you can talk some sense to your kinswoman then. No good can come of it. No good. Kings and queens, it's all quarreling and cattle raiding and taking of captives and buying and selling. Fun for the warriors, while they live. Me, I've been bought and sold more than once. My kin are the kine."

"I understand, *combrogo*," said Sarah. "I'd trust my horse over most people, any day. But would you, out of kindness, tell us if we are going the right way?"

"*Combrogo*, you call me? *Combrogo*. A word the queen likes. Keep going. Ride till the east darkens, and look for the left fork, if it's herself you want, the left fork."

He paid little attention to our thanks, and we rode on without questioning him further. Sarah dropped back and slowed her pace to ride beside me for awhile.

"We must be near," she said. "It sounds as though that man has actually heard her speak."

"Branwen said that when the Romans tried to disarm the tribes, Boudica went around and rallied them to rebel," I told her. "She probably gave lots of speeches then. Who knows how far afield she may have traveled."

"He did say, in that poetic way, ride until the east darkens. That will be in another couple of hours," she said, and when I did not respond she added, "You're nervous, aren't you, Mother?"

"Nervous?" I repeated. I had been avoiding naming the feeling in the pit of my stomach, the clamminess of my hands, but now that the subject had been raised, I might as well be precise. "I'm terrified."

Sarah said nothing for awhile, her eyes turned to the horizon, as if trying to gauge its darkening. The sun behind us found a break in the clouds and cast its rays on the clouds to the east, an effect I usually enjoyed.

"I suppose you have reason to be afraid," she said. "But I always think of you as fearless."

"You do?"

"It used to comfort me, all those years we were apart, to think of you being brave and fierce and coming to my rescue."

"I thought you hated me when you ran away," I ventured; this was territory we usually avoided.

"I forgot to after awhile," she said matter-of-factly. "And you did rescue me, eventually. I was right."

"I'm glad I had the chance," I said. "But I always think of you as the fierce and fearless one. Beating up all the boys in the village, and then leaving a trail of black eyes and bloody noses as you went."

"I'm tough," she admitted, "but not fearless. And not as foolish as you, either. Fearlessness and foolishness often go together."

She punctured the swelling of my maternal bosom.

"I prefer the word impulsive," I said.

"Whatever." Sarah waved away my semantics. "Have you thought about what you are going to say to Boudica?"

"I have thought about it," I told her. "However out of character you may find it, I don't intend to be hasty."

Sarah considered for a moment.

"What does that mean?"

"It means, it might not be wise for me to rush in and say 'I am your long-lost mother.' That's all."

"Then how *are* you going to present yourself?" she asked, reasonably enough.

"Well," I said, "as I told the cattleman, I am the foster daughter of King Bran. That ought to do it, especially since I have a message for her from Branwen."

"You do?" Sarah was surprised. "You never told me about that."

"Yes, I do," I said firmly. "I am to give her Branwen's love. Oh and Viviane's if I must."

"Right," said Sarah. "And you rode across the whole country to do that. And where are you supposed to have been all these years? What are you going to tell her about your life?"

I didn't answer. Clearly, I hadn't thought it through.

"What I'm asking," Sarah persisted, "is, are you, well, going to concoct some story?"

"I don't know yet."

"You just said you were on the side of truth."

"A story is true if it's well told," I fell back on my mothers' old axiom.

"You always said that to me when I was a child," retorted Sarah. "But you know what, Mother? That's a lie. Come on. Let's pick up the pace."

The truth is, she who has the faster horse has the last word.

There is no more delaying now. The east is darkening; the clouds have thinned enough that I can see the first star just east of mid-heaven. I can also just barely see the fork in the cart track. The right fork leads to a large torch-lit Roman villa, and the left fork leads to...more darkness.

"Can this be right?" Bele wondered after about a mile.

"We could go back to that huge villa and ask the way," suggested Alyssa.

"Just a little further," Sarah urged. "Just over that rise. I hear dogs barking."

My hands trembled so badly, Macha could feel it; she whinnied at my uneasiness, and the dogs barked louder. As soon as we crested the rise, we saw it: a large village of round houses behind a wooden stockade. In the next moment, half a dozen warriors arose seemingly out of nowhere; we were surrounded. Each warrior had an arrow or a spear aimed at one of our hearts.

"Who goes there?" demanded the leader. His voice sounded frail and elderly for a captain of the guard. "Who approaches the Queen's seat by night and by stealth?"

None of us answered for a moment. Bele and Alyssa didn't understand the language well enough. Though Sarah was a quick study with languages, she seemed, for once, to be waiting for me to speak first.

"We approach the Queen's seat by night only because the day has ended," I began. "We have no need for stealth. We come in peace."

"And if you do not, you will leave in pieces," the man rejoined.

(Yes, I know this is a pun only in English, but trust me, the Celts loved wordplay as much as swordplay, so let it stand.)

"State your lineage," the man commanded.

This could be tricky. My patrilineage was the same as the queen's. Well, my mothers never approved of tracing descent through the father, anyway. Boudica didn't know her matrilineage, so it would not be recognized. Plus, I would be telling the truth. So there, Sarah.

"I am Maeve Rhuad, daughter of the warrior witches of Tir na mBan."

I paused, remembering the name Tir na mBan used to cast warriors and druids alike into a trance of terror or longing. Men used to moan; their eyes would roll up in their heads, knees would buckle. So far as I could tell, these men were unmoved, except perhaps by impatience. Were they too far east to feel the proper awe?

"Go on," the man prompted.

"Daughters of the Cailleach, daughter of the goddess Bride—"

"Daughter of Dugall the Brown," the warriors began to chant (at least they revered Bride). I could hear women's voices among them. The guard was not all male. "ab Aodh, ab Conn, ab Criara, ab Cairbre, ab Cas, ab Cormach, ab Cartach, ab Conn. Each day and each night that I say the descent of Bride, I shall not be slain, I shall not be sworded, I shall not be put in a cell, I shall not be hewn, I shall not be riven, I shall not be anguished, I shall not be wounded, I shall not be ravaged, I shall not be blinded, I shall not be made naked, I shall not be left bare, nor fire shall burn me, nor sun shall burn me, nor moon shall blanch me..."

The warriors went on listing the benefits provided by Bride's lineage, and I joined in. We were all a bit breathless by the end, but I was sure we had bonded. What better credentials could I offer?

"Right, then," the man cleared his throat. "But who is your father?"

Who's the father, who's the father? That's all anyone ever wanted to know.

"Manannan Mac Lir," I said automatically. Sarah, next to me, gave me a small, discreet jab in the leg. "That is what my mothers always told me," I hedged. "My foster father is the late great King Bran of the Silures who gave his life to the resistance against Rome. Bran Fendigaid, ab Llyr Lleidiaith, ab Baran, ab Ceri Hirlyn Gwyn, ab Caid, ab Arch, ab Meirion," I launched into Bran's lineage, amazed that I remembered it. "...ab Ceiraint, ab Greidiol, ab Dingad, ab Anyn, ab Alafon–"

"You can stop now," the guard instructed me. "We all know of King Bran, may he rest in the Isles of the Blest and his bold sons after him. State your purpose."

Another tricky question. I was glad I had prepared for it.

"If you know of King Bran and his sons, then you know that he also has a daughter, Branwen, now a druid on the Isle of Mona where your queen once studied. I have a–"

"We will speak no more of this out of doors," the guard cut me off. "To show your good faith, you will disarm and cast your weapons on the ground."

Oddly enough for someone who wasn't all that keen on carrying a weapon in the first place, I felt balky. Queen Boudica had organized a whole rebellion to resist disarmament, but she expected her guests to make themselves, well, hostages. I looked at Sarah, waiting for her to object. To my surprise, she was unbuckling her sword, and Bele and Alyssa, after a moment's hesitation, followed her lead.

"It's the only way we'll get in," Sarah said quietly. "We've come this far. We'll just have to risk it."

We'll have to risk it, the same words I said long ago when a Samaritan with a sick man had knocked at Temple Magdalen's gates.

"All right," I agreed and laid my weapons down.

"Now," the guard continued, "you will dismount and follow me. My warriors will take your horses."

I did not even wait for my companions to protest.

"Take our horses?" I said. "I don't think so. Not until we see exactly where they are to be stable or pastured."

"Woman," the guard was indignant, "do you take the Iceni, a tribe renowned for our herds, as common horse thieves?"

I waited a beat.

"Not common."

Another beat; everyone tensed, the horses, too, and then the chief guard burst out laughing.

"By Andraste, if she had not said she comes from the west, I would swear this old witch is one of ours. A woman after our own queen's heart."

Yes, I agreed silently, after her heart.

"Come then," said the guard. "You will inspect your horses' quarters while we send word to the queen that you are here."

We dismounted and led our horses inside the stockade.

"Well done, Mother of Sarah!" Alyssa clapped me on the back. "Well done."

"How did you know it would work to insult them that way, Mother?" Sarah wanted to know.

I didn't, I started to say, and then I decided to take credit for having what Dwynwyn once described as nice impulses.

"Simple," I said. "They're Celts. Nothing like a well-turned insult to win their respect."

"Keep it up, Mother of Sarah," said Bele. "Keep it up."

CHAPTER SIXTEEN
FACE TO FACE

MY REST ON MY LAURELS was all too brief. We saw our horses to a shed where a young boy was summoned to rub them down and feed them hot mash, and then one of the guards returned with a message.

"Boudica our queen welcomes her *combrogos* from the west. Follow me."

No straight streets here, just winding round and round a cluster of round houses until we came to a large one, seemingly at the center. Our guide lifted the heavy plaid door covering and motioned for us to go in. I wanted to go last, but my companions conspired against me and I found myself stepping inside the familiar curved contours of a round hut, just a little larger than the one where I was born. The light came from a central hearth fire. In the shadows someone strummed a harp, a bit off tune in the damp. A cloaked figure sat on a low stool before the fire; nearby a young girl held a drop spindle. The girl leaned in and said something I did not catch to the cloaked one.

A woman.

She turned as she rose, slowly, majestically, an oak tree spiraling to full height. Thick gleaming braids fell to her waist, brighter than the bright plaid tunic she wore beneath her cloak, bright as the heavy gold torc around her neck. Just brighter than her eyes, red brown eyes, the color of a fox.

My father's eyes, her father's eyes. Lovernios alive again, standing before me in this strange, familiar form.

"I've got you," whispered Sarah, her arms around me, but she was trembling, too.

The young girl put down her spindle and went to stand next to the woman, a slender birch leaning into this massive greatness.

No one spoke. The harper stopped playing. The fire, too, seemed to quiet itself. Outside, rain began to fall, now and then a drop leaking from the smoke hole and hissing on the coals. I could hear my heart beating.

"Why. Have. You. Come."

She spoke like that, each word with its own separate weight, a low voice, stone rolling against stone in a cold rising tide.

"I wanted to see you again."

I heard my voice as if from outside myself. It sounded faint, insubstantial, like a wind seeking a way through a crack.

"Again?" she repeated.

I waited, waited for her to ask me what I meant by again. Waited for her to ask me what deep in her body she must know, waited for her to name me, to accuse me. I looked at her, silently beseeching her to say it. For a fleeting moment, I saw not my father's eyes, haunted, wary, but the infant face I had never forgotten. Little flame, little flower, the words sang themselves inside my mind. My arms lifted of their own accord, reaching for her.

Then, although I had not touched her, I felt hurled back. She herself looked startled, as if she had wakened suddenly from a dream. Just as my father once shook off his nightmare madness to become again a calm and reasoned druid.

"I am Boudica," she said, drawing herself up to an even greater height, so that her hood grazed the roof and fell back, revealing a gold crown of finely-wrought knotwork. "Queen of the Iceni, daughter of the great druid Lovernios."

And she began to recite her whole patrilineage...our patrilineage.

"This is my younger daughter, Lithben," she added when she had finished her recital.

Her daughter, my breath caught in my throat, my granddaughter. I noticed that Lithben's patrilineage was not invoked.

"We welcome you, *combrogos*," Boudica continued, "and we shall receive with gladness the messages you bring from the west. But first you must rest and take food and drink. You have had a long journey. Lithben, draw up stools for our guests, then tell the kitchens we are ready."

When we were all seated, Boudica regarded us silently, apparently feeling no need to put us at our ease with small talk or polite inquiries. I remembered Branwen saying that at school Boudica had been aloof and yet capable of great eloquence when she addressed a crowd. Apparently she seemed to feel she had made her welcoming statements, and the onus was now on us. Sarah concurred. After a few moments I felt her foot nudging mine. How it must madden her to have to let me be spokeswoman. And frankly it was a responsibility I wouldn't have minded shirking.

"I am Maeve Rhuad," I began, "as perhaps your guard has told you."

She scarcely blinked, just waited for me to continue with my lineage. Shit.

"Foster daughter of the late King Bran of the Silures." And scarcely pausing for breath I recited the whole long line farther back than I'd gone with the guards. By some miracle, I remembered accurately. If I hadn't, Boudica would have known, for she had stayed in school long enough to memorize the lineage of anyone who was anyone. By the time I was done, I had broken a sweat, and I prayed—yes, to Jesus—that she wouldn't ask about my birth father.

"And this is my daughter Sarah," I said. "I can recite her patrilineage. Upon request. It's very long and not one known to the druids."

I didn't look at Sarah. I could feel her glowering at me. And technically the druids did know Esus's lineage; or anyway they had heard it recited at admissions. Whether or not they memorized it I had no way of knowing. I wish I had thought to ask Branwen if the memory of Esus had been expunged from the college along with mine.

"And these are our *combrogos*, Alyssa and Bele," I added.

I hoped they had patrilineages handy. I had never thought to ask these daughters of the lost Amazonian tribes about their fathers.

"So," Boudica said after a moment of painful suspense. "Branwen is your foster sister."

Thank you, Jesus. I breathed a sigh of relief as Boudica moved on from the subject of patrilineage. But my relief was short-lived.

"I wonder how it is that I have never heard of you."

"Branwen never spoke of me?" I stalled.

"Never."

Now was the moment. Was I going to tell the truth or, as Sarah had put it, concoct a story? Surely there must be another alternative.

"Well," I said. "I suppose it might have been too painful for her. To speak of me, that is."

"How so?" Boudica was not making much effort to hide her wariness of me.

Then the gods in their mercy, or perhaps all the credit should go to Jesus, saw fit to have the food arrive at that moment. Lithben stepped in and drew back the blanket to let in half a dozen men and women, bearing pots and platters. Their garments were duller and more threadbare than the queen's, but I had no way of knowing if they were poor relations, servants, or captives that had been taken in a raid. Boudica, I noticed, thanked them but then dismissed them. She invited us to spoon a venison stew out of the common pot. There were also honey oat cakes and mulled red mead. We were all hungrier than we knew and fell to, not noticing at first the lack of conversation, how loud our slurping sounded in the silence, how intently our hostess watched us.

I stopped first and sat back, feeling sleepy and hoping Boudica might suggest that we retire to bed.

"Queen Boudica," I began. "We thank you for the feast."

"Simple fare," Boudica dismissed any excess gratitude, "such as we can hunt and grow for ourselves."

No Roman imports, was the subtext. I heard it.

"Tomorrow we will roast a pig in your honor. Then we will feast together."

"You honor us indeed," I answered.

I was about to make polite inquiries about the herds, the crops, the weather, when Boudica took up where she had left off.

"Tell me why it would have been painful for Branwen to speak of you."

There was no doubt who was queen here. This was not a question; it was a command.

"You know that her father King Bran was captured by Roman forces?"

"Yes."

"Did Branwen ever speak to you of him?" I took a gamble.

"Everyone knew what happened to him." Boudica frowned.

"But did she ever speak of him?"

"No," Boudica admitted.

I had guessed right. Branwen, poet though she was, would have found it painful to have her father made into a poem, a public legend sung by bards, someone that belonged to everyone. In order to keep her own memory of him, she would have kept silent. I understood that.

"Well, it was the same for her with me."

I felt Sarah stiffen beside me; I was teetering on the perilous edge of partial truth, a slippery slope on either side.

"You were also captured by Romans?" Boudica tried to follow my gist.

"Yes," and I breathed a sigh of relief at this unequivocal truth.

"How did this capture come to pass?"

Boudica was relentless and completely without delicacy or nuance. Her daughter, who had not yet spoken, looked at me round-eyed, fearful. I couldn't tell whether she was alarmed by me or by her mother's interrogation. I began to feel resistant. I considered saying: I don't like to talk about it. Not in front of children. After all, my capture did involve being drugged and raped, trussed and sold in the Roman Forum. Then my own daughter took the matter out of my hands.

"My mother was exiled from the Holy Isles in her youth."

I watched Boudica turn her gaze on Sarah, as if she had not fully taken in her presence before. She appeared to ponder her, not with curiosity, but with gravity, thoroughness. I turned to glance at Sarah's profile. I could see some tension in her jaw, but she sat absolutely still on the low stool, her legs crossed in front of her, her back straight. She had everyone's attention, including Bele and Alyssa, though Bele, bless her, did catch my eye and shrug. She didn't need to be able to understand every word to know that Sarah had, in effect, grabbed the reins.

"What authorities exiled her?" Boudica asked with eerie calm. Just another point of information about her guest. "For what crime?"

I felt as though I was in some awful game of hide and seek. Boudica was "it," and with each question, she got closer to my hiding place. Now here was Sarah poised to blow my cover.

"If you want to know what happened," I yanked the reins back, "ask me. Sarah wasn't born yet."

I readjusted my own posture so that my knee connected briefly and sharply with Sarah's.

Boudica nodded and duly turned to me again. And waited, waited for me to answer her question.

"The druids of Mona exiled me, if you must know," I finally said. "I interfered with a human sacrifice. I stopped it. Later, much later, after I was freed from slavery in Rome, I found him again and married him, the escaped sacrifice, Sarah's father."

Boudica continued to regard me in that unnerving way of hers, while Lithben's eyes darted back and forth from me to Sarah, who, as the daughter of an exile and an escaped sacrifice, took on quite a bit of interest for the girl. I caught her eye once and tried to smile at her, but she looked away and hid her face in her mother's massive shoulder.

"Do the druids of Mona know that you have returned to the Holy Isles?"

There were so many other questions Boudica could have asked, it was interesting that she chose that one. The druids of Mona were the authorities she revered; the ones she had obeyed despite her own desires. Did she fear that she was harboring a criminal, a traitor to the *combrogos*?

"Branwen knows and Viviane, too," I answered; at least they were druids in the plural.

Though her expression did not change, I could sense Boudica weighing this answer, considering whether or not it was adequate, whether or not she was obliged to probe further. I realized it had been that way the whole evening: advance and retreat, wanting and not wanting to know. Boudica was as ambivalent as I was.

"You said you had a message for me from Branwen," she spoke at length. "I would hear it now."

I took a deep breath for such a brief message.

"She sends her love."

"Her...love."

She said it that way, with a vast expanse between those two simple words, as if she could not comprehend them, as if the word love felt strange on her tongue.

"Yes," I said. "And Viviane sends her love, too. They say they both know you have always kept faith with the druids of Mona."

Sarah had warned me that this message was not adequate to explain the journey I had made, but what I saw in Boudica's face was nothing like the skepticism I expected or deserved. Her cheeks became blotchy, the bane of some redheads, and she abruptly turned her eyes from me, as to hide whatever strong emotion had overcome her. Again I had an urge to touch her, to enfold her, to protect this massive, awkward woman as if she were still my child.

"Do they know?" she spoke with that gravelly river bottom voice of hers, but I could hear it shaking. "Do they know how it is with us here?"

She looked at me again; tears stood in her eyes.

"I don't know," I said. "They told me they had not heard from you often since your return to Iceni country. They know you are queen. They hope for the best."

The tears began to fall. She let them, as if they had nothing to do with her. Her face remained still.

"How is it with you here?" I asked gently. "How is it with you, Boudica? Please tell me. I want to know."

She just kept looking at me, almost as if she knew, almost as if she remembered who I was. Then her tears stopped suddenly, as if a cold wind had blown them back, frozen their source. Her face became impassive again.

"You shall know," she said. "Tomorrow I will tell you. I will show you. But now you must rest from your journey. Lithben, show our guests to their quarters."

Boudica did not get up or acknowledge our thanks or good nights with more than a vague nod.

We were dismissed.

CHAPTER SEVENTEEN
CIVIL DISUNION

YOU MIGHT THINK that the four of us would have been eager to talk, that we would have pushed past our fatigue and stayed up analyzing Boudica's every gesture, every word. Maybe you wish we had. You would have liked to know what we said. But that is not how it went. Perhaps people spoke less in those days, at least when emotion was high, mystery deep. Perhaps the rain and the wind spoke for us, shrouding our silence with their own sound, making any tears or sighs of our own redundant, tossing back any reproaches before they could reach our lips.

We were wakened early next morning by Lithben as she ushered in a big pot of stirabout carried by two servants, who set about tending our hearth fire. After the night of rain, the dawn was coming up cold and clear. We made our way to and from the latrines, and I was pleased to see that Lithben was still there waiting just outside our hut when we got back. I wanted to get to know my granddaughter, and clearly Sarah wanted to know her niece. Last night Lithben had dashed away as soon as she had shown us to our door.

"Will you break your fast with us, Lithben?" I invited.

She nodded, still wordless, and held the blanket back from the door as we went in to eat by the fire. I realized I hadn't yet heard her speak. I hoped she did not have an affliction that had rendered her dumb. She was a slender girl who might yet be tall. Her hair was lighter than her mother's, more gold than red, and her eyes hazel...like mine. As she settled down next to Sarah, I suddenly saw that she looked a little like my womb mother, Grainne. The resemblance shook me and I found myself tongue-tied. There was too much to say—and not say.

"How old are you, Lithben?" Sarah took it upon herself to start a conversation.

"Eleven summers," she answered, her voice surprisingly low for a young girl's but with none of her mother's harshness.

"I am more than twice your age, then," offered Sarah.

"Is that old?" Lithben asked, doubtful and perhaps a little disappointed.

"Not too old. Not old enough to be your mother."

"But older than my sister Gwen."

"How old is your sister?" I decided it was time for me to enter the conversation.

"Almost fourteen."

"Where is your sister?" Sarah asked.

Lithben looked from Sarah to me, and then at her stirabout, but didn't answer.

"Maybe you should ease up on the questions," suggested Alyssa to Sarah in Greek.

"You're interrogating the poor kid," agreed Bele.

Lithben looked at the Alyssa and Bele curiously.

"They don't speak the language of your people," Sarah explained. "I don't speak it very well, either. But I spoke a language like it when I was a little girl living in the mountains far, far away from here."

Lithben's face lit up at the idea of far away and the hope of a story.

"The mountain people were called the Galatians. They are part of the *combrogos*."

"Oh," Lithben said, and I guessed this favorite word of her mother's made Sarah's distant origins less interesting.

"Tell her you ran away from home and became a pirate," suggested Alyssa, sensing the shift in Lithben's response. "Tell her you were the scourge of the Roman merchant navy."

"I think that might be too much information," I said sharply, not wanting my granddaughter to get romantic notions about running away from home. "Sarah has had an adventurous life," I turned to Lithben. "As I have, as your mother has."

Lithben could not make the connection.

"My mother only lives here," she said.

"I heard that she and your father once led a rebellion together against the Roman governor," I said. "That must have been an adventure."

Lithben stared at me. The rebellion had happened before she was born. Could it be that she had never heard this story before? Could it be that it wasn't true?

"I am not supposed to talk about my father," she said so softly that I almost couldn't hear.

Then she put down her bowl and got to her feet.

"Stay, Lithben," I pleaded. "We won't ask you any more questions."

"I am late for practice," she mumbled.

She was on her way out the door when she paused and turned back.

"Don't tell my mother."

Don't tell your mother what, I wanted to ask, but she was already gone.

* * *

We were all quiet for a moment, but this time there was no avoiding speculation.

"What is going on here?" Alyssa demanded. "You two, talk!"

"It's pretty clear there's some major rift between Boudica and her husband," Sarah said.

"I am afraid so," I agreed. "I don't know if any of you caught it, but Boudica did not introduce Lithben through her father's lineage last night."

"And she didn't mention her other daughter," noted Sarah.

"Actually, she did," I said, "at least indirectly. She called Lithben her younger daughter, so at least she is not denying the older one's existence. She hasn't disowned her."

"Lithben wouldn't say where her sister was," said Sarah.

"Seems like her mother keeps the girl on a pretty short leash," observed Bele. "I think Lithben is scared of her."

"I would be, too, if she were my mother," said Alyssa. "Boudica is positively terrifying, but in a magnificent way. She's like an old time Amazon queen. I'm not surprised she's given her husband the boot."

"Lithben is not allowed to speak of her father," said Sarah. "That can only mean one thing."

"Gone over to Rome," agreed Alyssa.

"It may be more complicated than that," I felt obliged to say.

"Not to Boudica," Sarah countered.

And I feared she was right.

Before we could speculate further, one of the guards who had challenged us last night came to find us. He was indeed well past his first, second or any youth. There seemed to be a dearth of young men in Boudica's village. Did she discourage men in general?

"The queen awaits you at the practice fields. I will guide you to her."

We followed the man through the muddy lanes of the village past the wooden stockade and the ditches and earthen fortifications. Though not exactly a hill fort, Boudica's village was on the highest ground for some miles around and clearly designed for defense. People from surrounding farmsteads probably banded together here when there was any threat.

Outside the village compound, our guide led us along the edge of a wide flat field where there was indeed practice of several kinds of martial arts underway. At the far end of the field a group of a dozen or so archers practiced hitting a semi-moving target suspended from a tree. There were several sets of people sparring with swords. And still others practiced casting the *laigen* while on horseback, also at targets suspended from trees. Alyssa and Bele, keenly interested, kept up a running commentary on the weapons in use, how they were different or similar to the ones they knew.

But the best was yet to come. Beyond a hedge row lay another field with a circular dirt track. In the center a huge woman on the back of an equally massive grey horse shouted instructions to two charioteers who drove their horses full speed around the ring. As they careened towards our end of the field, we could see that the drivers were women, or rather girls not much older than Lithben. In fact, as I looked more carefully, I saw that one of them was Lithben, her face white and rigid with terror, determination or both.

"Go, girl!" cried Alyssa, and she and Bele clapped their hands and burst into ululation.

Sarah watched intently; her silence louder than her friends' cheers.

As for me, for a moment I was back on Tir na mBan listening to my mothers shout at me as I first raced a chariot on the beach. All the intervening years fell away for a dizzying moment.

Then Boudica saw us and rode towards us, motioning to the charioteers to slow down. When she reached us, she dismounted, still topping the tallest of us by a head.

"You have rested well and breakfasted?" she inquired gravely as if it were a matter of state.

"We have, thank you, Queen Boudica," I said.

No one seemed to know what to say next, then Sarah jumped in, tactfully or not, asking the question I had not managed to form yet and might not have risked if I had.

"Is that your older daughter on the field with Lithben, Queen Boudica?"

"No," she answered shortly.

If her lips had been a door, they would have slammed shut; even Sarah did not dare to probe further.

"All the young women of the tribe are trained in the warrior arts," Boudica said after a moment, "if they are willing and show aptitude."

Or if you force them, I added to myself, for I wasn't sure that Lithben fell into either category.

"I myself oversee their training as much as possible."

"Do you train the young men as well or does the king see to that?"

Sarah was determined to push it. If I was close enough to kick her, I would have. I kept my eyes on Boudica's face, where admiration for Sarah's cheek warred with anger at this violation of her unstated rules.

"Do you see any men on the practice fields?" she asked Sarah.

"So those were all women," Sarah said. "I couldn't be sure from a distance. They might have been boys."

"There are no young men," Boudica stated. "Have you not noticed? No young men."

Then she turned from Sarah to me. She gave me a look I can hardly describe, both pleading and resentful at once, almost as if...as if I were her mother, someone who should have made everything better and had failed.

"Maeve Rhuad, foster daughter of King Bran the bold, you asked me to tell you how it is with us. The Roman occupiers conscript our young men into their armies by force, the ones that have not escaped and gone into hiding. Thank Andraste that despite the treacherous Brigantian Queen Cartimandua who betrayed Caratacus to the Romans and fought on their side (and small thanks she got and small thanks she deserved) the Romans still think she was a freak, an aberration, a monstrosity. They still do not understand that the women of the *combrogos* will fight, without their men if need be."

Apart from her recital of her lineage, this speech was Boudica's longest yet. I began to understand what Branwen and Viviane meant. She had no small talk, but if she chose she could command a crowd, just as my father could. But she had something all her own, something more elemental than his brilliance, some kind of barely restrained power that made you think of the muscles of a horse's neck rippling, nostrils flaring. She held herself in check, but only just. At any moment she could rear up and bring down her thundering, lethal hooves.

"And that is not all they take from us; that is not all."

We waited for her to go on. But as abruptly as she had begun she stopped, gathering her force back into herself. Then she turned and signaled to the young charioteers.

"Give your horses a rest now!" she called, her voice competing easily with the hooves and the wheels. "Take them out of harness. Walk them and rub them down."

I didn't realize until the chariots slowed and came to a stop and I let out my breath, how tense I had been. I resisted the urge to go and gather my granddaughter in my arms. With Boudica for a mother, she was going to have to be tough whether her temperament suited her to it or not.

"Queen Boudica," Sarah spoke again. "My two *combrogos* and I have some experience with horses and with chariot driving. We have also met Romans in battle before and know quite a bit about their weapons and how they use them. We would be honored if we could be of any use in warrior training while we're here. I am sure we could learn something, too. Will you allow us to join martial practice?"

Alyssa and Bele seemed to follow the gist of Sarah's offer and nodded with enthusiasm. But it was Boudica's response that held my attention. She turned her focus on Sarah so completely that I could almost see the edges of her vision darken and blur. She had Sarah in her sights, and nothing else existed in that moment. I remembered Jesus looking at a paralyzed man with equal intensity, as if he and the man were alone in all the worlds and that moment could suspend itself into eternity. But Boudica's intent was different, and I sensed that, paradoxically, Sarah herself did not matter. She was assessing Sarah's use. My blood (blood I shared with them both) slowed and cooled, as if it were not blood but something thicker and darker.

"Can you a shoot a bow or throw a *laigen* with any accuracy from a moving chariot?"

"I can," said Sarah.

"Good, you can coach my daughter. Lithben, fetch fresh horses. Meanwhile, I will show you the other trainings."

She strode off across the field with my women, as the general had referred to them. I could have followed, but I didn't. No one seemed to notice me, except Lithben, who cast a backward glance at me as she led the spent horses back to their pasture.

"I'll just entertain myself for awhile, shall I?" I said, though no one could hear me.

And suddenly I knew exactly what I wanted to do.

CHAPTER EIGHTEEN
MOTHER-IN-LAW

Clearly age and wisdom have not curbed my impulsiveness, not to mention my willfulness. I am afraid, as you have already seen, age was having just the opposite effect, and really wisdom is not synonymous with prudence, not in my opinion. Also, if it is true that people become more like themselves, even caricatures of themselves, as they grow older, that truth explains a lot about what I did, even if it does not excuse it. It was totally in character for me to investigate for myself the mystery surrounding the missing half of Boudica's household.

So I meandered across the fields, as if I were just taking a morning stroll. Once I was out of sight, over a rise, I turned and headed for the rutted track we'd followed last night, intending to retrace our route to the fork in the road, the fork that I was convinced marked the division between Boudica's traditional stronghold and the Roman villa we had glimpsed last night. By midmorning I reached the fork and made my way towards the villa, which was the center of its own small village, surrounded, like Boudica's stronghold, by fields, pastures, stables, buildings for various crafts and industries, but all square with tiled roofs in the Roman style. There were also barracks, like those I'd seen at Paulina's country estate, for housing slaves. Although the villa and surroundings were extensive, as I came closer I could see that the buildings were not in great repair. Tiles that had come loose lay haphazardly on the ground, and holes gaped. Weeds had grown up in the gardens, and a place that should have been bustling was strangely quiet. As I approached the main entrance to the villa, a railed wooden walkway to a small outer colonnade, I began to wonder if the villa had been abandoned. Then a guard stepped forth from the colonnade. Like Boudica's guards, he was not young. He was dressed in the Roman style and armed with a Roman spear, but he challenged me in the Celtic dialect of the region.

"State your name, lineage, and your business with Prasutagus, King of the Iceni."

Not again, I thought. I decided I couldn't bear to recite my maternal lineage only to be asked about the paternal. Nor was I sure that the lineage of a famous resistance fighter from the west would be welcomed as credentials here. As I stood pondering my answer, a gust of wind blew back my hood and loosened my hair from its never tidy knot. It floated on the wind, grey and wild. And for a moment, I fancied I could hear a necklace of small skulls rattling. Once long ago I had shape-shifted and taken the form of the old woman of Beara. It wasn't such a stretch now.

"I am the Grey Hag," I intoned. "My lineage is the holy earth of the holy isles, the very bones of her mountains, the breasts of her hills, the soft fertile flesh of her plains, the secrets hidden in her valleys, the lifeblood of her rivers, the cool bright reflection of her still waters, the ragged rocky edges of her shores, the breath of her tides, the depth of her seas...."

All right, I was getting carried away. The man looked visibly shaken, as if I had announced I was death on the doorstep. I didn't think I looked *that* bad. Still, I thought I had better come to the point.

"I seek the king of this land."

"R-right this way," he said.

At least I had achieved the desired effect.

The guard led me through the atrium where a dried up fountain sat forlornly gathering dead leaves. In Rome at this time of year, braziers might have been blazing and clients would sit waiting to call on their patron. There would have been sculptures garishly painted littered about the place. But the inside of the villa had the same neglected air as the outside. If Prasutagus had been bought off by Rome, where were his ill-gotten gains?

At the door of one of the rooms off the atrium, the guard paused and announced.

"King Prasutagus, the, uh, Grey Hag, daughter of the holy earth of the holy isles....what was the rest?" he turned to me.

"That's the gist of it," I said.

"She seeks audience with you, sir."

"The grey *what*?" a voice queried.

"Hag, sir."

"Did my wife send her?" he sounded both suspicious and oddly hopeful.

"Did Queen Boudica send you?" the guard relayed the question, as if I could not hear it perfectly well.

"Yes and no," I said, figuring one or both of the answers had to be right.

"Well, show her in," the king answered. "Old woman or goddess, messenger or beggar, it shall not be said that the king of the Iceni is lacking in hospitality, even were it his own end he must entertain."

Whatever concessions he had made to the Romans, the man was still a Celt at the core if he spoke like that.

"But you are in pain today," a woman's voice protested. "Surely she can wait."

Did he have a mistress, I wondered? Was that the cause of the rift?

"It is no matter," said the King. "Roc, send her in and fetch wine and something to eat."

Roc, as the king had called the guard, stood aside and I went into a small room warmed by a brazier and lit with oil lamps. The king reclined on a couch. I hardly needed to see his face, grey and slack, to know that he was ill. The charcoal could not cover the scent of the medicines he must be taking. I could feel the fire of the stars buzzing in my crown, flowing into my hands. Perhaps he would allow me to examine him, but it was too soon to ask. Beside him on a low stool, sat a young woman, really no more than a girl, her head bent to him as if to say or hear something not meant for my ears. Dark hair fell over her face, but then she turned to look up at me. Her face was pale from too much time indoors, and her eyes looked the darker and fiercer for it. It was the set of her jaw, the tension in her neck that gave her away. I had seen them both before and recently.

This was no mistress. This was my other granddaughter.

"Gwen?" I breathed.

She narrowed her eyes.

"How do you know my name? What do you want with my father?"

"Hush, Gwen, don't be rude. Help me to sit up. Then give your seat to our guest."

"As you will, Father."

The sullenness in her voice was clearly meant for me, not for him. With skill that must have come from long practice, she slid her hands under his armpits and helped him sit. Then she took her place next to him and continued to scowl at me. Now that they were side by side, I could see that she bore considerable resemblance to her father, but I suspected she was more like her mother in temperament.

"Pray, be seated, Grey Lady, and tell us, if you will, why you have come."

"I am a healer," I said as I sat. It seemed my most useful credential. "It may be that I can ease your pain."

"Who told you I was ill?" he spoke in a sharper tone than I had heard him use before.

All at once I remembered how serious it was for a Celtic king to be sick or wounded, code for impotent. Whoever his mortal wife might be, the king was wed to land itself, the goddess of sovereignty. If he were unmanned, the land would not prosper.

"Was it my wife, was it Queen Boudica?" Again that mix of longing and fear in his voice, in his face.

"No, the queen did not tell me."

"Then who did? It's important. I must know."

"I needed no one to tell me," I answered. "The Grey Hag knows all."

That sounded hokey even to my ears. And it wasn't true. I hadn't known. I had come here to snoop, to find out what tight-lipped Boudica wouldn't tell me.

"Actually, I didn't know," I confessed, "until I walked into the room. Then, if you will pardon me for saying so, it was obvious, at least to a healer, which I swear I am. Will you let me help you?"

"I don't mean to be rude." He used that word again. No wonder he was a client king. It wasn't greed; it was fear of giving offense. To anyone. "But if you did not know I was ill, why did you come?"

I sighed. Once again: the choice. Suddenly I was tired of spinning tales, spinning the truth, tired of spinning. They say deceit weaves a tangled web. But fabrication is an art form. The truth is the raw, and often unappealing, material.

"I wanted to find out why you and wife are separated."

"I thought everyone knew that," he said almost bitterly. "Who are you that you don't know what everyone gossips about around every hearth in the land?"

A reasonable question, especially considering that I had just claimed to know all. I sighed again, and then took a deep breath.

"I'm your long-lost mother-in-law."

There were no pins to hear drop and no angels dancing on pinheads who might have staggered to a stop, but it was that kind of a silence. Father and daughter stared at me, as if my face were a Rosetta stone, the map, not to a treasure, but to some fearful place that had never been explored or even discovered. Despite what might be considered unnerving scrutiny, I felt strangely calm. My secret was out. Whatever happened next was up to somebody else.

"Why. Did. You. Abandon. Her."

How had I not noticed that Gwen's voice was like her mother's, low, harsh, like something sharp being scraped against rock or bone. I looked into her eyes, bright as Sarah's, though their brightness had a different source. She did not look away.

"I did not abandon your mother, Gwen. She was taken from me by force. This I swear on my life and on my death."

It was such a relief, such a blissful relief to say this truth, this simple truth. For a moment I forgot the rest of story and all my reasons for keeping silent.

"Have you told her?" Prasutagus asked. "Have you told Boudica?"

And all my relief turned to dismay as it hit me all at once: to tell her estranged husband first was a betrayal, a huge betrayal. If I had not betrayed

Boudica before, I had now. Without a word, I rose to leave only to encounter Roc and a maid in the entry way bearing platters of food and a flagon of wine.

"Stay," the King said; it was the closest thing to a command I had heard him utter. "You asked if you could ease my pain. Stay then. Stay and hear me."

I turned around and sat back down on the stool as the servants placed the food on a low table in front of the couch—olives, figs, the foods I had been missing, imported foods, the kind that would keep. Given the condition of his estate, I suspected they were now delicacies. I accepted a cup of wine, also light, fragrant, tasting of the sun, air, and soil where the grapes had been grown far from this damp, misty place.

"Eat, drink," the king said.

He took nothing himself, I noticed, and Gwen only nibbled at a fig. I took a fortifying sip of wine.

"Now I will tell you," he began. "Boudica was right. She was right, and she will not forgive me."

"No, Father," Gwen protested. "It wasn't your fault. You couldn't have known. You did what you thought was best."

This exchange between father and daughter had a ritual quality, as if it had been repeated over and over. Each one knew their part by heart, and nothing was ever resolved, only temporarily relieved. I looked at the king, who even faded and ill was not unhandsome. He had a kindness about him that could be mistaken for weakness, or exploited as weakness.

"But I should have known," the king continued his part in the litany of reproach and reassurance. "Everyone knows about the Romans. They are conquering the whole world. The tribes of Gaul could not stand against them. They used the tribes against each other. I knew they would do that here, too. I knew the tribes would never unite. I did not want to see more slaughter. I thought to disarm the Romans, not by surrendering, but by coming to terms. I thought other tribes might follow my example, but I was wrong, wrong about that and wrong about Roman rule. I thought we could prosper under it. I thought they understood that our prosperity would be to their advantage, to everyone's advantage."

"Father," Gwen came in on cue. "Your reasons were noble, and for a time all was well. Don't you remember how it was when I was a little girl, the riches we shared with everyone, the great feasts? How happy we all were then!"

I sensed they had forgotten my presence and were speaking only to each other, or not even to each other, to themselves, to their loneliness. I wondered how Gwen, whom I could easily picture in a chariot, had come to be her gentle father's comforter, while Lithben, clearly more timid, was tethered to her relentless mother's sword arm.

"King Prasutagus," I remembered the question Lithben had not answered. "I have heard that you did revolt against the Romans when they tried to disarm the Iceni and the other tribes, that you and Boudica rallied the tribes and led the rebellion together. Is that not true?"

"It is true!" Gwen turned to me, for the first time without hostility, her dark eyes bright. "And they won. You won, didn't you, Father!"

"*Cariad*, no, we didn't win, though your mother married me as she agreed to do if I would fight beside her. And the cause was just. It is one thing to be a client kingdom, another to be disarmed and treated like slaves. So yes, I fought, fought hard. But even our bravest warriors are no match against an organized professional army."

"But you kept your weapons," I said. "The tribes were not disarmed. Is that not a kind of victory? Wasn't that the whole point?"

Gwen looked at me and nodded earnestly, for the first time seeing me as a possible ally in her (I feared losing) battle to glorify her father.

"Yes, that was the point," he conceded.

Then he fell silent and just looked at me, as if he wished I could read his mind, absolve him without his having to say more. I felt myself shaking my head, almost imperceptibly. There is no easy way, I spoke to him in my mind.

"Gwen, will you leave us?"

Perhaps if he had commanded her, she would have obeyed. But she was her mother's daughter—and my granddaughter—and she balked.

"Do not make me, go, Father. I am a grown woman now. Do not treat me like a child."

It was true, I thought, at almost fourteen there was very little left of the child in her—except her need to believe in her father's perfection.

"You do not have long," I heard myself saying.

And as soon as I spoke the words, I knew they were true. Even if I could ease Prasutagus's pain, I could not call him back from the death that waited for him, confident, patient. You could not call someone back unless he wanted to come.

"We kept our weapons, and I thought we would keep our peace, because...because of what I offered them."

He paused for a moment, as if winded. Gwen held a cup to his lips, and then wiped his forehead where he had broken a sweat.

"Your mother doesn't know," he said to his daughter. "Boudica doesn't know. Yet maybe somehow, without even knowing it, she does. Maybe that is why everything came to bitterness between us, even when we still prospered. Before they took everything we are and owned. They call it repayment of a loan," he explained to me, "what they first proffered as a gift, what some people called my price. The new procurator claims we owe interest, too. Interest *he* calculates, his own interest to which there is no limit."

The procurator, the man I had seen on the shore, waiting to greet the new governor, the man who did not know that governor was his father, just as Boudica did not know I was her mother. And I had twice taken that man's father as a lover, once knowing who he was, once not. I felt sick at the thought of all these secrets.

"But Boudica knows all that," protested Gwen. I noticed that she did not refer to her as mother. "She blames you. She's always blamed you for everything."

"And she is right, I tell you," said the king, "more right than she knows, more right than you know. My own body bears witness. Yes, I am impotent. I gelded myself."

Suddenly I felt impatient with the king's self-accusation. I looked from him to my granddaughter. Her father asked too much of her, more than Boudica asked of Lithben. Adoration, exoneration, things she tried desperately to give, yet he refused to receive. She gazed at him steadily, just a tiny furrow to one of her brows betraying any uncertainty.

"Tell me what you mean, Father," she said. "Please tell me. I will help you."

He put his face in his hands. I hoped he would not weep; I was afraid I would want to smack him. Then he straightened up, and turned to her, and I felt my respect for him, almost doused, flicker back.

"You cannot help me, dear child of my heart, brave daughter more fit to rule than I ever was. I have betrayed you, too. In exchange for keeping our weapons, for our being left in peace, I promised to will the country of the Iceni to the Roman Empire."

I looked as Gwen took in his words. I watched her tighten the muscles of her face so her expression would not change.

"And now my death is near," he went on. "What will become of you and Lithben? What will become of my people? What will become of my queen? Slaves, all of you, slaves."

Gwen lifted her hands and placed them on her father's cheeks. Only when his tears began did she allow her own to spill, and even then she made no sound.

"King Prasutagus," I said, unable to bear another moment of helpless witness. "When you made this agreement, did you sign anything?"

"Sign?"

He turned to me as though he could not remember who I was or how I came there.

"Sign," I repeated. "Put your name or mark to a document?"

"I know what sign means," he said, a bit querulous. "I know Roman ways well enough, the gods know, and to my sorrow. There was a document, a treaty. But I did not sign it."

"Then how can it stand?" I asked him. "How can you say you have given your kingdom away, if you did not agree?"

Gwen looked at me as if I might be a beam of dawn light slipping beneath a closed door.

"Ah, but I did agree," he said. "I gave my word. They wanted my mark, but I refused. Among the *combrogos*, I told them, word is sacred, word is law. If you will not take it, then leave it. I am still king here."

It was then that my own tears had their way, to think that this king had made one last stand on his word, on the power of the spoken word, when he had given everything else away.

"But, Father," said Gwen. "They have not kept their word to you. Did they ever tell you the gifts they gave were a loan? Did they ever say they would come due? Did you ever agree to such a thing by word or any other way?"

Here she was, her mother's daughter, after all, the granddaughter of the druid Lovernios, stuck in a ruined villa with a dying king, prepared to think her way clear.

"I did not," he answered slowly.

"Then, Father," said Gwen. "There is no harm done."

"No harm done?" he repeated bewildered.

He seemed at once a very old man and a young child, too tired to resist any more, willing to be put to bed.

"We will make a new will, your true will, a document. You will make your mark on it."

"I never learned to write," the king said.

"We will find someone who can, Father," soothed Gwen.

I could have slipped away then. If only I had.

"If you could write, what would you say?" I asked. "What would you will?"

The king looked at me as if he wished he had never seen me, as if I were indeed his death, a rude and impatient death, jostling him out of life as he knew it.

"Would you leave it to my mother?" Gwen asked in a tight voice. "Would you leave the tribe to Boudica's rule?"

The king let out a long sigh, as if he could exhale all the sorrow and futility of his life.

"If only I could, I would. She is a better, braver leader than I am, but the Romans would never let her rule; they know she is sympathetic to the resistance. There would be a legion here before my body was cold. She'd fight, I know she would, she'd welcome a fight, but she could never win. And if they took her alive—"

His voice broke again; I did not blame him. I had lived in Rome. I had seen with my own eyes what happened to celebrity captives. I knew how they were shackled so they could not kill themselves to avoid the humiliation of being paraded before the crowds.

"Then, Father," Gwen took a breath in, as if gathering up all the defeat of her father's sigh to change it, to charge it with purpose again. "Leave the rule of the Iceni to me. To me and Lithben. We are your daughters. We both know how to fight in battle, but you have trained me in diplomacy as well. Lithben will be guided by me. We know the old ways and the new ways. The people know us, they will trust us. And surely the Romans will respect that we are your heirs."

"They will not," I cried out, alarmed by where my impulsive question was leading. "They hate and despise women who rule. They still haven't gotten over Cleopatra. They will never tolerate it."

But Prasutagus was no longer hearing me or even Gwen. He was gazing into the middle distance, as if he could just glimpse something that had been for so long out of view, out of reach.

"I know what to do," he spoke at last. "I know what to will. Find me someone who can write, Gwen, however long it takes, however far you have to go."

"Yes, Father," said Gwen, and she rose to go, clearly prepared to seek to the ends of the earth, and brave a Roman legion if need be.

"I can write," I heard myself say.

And as soon as I spoke, I wished I had never learned. I wished I had told Joseph where to stuff his fantasy of the literate hetaera. No good had come of the written word, as far as I had ever been able to tell. No good would come of it now.

CHAPTER NINETEEN
THE HERO'S CUT

BY THE TIME I left, the sun had journeyed to the west, and all the shadows of grasses, trees, small rises and hollows stretched in the opposite direction than they had when I set out on my impulsive morning jaunt. My mood had also reversed itself, my feet and heart so heavy it was a wonder I could walk. I had set forth with only my own secret, now I carried the confession of King Prasutagus as well. He had promised me that he would reveal his will to Boudica before his death and pleaded with me to keep his confidence. I had agreed, reluctantly, feeling that I had meddled more than enough. But I was already having second thoughts, and I was deep in them when Lithben stepped out from behind a tree at the crossroad and into my path.

"Child," I caught myself just before I stumbled. "You gave me such a fright. What are you doing here?"

"I was waiting for you," she said, and she surprised me by slipping her hand into mine. "I know where you went."

We fell into step together, walking along the rutted track to Boudica's compound.

"Does anyone else know?" I asked trying, unsuccessfully, to sound offhand.

"No. I told them all you were tired from your journey and had gone to rest."

Resourceful child, I thought, feeling relieved, and then my relief immediately gave way to remorse that I had unwittingly dragged this child into a secret.

"Is my father well?" she asked.

I hesitated a moment and decided on the truth.

"He is not well," I said as gently as I could. "But your sister is taking very good care of him."

"I want to see him," she stated.

"Of course you do," I answered.

We walked the rest of the way in silence, hand in hand.

"Your mother has been looking for you, Lithben," the watch told her when we approached the gate. "She is overseeing the preparations for the feast. You are to report to her. And your daughter is looking for you," he said to me. "She is waiting at your quarters."

I reckoned we were both in trouble.

* * *

I found Sarah sitting cross-legged on the ground outside our hut, blunting the blade of a sword to be used for practice.

"It's one thing to wander off," she started in without even acknowledging me, "though it's a foolish thing to do in country you don't know. It's another to ask a child to lie for you."

"I did not ask Lithben to lie for me, Sarah," I sighed, suddenly feeling very tired.

"No?" she looked up at me and raised an eyebrow. "But you seem to know what I'm talking about."

"Lithben came and found me," I explained. "Now if you don't mind, I think I really will go and have a rest before the feast."

"But I do mind," she said, and I instantly regretted my phrasing. "Found you where?"

I plopped down beside Sarah. I ought to put Sarah in her place, refuse to answer any questions, but it seemed too much effort. Also, I was tired of secrets. I needed someone to know.

"On my way back from visiting King Prasutagus."

"I *knew* that was where you had gone!" she said, as if it had required great powers of deduction.

"Then why did you ask?" I said, feeling querulous.

"I wanted to see if you would lie."

I was silent for a moment, listening to Sarah scrape away at the blade and wondering how and when I had gotten a reputation for deceitfulness. I had always thought of myself as being honest and outspoken, perhaps to a fault. But Sarah had her own view of me, which did not always square with mine, and was often not very flattering.

"Stop testing me, Sarah," I said without much heat. "Just ask me what you want to know and I'll tell you."

"Well, everything," she answered. "Obviously."

But I could not tell her everything, I realized. I had the confidence of a dying man to keep.

"The king is very ill," I said. "Gwen, the older daughter, takes care of him, rarely leaves his side."

"What's she like?" Sarah asked, and I heard more than idle curiosity in her tone, questions she would not voice: what's it like to have a father you can see and touch and tend?

"She's very smart and strong-willed," I said. "She doesn't look like Boudica, but she is more like her than Lithben is. She believes—or wants to believe—that her father can do no wrong."

Just as Boudica believed in her legendary father.

"But Prasutagus has done wrong," Sarah asserted. "Boudica told me. The price he received from the Romans for accepting their rule is now a debt. The tribe is bankrupt."

"I know," I said. "Prasutagus told me the same thing. She can't reproach him any more bitterly than he reproaches himself. I wonder if Boudica knows how remorseful he is?"

"I doubt she would care if she did," Sarah shrugged.

"But they need to talk, Sarah, they need to talk before it's too late."

"What would talk accomplish?" Sarah was skeptical. "Talk can't undo what's done. Talk can't drive away the enemy he let in the door. She wouldn't talk to him unless he's ready to fight."

"He's dying, Sarah. They need to talk about what will happen when he's dead. They need to prepare. They need to talk about their daughters, how to protect them."

He needs to tell her what he said in the will, the will I helped him write, against my better judgment, I added silently.

"And Lithben needs to see her father before he dies," I added.

"There is that," said Sarah quietly. "What will you do about it, Mother? Do you intend to meddle?"

"Me?" I attempted to make light of her question.

Sarah looked at me shrewdly.

"Tell the truth," she said.

"There are some truths that are not mine to tell."

And with that, I went inside to a well (or un) deserved rest.

Roman occupation and bankruptcy notwithstanding, Boudica's feast was a fine one, not excessive like a Roman feast with all sorts of exotic delicacies such as lark's tongues baked in pastry, not like a Temple Magdalen feast, bread, olive oil, figs and grapes, fresh fish and maybe a goat or spring lamb. Boudica feasted the way the *combrogos* always had: a whole roasted pig on a spit, stuffed with apples, onions, and root vegetables. There were barley and oatcakes in abundance sweetened with honey. She eschewed imported wine, but strong mead and barley beer flowed in abundance in a feast hall under the heavens, for the night was a fine one.

It seemed the whole village had gathered. Just as the pig was being lifted and carried to a carving table, men, some young, some a bit older, all armed, began to steal in from the shadows, in ones, twos, small groups, from all directions. All of them first paid respects to Boudica, saluting by holding their spears aloft, and she answered the gesture with her own upraised spear. Then many turned to seek out mothers, sisters, and grandfathers.

"These must be the warriors who went into hiding to avoid conscription into the Roman army," said Sarah. "I saw a couple of the women riding out earlier. Boudica must have a system for getting word to them quickly."

"But can it be safe?" wondered Bele. "Couldn't the Romans ambush us here? Now?"

"I'm sure Boudica must have sent scouts out," put in Alyssa. "From what we've seen, the Romans have pretty much plundered the place already and gone back to the south."

"Also," I added, "it's not one of the known times for a tribal gathering. The Romans probably keep an eye on those. This is an impromptu feast."

"In our honor. Or maybe I should say your honor," Sarah added a bit ominously.

I reached for a horn of mead and took a generous swig. Then all our attention was drawn to the roast pig. Boudica stood over the sizzling carcass. With great precision, she sliced into a haunch, making what I recognized as the hero's cut. Before she could even finish two young men had drawn their swords.

"Do you dare to claim the hero's cut, Dylan, you son of horse thieves, who would steal the fastest steed and ride like the wind—away from the enemy?"

"Who else could claim it? Not you, Brian, who is always first among men, in retreat. You accuse me of your fault."

"What are they doing?" Bele asked.

"I think they are about to fight, I hope not to the death, over the hero's cut of meat," I explained. "It's something Celtic warriors do."

The insults went on and on, one jumping in whenever the other took a breath. Meanwhile, Boudica carved on unperturbed, nodding impartially whenever one or the other scored a point. Everyone else watched as if the duel were a part of the entertainment.

"Well, if they are going to kill each other, I wish they'd stop yammering and get on with it," grumbled Alyssa. "I'm hungry!"

"Yes," I agreed. "It's worse than prayers, but that's how it's done. A fight isn't worth anything without the challenge first."

Then all at once, the swords were clanging and the fight was in full swing, with people shouting encouragement from the sidelines. At first blood, not a serious injury, just a scratch on the face that might result in an interesting scar, Boudica stepped between the men, who fell back, confused but deferent.

"Well done, Dylan and Brian. It is good to keep the old traditions alive, but I can't afford to lose either of you. Tonight the hero's cut will go to our honored guest from the west. Though she is not a warrior, she is the mother of warriors, and after we feast I trust she will in turn honor us with a hero's tale."

And before I could quite take it in the full implications, Boudica approached me, unsmiling for all her cordial words, and presented me with the hero's cut of meat.

Honored guests or not, Boudica paid scant attention to us during the feasting, but spent her time conferring with the warrior leaders. Bele, Alyssa, and I sat with the women and girls (those who had not slipped away for amorous visits). My three companions, who had spent the day on the practice fields, seemed to have made friends. Sarah had pretty much mastered the local dialect, and Bele and Alyssa were making admirable progress, since the main subject seemed to be weaponry and fighting. Lots of animated gesturing filled in any linguistic gaps. Eventually some young men sidled closer and joined in what became a bragging contest, with my women being as full of hyperbole as the brashest of the men. None of them, I noticed, had the least inclination to flirt—at least not with the men who seemed to hold no interest for them except as fellow warriors. I had never asked, because Sarah could be prickly about what she perceived as prying, but I suspect she preferred women as lovers, though as far as I knew she had never given her heart to anyone.

I sat back, replete after the huge cut of meat, which was as succulent and savory as any I have ever eaten, content to watch and listen. I must have dozed off, for I did not notice Lithben coming to sit beside me till her question startled me fully awake.

"Who is your other child, Maeve Rhuad?"

"My other child?" I repeated, not sure what she meant.

"My mother called you the mother of warriors," explained Lithben. "So I thought you must have another child or maybe more than one."

This child didn't miss a thing. Boudica *had* said mother of warriors.

"Perhaps she meant that Bele and Alyssa are like daughters to me," I ventured.

I glanced at Lithben who was frowning and gazing into her lap, then suddenly she looked up at me, her expression sweet and grave and so like my own mother's face it took my breath away.

"Then you have no other child?" she asked. "No other child than Sarah?"

How could I lie to her and imply her mother was mistaken or speaking only rhetorically? Perhaps she hadn't meant Bele and Alyssa at all. Was Boudica trying to tell me something and only her daughter had heard it?

"I did have another child once," I answered carefully. "But she was taken from me and sent out to foster when I was exiled."

Lithben regarded me, her eyes filled with a sympathy that seemed beyond her years.

"Maybe my mother knows her," she said. "Maybe she can help you find her."

"Maybe," I said, not able to get more words past the lump in my throat.

It was not a good moment to be called on stage.

CHAPTER TWENTY
HERO'S TALE

"MAEVE RHUAD."

Boudica's voice was like a catastrophe starting, an avalanche, a flood. Everyone hushed, hairs standing on end—or at least mine were.

"Foster sister of the renowned bard Branwen and foster daughter of King Bran. You were at school with Branwen for a time, I believe. Surely you have some tales by heart. It would please me to hear you tell one, a hero's tale."

There were a lot of excuses I could have made and thought of making. That was a long time ago. I never finished my course and earned a silver branch; I barely lasted a year. Before I could begin to demur, Boudica spoke again.

"Your daughter Sarah tells me you are an excellent storyteller."

I did not know whether to feel flattered or set up. I turned to look at Sarah. She looked back at me, but I couldn't read anything in her face, neither hint nor warning. Her eyes shone with reflected firelight. Boudica rose, crossed to where I was sitting, and extended a hand to me.

"If you stand here," she said, raising me to my feet and moving me to what would become center stage, "we will gather round you and everyone will be able to hear."

The reconfiguring of the expectant crowd gave me a moment to collect myself, which is to say, panic. I ransacked my brain for tales of cattle raids, elopements, wonder voyages, heroes doomed by *geasa*, standard bardic fare. I had stood like this before, mind suddenly blank, during my first recital when I could not remember the tale I had memorized and had winged it instead. I had told my own story, the story of Maeve and Esus. It had been a crowd pleaser, even though my departure from tradition had got me placed on academic probation. The tale I had told long ago had barely begun. Now I knew the end. Or did I? How do you know when a tale has ended?

People rearranged themselves, and at a sign from Boudica, the talk and laughter subsided again. Then she took her seat between Sarah and Lithben, the three faces with all their differences and similarities, side by side. My knees shook, but my voice, as I began to speak, held no tremor. If she wanted a hero's tale, a hero's tale she should have.

"Once upon a time, and timelessness, on an isle faraway and yet as near as your dreams, there lived eight warrior witches who knew all the heroic arts and the arts of love, and yet they lacked one thing: a hero to train. Every day they scanned the curve of sea and sky for a hero-bearing boat bound for their isle, but none ever came until one of the witches, who would not wait for fate, called a great storm that blew a small boat off course where it shattered on the rocks, and a young man, more dead than alive, washed up on their shore."

I paused, not for effect as my audience no doubt believed, but because I had never begun the story this way before, with my mothers' drastic action, the wreck of my father's ship. The story had always begun with me and Esus, but that was not the story I was telling now. I glanced at Sarah, whose eyes were round and rapt as when I told her stories as a child, this same story and not this story. She gave me an almost imperceptible nod: Go on. And I did.

After awhile I was hardly aware of my own voice, I was so inside the story, seeing it from my father's point of view. I experienced his humiliation, how the thwarting of his ambition turned to madness. I was with my mothers, too, and I felt the tensions mount between them as the dream of a hero to love and train became as wrecked as his boat. I told parts of the story I had never known, how my mothers turned a blind eye as the man scrabbled for drift wood among the rocks and cobbled together a boat and finally left one dark moon night riding the tide out to sea.

"And from all this wreckage and sorrow, a child was born, a girl child, with hair as bright as flame, and so they called her Little Bright One. The witches resolved that she would be their hero child, and they also swore they would never tell her the truth of her begetting. Instead they wove pretty tales for the child of how her father, the god of the sea, came in the night to court the fairest of them all. And their daughter grew strong and lived happily in their midst."

I paused again, wondering if I could possibly get away with ending the story here. If I kept on, the story could go on all night, and who knew where it might end. Well, I knew. That was the trouble.

"Did she grow up to do heroic deeds?" Queen Boudica prompted when I had waited too long. "Did she ever find her father?"

"Yes to both questions, Queen Boudica," I answered. "But the tale is a tragic one, and the hour is late."

"Heroes' tales often are tragic," observed Boudica. "We would hear this tale to the end."

I looked at Sarah again, sending her a silent question.

The truth, answered Jesus's daughter.

Help me, beloved, I prayed silently. It is your story, too. Help me.

And so I resumed the story where, for me, it really began, with the young hero-to-be running away from her mothers and glimpsing her beloved across the worlds in the well of wisdom at the heart of the holy island. When the two met later at druid school, I did not give a location, but I noted a change in Boudica's expression, a shift from benign interest to wariness. As the plot thickened and a brilliant but disturbed druid began to menace the young pair, wariness gave way to alarm. She had no chair with an edge to sit on, but when I came to the part where the young girl decided to trespass in the sacred grove during her beloved's initiation rite, I saw Boudica's hands gripping each other; her knuckles were white.

"Why would she do that?" Boudica suddenly interrupted the narrative with a voice that was almost a growl, as if the trespass was happening now on her watch. "She knew the rules, and she was forbidden expressly. The druid warned her!"

In the silence that followed her outburst, I could hear the hissing of the coals as the fire burned low. An owl screeched, and people shifted uneasily and exchanged furtive glances. The evening's entertainment was more than they had bargained for. I sensed everyone wondering what I was doing—and if I knew what I was doing. Mine was no predictable tale to be recited to the reassuring strains of a harp.

"She was a hero," I said quietly, looking only at Boudica. "Heroes often do foolish things, and sometimes terrible things happen to them."

The owl cried out again, and someone rose to stir the fire. It was a moment of decision, Boudica's or mine.

"Go on," she said grimly. "I would hear this tale to the end."

It did not escape me that she said *I* this time instead of *we*.

"Sarah," I said, "you know the story already. Will you take Lithben to bed? Mothers with children, I wish you good night now."

You might have thought Lithben or the other children would have protested. They had been caught up in the story so far, for until now the boy and the girl had been children, like them. But everyone sensed Boudica's ominous mood. They were afraid, even if they didn't know of what, and glad to be taken away and comforted with familiar beds and embraces. Lithben slipped her hand into Sarah's and followed without a backward glance.

I took a deep breath and sent my roots into the earth and my branches to the cool burning distance of the stars. Then I let go and gave myself to the story, telling not only what I remembered but what my father might have seen and felt. There was that girl, his nemesis, following him, plaguing him, pulling him back into helpless chaos. I felt his rage towards the witches, towards her, I felt how hot and wild it made him. I felt him throw the girl down and tear her open. Then I knew his horror when he came to himself again, his self-loathing that made him loathe her more.

Someone screamed then. I do not know who it was.

I stopped and looked at Boudica; her eyes were cast down, and then she lifted them to me, lifted her chin. With the barest flicker of an eye, she said: "Go on."

So I told how the girl almost lost her mind, even while a baby grew inside her. When I came to the part when the boy healed the girl, I saw that Sarah had returned. She reached for Boudica's hands and held them in her own. Boudica did not seem to notice, but I saw her grip Sarah's hand hard as I revealed how the girl learned that the druid who had raped her was her father, how he tried to kill her then. Even with my new understanding of my father, how he could see the boy as both salvation and nemesis remained, to me, a strange and twisted thing, true and distorted at once. When I came to the part where the druid plotted to kill the boy by rigging the lot for sacrifice, Boudica sprang to her feet.

"No! No druid of Mona would ever rig a lot. No druid of Mona would interfere with the will of the gods."

There was no point in saying I had never mentioned Mona. She knew; I knew. Now everyone knew.

"You are mistaken," she informed me.

For a moment I was shaken; it was as if all my years fell away and I was standing before the druid court. Could I be wrong? Could I be making it all up?

"Perhaps," I said, closing my eyes, seeing again from my father's point of view. "Perhaps it comes to the same thing. The druid believed the young man was the chosen one, the one destined for the god-making death. In this he was not altogether wrong."

When I opened my eyes, I saw Sarah. Her gaze was so golden, so unguarded. For a moment I was back in the garden, standing with my beloved under the tree. She smiled and nodded. I had done something right, even if I wasn't sure what it was. Slowly, very slowly, the way a mountain might wear away, Boudica took her seat again.

And I went on with the story, or the story went on itself, the point of view shifting unpredictably back and forth, so that I was not only the girl calling the tidal bore as her lover made shore on the other side of the straits, I was also my father dismounting and walking straight toward the wall of water. This time I heard him, or thought I heard him, singing to the wave.

I will go back, back to the sea
sea that has been the ruin of me
sea that will be the death of me
there my life will be, under the wave
under the sea, there my death will be
to Tir fo Thuin I go now,
to Tir fo Thuinn I go.

And I was startled to hear my voice singing the song, and to feel my own tears slipping soundlessly down my cheeks.

"You killed him."

Boudica did not stand to accuse me, but everyone heard her.

"You killed him."

Everyone waited for me to say something, but my story had come to a dead stop.

"You killed him."

Then to my amazement, it was Sarah who rose to her feet and stepped between Boudica and me.

"My mother did not kill him," she stated. "He killed himself. My father tried to save him; my mother did, too. He chose the wave. He chose it."

Boudica rose and faced Sarah; I could not read her expression. She just looked at her, as if she were an obscure augury, a garbled message from the gods.

"Will you hear the rest of the story?" I asked softly, a hint of pleading in my voice. "Will you hear about the birth?"

Boudica turned to me and gave me a look I had only ever seen on one face before.

"I will not," she said. "We will speak in the morning."

And with that she walked past me into the night.

"You didn't kill him," Sarah turned to me, needing reassurance as much as giving it.

"I didn't kill him that day long ago," I said slowly. "But my story killed him tonight."

CHAPTER TWENTY-ONE
BETWEEN STORIES

If Boudica could have called a tidal bore to Iceni country, I swear I would have flung myself into it, joining my father, our father, under the wave. Sarah, shaken as she was herself, must have sensed that urge. When we got back to our hut, she had a whispered conference with Bele and Alyssa in which I believe it was agreed that someone would be awake and watching over me at all times. At the moment I hardly noticed. I might as well have been underwater, I was so deep in loss, misery, and self-reproach.

Sarah's must have been the first watch, for soon I sensed her near me, not touching me, but sitting close to me, offering an almost animal kind of comfort. I felt myself relaxing into her warmth, but I would not let myself have the relief of sleep. After a while, I sat up, so Sarah would know I was awake.

"I am sorry." Sarah's words startled me. "It was my idea."

"Your idea?" I repeated, not knowing what she meant.

"It was my idea that you should tell her the truth. You were the one who wasn't sure, who knew what the truth might cost her."

Sarah, my Sarah, reproaching herself for something that utterly was not her fault.

"It was in no way your idea to tell the whole story in front of her whole tribe!"

"I encouraged you," she was stolid. "I share the blame."

"No," I said. "I'm the mother, yours, hers. What I have done, I have done."

We sat in silence for a time. I was just about to tell her to go to sleep, to promise her that I wouldn't do anything rash, (though admittedly she would have little reason to believe me) when she spoke again.

"I don't know that you could have told her any other way."

"Of course I could have," I resisted her kind attempt to exonerate me. "I could have told her privately. I could have told her right away."

"She would not have believed you," Sarah spoke with certainty. "She believed you tonight, because you gave her a choice. And because you told the story well, better than you have ever told it before."

"Thank you," I said. "I think."

We let the silence fall again, but it had a different quality this time. It was more spacious.

"But Sarah," I said slowly. "I destroyed her father for her, and for the *combrogos*."

"Maeve Rhuad." Sarah had never called me that before. "He destroyed himself."

"But why does anyone need to know that?"

"Because it's true."

In the dark, I shook my head.

"And the way you told it," she went on, "you could understand him, you could feel what he felt. He was a hero, a flawed hero, as much the hero of your tale as you or my father."

I picked up Sarah's hand, kissed it and pressed it to my wet cheek.

"Daughter of Esus," I said. "You are wise beyond your years."

Sarah and I did doze for a bit after that, leaning against each other, holding hands, closer than we had been since she was a little girl. But the respite didn't last for long. Boudica's summons came at dawn.

The guard, the same one who had challenged me the night I arrived, did not guide me to her hut where kinsfolk and servants would have been stirring, but to the chariot field, empty now and as flat and bleak as the sky where clouds had settled low. I saw her waiting at the far end, almost small in that expanse.

"She wants to speak with you alone," the guard stated the obvious.

And he left me to walk across the field by myself, one of the longest walks of my life. Boudica kept her back to me, which would have been unwise if I had been a fellow warrior, but I suppose she did not consider me dangerous in that way. My damage was already done. When I was within five paces of her, she turned to face me, and I stopped where I stood.

I don't know how long we stood looking at each other; there were no shadows, no shifting light to measure the time. It was long enough for me to let go of my own remorse and longing and simply see her, a woman between stories, a woman who did not know anymore who she was, who she should be. In that way, she was like an infant, but not one I could hold, and never one I could protect.

"I will not call you mother," were her first words.

They did not seem to call for any response, so I just nodded and waited for her to go on.

"Why did you come?" she asked, a slight alteration of the question she had asked the first night, but with a seismic shift in her tone which held not just anger now but anguish.

"I wanted to see you again," I repeated the words I had said that night. When she didn't answer I went on. "I wanted you to know: I did not abandon you; I did not give you up. The druids took you from me by force."

She continued to regard me as if my words were still incomprehensible.

"Then why?" she said at length. "Why did you wait till now to tell me?"

"I was afraid," I admitted.

"Afraid of what, afraid of me?" she asked sharply. "Am I so fearsome?"

Yes, I wanted to say. You are an angry, wounded woman who does not know herself. No, I wanted to say, you are still my baby. I am still holding you to my breast, whispering your name in your ear.

"I was afraid for you," was all I said.

"Afraid for me?" she repeated.

"Afraid that if I told you the truth, you would lose your pride in your lineage. I did not want to take that from you."

"Then why did you?" Her voice was cold and raw as the wind, her face as bleak as the sky.

There were so many reasons—or excuses—I could have given. None of them seemed adequate. And there was another truth I needed to tell her.

"I did something thoughtless yesterday that I had no business doing. But it is too late now to undo it. I think you ought to know."

"Go on," she said when I hesitated.

"I went to see Prasutagus. Your daughter Gwen was there, too. I just blurted out who I am. Prasutagus asked if you knew. Gwen demanded to know why I had left you. I felt that I had betrayed you by telling them first."

I don't know what I expected her to do. Lash out at me, turn away, freeze or blast me with her rage. Instead she looked suddenly vulnerable, almost as if she might burst into tears. Could it be that she still had some feeling for him, or that she was moved by her daughter's anger on her behalf? Whatever it was, I decided to seize this rare moment of openness.

"I know you are estranged," I waded right in. "For what it's worth, Prasutagus puts the blame entirely on himself—"

"It's worth nothing!" she interrupted, but her voice wavered and she did not tell me to stop.

"Be that as it may, he is dying, Boudica. Lithben needs to see her father before he dies or she will suffer even more when he does. And you, you need to speak with him."

Her face closed again, not violently, but slowly, with deliberation.

"I will never reconcile with him."

"He does not expect that," I said. "But he fears for you and for his daughters, as you should also. Feeble as he is, he is all that stands between you and ruthless military domination. You are still free now, even if you are poor. When he dies, you will be in danger. Your daughters will be in danger. You must hold counsel with Prasutagus and do what you can to safeguard the lives of your daughters and your people."

She looked at me coolly, almost with contempt.

"He is *not* all that stands between my people and Roman domination," she countered. "I stand. I stand. I stand!"

And tall as she was, she appeared to grow taller, tall enough to reach up and pull down the whole sky, if she chose.

"I will never be a Roman whore!"

I was stunned, as if she had dealt me a blow. How did she know, I wondered, how did she know? Then I realized she meant Prasutagus, not me. But still her words shook me.

"No," I agreed. "You won't. But don't be a fool, either. Go to him, Boudica. Be armed with knowledge as well as weapons."

She looked at me thoughtfully, as if some plan were forming in her mind.

"Heroes often do foolish things," she said, echoing the words I had said to her last night, "and sometimes terrible things happen to them."

And as she spoke, more softly than she ever had, I suddenly heard a roaring in my ears, pierced with terrible cries and clashing metal. And then the stench: fear, smoke, blood, loosened bowels, death.

"No!" I cried out. "No!"

I must have looked as if I was about to swoon. I don't think Boudica would have willingly touched me otherwise, but suddenly her arms were around me, arms strong and muscled as a man's, pulling me to a breast that was surprisingly full and soft. Oh Boudica, I thought, my dear lost child.

And then I really did faint.

When I came to, I was back in the guest hut with Sarah, Bele, and Alyssa. If it hadn't been for their anxious hovering, I might have thought my encounter with Boudica had been a dream.

"Are you all right?" asked Sarah, whose dark skin looked almost pale.

I nodded, though when I sat up, I still felt a little dizzy.

"Rest, Mother of Sarah," said Alyssa, sitting behind me to prop me up.

Bele brought me a bowl of broth, but Sarah stayed right where she was, close to me but facing me.

"Boudica was afraid it was your heart," said Sarah. "She carried you back, you know, as if you weighed nothing. She has sent for a healer. Do you have pain anywhere? Can you speak?"

"No pain," I said, though my tongue felt a little clumsy. "I don't think there is anything wrong with me, other than the usual."

Sarah frowned, her eyebrows drawn together so they almost met, just the way her father's had.

"Did Boudica say something to upset you?" Sarah wanted to know.

"No, I mean, yes." I paused and tried to reconstruct what had happened. "Well, it wasn't the easiest conversation, but it wasn't what she said, it's, it's what I saw."

"Oh," said Sarah. "You had another vision."

"Yes." I closed my eyes to call it back, then opened them. I did not want to see it again. "It was like the one I had before when we were in the valley near the fort, only worse."

"Worse?" prompted Sarah after a moment.

"Yes, worse," I repeated. "Because Boudica, Boudica...." I found I couldn't finish.

I did not know I was weeping until Sarah put her arms around me and held me close. Two embraces from two daughters in one morning and yet no comfort, for I felt powerless to protect either one.

Boudica's healer confirmed that I suffered only from fatigue, which made sense. I tried vainly to persuade myself that my vision was only a waking nightmare brought on by nervous exhaustion. I spent most of the day resting, with one or the other of the young women in attendance. Boudica herself did not come to see me, but when I woke from a nap in the late afternoon, I found Lithben sitting beside me.

"I brought you honey cakes," she greeted me.

"That is just what I wanted," I told her sitting up. "How did you know?"

"It's what I like to have when I am sick," she explained.

"Have some with me," I said sitting up. "I am not sick. I was just a little tired, so this can be a party instead."

She accepted the offer, and we ate companionably for a bit, licking our fingers as daintily as the cats of Temple Magdalen licked their paws after a treat of fish. When we were done, she looked at me solemnly for a moment, her face and manner so like my mother's I almost had to look away.

"You are my grandmother," she pronounced at last.

"Did your mother tell you that?"

"No one told me," she said. "I just know. You are, aren't you?"

"Yes, I am your grandmother, your mother's mother. And you are my granddaughter, which makes me very glad."

I waited for her to ask the same question her sister had, but instead she was full of information.

"Your mothers were witches," she stated.

She had heard that much of the story and had figured out who the girl hero really was.

"Yes," I affirmed. "Warrior witches. They taught me to race chariots, just as your mother is teaching you."

She said nothing, but gave a little dismissive shake, like a dog shedding water from its fur. That is not the story we are telling right now, she might have said.

"Your mothers stole from your father to have you."

A succinct way of putting it.

"And so he hated you. But it was not your fault."

"I thought Sarah put you to bed last night," I said with as much severity as I could muster. "Did you sneak back out to hear the rest of the story?"

She shook her head again, vehemently.

"I just know," she said again. "Something bad happened. Will you tell me what it was?"

I considered. Should I tell this child? She had already figured out that the druid in the story was my father. But should I tell her this father raped his daughter and made her pregnant with this child's mother?

"Here's what happened," I said slowly. "My father was so angry with my mothers that he stole back. He stole from me. But the good part is that I gave birth to your mother."

"Why is that good?" she asked.

As relieved as I was not to have to explain rape, I was also startled by her question.

"It's good, because your mother is strong and brave, and because she is your mother and your sister's mother."

"Oh," said Lithben.

She fell silent again, reached for one of her braids and began to suck it as she pondered, a childish habit she had doubtless been scolded for. But I was her grandmother, and I let her be.

"Will you stay with us now? Always?" she asked.

Before I answered her, I did my best to shut tight whatever eyes had the second sight. But really I didn't need the sight to know this child would suffer, with her father dying, her mother fanatically defiant, a rapacious empire at the door, unless....a beautiful desperate idea took form...unless I took her with me when I went. For all at once it was clear to me: I had to go.

"*Cariad,*" I said, and I touched her soft cheek, still round with her baby flesh. "I don't know yet what will happen."

And for a moment, at least, that was the truth.

CHAPTER TWENTY-TWO
HEART TO HEART

"No!"

Boudica and I were in the guest hut where I had asked to sup with her alone. Her answer to my request that I take Lithben with me to Mona was thunderous. You could practically smell lightning in the singed air between us. I was surprised I hadn't been struck dead. I did not expect her to say more.

"How could you?" she spoke again, her voice quieter now but just as full of fury and something else, not so easy to identify. "How could you even ask?" She did not wait for me to answer. "Has there not been enough separation? You lost to your mothers, me stolen from you, your younger daughter running away from you, lost to you for years. And now you want to take *my* daughter from *me*? Enough, enough! The curse of this matrilineage ends here. My daughter stays at my side where I can protect her as no one else can."

The silence after this speech was so charged, I did not want to touch it. I sat in it hardly daring to breathe. There seemed no opening for simple explanations, like: I want to take her out of harm's way. Besides, in truth it might not be safe for her to go to Mona, or not safe for those left behind. Hadn't her mother been called away from druid school, because that association was dangerous? And hadn't Dwynwyn prophesied terrible things for Mona? Still, I couldn't shake the feeling there was greater danger to Lithben here—and to her sister.

"What about your older daughter?" I found my voice again. "If you want to end what you call the curse of our matrilineage, which I think is overstating the case, why are you estranged from her?"

I had hit her in an undefended place.

"I am not estranged from her," Boudica said; this time the pain in her voice was unmistakable. "She is estranged from me. She took her father's side. She chose to stay with him. There was nothing I could do. There is nothing I can do."

I waited a beat.

"That is not true, Boudica, and you know it."

Both of us had been speaking without looking at each other. Now our eyes locked and our wills.

"How dare you chastise me?" she demanded, and underneath the outrage, I thought I heard wonder.

"I am your mother," I said lightly, almost as if it were the punch line of a joke.

If only we could have laughed. Would everything have changed? But we didn't.

"You are my mother," she repeated, sounding so bereft it broke my heart.

"I am sorry," I said.

"Don't be," she had the grace to say after a moment. "It's just hard to get used to. Everything has changed, and yet nothing has. I don't understand."

"I don't either," I agreed.

Our silence this time was not peaceful, exactly, but slower, like water seeping through ground layers, becoming cool and dark and clear again.

"Will you do something for me?" she said at length. "For us?"

Oh my dear lost beloved child, I did not say out loud.

"Of course."

"I can't let you take Lithben. I can't. But if you are going back to Mona, tell the druids what is happening here. Tell them about the payments and the conscriptions. Tell them about Prasutagus. Tell them to send us help."

I dared to reach out and take her hands. She let me.

"I will. And I will also ask you to do something."

"What?" she said warily.

"Take Lithben to see her father. Go see your daughter. The four of you need to be together again before it's too late."

She let out a long sigh, and then she astonished me.

"All right, mother. If you say so."

"So soon?" said Sarah

The four of us were together in our quarters later that night. I had just told them I wanted to leave as soon as we could provision ourselves.

"We just arrived two days ago," Alyssa agreed with Sarah. "It seems to me we could make ourselves useful here."

"Boudica has asked me to go on her behalf to the druids of Mona," I explained.

"Who are as likely to exile or execute you as listen to you," Sarah pointed out. "Surely she could send a more welcome and well, reliable, ambassador."

"She can't spare any warriors," I pointed out. "Even the older ones."

"Maybe she just wants to be rid of you, Mother of Sarah," fretted Bele. "Have you thought of that?"

"That's possible," I agreed, "but if she does, that is all the more reason for me not to impose on her hospitality. Besides, I want to go back to Mona."

I did not tell them of the vision I'd had on the Tor of myself standing on Dwynwyn's isle wearing her robes, looking out at the blood-red straits. It was not a happy vision, but no less compelling for that.

"Isn't that carrying nostalgia for your youth a bit far?" suggested Alyssa.

"You need not come with me." Then I surprised myself by saying, "In fact, you must not come with me."

Bele and Alyssa sputtered and protested, but Sarah just looked at me, as if she were trying to see into my mind's eye.

"Bele and Alyssa," Sarah spoke at length, "if Boudica will have you, I think it would greatly relieve my mother's mind to know you are here to look out for Lithben and befriend Gwen."

"Yes," I agreed, and then suddenly everything became clear to me. "Sarah, you must stay, too. You are their kinswoman."

There was a perturbed silence as everyone took in that I meant to go alone.

"But Mother! That is a long journey," Sarah objected. "And you are an old—"

"That's right," I cut her off.

I stood up and the little hut filled with a wind that swirled my garments. I loosed my hair and let it float.

"I am the Grey Hag. I am the daughter and mother of the holy earth and the holy isles, the mountains are made of my bones. I am the ragged edges of her rocky shores, the breath of her tides, the depth of her seas. Whoever harms me brings down my curse and whoever lends me aid is blessed."

I'd intended to mock myself by intoning the lineage I'd boasted the other day, but suddenly my claim seemed true.

"You're scaring me, Mother of Sarah," said Bele.

"I believe that's the idea," answered Alyssa.

"Right," I said, and the strange wind I'd called ceased as suddenly as it came. "If I have enough provisions, I can ride straight through. It's not all paved Roman road, but I believe the Wyddelian will take me all the way to the Menai Straits. If you would see me back to the main road, I will go on from there alone."

"Mama," Sarah hadn't called me that since long before she ran away. "I can't. I can't let you go."

I sat down again facing her and she flung herself into my lap.

"You can, *cariad*, Colomen Du," I said, stroking her hair, her black springy hair that like her father's seemed to have a life of its own. "You can let me go, for a time, for a little time only."

Though we both knew it might be forever.

Sarah sat up and looked at me quietly. I lost myself in the golden light of her eyes. Maybe we both traveled back to the tree in the garden of Tir nan Og where I had stood with her father, and with her, too, just conceived. Then slowly and so subtly I almost didn't see it, she nodded. And she sang me a blessing I had taught her as a child, the one I had given her father long ago.

The blessing of Isis go with you
queen of stars, mother of grain
she whose tears are the rain
she whose embrace is the sky
her wings of protection enfold you
her breast be your place of rest
her river with you wherever you wander
her river to guide you home.

PART THREE

Earth
The Song Of The Stones

CHAPTER TWENTY-THREE
GREY ONE, RED ONE

EVEN AT THE HEART of Pretannia, you are never far from the sea. And in this misty land there are rivers everywhere. Many of them run with the Wyddelian for a time. In their rush or quiet flow, I hear Sarah singing to me and I sing myself, the song becoming an invisible river running between us.

I soon lost count of the days, though the moon, when the night was not overcast, kept a record for me, waxing from new to full to waning again. I encountered other travelers on the road, and sometimes, if the night was cold or wet, sought hospitality at a village or farmstead. No Celt would turn away a wandering old woman, Grey Hag or not. No Roman soldier or civilians molested me, though some looked at me curiously or askance. And to my great relief no one tried to commandeer Macha, for though a good sturdy horse, she was old and grey like me.

Sometimes for hours I would see no other human. My days as a hermit in the cave stood me in good stead. I slipped back into solitude as if I had never left it. Yet it was different now. In the cave, memories and old friends, dead and living, had often visited, especially in dreams. Maybe it was being in motion, riding, riding, riding to the west, but even memory fell away. At times, I could barely remember who I was. My name, when I thought of it, seemed unfamiliar and arbitrary. I did not know why it belonged to me. Perhaps I was going a bit mad, but it didn't trouble me much. I simply felt free in a way that might have frightened me when I was younger. Free of myself, free of my story. I had shifted beyond any recognizable shape.

Alas, my blissful amnesia was all too short-lived.

The day I saw the Roman fort rising from the plain, it all came back to me. Wary of riding right past the gates, I decided to leave the Wyddelian for a bit and urged Macha up the ridge, so that I could survey the fort unseen. Unlike the last time we had passed this way, the fort was bustling: a flow of supplies converging on the gate, soldiers practicing maneuvers on the plain, and the constant sound of sawing and hammering. The flag of the general's own Fourteenth Legion, twin thunderbolts, was flying from the watchtowers. None of this activity augured well for the west. I would have more than Boudica's news for the druids of Mona—if they would hear me.

And if I ever got there.

For I suddenly had an idea, no doubt a crazy idea, but Sarah was not here to stop me. If she knew what I was contemplating, she would kick herself for letting me go alone. But she didn't know; she would never know unless I succeeded, and perhaps not even then. I turned Macha and headed back down to the road. Whatever the dangers of approaching the fort, at least I would avoid that valley this time, and there was the slimmest possibility that what I was about to attempt could undo the disaster I had foreseen.

My request to see General Suetonius was met with scorn and even a guffaw from the guards at the gate, which I thought was very bad form, but I am afraid Roman military discipline did not extend to manners. Who should know that better than someone whose husband had been tortured and ridiculed en route to his crucifixion where the soldiers played dice while they waited for him to die?

"At least she speaks decent Latin, which is more than most of these natives do."

I was glad he left out any adjectives before the word native.

"I can speak Greek, too, if it's any easier for you to understand," I added. "Not to mention Aramaic and dozens of Celtic dialects."

"What? Are you applying for a job as an interpreter? Or perhaps an informer?" he asked sounding slightly more interested.

"It could be. That is for the General to decide. After I speak with him. Alone."

"Look here," said the other guard impatiently. "The general is a busy man. No one gets an audience with him, unless he asks for it. Not the other way around."

"He will ask," I said with more assurance than I felt, "when you tell him I am here."

"And just who might you be?" he asked, his voice full of condescension.

How I wished the man was a Celt, and I could wow him with one of my lineages—my descent from the goddess Bride, my relation to a hero of the resistance, my Grey Hag number, but none of those would help me here, and might well land me in the brig. And I had no intention of giving these men my own clearly Celtic name.

"Tell the general," I began, not knowing what I would say, "tell the General that the woman you have kept waiting at his gate is...the lover of the world!"

I expected renewed sneers and rude laughter. Instead both the men looked terrified; blood drained from their faces. I swear I could hear armor rattling. Then the wind lifted, and blew back my cloak; out of the corner of my eye, I glimpsed a flash of bright red hair.

I was the one who laughed.

* * *

"You shouldn't go around doing that!" the general fulminated when I was whisked away to his private quarters. "Soldiers are superstitious and easily spooked. Now they'll be running after—or away from—every old woman they see."

He, for one, wasn't looking at me, but rather pacing while I took my ease sipping the wine he had ordered, eating dried figs and enjoying the warmth of the charcoal brazier.

"And I will admit, it disappoints me to discover it's just a cheap trick when I thought—"

"You thought I would only shape-shift into a ravishingly beautiful young woman for you?" I cut him off. "Well, it was for you. They weren't going to let me near you otherwise. Besides, whether or not you believe me, it isn't a cheap trick. I didn't do it on purpose. It surprised me as much as it surprised your soldiers."

Finally he stole a glance at me, as if fearful of what he might see. Which form alarmed him most, I wondered?

"You can't do it at will?" he demanded.

"Perhaps I could learn. But it may be that some circumstance has to call forth the change. Or some person," I suggested.

He sighed and stopped pacing abruptly, sitting down on a stool, facing me on the couch where I reclined, and he finally looked at me, as if I were a conundrum, a pending battle on treacherous ground. Or maybe that is how he looked to me.

"Why are you here?" he finally asked.

For a moment I forgot or maybe I just didn't want to remember, didn't want to think about the enmity between his people and mine, our problem children. I am here because you're here, I almost said, because you remind me of my beloved, and yet could not be more different. Because I want to go to bed with you again right now.

"Stop doing that," he said sharply.

But he didn't mean it. The next moment, he was on the couch with me, kissing me as if he was starving and only my mouth could feed him. He pulled back my cloak and I glimpsed my hair again, grey as clouds, and I saw my hands on him, thin and spotted with age. I looked at him, confused.

"It doesn't matter," he said.

"What doesn't?"

"Whether you're red or grey. It doesn't matter."

And it didn't.

* * *

"Where is the rest of your company?" he asked.

We were enjoying a late night feast after he returned to his quarters from his rounds of inspection. Until we stopped to eat, we hadn't spent much time talking.

"They have stayed on with my daughter, my older daughter."

"So you found her," he said. "Why aren't you with her, too?"

Of course we had to have this conversation, this delicate, tricky conversation.

"I am not with her," I began, "because I am here."

He gave me a look of mixed wariness and amusement.

"And you are here because?"

I gestured at our mutual state of undress. He smiled the way he often did with just the corners of his mouth and eyes as if showing his teeth would give away too much.

"The other reason," he persisted.

I sat up and pulled a shawl around me. I did not think I should be so naked when I broached the subject of his son.

"I wanted to tell you something," I began. "About your son's financial policies."

He also sat up and instinctively felt for the whereabouts of his sword, though he did not close his hand on it.

"You mean the policies of the procurator of Pretannia," he corrected me. "How would you think that as governor I would not be fully aware of them?"

"Well then, you must be aware that his policies are rapacious."

"Why do you say so?"

"If you give someone a gift and later declare it a loan to be repaid immediately and with high interest, what do you call that? That is what the procurator of Pretannia is doing to the tribes who cooperated with the invasion of their land. He is bankrupting them, taking all their wealth as so-called payment as well as conscripting their men into the Roman army by force. Are you aware of *this* policy!"

He didn't answer right away, but just gazed at me, almost losing focus. I wondered if I had shape-shifted again. If he dared to say something like, You're so beautiful when you're mad, I might have to run him through with my own sword (which yes, at Sarah's insistence, I had brought with me, and which was close to hand).

"I asked you a question," I prompted him. "Are you aware of this policy?"

"Yes," he said at length. "And as you note, it is his policy, and he was appointed by Emperor Nero to make all such civil policies, just as I am appointed to command the army and protect the peace. They are two distinct offices. As I'm sure you are aware."

If he meant to appease me with a nod to my knowledge of the inner workings of the Empire, his attempt failed.

"Of course I am aware," I said. "But I am not stupid, and I didn't think you were. Your job of protecting the peace is going to be a lot harder if civil policies oppress the tribes, even the friendly ones. If Rome wants people to accept the Pax Romana, which is a pretty bitter draught in the first place, you'd better sweeten the deal, make it worth their while, give them something to lose."

"You don't need to lecture me on Roman foreign policy," he said stiffly. "I know perfectly well how it works. Put simply: people who cooperate are rewarded; people who don't are dealt with. Swiftly."

"But that's just the point," I argued. "Plenty of tribes did cooperate, and they are being punished anyway. By your *son*." Wisely or unwisely I drove the point home.

We sat silently, alternately glaring at each other, then looking away, like cats trying to decide whether to have a full out fight.

"And you came here," he said, "to ask me to do something about it, to influence the procurator."

"Why do you call him that?" I shot back. "As if you had no other relation to him."

"Because I don't," said the general shortly. "No matter what I told you in a moment's madness in the moonlight, no matter what I believe to be true, another man lifted him to the knee, accepted him as his son and raised him. According to Roman law that man is his father."

I knew that law well. To raise a child to the knee was to acknowledge paternity. If a man refused to do it, a child could be exposed and abandoned. Once it was done, it was binding, no matter what a man subsequently believed. That was how my erstwhile nemesis Paulina became the daughter of a horrible Roman senator who discovered too late his wife's liaison with a slave.

"I understand," I spoke more gently. "So you have not told him."

"Have not and will not."

I felt at an impasse. There was too much emotion roiling around to continue a policy debate. It occurred to me that the general might be ashamed of this man who was son in blood if not in name. Yet this unacknowledged bond might also make him hesitate to challenge or even advise the procurator as he might if he were merely a fellow official.

"And what about you?" he asked. "Did you tell your daughter who you are?"

I hesitated, aware that we were now entering treacherous water, cold with strong currents and slippery rocks.

"I did," I said. "Perhaps not wisely or well, but I did."

"She was not pleased with the news?"

"It was bittersweet," I answered cautiously. "It did not match the story she had always been told."

"But she believed you?"

"Yes, she believed me."

There was another silence, and I sighed with what turned out to be premature relief.

"And is your daughter's tribe one of those oppressed, as you so dramatically put it, by the procurator's policy?"

I raised my eyes to his. He looked back, his expression carefully noncommittal. Did he think I would open my mouth as easily as I opened my legs? He could think again.

"There are few tribes that are not. Travel to the east and see for yourself. Leave someone in charge here. Go see the procurator. Speak to him, sway him before it's too late," I sounded my theme again. "You are older, more experienced. Surely he must defer to you."

He gave a harsh laugh that got caught somewhere in his throat.

"I thought with your experience you would know men better than that," he said. "I am the old dog. He is the new dog. Best we keep to our own turf, unless one of us is willing to roll over, expose his neck."

And I understood. He would not do that to his son, even if he didn't call him son, and even if he could. And so he was off, as I could guess only too well, to subdue the west instead.

"What will you tell your daughter when you return to her?" he asked, assuming more than I had told him, an old trick for getting information. He wanted to know if I had been sent here; he wanted to know who my daughter was.

"Nothing," I said.

"Nothing?" He gave me a skeptical look.

"Nothing," I repeated, and then decided to toss him a tidbit. "She does not know I am here. No one knows I am here."

"How will you explain your absence?"

I could not help it, I smiled. He thought I was going back; he thought I was going east, and I would—until I lost any tail he put on me and doubled back.

"I will think of something," I assured him.

"Let me give you safe escort," he urged. "You should not travel alone."

I gave him the look he deserved for such an obvious ploy.

"The Grey Hag's only companion is the wind," I tried it on for size.

"What is that supposed to mean?" He seemed singularly unimpressed. That was a Roman for you. Where was his Etruscan spirit?

"It means I can take care of myself."

"On the contrary, it seems to me that whenever you venture out on your own you get into trouble."

He gave me another of those almost smiles.

"Is that how you describe yourself?" I shot back.

We were playing, and I couldn't resist, even though or maybe because the world around us, our clashing worlds, were in such dire condition.

"Upon consideration," he said, "I'd say that's how I would describe you."

"I see." I smiled and stretched out on the couch, letting the shawl fall away and expose breasts that could never, no matter what age or shape I took, be described as anything but ripe, round, glorious. "And would you like to get into trouble again?"

"I would," he said, and he reached for me, but his playfulness was gone, and there was such sadness in his face, I caught my breath and touched his cheek.

"What is it?" I asked him. "Tell me."

"You know," he said. "You know."

I closed my eyes and saw that valley again; it was dark, and we were alone there. All the din and death as yet unborn.

"It doesn't have to be that way," I told him. "It doesn't."

"You have your fate," he said. "I have mine."

"Fate doesn't have to be fatal," I insisted.

He shook his head, "Of course it does, in the end. Didn't your husband teach you that?"

"No," I told him. "No, he taught me that love is as strong as death."

"But not stronger," the general said. "Not stronger."

We looked at each other, suspended, at a draw. Two wrestlers evenly matched. Yes, wrestlers, locked in that close fighting form that could turn at any moment into an embrace.

"He also said to his followers, Love your enemy."

And I drew my enemy into my arms. Tonight, at least, I would win.

I left the next day not long after dawn. The general had had Macha fed and curried, and her saddle bags were filled with fresh provisions. He himself walked me to the gate. As we crossed the near deserted courtyard, I looked at the construction-in-progress, idle now at this early hour. It was at too unformed a stage to be sure what was being built, but I noted lots of oak boards, and some wood being soaked so that it could be shaped into what looked like the prow of a...boat.

"What are you building here?" I asked, trying to sound merely curious.

"Boats." He didn't bother lying.

"Boats for what?" I pressed.

He shrugged.

"Pretannia is an island. Everyone who lives here needs boats."

"I suppose they do," I said lightly.

But not everyone built them at a fort on the western front, and not all boats were constructed with flat bottoms, as these appeared to be, to make it easy to maneuver them in very shallow waters.

We did not speak again until we reached the gate. He helped me mount Macha, and then we looked at each other, each silently making our case one more time.

"The gods protect you and yours," he said.

I don't know why, but I found I could not repeat his words back to him.

"Peace," I heard myself saying. "Peace be with you."

And then I headed east on the Wyddelian road.

It wasn't long before I sensed I was being followed. Whenever I stopped to listen, I could hear the footfall of another horse behind me stopping a moment or two after I did. It might not have been a pursuer, but I decided to take no chances. For an experienced weather witch, the solution was simple. I gathered the mists still hovering over the river and the streams, the boggy places, and put quite a thick fog between me and whoever rode behind me. Then I rode on swiftly till I came to a stream running down from the ridge, shallow and rocky enough for me to follow it up into the cover of the wood without leaving any hoof prints. The great thing about a hard paved Roman road is that no one would be able to see where I departed from it. From my hidden post on the ridge, I thinned the fog so that I could glimpse the other rider; he was dressed in a plain tunic as if he were a farmer, but his horse was no plough horse, so I felt confirmed in my suspicions. I watched to make sure he kept riding east, then I sent the fog after him, and I followed the ridge west, going out of my way to avoid the wedge-shaped valley where I had foreseen the horror that I still hoped against hope to prevent.

CHAPTER TWENTY-FOUR
INHERITANCE

THE ROAD BECAME wilder and less Roman the farther west I went. Even after the paving stopped, I managed to follow it through the steep mountains that made the west so difficult for the Romans to control. A great country for ambushes. Now and then, I caught glimpses of roaming warrior bands, but they were all heading for their winter places now. In the mountains the snows had begun, and more than once Macha and I had to wait out a blizzard in a cave. These were the mountains I had gazed at when I was a student on Mona, the mountains my beloved had disappeared into when he escaped with the Hibernian outlaw women, an escape too swift and mountains too rugged for a young girl about to give birth. They were a bit rugged for an old woman and an old mare, slowly picking their way across narrow valleys and narrower passes with no companions most of the time but each other—and the rocks that at dawn and dusk looked like giant creatures, watching, waiting, deciding whether to open the way or obstruct it.

Then one morning early, with the sun rising behind us, we crossed the last pass and Mona lay below us, still lush and green and ripe, floating in a sea of dawn light.

"Oh, Macha!" I said aloud, "Just look at all that rich grazing! Just think of all the oats and barley mash you will have."

Of course Mona fed not only horses but armies, I realized. No wonder the druids had made it their stronghold and the base of resistance to Rome. I thought uneasily of the boats under construction at the fort. It would be no mean feat to cart them over these mountains or to maneuver them around the long intricate coast, but the general had the winter to prepare equipment and troops. For what it was worth, he did not know that I would warn the druids.

Macha whinnied, impatient of my interest in the view, and we started our last descent.

By the time we got to the shore, it was midday and the tide was high. We stopped and rested for awhile and then, as the tide ebbed and the sun went west to the Hibernian Sea, I searched for the best place to ford the straits. Even at the lowest tide in the shallowest waters, the currents were tricky and quicksand was a danger. At last I fixed on a course and prayed to Bride and Isis to guide us safely across. But I believe it was my beloved who led me. In the late afternoon light, I could see that we were splashing ashore at just the spit of sand where I had let him go, no, commanded him to go in the name of his god. I slipped off Macha and just stood there with my eyes closed, listening to the same wind blowing over and over the island, the same tide going out like a last breath. My beloved was long gone; he was just here.

I didn't really have to think what to do next. I mounted Macha again and turned her west towards Dwynwyn's Isle. As if sensing she was almost home, Macha galloped down the sands like a horse half her age. At dusk, we crossed the tidal spit of land where we were greeted by a small flock of sheep, with complicated horns. Dwynwyn's own breed. They regarded Macha with equanimity and silently invited her to feed, which she did with a big horsey sigh, while I unloaded her saddle bags and went in search of the cave. I wanted to settle in before full night was upon us.

I picked my way in the gloaming, stopping at the well where Dwynwyn's famous eels swished, a flash of darkness in the silvery pool. The cave, if I remembered right, was on the other side of the highest hillock on the little island. When I walked around it, I got a shock. There was Dwynwyn's cauldron where it had always been, just outside the mouth of the cave—and someone had just lit a fire, for I had not seen or smelled smoke when I set foot on the island.

"Dwynwyn?" I cried out. "Dwynwyn, are you here?"

Then I fell silent abruptly, feeling cold despite the heat from the fire. What if someone else was here, what if someone had taken her place? Whoever they were—or weren't—they couldn't be far away. Most likely they were inside the cave.

"Is anyone there?" I crouched by the entrance and peered inside.

By the firelight I saw the red tunic, laid out on a pallet on the floor. The necklace of white skulls gleamed against the blood red of the robe.

"Dwynwyn?" I whispered. "Is that you?"

But I already knew it wasn't. I crept into the cave and touched the fabric, a strange fabric, heavy and light, smooth and coarse at once. I brushed my fingers over the skulls; they made a sound between a rattle and a bell.

"Is this for me?" I asked, not knowing if I spoke aloud or silently.

"Of course," the answer came from somewhere, from the tide creeping back, the wind in the wild grass, the crackling of the fire. "I told you I would leave my red tunic for you. But before you put it on, you'd better stir the pot. The rutabagas are sticking to the bottom."

I laughed out loud, and then got up and did as I was told.

* * *

The red tunic was as wonderful on my body as it had felt to my touch; in the days to come, it adjusted itself to the temperature, cool when the weather was warm, which it seldom was as autumn advanced, and warm when it was cold, and wonderfully dry in the inevitable damp. It felt then as though I had picked it up from a sun-warmed rock and put it on. Weather magic woven into fabric. When I was a girl I'd had no idea that Dwynwyn enjoyed such luxury. The time I had changed shapes with her, she had made sure I felt all her aches and pains but none of this ease. Or perhaps it was only that I had worn a grey robe then, the better to appear as the Grey Hag and not Dwynwyn in particular, who had a habit of annoying the druids with her scorn for their authority. They had no jurisdiction over her and could not prevent people, including students, from coming to consult her eels about their love luck, something the druids considered frivolous, but we girl students had taken very seriously.

When I woke that first morning after a long, comfortable sleep, I stoked the fire under the cauldron, and went outside to relieve myself. The day was bright and clear; though it looked as if clouds might be moving in from the east. I whistled for Macha, whom I hadn't tethered, and she ambled around one of the hillocks, looking as well-rested and better fed than me. Her mouth full of grass, she had clearly been breakfasting for awhile.

I went to the cauldron, hoping I'd find stew left over from last night's supper, and to my surprise (well, not as much surprise as you might think) I found the cauldron full of stirabout flavored with fresh apples. I heaped some in a bowl, and then sat down cross-legged, looking out at the straits where the tide was ebbing again.

"If you had a magic cauldron," I said to Dwynwyn, "why were you always pestering us about bringing something for your pot and scolding us if our offerings weren't up to snuff?"

"You can't give divination away for free," she said. "No one believes in it if you do. Haven't you learned that, sweet pea, in all your worldly travels?"

Had I? I was suddenly finding it hard to remember the details of my life, where I had been, what I had done. I had been a whore and a slave for awhile, I thought, and then later I had embraced men of my own free will and healed people for the asking. But there had always been food, I seemed to remember, or coins to buy food. They fed me on the ships when I whistled up the wind for them. Why did it all seem like a dream?

"Besides, I am spoiling you now. Soon you'll have to fill the pot for yourself. Don't worry. You'll have plenty of business. Some things never change."

All at once, I felt dizzy and confused, as if I had fallen into some vortex and landed here on this timeless tidal isle without knowing how.

"Dwynwyn," I cried out. "Why I am here? Why must I take your place?"

"If I knew the answer to that, mutton chop, you wouldn't be here at all. You're here, that's all I know. We'll just have to find out."

Then I realized with a jolt that Dwynwyn's words were coming out of my mouth.

Was I Dwynwyn or was I myself?

I stood up suddenly, upsetting my bowl of stirabout, pulled back my hood and loosed my hair on the wind. It was still grey as clouds, not that gorgeous mist-by-moonlight white Dwynwyn's had been.

"Damn," I said, relieved and annoyed at once.

"You can't have everything," Dwynwyn retorted, in whose voice no longer mattered.

Over the next few days I got used to this strange relationship within or around whatever I called myself. I tended Macha and the sheep, whose needs were few beyond a trip to the mainland for fresh water (the eel well was brackish). The pot continued to have something in it, but I also added fresh fish I caught with a net I found in Dwynwyn's cave. I found a smaller pot and made tea from wild rose hips. A couple of times I rode with Macha to an orchard a mile or so away and gathered apples.

Periods of what might almost be described as amnesia (or perhaps the beginning of senile dementia?) were punctuated by memories so vivid it almost seemed as though they were not memories at all. The future, too, troubled me, what with Dwynwyn's maddeningly vague prophecies of the terrible things to come and visions that hovered at the periphery of my second sight. Nor did I forget that I had come to Mona with a mission to fulfill, though I sometimes could not remember what it was. And whenever I thought of leaving the tidal isle to seek out the druids of Mona, I felt a stop in my mind.

"It is timing," said the Dwynwyn part of me, "it is all a matter of timing. You will know when to go to them. Otherwise they will not hear you."

"They?"

"The druid boys," she said.

"There are druid girls now, too," I reminded her.

"Hard to tell unless you lift their tunics."

We cackled. I suppose you would have to call it that.

"I have things to tell them," I said, "urgent things to tell them. Will I remember?"

"When the time is right," reassured Dwynwyn, "when the time is right."

* * *

Time wheeled over the island, the sun hurrying west each day a little sooner, the nights bristling with stars and frosts. Then there came a day, when summer seemed to let out its breath one last time, slow and soft. The wind rested in the grass, and the tidal pools were still. I was lying on the side of a hillock, soaking the sun into my tunic. I heard their voices from a long way off, geese, I thought, but hadn't the geese all flown away? No, the sound came from girls, girls laughing and talking. I sat up and saw them walking down the beach, their sandals in their hands. Every now and then they broke into a run or stopped to splash each other.

"Your first customers," Dwynwyn said. "Don't be too easy on them. Put on a good show."

Despite gaps in my memory, I could vividly recall tiptoeing around the island with the other first form girls till we came upon Dwynwyn sitting cross-legged and barefoot by her cauldron. She had worn a black cloak over the red tunic, all the more dramatic with her white hair. But the day was warm, so I sat uncloaked, my hair wilder than Dwynwyn's, my feet, despite or maybe because of all my travels, still quite shapely, I thought. I waited for the girls to find me.

When they did, standing in a semi-circle at a safe distance, I tried to beetle my brow and glare at them ferociously, but I found myself distracted. They were so young, was I ever that young, young as babies, young almost as Lithben. But they were clearly girl-druids in the making, wearing the same green tunics we had, green for their greenness.

"What have you brought for my pot?" I demanded.

These girls were better prepared than we had been. We hadn't known the custom, which elicited disparaging remarks from Dwynwyn about the detrimental effects of over-education. When I had proffered some hazelnuts from my pocket, her remarks had been memorably crude.

"Hazelnuts!" she'd scowled. "What? Not a fish or a rutabaga for an old woman? Something to slide easy down the throat? I suppose you expect me to crack all those nuts, hard as they are. Hard as a young man's head, though with more wisdom inside. Hard as a young girl's heart, though with more sweetness inside. Don't give me that dewy, doe-eyed look. Of course you have hard hearts. All hearts are hard till they're broken. Then they're a bloody mess! Though not bad tasting if you cook and season them properly.

"Save your hazelnuts for the Samhain *fires," she'd said. "Though for all the good you'll get of them you might as well stuff them up your pussies and let them pop there. Such a waste of wisdom."*

I wasn't going to have the opportunity to make such a colorful speech. The girls dutifully, if warily, approached me with barley and oat cakes, leeks, rutabagas (Dwynwyn's favorite vegetable) a hunk of salted pork, a bowl of late blackberries, a basket of apples, some hazelnuts thoughtfully shelled, a jug of mead (praise goddess) and a dripping piece of wild honeycomb that left the bearer's hands quite sticky. A red-head, the girl licked her fingers as delicately and discreetly as possible. I tried to restrain my inner Dwynwyn from smacking her lips and forgetting all about her guests.

"That will be acceptable," I informed them. "Now I suppose you want to consult those slippery little sods about your love luck?"

They all nodded, still speechless.

"Come then," I rose to my feet with impressive agility; the necklace of skulls tinkling merrily, so to speak.

I wondered if the girls had made this trip on a dare from older initiates. Well, whatever Dwynwyn would have done, whatever the eels had to say (and come to think of it, I didn't know how to interpret eels' movements) I intended to put the best spin on their fortunes I could. I led them to the well. We gathered round the dark water, shadowed by rocks, churning with the restlessness of the eels, and the subtle ebb and flow from the underground channel to the straits. The girls cast glances at me, waiting for some kind of instruction, but I only gazed in increasing horror at the pool.

The straits, red with blood, the smell of smoke, and over the sound of wind and battle, the heart-shattering wailing of women.

When the sound stopped, I looked around me, and all the girls had gone away, except for one, still standing poised to flee but riveted on me. The red-head, her hair as red as mine had been, as red as Boudica's, her boldness stronger than her fear.

"What happened?" I asked.

"You screamed," she said. "And screamed. The others all ran, but I had to know. What did you see?"

"You're a brave one, colleen," I avoided her question. "What is your name?"

"Maeve," she said. "I am from Hibernia, and I am named for Maeve the Brave, Queen of Connacht."

"So am I!" I exclaimed before I could think. "And did she name you herself?"

The young Maeve took another step away from me.

"I don't know what you mean," she said. "I thought your name was Dwynwyn."

"Oh yes, well, it is, I suppose. Or was. Or will be," I answered, feeling dazed, almost seasick from riding the heaving swells of time and identity.

Young Maeve stared at me with wide eyes the color of dusk sky; in the fading light her bright hair still glowed.

"Today is *Samhain*," she said. "We brought you the last berries picked yesterday, the last apples, the last honeycomb. What did you see between the worlds?"

I opened my mouth but closed it again; the scream was still in my throat.

"Run, Maeve," was all I could manage, "before the tide comes in. Go with Bride's blessing."

I watched Maeve disappear over the hillock. Then out of the corner of my eye, I caught a flash of red hair in the well, but as a face cohered, it wasn't the girl's. It was Boudica's, watchful and strained, waiting.

"Tell them," I heard Boudica's voice clearly now in memory. "Tell the druids how it is with us here."

"It's time," said Dwynwyn. "Go."

I went to fetch my own grey cloak. I climbed the hillock and looked east where the full moon was rising. Maeve had just made the tide. I could see her running as fast as she could down the beach. Cold waters rushed in, cutting off the island from the mainland. I might be able to cross on Macha, but as I pondered, the wind suddenly rose. And before I knew what was happening, I rose with it, my doves' wings brushing the edges of my vision.

CHAPTER TWENTY-FIVE
THE RETURN OF MAEVE RHUAD

IT WAS NOTHING new for me to find myself in the form of a dove. I had made this very flight from Dwynwyn's Isle long ago when my father tried to kill me. Or was it long ago? It is hard to think when you are flying; really there is only wing beat, heartbeat, wind that is with you or against you. The wind was with me this time. I rode it, I rowed it like a stream. It carried me over the sands, then shifted and bore me inland where I saw it toss the crowns of the great trees of the teaching groves, till it quieted and set me down at the edge of a wide empty field ringed with ancient beech and oak.

I stood in the shelter of a beech, adjusting again to my human form, wondering where I was, when I was. I touched my face, still worn and lined, so I concluded I had not traversed time. I was not sure what to do next; whether I should try to find my way to the college and look for someone I knew.

"Just wait," said Dwynwyn. "Watch."

And so I did, for what seemed like a long time. Dusk deepened into full night, the moon sailed into the open sky. By its light I could see that a bonfire had been laid, and waited, ghostly in the moonlight, for a torch to bring it to life. Chill crept up from the ground, though I felt warm enough in the red tunic and my grey cloak. Still I could not help thinking with longing of the feast I'd left behind on the island. I wished I hadn't flown away so hastily.

"It's hard to fly on a full stomach," remarked Dwynwyn. "You're an old woman now; you don't need much food to keep you going."

"You're one to talk!" I retorted. "When did you ever think of anything but filling your pot—and your belly?"

"Hush now," whispered Dwynwyn. "Pay attention."

It felt as if the trees had heard her, too, as if they had woken suddenly from some dreaming state and now leaned in a little closer, waiting for what would happen next. Then from the opposite side of the clearing, a procession entered bearing torches, chanting words I could not quite catch, but by the light of their torches I could see that they wore masks and headdresses. Feathers abounded, and there was one impressive rack of antlers.

The faculty of the druid college of Mona in full regalia.

Beeches are the most accommodating of climbing trees. I accepted the low slung branch the tree extended to me and climbed high enough to get a good view.

The druids ringed the still unlit pile of wood, the first circle, the inner circle, always closest to whatever mystery was at hand, fire, water, stone, or blood. Then the students of the college followed. I spotted Maeve, her hair orange in the full moonlight, and for one disorienting moment, I thought it was my own younger self, flanked and supported by Branwen and Viviane after my breathless flight and narrow escape—and the sudden almost incomprehensible knowledge that I carried my father's child. But young Maeve was not me. I had seen her running back in ordinary human form along the sands. I was here to help her, I remembered. I was here to warn them all. It was not too late.

Now the rest of the *combrogos* flooded into the field: warriors, chieftains, farmers, metal workers, not as big a gathering as *Lughnasad* and *Beltane* when winter weather did not threaten. But enough representatives from enough tribes for every word said this night to travel, just as the flames of the *Samhain* fire would travel to every far-flung hearth, uniting the *combrogos*. For now that mass of people was as silent as the trees, more silent, for their limbs did not sway and creak or whisper the words of the wind. Then the antlered one, the archdruid, no doubt, stepped forward and ignited the blaze. The wood caught quickly, flames towered like waves, sparks flying into the night, holding their light till they seemed to turn to stars. A human roar competed with the roar of fire. Drums pounded and pipes wailed.

The archdruid lifted his arms, as if with his staff he conducted the sound, served as its conduit to the Otherworld, and then he lowered his arms and sound ceased again; even the wind subsided, and the flames, still bright, burned more softly. With his staff in hand, he slowly circled the fire, stopping to call the quarters. When he came back to center, or as close as he could without standing in the fire, I had a view of him in profile, and I was able to hear his voice.

"Here now," he said plunging his staff into the earth, "is the center of the world."

I felt disoriented again. I did not recognize the man's voice, or rather I did, vaguely, but it was not the voice of *the* archdruid, the voice that still sounded so vividly in my memory pronouncing my sentence of exile beyond the ninth wave.

"Of course it's not him," Dwynwyn said. "The wily old coot died more than ten years back. Of a bad cold!" This fate seemed to amuse her. "He had a terrible case of laryngitis; couldn't make any deathbed pronouncements. There's justice for you. I outlasted him."

I thought she would burst into a playground taunt any minute.

"Only one Crow lady still left at the college," Dwynwyn added grudgingly, "tiny, a dry stick of a woman. Next strong wind will take her."

"Really? Which Crow?"

"Don't ask me. Never could tell them apart."

We students hadn't been able to either; they hadn't wanted us to, really. They were a collective entity, like a cluster of rocks or trees. Still, I was glad there was one left. I hoped it was Moira, the one who had distinguished herself through kindness to me after Boudica's birth.

"Who is the archdruid now?" I asked. "Why does his voice sound familiar?"

"That would be Ciaran under that rack of antlers, of the formerly blue-black hair. What a nuisance he was for the eels in his youth, all the girls in love with him."

One of my classmates now in charge of the college? It was shocking to think he was old enough. But then Ciaran was actually several years older than me; he'd been in ovate studies when he and Viviane had run off for their trysts in the moonlight, the fruits of which had almost killed Viviane, would have killed her, if I hadn't halted one of my own escapades to save her life (for which she was eternally grateful and resentful). I wondered how Viviane felt about Ciaran being archdruid.

"She fought him for the succession," supplied Dwynwyn. "Wanted the job for herself. Terrible controversy, many undergarments in a wad over it. She finally deferred for the sake of the college and of course the *combrogos*."

"How noble," I murmured.

"It's worked out," said Dwynwyn. "He respects the hell out of her. Truth to tell they've been a bit of an item again since she went through the change."

I felt a twinge of jealousy, that Viviane and Ciaran were still here together where they'd always been when I had lost Esus so long ago, then lost him again so long ago. But it passed quickly. They were in no enviable position, as I must soon let them know. When, I wasn't sure. Ciaran was still addressing the crowd, though I hadn't been able to follow him, with Dwynwyn gossiping in my brain.

"You haven't missed anything," muttered Dwynwyn. "Some things don't change. The druids are still full of gas. But pay attention now. Your cue is coming."

The archdruid, as I might as well call him, fell silent for a moment. Taking up an unlit torch, he touched it to the fire, ignited it, and raised it, and then he chanted:

Spark to flame
flame to hearth
hearth to heart
the *combrogos* stand as one
the *combrogos* stand as one.

As the flame moved from torch to torch, people took up the chant, turning it into a song; the pipes and the drums added deeper wilder notes, and my hairs stood up along my arms. I had never heard this chant when I was a student. Roman invasion then had been only a threat; now it was fully established in the east, making its way west, battle by battle, tribe by tribe. This chant was a call to resistance.

"Tonight," the archdruid spoke again when the chant had risen and fallen again to deeper silence, "is the holiest night of the year. The veils between the worlds are thin. The dead can bring messages, and the unborn can speak. We can ally with spirits of the earth that the Romans cannot conceive, for they are strangers here. This soil did not feed them; this earth does not cradle the bones of their dead. I call now upon the spirits kindly to our cause to speak, speak to us, speak through us. Come to our aid."

"Go on," whispered Dwynwyn. "That's you."

"I'm not a spirit," I protested. "Am I?" suddenly not so sure.

"You'll get a better audience if they think you are. They never listened to me when I was alive. Now go on, you old Grey Hag, go."

I slipped down from the tree and made my way towards the crowd, regretting the lack of a staff of my own. It would have made a helpful prop, better than elbows for pushing people out of the way. I had to make do with theatrical muttering.

"Make way for the Grey Hag. The *combrogos* have called for me, make way."

Something about me must have been convincing, maybe the grey cloak itself, for people did as I said and soon I stepped into the pool of light around the fire and faced off with the archdruid, who, considering he had just invoked me, seemed a bit flustered. I expect he would have preferred to channel (and edit) any Otherworldly messages himself. And here I was about to upstage him.

"*Woe!*" I astonished myself by saying. "*Woe unto the inhabitants of the Holy Isles, even unto the druids of Mona, I say woe!*"

Where had that come from? Even as I asked myself, I knew, and underneath their masks, I sensed the druids turning pale. They knew, too. Most of them had been there the day Esus had fallen into a fit and prophesied doom. Surely his words sounded in their memories, as they did in mine.

Yea, the day is coming when the Menai Straits will run red. Black-robed priestesses will stand in the turning tide and shriek their curses, yet devastation will come. A great host will ford the waters. Blood will spill. The groves will burn. The heavens will turn black with smoke, and the earth bitter with ash, and the druids will be gone forever from Mona mam Cymru.

"Um," I stalled. "I didn't quite mean it that way."

Surely I had come to prevent, not predict.

The archdruid took a step closer to me, surreptitiously lifting his mask a bit, which skewed his antlers. He grabbed hold of his headdress just in time to keep it from sliding off.

"Who are you, spirit?" he addressed me sternly. "Make yourself known to us, if you have business with the *combrogos*. Or else be gone from here, return to your own side of the veil."

Right then, I'll just be going, part of me wanted to say, but then a voice cried out.

"It's Dwynwyn." Young Maeve pushed her way to the fore of the crowd, as recklessly as I had done many times at her age. "I saw her today. She looked in the well. She had a vision."

"Dwynwyn?" I could hear the archdruid frowning. "Dwynwyn is dead or, er, at least departed from the tidal isle she used to call her own."

"The veil between the worlds is thin," I retorted. "Spirits will be spirits."

"There was smoke, smoke from her cooking pot," Maeve insisted. "We went to see her. We saw her with our own eyes. She was going to tell our fortunes, but instead she screamed and screamed."

"That will be enough now, Maeve."

I thought he was dismissing me, until he signaled a priestess to get my first form namesake to pipe down. Then, before I knew what he was doing, the wily old coot, as Dwynwyn had called his predecessor, whistled up a sudden breeze, just strong enough to blow back my sheltering grey hood and reveal my hair and face for all to see.

The druids looked at me in confusion, for they all knew Dwynwyn by sight. I did not have that theatrical mantle of white hair. I also had two matching eyes, whereas Dwynwyn had a cloudy one that wandered.

"Take off your cloak," Dwynwyn urged. "I love to see them flummoxed."

Since it was quite warm this close to the fire, I took her suggestion. The red tunic looked even redder by firelight, and the necklace of skulls gleamed. I gave them a provocative little shake.

"You are not Dwynwyn's spirit." The archdruid tried to sound authoritative but failed.

"Actually, I am afraid I am, or the next thing to it. She seems to have gotten lodged in my skull. She talks all the time."

"That is not true," objected Dwynwyn. "I only speak when I have something important to say."

I didn't bother to relay that remark to the archdruid.

"I called for the spirits of the land. But you...appear to be incarnate." Again he sounded more uncertain than he might have wished.

The *combrogos* sensed it; a murmuring began that could easily get out of hand.

"Is that a problem?" I asked.

"It depends on who you are."

"It doesn't matter who I am," I jumped in before he could ask me my name and lineage.

I had not been able to pick out Viviane or Branwen in the masked circle, but surely they were here somewhere. If Viviane hadn't outed me, I must still be persona non grata on Mona and be in enough danger that she felt bound to protect me.

"It only matters what I know. Hear me, my *combrogos*."

I grabbed the reins from the archdruid and turned to address the crowd.

"Atta, girl!" crowed Dwynwyn.

But suddenly I felt at a loss. What was I to say? You're in danger from the Romans? They already knew that.

"Long ago, and not so long ago," I began, "a young stranger walked in your midst, a stranger sent by the gods, a stranger you tried to send to the gods, because he told you truths you did not want to hear. He told you that when you buy and sell each other, Rome has already won. He foresaw the end of the druid college at Mona."

The crowd was quiet now, a dreadful eye of the storm quiet.

"I have seen it, too," I said more softly, but everyone heard me. "I have seen it, too."

"We will hear more of this," the archdruid said to me in a low voice. "In council. You must not sow fear in the hearts of the *combrogos*. Speak words of courage to them. Now!"

A command performance, if ever there was one.

"Long ago and not so long ago," I said again, "far away and as near as my heart, that young stranger went to his death, the god-making death. I have seen him in Tir nan Og. I have stood with him at the world's heart under the tree of life, the golden tree with leaves that shine with their own light."

I held out my hands towards the druid's staff and felt the fire of the stars flowing through them. I heard the crowd draw in its breath as they saw the tree, so huge, so bright, the fire paled. Then I saw something more wonderful still: my beloved standing under the tree, looking even younger than he had that morning outside the tomb, young as a boy, as the young stranger Esus. He held out his hand and beckoned to me to come and stand with him under the tree.

And I did.

I could not see the crowd anymore; I could not hear the roar of the fire. But I could feel the earth cool and damp with dew; I could smell the sweet, spicy air.

"Maeve, *cariad*," he spoke, to me or within me; it didn't matter. "You are in trouble with the druids again."

I could hear the laughter in his voice. I wanted to laugh, too, but the joy was so deep it welled up in a different way.

"There's nothing to fear, Maeve."

Then he was gone again and the world hurtled back as a tiny woman in black stepped forward, her ragged wings unfurling as she raised her arms.

"She has returned. I have lived to see it. Maeve Rhuad has returned!"

I stepped forward and embraced her; it was like holding a feather.

Out of the corner of my eye, I could see the druids conferring in their secret code, forming *ogham* by placing fingers on the bridge of the nose. It seemed there was general consensus. The archdruid began to disperse to the crowd.

"My *combrogos*, powerful messages–and messengers–have come to us tonight from beyond the veil. Away to your own hearths now, to your own tasks, be they humble or heroic. And we to our work of discernment and divination. May the Mighty Ones be with us and protect us all."

Before anyone could object the druids started up the chant again and the drums and pipes carried the crowd on its way.

Spark to flame
flame to hearth
hearth to heart
the *combrogos* stand as one
the *combrogos* stand as one.

And I was left alone with the entire faculty of the druid college for the first time since my trial.

CHAPTER TWENTY-SIX
THE DRUIDS OF MONA: REPRISE

"WHAT IN THE THREE WORLDS was that all about?"

The archdruid pulled off his antlers and mask and ran his hands through what was left of his hair, sweaty and plastered to his skull. I had to bite my lip to keep from giggling at the sight of Ciaran of the blue-black hair nearly bald. At a signal from him, the others doffed their masks, too. It seemed I was in with the in crowd. Or maybe they were just tired and cranky, wishing they could be heading for their beds instead of dealing with me. I glanced around the circle. Viviane was scowling ferociously, and Branwen was beaming.

"What was what all about?" I asked.

"Sit down, everyone," said Ciaran. "This could be a long night."

When we were all seated cross-legged on the ground, the archdruid turned to me.

"Maeve Rhuad, if that is who you are, perhaps we should establish your identity first, or your identities. You have claimed more than one."

He made it sound like a criminal act, but then on Mona I was a criminal.

"I am Maeve Rhuad," I stated. "I am also called by some the Grey Hag, which is a more accurate description of my appearance. And Dwynwyn does talk to me. As you see, I have inherited her tunic and her...accessories." I rattled the skulls for effect. "Is everything clear now?"

Across the circle, Viviane frowned at me even more deeply and shook her head slightly. Was she warning me not to be cheeky with the archdruid or did she think I was flirting with her old/new beau?

"Perfectly," answered Ciaran.

He was still so suave. I found myself remembering the time he and Esus had come upon Viviane and me brawling over my rock-painting with menstrual blood. He had restrained Viviane and Esus had exposed himself to horrific uncleanness by restraining me. I found myself blushing decades after the fact.

"Just as it is perfectly clear that you are here in the Holy Isles and on Mona unlawfully. You were exiled and excommunicated for life."

I am afraid I shrugged, rolled my eyes (subtly I hoped) and stopped just short of saying, So? What are you going to do about it? Facing authority figures I had last seen when they were teenagers was having an odd effect on me.

"Pardon me, Archdruid," Viviane spoke up, "I am afraid that is not perfectly clear from a legal standpoint."

My jaw almost dropped. Viviane was going to stick up for me? Against her boyfriend?

"Speak on, esteemed *brehon*."

I understood. This formality was their secret love language. Later tonight they would tear each other's tunics off.

"As I recall" (and everyone present knew Viviane's recall was perfect) "when your predecessor pronounced sentence on Maeve Rhuad, he used these words: *Having broken the laws of this college, which are the laws of life, having meddled in high mysteries, having willfully endangered the* combrogos, *you shall from this moment forward be excluded from all our rites and sacrifices. You shall furthermore be exiled from the shores of the Holy Isles and sent beyond the ninth wave, there to meet the judgment or mercy of the sea.*"

I must admit, it was chilling to hear those words again, even in Viviane's voice.

"Precisely. An unambiguous sentence of excommunication and exile," said Ciaran.

"You are overlooking the fact that your predecessor left final judgment to the sea," argued Viviane. "The sea ruled in her favor. We have debated this question before without conclusion, because until now no one has ever returned. Now we must decide what to do in a case that is in fact without precedent."

This really was shaping up to be a long night. An argument like this one could go on for days, for weeks, for years. I had to distract them from this legal quagmire that could suck us all down while, back at the fort, General Suetonius's troops hammered away at their flat-bottomed boats and each breath Prasutagus took brought him closer to his last.

"It doesn't really matter what becomes of me," I spoke before the Archdruid had time to make a considered reply. "I didn't come here to ask you to reverse my excommunication or my exile. For all I care, you can put me out to sea again or kill me three times over or just pound me into the pit. As long as you listen to what I have to say first. I came here with a message."

"I thought you already gave it," said the archdruid. "You prophesied doom, did you not?"

"She also showed us the tree of life," Branwen defended me. "She brought us all to Tir nan Og. She and the Stranger. She and Esus."

"Who is long dead, if I understand Maeve Rhuad correctly?"

Ciaran actually sounded sad; Esus had been in his form. They had been friends, I remembered.

"Who is long dead," I acknowledged. "And who lives. He has become a Mighty One."

"Is your message from him?" Ciaran asked. "Will he intercede for us, even though he is the one who condemned us, who foresaw our end so long ago? Even though we tried to kill him?"

That *was* a count against the college, I might have said, but Jesus had never held a grudge against the druids for attempted murder by triple death. Still, even though his followers were always invoking his authority and praying for his intervention, I had never felt comfortable speaking for Jesus or telling him what to do. I decided to dodge the question.

"My message is from Queen Boudica," I stated.

"Queen Boudica!" The archdruid was taken aback. "You have seen Boudica?"

"Yes, I have seen Boudica, my daughter, to whom you druids lied shamelessly–and shamefully. And by the way do I look like a silkie to you?"

I was getting a little hot under my red tunic. I might be a returned convict, but I had grievances of my own with the druids.

"Maeve," Viviane spoke up. "You know none of us here concocted that story."

"But you all perpetuated it! You all knew the truth."

There was an awkward moment during which I hoped the druid faculty examined its individual and collective conscience.

"Whether we were right or wrong in sustaining a deception deemed necessary by my predecessor," resumed Ciaran, "we are not on trial here."

"Neither is Maeve Rhuad," spoke up Moira. "A court has not been convened. Let us hear the message she has crossed the Holy Isles to give us."

"Proceed," nodded Ciaran.

"Queen Boudica asked me to tell you how it is with her and with the Iceni."

And as the moon fled the clearing, and the cold tightened our circle, I told them everything I could about the Roman procurator bankrupting the tribes by calling in the loans, about the conscription of young men, and the warriors in hiding, about Prasutagus' illness. I told them about everything but the desperate compromise in his will, which he had made me promise to keep secret.

"She asks you to send help," I concluded.

There was another silence. It settled in my stomach like something heavy and unwholesome.

"What kind of help?" Ciaran asked at length.

I supposed Boudica wanted warriors from the free western tribes to stand with her when Prasutagus died, to protect her claim—or her daughters' claim—to her land, but in point of fact she hadn't spelled it out.

"She just said, send help. Figure it out for yourselves!" I said suddenly exasperated. "She will soon be a widow with two young daughters and a meager army! Aren't there warriors at your command? Could you give her family asylum here, if they had to flee? She trusted you once. She revered you. She left Mona against her will; she made the best of a bad situation. She married a king who promised to stand with her against disarmament. She led a rebellion. It was no fault of hers that he made a bad bargain with the Romans in the end. But she will be left with the debt. Could you not send gold at least?"

The druids controlled the gold route from Hibernia's Wicklow Hills to the rest of the world. In my youth, I'd seen votive offerings—torcs, mirrors, weapons, whole chariots—tossed into a boggy lake. The druids could just go trolling for it if they ran short, though I supposed it would be considered bad form to steal from the gods.

"Maeve Rhuad," said Ciaran, "perhaps word has not reached the eastern tribes of the heavy losses to the Ordovices and the Silures. They have been beaten back to their borders. To the north the Deceangli are now under direct Roman control. The western tribes have never fully recovered from the defeat and capture of Caratacus."

I glanced at Branwen, who kept her face impassive at this mention of the defeat that destroyed her brothers. But I could sense how much pain she concealed.

"As for gold, it has all gone to the border tribes to keep them in arms. We would of course offer Boudica such asylum as we can provide, if she wishes to return here, if she can make her way through the occupied territories."

Now I was silent. They knew and I knew that Boudica would fight first and that her chances of slipping through enemy lines were nil.

"I am sorry, Maeve Rhuad," Ciaran said at length. "I had hoped for a different message from Boudica. We thought, at one time, she might be able to unite the eastern tribes against the Romans and that between us we could drive the Romans out."

I felt an odd little shiver run over me, a sense of déjà vu that I could not keep hold of.

"She tried," I said sharply. "Her husband was never of the same mind. I told you: they've been estranged for some time. She lives in the old way, refusing all Roman luxuries. She's kept faith with Mona. What have you ever done for her?"

Ciaran looked at me for an uncomfortably long moment, as if weighing some decision—about me.

"The truth is, Maeve Rhuad, ever since the capture of your foster father, King Bran the Bold, the druids of Mona have sensed a fissure in our stronghold, in our power to protect the *combrogos*, one my predecessor sought to seal with the quinquennial sacrifice."

That you prevented, he did not say. But the words, unspoken, charged the air and stirred the old guilt I'd never quite let go. It's your fault, guilt whispered: the Roman invasion, all the death and suffering and oppression to this day and yet to come. It is all your fault.

"Archdruid," protested Branwen. "On behalf of my father, whose name you have invoked, I must object—"

"It's all right," I interrupted. I could not bear for Branwen to defend me. "I did stop that sacrifice. If what you imply is true, then it is fitting that I am here with you now, to be of what use I can, to share with you whatever end awaits. That is, unless you would prefer to sacrifice me. I'm quite willing."

The archdruid let out a heavy sigh.

"It's not a quinquennial year," he pointed out. "And besides, as I recall, you were rejected as a sacrifice before. Now you are a criminal or at the very least an excommunicate and returned exile. Sacrifices must be perfect, without blemish in body or character."

Just like at the Temple of Jerusalem, only there the rules applied to doves, goats, and bullocks.

"Have it your way," I shrugged.

"Now about your prophecy of doom," the archdruid resumed, as if it were merely by the by. "The Menai Straits running with blood and all that—"

"I didn't get that far," I interrupted. "All I said was Woe unto the druids of Mona. But it jogged your memories. It was Esus, the one you called The Stranger, who made that prophecy. And you remember, you all remember it perfectly."

I paused, wondering at my own insistence.

"But you said you saw it, too, this end. And the girl said you shrieked instead of telling those silly fortunes. Come clean now, if you want to help. Tell us what you saw."

I nodded. There was no point in fighting with the druids. That was just a distraction, just a way of trying to hold on to a past that was already gone, a way of avoiding a future that looked unbearably grim.

"I did see it when I looked in the well of eels, the Menai Straits red with blood just as Esus described it long ago. I did shriek, just as I will when that day comes."

No one spoke for a time.

"Must it come?" said Viviane at last. "Maeve, must it?"

"I don't know. It is so hard to say with visions." Though too many of mine have come to pass, I did not add. "Perhaps it is only a warning. But there is something else I must tell you that is not a vision at all. You know there is a new governor?"

"Yes," said Ciaran. "He has a reputation for ruthlessness. Maybe that is just as well; there will be no temptation to bargain with him."

I felt a little sick as I remembered my attempts to do just that, and I feared, if they knew, the druids would not regard me as a diplomat.

"Well then," I went on. "It should hardly surprise you to hear that the governor is spending the winter building boats. Flat-bottomed boats."

To my relief, no one asked me how I knew, though if they had I would have told them. I sensed a shift in the atmosphere. All our self-importance, all our defenses were falling away. We were just people, once young, now old, who might have to face death together.

"We have heard and seen enough for tonight," announced Ciaran. "Away to our dreams and in the days ahead we will continue to divine and deliberate in council. Maeve Rhuad, it is a long way back to Dwynwyn's Isle. The college will offer you hospitality for tonight."

"Take him up on it, honey lamb," Dwynwyn spoke up again. "It's hard to shape-shift after a long meeting with the druids."

"And after tonight?" I asked.

"Don't push it, Maeve."

He sounded as tired as I felt.

I spent the night with Branwen and Moira at Caer Leb in a hut they shared with some of the girl students (radical co-education had been modified since my day). I woke when it was still dark, confused for a moment about where I was—or rather when. My life felt as if it had collapsed in on itself. I had come, not quite to the place of my beginning, but damn close. I was Maeve Rhuad again, and I longed for Esus. Our younger selves were so vivid here. It was hard to believe I could not slip away from Caer Leb to meet him under the yews. It was hard to remember all the long years without him and the brief, brilliant years with him. How could it be that the unborn child he valiantly offered to claim as his own was now an angry queen befriended by his own grown daughter, whom he'd never met in the flesh? And how could I have left both these daughters behind? But here I was with time sitting on me like a study stone. What lessons were mine to sing over? What poem might I make at last?

"Dwynwyn," I spoke to her in my mind. "Are you there?"

But she was silent; my head felt empty as a scoured skull with the wind blowing through it. Maybe she'd gone back to haunt her island. Or, the thought struck me, maybe she was just gone; now that I was here...to take her place.

"I'll be with you when you need me, cabbage." Dwynwyn spoke, but her voice seemed to be coming from somewhere far away. "You're a big girl now, Maeve Rhuad. An old woman, to be precise, though you've still got the fire in the head–and in other places."

Even at that distance she managed to cackle lewdly.

"Wait," I said. "No one asked me if I wanted to take your place."

"Haven't you learned yet, pigeon pie? Life really doesn't care what you want. Neither does death."

And she was gone again. A little dawn light seeped under the plaid. I got up quietly, clutching the necklace of skulls so that it wouldn't rattle, and went out to greet the day.

Outside in the chilly air, I knew what age I was. Moreover, my wing pinions ached. I stood gazing east over the straits, which looked not red but rosy and silver, peaceful, the tides coming and going, minding their own business, indifferent to the plots of human beings.

"Maeve Rhuad."

I startled. I hadn't heard Moira come up behind me, silent as the shadow she appeared to be.

"Come walk with me awhile before the whole college wakes up. I've got an oatcake for you."

That was thoughtful of her; she looked as though she herself never ate at all.

"How is it you are still alive?" I asked.

And she laughed, or I think she laughed, a sound like a tree branch rasping in the wind.

"I'm sorry," I said. "That didn't come out quite as I meant it."

"I am too old an old Crow to be offended," she smiled. "Yes, I know you girls called us old Crows. And quite right, too. We were very old even then; we are beginning to suspect we are immortal."

She sounded a little wistful, I thought.

"Dwynwyn was very put out that you outlived her," I said. "I think that's what she was going on about. She predicts your demise with the next strong breeze."

Moira's laughter creaked again.

"Dwynwyn was always so hostile to the druids, and so competitive with us. She needn't have been, though I suppose she enjoyed having something to be cranky about. She thought we sold out to the druids; she never understood what we did—or what we are."

I wondered if anyone understood. I remembered the first time I saw the black-robed priestesses standing on the cliffs of Holy Island, the western tip of Mona, an island unto itself. Their sleeves whipped into wings by the wind, they looked like crows indeed as they watched my mothers bring our boat about to make for shore. Then, at the interminable admissions procedure, they had blown in on a damp wind to secure my acceptance by standing surety for me. Later, when the presence of girl students proved more disruptive than the druids had bargained for, three priestesses came from Holy Island to tend to our peculiar female needs and natures, in other words to keep us in line—with questionable success in my case.

"Where are the other two?" I asked. "I'm sorry I never knew their names."

"It's all right," said Moira. "We hardly knew our names ourselves. Names were only for the convenience of others. My sisters went back to Holy Island when the girls in your form became full-feathered druids qualified to teach. I am the only one who chose to stay."

"Why did you?" I asked, curious.

She stopped walking and turned to look at me, so crow-like, with her eyes bright and beady, her head cocked to one side.

"It is your fault," she stated, though without apparent bitterness. "I got caught up in your story. It made me...more human."

"But my story, my story here, that is, ended so long ago," I said.

"Ah, but it didn't," she contradicted. "It hasn't. And there was your daughter, coming to us at just the age you did. Coming back. Surely you have not forgotten. I was there when she was born. I held you while you pushed her into this world."

I took the tiny Crow lady's tinier hand, so frail but so strong.

"I have not forgotten," I assured her. "And I have not forgotten that you went against orders from the druids and told me my daughter would foster with the Iceni, a wealthy tribe, you said, known for their horses and their strong beautiful women. I carried that comfort with me all over the world. And how could I ever forget that you stood up for me at my trial."

"I would do it again, Maeve Rhuad. I would do it again. But there will be no need."

"What do you mean?" I asked.

I looked at her face, getting lost in its ancient geography, the ritual inscription of tiny lines crossing tiny lines and then the deeper caverns, river beds made by her bones and hollows.

"The time of trial is at hand; we will all be tried. All of us together."

We fell silent then, silent enough to hear the tide pause before it turned, silent enough to hear the wingbeats of a flock of curlews scattering themselves across the brightening sky.

"Will you give Branwen and the other druids a message for me?" I asked at length.

"I will," she said.

"Tell them, when they need me, they know where to find me."

She nodded. Then releasing my hand, she turned and began to walk back up the hill. After a few steps, her black sleeves billowed into wings.

Or maybe it was just the wind.

In case you are wondering, I walked the seven miles back to Dwynwyn's Isle. I had tried raising my arms and flapping a few times, but shapeshifting, it seemed, was only for emergencies. At least in my case. Perhaps if I hadn't gotten kicked out of school so soon I might have been more adept. Oh, the wasted opportunities of my youth. The walk was not unpleasant, the day was cooler than yesterday, but the sun was bright. My trek would have been pleasanter if I hadn't remembered the taboo about picking berries after *Samhain*, but I did remember. And Anu knows between druids and Roman troops I had enough trouble without arousing the ire of the Fomorians. I was cheered on by the thought of all the edible, drinkable gifts the girls had brought me and dismayed when I reached my tiny tidal isle to find I'd have to wait for low tide.

Worn out, I wrapped myself in the cloak and lay down for a nap in the dry, sun-warmed sands. I woke to find Macha, who'd been foraging on this side, ready to take me on her back across the waters to our tiny isle, our home now until the time of trial.

CHAPTER TWENTY-SEVEN
THE MOTION OF TIME

WHEN YOU LIVE alone, more out of doors than in, you understand that time is motion, heavenly bodies moving through space, the sun, moon, and stars hurtling past, the tides following the moon. Under a huge sky, you know the world is round, everything is round; everything is spinning. I had lived alone in my cave for three years, but I felt the motion of time more keenly on the island. In my cave, I could forget or remember as I chose. There was nothing I had to do, nothing I had to know. Now I could not escape knowing that the druids' time on Mona was running out.

As the days grew shorter and colder, I spent more and more time curled in my tiny cave in a state between sleeping and waking, almost always dreaming, dreams so vivid I believe I left my body and went traveling in both space and time.

One night near the longest night of the year, I dream Jesus and I are walking together along the shore by the Sea of Galilee. Where Temple Magdalen should have been there are only the wild roses, the spring that I first found there, and the ruins of the tower.

"Where did it go?" I cry out. "Who destroyed it?"

"I am showing you what will be."

"Why must it be!" I demand.

"All things rise, all things fall. Not one stone will be left on stone and yet the stones will sing. Look."

And he points across the water, which has become the Menai Straits full of Galilean fishing boats.

"Cast your nets to starboard!" Jesus calls across the water. "I will make you fishermen."

For suddenly I see that they are not fisherman at all. They are Roman soldiers rowing their flat-bottomed boats closer and closer. General Suetonius rises to his feet and steps out of the boat, and the two men walk across the water to meet. I am close enough to see their faces, one helmeted and shaven, one with wild hair whipping on the wind. But they are brothers; it is undeniable. I want to tell them. I think: if only they know, everything will be all right. I step out onto the water, but I sink immediately. The tide is so strong, I can't swim against it. And the water turns red and roils around me.

At last Jesus comes back for me. He picks me up and carries me as if I were light as a child, over water, over mountains, until he sets me down on the Mount of Olives overlooking the Temple of Jerusalem, the beautiful gates shining golden as the tree of life, as Sarah's eyes.

"This Temple will fall, too," he says. "Tell the druids everything is in the hazelnut. Tell them, Maeve, and then they will know what to do."

Then he leaves me, as he did before, walking across the valley towards the beautiful gates.

"Let me go with you this time!" I call after him.

He turns and smiles with such tenderness that I can hardly bear it.

"Your time is near, Maeve. But not yet. You still have to learn the song of the stones."

I woke just before dawn to the sound of pebbles on the shore being rolled by waves. When the tide went out, a young man, a second form student, crossed to my isle with a summons from the druids of Mona. I was called to their counsel. They wanted, the young man said, the benefit of my wisdom. I don't know if he understood why I laughed.

I rode Macha to the college, thinking she could use a supplement to her diet of wild grass. The sheep with their strange horns like Celtic knots decided to come along, too, so I had quite an entourage when I rode into Caer Leb. A phalanx of druids and a crowd of curious students greeted me. As soon as I dismounted, some first formers took Macha off for a luxurious session of grooming and a bucket of hot mash. The sheep followed her and were, I understood, to be fed some hay. As for me, I was handed a cup of hot mead and led off to refresh myself in Branwen and Moira's hut. Viviane, who had her own quarters with the more advanced students, came along with us.

"So," I said when I was seated before the fire with a bowl of leek and barley stew. "Have the druids decided not to off me or exile me? Is it official?"

"Not as official as I'd like," Viviane frowned. "We made no formal ruling, which I had hoped we would in case there are other cases like yours."

The law was Viviane's first concern. She didn't like loose ends, especially ends tangled with ambiguity.

"But there will be no other cases like Maeve's," Branwen pointed out. "Maeve is Maeve, and now she has also taken Dwynwyn's place. Dwynwyn was always beyond the jurisdiction of the druids. Isn't that what the archdruid concluded?" She deferred to Viviane's more intimate knowledge of him.

"More or less," admitted Viviane, still disgruntled. "But no one has found a law triad to fit the case; no one has made a pronouncement. Ciaran is pragmatic to a fault. What it comes down to is you're the least of our problems. He doesn't want to spend time and effort on your case."

Very sensible, in my opinion, but I did not say so.

"My handsome young escort told me that my wisdom is in demand," I said instead.

Viviane snorted, not very delicately.

"It is obvious that you have sources of information," Viviane conceded, "in this world and in the Other. We want to know more about what you know. You have a chance to make yourself useful, to make up for all the trouble you've caused."

Trouble *I* caused! I almost protested before I remembered that the Roman invasion of Pretannia was my fault—or could be argued to be.

"But I don't know any more than I've already told you. I don't even know that much for certain, but it makes sense that the Romans would attack Mona. They know the druids fund, feed and direct the resistance."

"True, true!" Moira agreed, sounding very owl-like.

"What we don't know," put in Branwen, "is what to do about it. We want you to sit in council with us on the longest night, Maeve. We want you to divine with us, to dream with us, to make a way out of nowhere."

The four of us sat quietly for a time watching the fire. Viviane had nothing to add and no dispute. Outside the wind picked up and circled, and the walls of the wattle and daub hut, made of willow, mud, and dung, shivered like any living thing. We all moved a little closer together, and Moira began to sing in the same pitch as the wind.

A way out of nowhere, a way
the path of the sea, the path of the moon
the path of the bright sun over the earth
the path of the birds, the path of the wind
a way out of nowhere, a way.

"The night before he died," I said, when Moira's song subsided, "Esus told us, I am the way."

"What do you suppose he meant by that?" Viviane asked.

"I don't know," I said. "Maybe he meant the way out of nowhere, the way you go when you can't turn back, when you won't turn back."

Branwen reached for my hand. "At least we'll be together. I am glad for that."

* * *

The shortest day dawned. The druids gathered mistletoe and the bards who would fill the night with stories practiced their tales and songs. The air was loud with the sacrifice of pigs for the feast. I had no tasks to perform, nothing I needed to oversee, so I stole away, for the first time since my return, to the Yew trees where Esus and I used to meet in that other lifetime that seemed so close.

So often, things seem smaller when we return to them years later. Not the yews. They had grown and the grove had spread, the branches rooting and rising again, resurrection after resurrection. I ducked under branches, traveling further in till I came to a very old tree, mother of many, the one that had sheltered Esus and me on the shortest day long ago, the day my unborn child had quickened. I had reached for Esus's hand and placed it over my womb. "*Who went in unto you?*" he'd demanded to know. And we fought until I finally screamed the truth I barely comprehended myself. He held me close till I quieted. Then at last we became lovers, and the cold winter world grew warm and green around us. We did not know till later, too late, that my father had seen us, that he had conceived that day his plan to sacrifice Esus.

Now I sat in a lap of roots and leaned back against the tree. There was no snow on the ground that was still soft here under the shelter of the branches. I picked up a stick and scratched *ogham* in the dirt, the same ones my beloved had written in the dust of the Temple of Jerusalem the day he saved me from stoning. Maeve and Esus. I traced the *ogham* over and over, as if I could conjure him, conjure our youth, make time reverse, as Esus had once expressed it, like a tidal river.

"Are you sorry now that you didn't run away with me when I asked you to?" I spoke aloud.

I had asked him that day, begged him, but he'd refused. He told me we had to stay for the sake of justice, for the sake of truth, that we could not let my father get away with what he had done to me.

"*But no one will believe me,*" I had argued.

"*Is that the measure of a truth?*" he'd asked.

"I was right," I said again to the silent grove. "They didn't believe me."

A wind found its way into the sheltered branches.

"*They believe you now, Maeve,*" said a voice, his voice, my voice, the voice of the wind.

"They believe I am to blame for everything," I said. "But I would do it again, *cariad*, I would save you again. That's all I know of truth."

I dug our names deeper into the dirt.

"*Cariad,*" his voice tender and amused, "*how about this time I save you?*"

"Save me from what?" I asked. "Save me for what?"

This time only the wind answered.

CHAPTER TWENTY-EIGHT
IN THE DARK

THE LONGEST NIGHT had already been going on for a long time when the archdruid gave the signal for the druids to withdraw from the revels. He led us by torchlight away from Caer Leb on a path that wound with the Afon Braint in the direction of the deepest, darkest of the groves, forbidden to the uninitiated.

I had walked this way before. I had trespassed here before.

"Branwen," I whispered. She was walking just ahead of me, and she turned and paused so I could catch up with her. "We're not going to Bryn Celli Ddu, are we?"

The Mound of the Dark Grove is the poetic translation, a burial chamber built thousands of years before the druids arrived.

"We are, Maeve. That is where we spend the longest night. We are reborn with the sun."

Death (symbolic or not) and rebirth, everyone's favorite rite.

"But I am not an initiate," I pointed out.

"Oh, Maeve," said Branwen. "If you are not, no one is."

I supposed that was true. Druid or not, I was the only one who had actually resurrected someone from a tomb. Somehow that knowledge did not make me feel any better about approaching the site just outside the mound where I had conceived a child by rape while my beloved, undergoing his own initiation inside the mound, foresaw his excruciating death to come.

"Isn't life just jolly," I muttered to myself, aware that with this fit of irreverence, I was fending off dread.

"What was that, Maeve?" asked Branwen.

It dawned on me that no one, not even Branwen, knew that the Mound of the Dark Grove was where Boudica's story began. Who knew how it might end?

"No matter," I said.

And we walked on in silence while a waning sickle moon sliced through the twisting branches.

It had been a full moon night in summer when I approached the mound before, a bright roundness rising from the dark grove. Now, with the trees bare and the moonlight dimmer, the mound was more like a different shaped darkness, and the shadows of the trees were more a blur than a tangle. As we filed towards the entrance, something made me look to my left, and I swear I saw him there, tall, bright-haired, frozen.

My father.

I stepped from the line and let the others pass me.

"Maeve," Viviane spotted me. "What are you doing? Come along."

"Just give me a moment," I said. "I'll follow."

The mound swallowed up the druid faculty and I faced my father's ghost alone. I cannot say that we spoke. He never even moved. And yet I swear he was present, and his presence was one of grief so overwhelming I thought I might drown in it.

Make a way, a voice inside me said, make a way out of nowhere.

And in that thin, cold light of the darkest night, I made my hands into a cup and let the wave fall through my fingers and melt the frozen ground. I bent and touched the soft, wet earth.

"Be at peace, Lovernios," I said aloud. "It is finished."

And I turned and followed the others down the narrow passageway into the heart of the mound.

It was pitch dark inside. I moved carefully to avoid stepping on anyone, and found a place to sit nestled between warm bodies on all sides. If the chamber had been lit, I might have felt claustrophobic. Jesus's tomb had been palatial compared to this. But as it was, all of us pressed together, it seemed like children playing a game in the dark. I am not the only one who felt that, for among that august body, with no one much under forty, there were quite a few giggles and even now and then a guffaw as we all got settled.

Then the archdruid's voice rang out, calling the quarters and proclaiming at last:

"Here now is the center of world."

Instead of his planted staff, the center was a stone standing in the middle of the chamber, a stone I sensed rather than saw. I felt us all quieting, deepening, taking on the qualities of the stone. The only sound was our breath, almost inaudible as we caught each other's rhythm, so that soon we were breathing as if we were one body.

"We know the danger that is almost certainly coming to our shores," the archdruid said at length. "There is no need to debate it. The question before us is how shall we face it? Let us listen for answers in the silence. In the holy darkness, let our inward sight be clear. When words come, let them be words of wisdom and power."

The silence spread over us again: fallen leaves over the earth, snow over leaves, stars over stone. Time got lost in the darkness; the confines of space that held us close together dissolved. We were sitting inside the vast womb of night, waiting for words to be born.

"We must fight," a man chanted rather than spoke. "We must fight. We must face down the *geis* laid upon us against druids bearing arms and go bravely to our doom."

The silence bubbled into words like a pot coming suddenly to boil.

"Let each voice be heard," said Ciaran. "Let silence fall around each speaking."

And it did fall, a loamy silence that absorbed any agitation and anger and restored calm before the next voice rose.

"We must defy doom," sang another voice, a woman this time. "Defy doom and never break our *geis*. Let the Romans come and we will stand. We will defeat them with our power. We will call the gods to our side. We must keep faith, keep faith with our ways."

The silence now was like a river, bearing us along on a strong current.

"The Romans' ways are not our ways, their strength not our strength. They are a fire raging, a wind driving. We are water and stone, secretive, enduring. We must fight according to our nature."

Again the silence, a pause between breaths, a wind stilled.

"We need not stand alone, not alone. The Romans work to turn the tribes one against another. They did it in Gaul; they are doing it to the east and south. We must gather the tribes that are left, call them to stand with us as one people."

In this silence unspoken words sparked and crackled.

"So that we can all be slaughtered as one, all at once?" someone burst out.

And the fire caught.

"Ask warriors to die for us who refuse to bear arms!"

"Why not? Whose wealth supplies their arms? Whose laws unite them? Who remembers their lineages, their stories? We are the head, we are the mind. Without us the *combrogos* are lost."

"That's exactly why they want to destroy us. Not just exile us, drive us underground. Destroy us."

Talk became a conflagration, words leaping and singeing the walls, the air becoming scarce.

"Silence," the archdruid called out. "We are druids, not panicked rabble. Listen, listen more carefully, listen more deeply."

The renewed silence was a relief, at least to me. It was tempting to let go, to sink down into it and not return. To let it all become a dream. For a time I drifted between waking and sleeping. That's when I heard Esus's voice.

"*Everything is in the hazelnut.*"

"Did you hear that?" I spoke for the first time. Esus's voice had been so distinct, as if he were here in the chamber with us, his voice echoing off the walls.

"Hear what?" asked the archdruid. "Speak, if a message has come to you for us."

"Yes," I said. "Yes, it is for you. I remember now. I dreamed it before. And now he is telling me again."

"Who? Who is speaking to you?" several voices clamored now.

"Esus," I said. "The one you called the Stranger. He said: Everything is in the hazelnut. He said, Tell the druids and they'll know what to do."

The silence that followed was clearly perplexed.

"The hazelnut will tell us what to do about a Roman attack?"

Rumination followed as druids searched their voluminous minds for poems, law triads, stories, for an interpretation of this pronouncement. The longest night would never be long enough to exhaust the possibilities. I didn't even try to follow the nuances. I closed my eyes again, though it was hardly necessary in the darkness. I slipped into the dream again.

Esus and I are on the Mount of Olives, the Temple is burning. Soldiers swarm in the Kedron Valley, and the air is full of wailing and smoke.

"*All temples fall, Maeve,*" he says again. "*You'll have to tell them, if they can't figure it out for themselves. It's all in the hazelnut.*"

And all at once, I understood.

"My *combrogos.*" My voice cut through the cacophony. "Why did the salmon eat the hazelnuts from the well of wisdom?"

"Why, because they contained all wisdom and knowledge, of course."

"What does the skull of a druid contain after a full cycle of training?"

There was a brief, appreciative silence.

"Knowledge and wisdom!" everyone chorused.

"My *combrogos,*" I said. "In the lands where I have lived in my long exile, there are huge buildings full of scrolls where Romans, Greeks, Egyptians, and other peoples store their knowledge and wisdom. If anyone put a torch to these buildings, their knowledge would be lost. The same thing will happen to the *combrogos* if the druid faculty is hacked to pieces by Romans swords, not to put too fine a point on it. Or perhaps they would take you captive and crucify you, that is, if there was anyone left to gape on you. I am sure you are all brave enough to face such a fate—but do you want that fate for the wisdom and knowledge inside your skulls?"

I could sense my deliberately graphic description was having an effect.

"Since, as we have all agreed, that this is exactly what the Romans intend," resumed the archdruid, "how is this, uh, message instructive?"

"Wisdom and knowledge," Dwynwyn snorted, speaking in my head for the first time since *Samhain*. "When it comes right down to it, they're not very bright."

"Here's what I think Esus means, and why none of us has thought of it before, I don't know. It's so obvious. You've got to take your hazelnuts," here I rapped sharply on my own skull, "and go. Long before the Romans get here. Begin now, in ones and twos, in small boats, so that even an advance scout would not suspect an evacuation, but go."

The murmuring now held notes both of excitement and consternation, but I could tell the idea had caught their attention.

"Where? Say we follow this plan, where would we go?" someone raised his voice above the others.

"The answer is obvious," Dwynwyn spoke up again. "They're just not thinking clearly. Tell them." To my surprise I did.

"You must not all go to one place," I said. "Some will go to Hibernia, some to the remote isles of Caledonia. west and north, to the places the Romans haven't gone and may never reach. The youngest students must be given the choice to return to their families. The other students must choose teachers to accompany. The teachers must gather again in threes, so that all the branches of wisdom will root and rise in a new place, just as the Yew trees spread their branches and root."

No one questioned or protested; I sensed they were as astonished as I was by my sudden authority.

"See on, Maeve Rhuad," the archdruid said. "Say on."

"In this way," I continued, hardly knowing what I would say next, "in this way you will defeat the Romans. They will come; they have already come, and one day they will go. Later they will come again in another form, but the wisdom preserved will rise again and go underground again and rise again. And so it is and always will be."

I did not know then that I spoke prophetically of the coming of the Roman church; that my old nemesis would conquer, that I would be cast a penitent whore, that the church would build houses in my name and enslave women in the guise of reforming them. I could not foresee the church and all its abuses of the people, of women, of children. And am I to blame for that second invasion, too, because I saved my beloved's life long ago on the Island of Dark Shadows?

"There is wisdom in this plan," the archdruid spoke again. "But here is what I wonder: if the Romans come and find the place deserted, will they not pursue us? Invade Hibernia which they have left alone till now. Can we bring such danger to our *combrogos* to the west?"

Voices rose again in consternation. My head began to ache. I buried my face in my hands. I was suddenly so tired. If only it could be over, if only whatever it was could be over.

"They will not find Mona deserted," a voice spoke, a voice insubstantial as smoke, light as feathers. "The priestesses of Holy Island will stay to meet them, and welcome to stand with us are the oldest of the old, any druid or any other who has passed along all his wisdom, or anyone who cannot bear the hardships of the journey nor has the will to make a life in a new place."

A depthless silence followed as if we had all fallen headlong into a deep well and were falling still.

"What of the *combrogos* who make their living from this land, what of the warriors?"

"They must choose," said Moira. "To go to a new place or stay and die. They must understand that death is almost certain. To stay is human sacrifice not chosen by lot. To stay is to give blood to the ground, to the sea, to give life to those who must live. To stay is to go to the Isles of the Blest and live among the Mighty Ones."

Now a wailing began.

"Let us all stay!" someone sobbed. "Let us all die together."

"No!" the archdruid's voice rang out. "Maeve Rhuad and our sister from Holy Island have shown us the way. Tomorrow we will begin the task of discerning which of us must go and which stay, according to our responsibility to the *combrogos* and not our desire for life or death. Others may choose, but the druids must be chosen carefully, each for his particular task. If anyone dissents from this plan, let him speak now."

No one did. Eventually the sobs subsided and the silence settled again. We moved even closer to each other, arms wrapped around whoever sat in front of us, head resting against the breast of the one behind. The pounding in my head eased. It would be over soon. I had no doubt of my task. I knew exactly where I would stand. I think I dozed off then. We all did, till the sun, reborn, shot its first ray down the passage grave and we rubbed our eyes and rose, stiffly, again.

CHAPTER TWENTY-NINE
OVER THE RIVER HARD TO SEE

I STAYED ON at Caer Leb to be of what help I could as the druids set to work at once with great efficiency and discipline deciding who would go, in what combinations, when, and where. There was some debate about what messages should be sent to which tribes or if they could be dispatched at all, given the treacherous condition of the mountain passes in the winter. If word of the evacuation got into the wrong ears, the plan could be ruined; on the other hand, the druids felt the closest tribes should be warned of the coming attack and choose for themselves how to respond. After heavy losses in the last years, the Ordovices and the Silures did not have enough warriors for an open battle, but if the general's army came through the mountains, they could pick off some troops by ambushing them. There was no discussion of going further east into occupied territory. The tribes under Roman rule no longer sent their children to the college; ties were already weakened. If I wanted to get a message to Boudica and Sarah, I would have to go myself.

"Maeve Rhuad," said the archdruid when I brought my concern to a meeting in the archdruid's hut some days later. "You are of course free to go. You wear Dwynwyn's mantle now and have no need to petition us. But since you have brought the matter here, I will make bold to express an opinion."

He was getting almost as longwinded as his predecessor, I noticed.

"You probably wouldn't survive the passage through the mountains. If you wait till Spring, it will be too late."

"In other words," Viviane decided to translate, "you're stuck here."

"Unless she comes with us to Hibernia," said Branwen wistfully.

I shook my head.

"Maeve Rhuad," resumed Ciaran. "Far be it from me to volunteer anyone for human sacrifice, but I rather thought that was what you had in mind. And a very suitable and, dare I say, poetic end it would be."

"Do you think so?" I personally thought that was carrying aesthetic appreciation too far.

"I do," he said. "A sacrifice stolen, a sacrifice–"

"Enough!" interrupted Branwen; she was rarely angry, but now her usually pale cheeks were actually red. "You said yourself Maeve Rhuad is not under our jurisdiction. She has suffered enough, if any of you cared to know her story at all. Because of Maeve, my father died in peace. I don't want to hear one more word about poetic justice from anyone, not *anyone*!"

A respectful silence followed her outburst.

"Thank you, Branwen," I said at length. "It's not a particularly noble decision on my part. It makes sense, that's all. It's just my daughters, I wish—"

My voice broke as I took in fully for the first time that I would likely never see them again in this life.

"They would understand," I added after a moment. "I just wish I could tell them."

"Oh, Maeve Rhuad, silly girl," said Moira, the only one old enough to call me that. "Why climb mountains and brave blizzards. Send your spirit out, girl. Send your spirit. They are your blood; you carried them both beneath your heart. One was born here, and here you met the other's father. Send your spirit to them. They will hear."

Isis knows, Jesus knows, my spirit was more than willing, but in my flesh I wept.

I did not try to reach Sarah or Boudica while I was still at the college in the midst of all the preparations for evacuation. I stayed longer than I intended, relishing my friendships, the comfort of sleeping next to Branwen just as I had in my youth. But after the morning festivities of Bride's day, unusually subdued because so many had already left, I rode Macha (laden with supplies for us both) back to Dwynwyn's Isle, my isle for a little while, the sheep trailing after me, one with two new lambs. Spring was still hidden under the ground, but that ground was softer, and so was the air. Spring was starting its journey north, and it would not be the first Spring of my life to bring sorrow or sacrifice.

I found my cave remarkably cozy and dry, and I had an ample supply of dried driftwood and seaweed for a fire (though by the time I struck a spark from my flints, I'd already worked up a sweat). I had root vegetables and dried fish ready to be made into stew and, best of all, I still had a keg of red mead. At sunset I sat down to an ample meal and the comfort of warmed drink. The waxing crescent moon drifted down the west with Venus huge and brilliant close by, just as they had been when I was sent beyond the ninth wave in my tiny coracle. I sang the song to the new moon that my classmates had chanted into the night, the song I had sung to Sarah when she was a baby, the song I would have sung to Boudica. The song of the young moon, the daughter moon.

Hail to thee, thou new moon
Jewel of Guidance in the night
Hail to thee, thou new moon
Jewel of Guidance on the billows
Hail to thee, thou new moon
Jewel of Guidance on the Ocean
Hail to thee, thou new moon.
Jewel of Guidance of my love.

But my daughters were not in the west with the setting new moon. They were both to the east where night had already come, beyond the straits, beyond the sharp-toothed mountains, beyond the long, hard Roman road. I wondered if they had celebrated Bride's day together. I wondered if Sarah would tell Boudica about the Bride's day when Paul of Tarsus had killed a snake, and he and I had quarreled publicly, and Sarah had run away from us both. Boudica could have told a Bride's day story, but I doubted anyone had ever told her about how, in a trance, I had revealed my pregnancy to the druids and for a moment become the goddess herself. That night Sarah's father had stepped forth to protect me, willing to be named as Boudica's father if need be. How much more bound they were than they could know. Or maybe at some level they did know. They had chosen to band together. Together they had let me go where I had to go.

It was time, time to send out my spirit, to both, to each.

Wrapping myself in Dwynwyn's cloak and my own, I left my cave and walked over the small hill to the other side of the isle where the well of eels gleamed faintly with reflected stars. I crouched before it, waiting for the dark water to open the way to whatever I needed to see, whatever I needed to know.

"Boudica," I spoke her name to the wind. "Boudica."

But I could not see the angry, wounded woman she had become, the woman who had relented enough to ask me to carry a message for her. It was as if I had gathered her back into my womb, dark as this night, rocked by the waves and the tides.

Then just as I was about to give up and go back to my cave, seek her in dreams, I saw a flash of light, a sweep of red hair by torchlight, a curtain across a face. Then for a brief moment a whole scene, distinct, clear: Boudica sitting at the foot of her husband's bed, as still as he was. His eyes were closed, but his chest still rose and fell. He was alive, just barely. Part of him already hovered outside himself, ready to go, part of him still clung to this woman, fiercely, protectively, but the battle couldn't last long.

"Boudica," I spoke to her in my mind. "Boudica."

"Mama," another voice answered. All at once I was awash in warmth, in gold. I couldn't see Sarah, but I could feel her presence all around me, huge, strong, comforting. "She can't hear you now. I'm here. Speak to me."

"Oh, Sarah, Sarah."

I don't even know if I spoke. I was a river carried by my own current.

"I am here," I said in whatever language was available to me. "On the druid isle. Tell Boudica I delivered her message, but there is no help for her from the druids. Sarah, you must not come here, either. Stay with Boudica, for her sake, for my sake. The Romans are on their way to Mona. The druids are going into hiding across the water. Only a few will remain, the old ones. I will be with them."

Then the river broke its bounds, love and loss a flood plain, tossing on it all the jumbled bits of memory and regret, funny, poignant, bitter, achingly sweet.

Sarah, oh Sarah, oh my Colomen Du.

All words went away, but we both saw what was to come; only in the vision the straits were not red but gold and a bird flew high above the battle din. Then I heard Sarah's voice half speaking, half-singing.

O my mother, my little mother
be brave, my mother, be brave for me
fear not, my mother, my little mother
fear nothing, for we have lived gladly
and gladly we will die, fear nothing
little mother, though I am far away
I am with you, and you are with me.

And I wept to think that my daughter, my little daughter, would sing comfort across the worlds to me.

It is a strange thing to wait for death while all around you the earth is coming back to life, trees leafing, flowering, shining, breezes carrying such a richness of scents, onion grass, apple blossom, sheep manure, the scent of new turned earth, and of course for me, the scent of the sea, seaweed in the sun, warmed tidal pools. Every day another kind of seeding took place, coracles and fishing boats blown across the water to isles too tiny and distant to find, remote caves, crevices in rock. Also, in ones and twos warriors began to arrive. I watched all the coming and going from my isle. And the oracular well and I gave what help we could to the other inhabitants of Mona as they struggled to decide whether to go or stay, whether to plant crops that might be trampled or burned, what to do with animals that might be stolen or slaughtered. Where to go, if they went.

It is an even stranger thing to know personally the man who will kill you or at least orchestrate your death and the death of everyone around you. Stranger still to think he might be related to the man whose death in this very place I had prevented. I did not know what to do with this knowledge, so I did my best to set it aside as I waited for this death, both known and unknowable, to arrive.

One afternoon, I had some other visitors. I was sitting in the shelter of a hummock, gazing across the straits, when I heard footsteps. My hearing was still sharp. Before I even looked, I knew that two people approached. I guessed they were not young, not used to walking so far, but still fit, with light steps. I turned and saw Branwen and Viviane stop at the top of the hummock to scan the isle for me.

"What have you brought for my pot?" I stood up and called out to them.

"Nothing, you old witch," Viviane called back. "We are not in the least interested in our love luck."

"Of course we did!" countered Branwen, and she held out some wild ramps she must have dug up along the way.

"These will give the stew some savor," I accepted them and walked down to the water to rinse them.

"We came to say goodbye," Viviane said.

I didn't answer, just kept walking to the pot, knowing they would follow. At my cave, I picked up a knife and sliced the ramps and added them to whatever simmered there, a perpetual flame, a perpetual feast.

"Sit," I commanded. "Eat."

"You are getting more and more like her," complained Viviane. "All you think about is your stomach. We don't have long. We sail with the tide at dusk."

But they both sat down. I ladled stew into a common bowl, and we broke a small loaf of barley bread together. I remembered at Temple Magdalen Judith always had people sitting and eating within moments of their arrival. And Jesus had said, "Whenever you break bread together or share a cup of wine, I'll be with you, in your midst." The three of us sat and ate silently, companionably. Surely Jesus was with us, and maybe many others in my life that I had not known I would never see again. I thought of Dido and Berta, especially. I had seen them last when I was hot on Sarah's trail. Now I didn't even know if they were alive or if Temple Magdalen was still standing.

It is strange to know when a goodbye is final. It is a gift.

"Are you afraid, Maeve?" asked Branwen.

She had never been one for small talk and certainly now was the time to say only what mattered or nothing at all.

"Not yet," I said. "But I might be. I don't think I'm afraid of death. But dying can be a nasty business."

I had seen Jesus die; felt his dying pains. If I was lucky, my death would be quick and I wouldn't live to see many others.

"Do you wish you were staying?" I asked.

"Yes," said Branwen.

"No," said Viviane.

"We've been all over it, and over and over it," sighed Branwen. "For me it is a sacrifice to go, for some it is a sacrifice to stay. We each have to do what we have to do—"

"For the good of the *combrogos*," I completed her sentence. "I'll never forget when the archdruid said those words just before he sent me off beyond the ninth wave. He was having such a good time being noble and regretful. He even manufactured a couple of tears. Did you know that? At least Ciaran isn't quite such a stagey hypocrite."

Viviane made a noise that could be loosely translated as "harrumph."

I glanced at her, and she turned her face away, but not quickly enough. I could see that her eyes were red, and there were tear tracks she had forgotten to cover.

"You are not all going together?" I suddenly guessed. "The three of you?"

"No," said Branwen. "Viviane and I are going today, but Viviane will stop at the Isle of Mann and I will go on to Caledonia. We will both join groups already there. Ciaran will follow soon, but he will go far west to Hibernia."

"We have different strengths, but each one of us has all the knowledge, all the wisdom," explained Viviane. "Each one of us is qualified to be an archdruid of a college. We have to spread out, just as you said, for the good of the *combrogos*," she concluded, her voice both wistful and defiant.

"So you see," said Branwen, "it is goodbye for all of us."

"I see," I answered.

And I reached for their hands as they reached for each other's, and we sat together, a living triad with no need for rhymes or study stones to commit each other to heart.

"Do you remember," asked Viviane, "when we first came to this isle and Dwynwyn spoke prophecy over the three of us? The poet, the lawgiver, and the lover, she called us."

"Don't forget the word great," I reminded her. "Great poet, great lawgiver, great lover."

"Do you think her prophecy came true?" wondered Branwen.

"Yes," I said without hesitation.

And we all laughed for as long as we could. And then we wept. At last we helped each other to our feet.

"It's only for a little while," said Branwen.

She let go of us and held her hands up to us in blessing:

Bride be taking charge of you in every strait
Every side and turn you go
Bride be stretching out her arms for you
Smoothing the way for you
When you go thither
Over the river hard to see
  Oh when you go thither home
  Over the river hard to see.

"Come," said Viviane. "The tide's turning."

Almost violently she flung her arms around me and gave me a kiss like a blow. Then Branwen and I held each other softly and easily. At last she and Viviane took hands and made their way to the shore. I climbed the highest hummock and watched my two oldest friends in the world walk hand in hand down the sands until they were out of sight.

CHAPTER THIRTY
THE ORDER

I WON'T LIE. I was bereft after they left. Of all the partings in my life, this one was one of the hardest. My beloved was dead; Joseph was dead. I had left Miriam near death in the care of John, a lover I would never see again. Nor would I see any of my friends from that world, or ever know if they still lived or had died before me. Anna the prophetess had told me long ago that there is nowhere else but here; everything is here. But while you're still in the flesh you can't always see it or feel it. While you're in the flesh, you want flesh, arms to hold you, hands to clasp. This phase of life when your friends and lovers are lost to you, for whatever reason, comes to everyone who lives long enough. Now it was my turn, and I just want to say, it felt different from my chosen solitude in the cave. It felt lonely, and sometimes I felt afraid, not of death exactly, just afraid. Tending the sheep and Macha was some comfort. I think they tended me, as much as I did them. And all the while, across the straits, the snow melted in the mountains, the passes opened and the green of Spring took root on the rocky slopes.

Then the dreams began, the dreams that were not dreams.

I do not recognize the place; it could be anywhere in the Roman Empire, a dining room off an atrium, some dozen or so guests (or clients) reclining, enjoying the remains of a modest feast, various dishes set forth on three tables, slaves removing empty platters, bringing fresh ones, keeping the wine flowing, while the men hold forth, all at once, interrupting each other, as people do when they are at that stage of tipsiness.

Then there is the sound of feet crossing the atrium, and a man steps into the dining room. He is clearly not a slave or a mere messenger; he's too well-dressed for that, in a fine linen tunic, new sandals. He has a sword at his belt and epaulettes on his cloak. I reckon him to be a centurion.

"Lord Procurator," the newcomer addresses a man at the central table.

I recognize him then. He was not just any Roman, anywhere in the Empire, the Procurator of Pretannia, Catus Decianus, the one who has been bleeding the tribes dry, the one the general refuses to confront, his secret son. There is some faint resemblance around the nose and mouth, but character and circumstance have made it hard to see. The father looks grim, the son querulous and petulant.

"I bring you news of the Iceni king."

"I suppose I must hear it then. Excuse me," he says to the company, as he rises ungracefully from his couch. "This shouldn't take long."

The two men cross the atrium to a smaller room, the procurator's private office.

"So, did old Prasutagus finally kick the bucket?" the procurator asks, reclining again and gesturing for the messenger to sit on a stool beside him.

"He died this morning, Lord Procurator, with his family surrounding him."

"So touching," says the procurator. "Well, I sorrow, too. He was one of the easier ones to manage. Understood what a client was, didn't get above himself. Didn't quibble too much about his debts. Almost civilized."

"He had a reputation as a reasonable man," agrees the centurion.

"What about the wife? Heard she's a savage bitch who prefers a native hovel to a villa. She going to be any trouble?"

"Sir, there is a complication. As you know, King Prasutagus was granted the status of a Roman citizen, for being such a cooperative client."

Catus Decianus groans and shakes his head.

"I've never agreed with that policy. Takes things too far. Gives natives an exaggerated sense of entitlement. Still, he's dead now. What's complicated about that?"

"It seems he had a will drawn up, an official will, written, witnessed, signed, sealed. Here is the copy to be sent to Rome. But I have read it, read the copy his wife holds."

Although I am not present in the scene, I feel sick. The will, the plaguing will that I helped write for Prasutagus's peace of mind.

"His wife! Surely he didn't leave anything significant to his wife. What does he have to leave her anyway but the balance of his debts? He understood that on his death his lands come under direct Roman rule. I recently went over that with him myself. He made no objection. After all, he has no heirs."

"He has daughters."

"As I said, he has no heirs," Catus Decianus reiterates.

"Well, sir, it seems King Prasutagus was in disagreement on that point. He has willed his kingdom jointly to Emperor Nero and to his two daughters."

The procurator's eyes bulge unbecomingly, making him look like a surprised toad that swallowed something unexpected.

"Utter cheek," he says. "I suppose the bitch wife is behind this."

"Begging your pardon, sir, but the wife is not mentioned in the will at all. She seemed stunned and withdrew almost immediately. Whether she was overcome by rage or grief, I could not say."

"What of the daughters?" Decianus asks. "Are they young enough to be ruled by their mother?"

"They are young, but the older one is certainly of marriageable age. Perhaps something suitable could be arranged, some noble from one of the friendly tribes who understands the way things work. Maybe even one of our retired soldiers in Camulodunum who could settle everyone down."

"Perhaps," the procurator says, sounding thoughtful in an odious way; or maybe that is just the effect of his sucking the tip of his forefinger as he ponders. "But I think they must be taught a lesson first. This sort of arrangement cannot be allowed to stand. It can't become precedent. It won't do to have all these petty tribal kings thinking they can dispose of Roman property as they please. I'm afraid we must make an example of these so-called heirs."

The centurion looks as though he is wrestling with himself. I can tell he doesn't like the procurator much, but it goes against his training to oppose a superior, even if that superior is a civilian and a disagreeable self-serving one at that.

"Sir, perhaps that is for the Emperor to decide, since he is named as co-heir in the will."

"Co-heir!" The procurator clearly does not like to be questioned. "Do you hear yourself? Emperor Nero co-heir with a pair of girls to land he already rules? The emperor is not to be bothered with such nonsense. I am appointed here to take care of petty nuisances like this laughable will. No, they must be put in their place, and you and your century shall put them there."

"Sir?" says the centurion.

"Don't play the innocent with me. They are women. Discredit them, ruin them, humiliate them in the eyes of their people, make them unfit to rule. You know what to do. Standard procedure."

Again the centurion struggles with his better judgment.

"Sir, begging your pardon again, but I am a military man. The action you suggest might lead to trouble. It might be better to wait until Governor Suetonius—"

"We can't wait. The governor is on an important campaign on the far western front, as you know, and he may be gone for months. I command the home guard in his absence. Do not question me again. You will go at once while they're still wailing over their dead king, before they can get up to anything. You will deal with them swiftly and thoroughly. Do you understand your orders?"

"Yes, Lord Procurator. I understand."

* * *

I woke in a cold sweat, uncertain for a moment where I was. The dream had been so vivid, not like a dream at all. When I saw the glow of my cook fire, banked for the night, and heard the waves lapping at the shore as the tide came in, I felt momentary relief at recognizing my surroundings. Then I was overcome by sickening horror. If the dream was real, then Boudica and her daughters, and very likely Sarah, Alyssa, and Bele, were all in imminent danger. I wrapped myself tighter in my cloak and closed my eyes, willing myself to dream of them, to dream to them, but I was much too tense to go back to sleep. After a little while, I got up and felt my way in the dark to the well of eels.

A waning moon gleamed. From time to time, the eels surfaced, breaking up the moon's reflection with their sinuous darkness. I gazed until my eyes grew heavy again, but saw nothing in the shifting patterns of dark and light. Eventually I slept again and again I dreamed—or did not dream.

She has brought Prasutagus to her home. He lies on a raised pallet, dressed as a king, complete with a gold crown that looks like a wreath of vines. He is wearing a plaid tunic beneath a woolen mantle, clasped with a brooch. His sword has been placed in his hand at his side. There is no remnant of anything Roman about him. Boudica, bare-headed, her face streaked with red as if she had torn at it with her fingernails, sits on a stool beside him. Gwen and Lithben are at his feet. Gwen, worn out with grief and months of nursing her father through his last illness, has fallen asleep with her head on his legs. Lithben, too, rests her head against her father. Boudica is awake, her eyes wide and unblinking, as she stares past her husband, her lips moving. At first I can't catch any words, but gradually she speaks louder or my hearing sharpens.

"You did wrong, you did wrong, you did very wrong," she says over and over. "You meant to do right, but you did wrong. You thought you could save us with deals and compromise, but you did wrong, you did wrong, you did very wrong. Never mind, my dead one, never mind, my long ago love, my lost false love, who betrayed me. Never mind. The Roman wolf will not win. I am the mother bear, the wild mare, the leaping hare. I will never let go, I will never give in."

She goes on and on, rocking slightly with the rhythm of her words as she repeats them over and over again.

"Boudica," I call to her, hoping I am here in this dream, whosever it is. "Boudica, can you hear me? Listen."

She keeps on talking and rocking.

"Boudica," I say again.

"Grandmother?" Lithben lifts her head and turns toward me. "Grandmother, I knew you would come back."

Lithben gets up and comes to me. For a moment, I can feel her warmth, almost feel her solid young body, but then I can't.

"Grandmother, are you a ghost?" she says with surprising calm. "Have you seen my father's ghost?"

"Dearest child," I say, longing to gather her into my arms. "I am not a ghost or at least I am not dead. I am still far away to the west, and I can't come to you any other way. We're having a dream together, *cariad*. You must listen to me and tell your mother and sister what I say."

Lithben nods, looking grave and sweet, young and wise all at once.

"Do you know about your father's will?"

"Yes," she says. "Gwen and I are to be queens together. Our mother doesn't mind about not being heir. But the will says we have to share with the Roman Emperor. Gwen and mother are already arguing. Gwen says we have to make peace with the Romans. And our mother says absolutely not. I wish they wouldn't fight. My stomach feels sick when they do. I wish my father was still alive."

"So do I, *cariad*, so do I. Listen, Lithben, you are almost grown and you are a queen, so I know you will understand what I am about to say to you. The Roman procurator of Pretannia doesn't want to share the land. He is sending soldiers to do harm to you and your sister and mother. You must leave now and go into hiding where they can't find you."

Lithben's eyes grew wide and she glanced at her mother, who continued to rock and mutter.

"I don't think...I don't think Mother will listen to me," whispers Lithben.

"Get someone to help you with her. Get Sarah."

"Sarah is not here."

"Not here?" I am dismayed. "Where is she?"

"My mother sent Sarah and Alyssa and Bele and lots of the others to get word to all the Iceni about my father. And they are going to some of the other tribes, too. My mother wants them all here when we bury my father. That is the one thing she and Gwen both agree on."

If she had dispatched most of her able-bodied guard, the danger was even more serious. Not that they could hope to hold off a Roman century even if the village was fully armed and guarded.

"Will Gwen listen?" I ask Lithben. "Can you wake her now?"

Lithben nods and goes to her sister, touching her shoulder and whispering to her, though Boudica pays no attention. Her eyes have closed and she seems to be sleeping bolt upright.

"Grandmother wants to talk to you," says Lithben in a low voice.

"What are your talking about?" Gwen rouses herself and rubs her eyes. "Our mother's mother left months ago. Has she come back?"

"She's over there," Lithben points to me.

Gwen looks right through me.

"There's no one there, Lithben," Gwen says, kindly for one who is so exhausted and grief-stricken. "You must have had a dream. You should go lie down and sleep. I will stay by father."

Lithben turns and stares at me as if to make sure.

"It's all right," I encourage her. "She may not be able to see me. Just tell her, tell her about the danger. Tell her you must all find a place to hide."

"Maybe it was a dream," Lithben says with impressive control. "She even told me it's a dream. She says it is the only way she can come to us from all the way in the west. She says to tell you the Romans won't share with us, like father wanted. They want to hurt us. She says we must find a place to hide."

"If she's in the west," says Gwen all too logically, "how can she know what the Romans in Londinium plan to do?"

Lithben wrung her hands in the air, tugging at frustrations that must have plagued her all her life as the younger daughter.

"Because she's magic, Gwen! She knows things. She had eight mothers, all witches."

"Well, she may not know as much as she thinks she does," says Gwen. "We are civilized people, Lithben. We will not run and hide from the Romans like guilty fugitives. We will meet with their ambassadors. We will negotiate the terms of our rule, just as our father did. That is why he left us in charge, and not our mother. If you see her again in your dreams, tell her not to worry. Now get some sleep."

Lithben turns to me again and shakes her head.

"Gwen," I try again. "Gwen. Listen to me! Please."

But she just sits quietly, head bowed, one hand resting on her father's leg.

"Who's there?" Boudica comes out of her trance; in seconds she is on her feet, sword in her hand. "Who dares disturb the peace of this royal chamber?"

At their mother's alarm, Gwen and Lithben rise, too. For the first time all three face me.

"Boudica," I say. "Boudica it's me, Maeve Rhuad, your mother."

"Who is it?" she repeats.

"There's no one there, Mother," Gwen insists. "Lithben had a bad dream."

Lithben, goes to her mother, puts her hand on her arm and points to me.

"Can't you see her," Lithben pleads. "She's right there."

"Who is there?"

"Grandmother."

"Grandmother?" Boudica repeats as if the word had no meaning to her at all.

"She had a dream," Gwen explains. "She thinks your mother is here."

"The woman," Boudica says. "The woman behind that stupid treacherous will."

"It is my father's will," Gwen says sharply, defending him, I guess, not me. "She only wrote it for him. She even argued that the Romans will not let us rule. We shall prove her wrong, won't we, Mother?"

She makes a roundabout appeal for solidarity.

"Won't we, Mother?" Gwen repeats, sounding more like a child than I had ever heard her.

"No! Grandmother says they are going to hurt us!" Lithben tries one more time. "She says we have to hide."

"That is out of the question," snaps Boudica. "We are going to bury your father as befits a king with all the tribes and warriors attending us. Then we shall see what we shall see."

All at once her eyes widens and her mouth opens. I know, for an instant, she sees me.

"Boudica," I call to her with my heart, my voice, "Boudica, save your daughters, Boudica!"

And I woke to the sound of my own voice calling in a cold, bitter dawn.

CHAPTER THIRTY-ONE
A MORNING'S WORK

THE DAY AND NIGHT that followed gave between-the-worlds a whole new and horrible meaning. I was not here; I was not there. Waking and sleeping both held dread. There was no escape from my helplessness; there was no escape from my knowledge. You could say that I prayed with every breath, with every agitated step. But my prayers brought me no peace. If my beloved was with me, I could not sense him. I have never felt so alone and so not alone. Between the worlds were cords that bound me to my daughter and my daughter's daughters. I could not and would not cut those cords, and yet they did no one any good. So I paced and prayed until I dropped.

The dream begins with the sound of hammering, dull and methodical, and a workman whistling softly, tunelessly, just doing his job, his job of nailing a man's wrists to a wooden cross piece. Women cry out and then try to stifle their cries for his sake. I am one of them. And the awful hammering goes on. Now the workman has secured the wrists. One huge spike will do for both the heels. Still whistling, the workman drives it through.

The soldiers arrive at Boudica's compound just before dawn. I see them hidden behind the hedgerows in the fields surrounding the village. The centurion, as official envoy, approaches the guard, who demands to know his business.

"I have a message for the royal family from the Procurator of Pretannia," he announces in poorly pronounced Celtic.

I sense the centurion taking stock of the sleeping village, how poorly defended it is, how pathetically easy his job will be. Even now his men have surrounded the village, quietly dispatching a few early risers on their way to work who might have sounded the alarm.

"The royal family is in mourning, sir," protests the guard. "They are not to be disturbed."

"I am afraid they must be," says the centurion. "Will you fetch them out, or shall I?"

I feel the guard's dawning horror. He knows how few armed people there are in the village. He guesses this centurion is not alone. Should he draw his sword now and sound the alarm or should he go to Boudica first?

"Wait right here," the guard says. "I will see if the queen is willing to receive you."

The centurion does not bother to say, there is no queen here anymore, and if there were, her will is irrelevant. Let the man have his last shred of dignity. This is a job, only a job. It'll be over quickly enough.

"Send the word along the lines," the centurion says to his aides, " to be ready at the signal."

"Queen Boudica," says the guard, lifting the heavy plaid across the door to her hut. "I wouldn't disturb you for the three worlds, but I must. There's a Roman here, a centurion, I think. He says he has a message from the procurator."

Inside the hut, Boudica rouses herself but does not get up.

"Tell him to go away, Geraint. I will see no one till after the burial rites. No one."

"Queen," says Geraint, "I have told him so already. I am afraid he is not alone. You know how poorly defended we are right now. I am willing to fight and die at your bidding, as are all your people. But if you will meet with him, maybe we can forestall him till the warriors arrive, till we have a fighting chance."

"Their demand is not seemly," says Boudica. "Already they show their contempt."

"Mother," Gwen rises to her feet. "You forget. I am Queen of the Iceni now. I will not risk our people's safety for your pride. If the man is bringing us a message, I, for one, will go to receive it. Lithben, will you come with me?"

Lithben looks from one to the other and seems to search the dim hut for someone else, for me.

"Courage, *cariad*," I whisper in my heart, to her heart. "Courage. I will be with you."

"Very well, we will all go," decides Boudica, wresting back her authority from Gwen in the only way she can.

Boudica stands, then turns and takes Prasutagus's sword and shield from his body.

"Mother!" Gwen is horrified. "You complain of the Romans, but you desecrate my father's body. My father's honor."

Boudica actually shrugged.

"He won't be needing these now. And if he had made better use of them in his life, I might not need them either. Come on, let's go."

And before Gwen can protest, Boudica thrusts aside the plaid and steps out into the dawn.

* * *

"You come with sword drawn, *domina*," says the centurion. He refuses to call her queen. "That is not a wise way to welcome an envoy of Rome."

But it will make my job easier, he is thinking.

"You are not welcome," states Boudica.

Gwen, to her mother's right, draws herself up, while Lithben on her left hangs back.

"I am the Queen of the Iceni," says Gwen. "You may deliver your message to me."

The centurion looks at her, almost with pity, almost but not quite, and then he gives the signal.

Everything happens so quickly, it is a blur, and yet I also see each detail. Boudica's skeleton guard is outnumbered and quickly overwhelmed, all but Boudica, whose sword swings and whirls as if she had eight arms. The centurion watches almost wearily, then gives another signal. A cluster of men rush Gwen and Lithben, hurl them to the ground and pin them there.

No. Not this.

For a moment I am enveloped in silence. Then I see my beloved's cracked lips, the cracked sky. My beloved opens his eyes and looks at me from the cross, just looks.

And I know what to do.

Lithben, I cry out with my whole being, Lithben, fly!

Just in time I am there, in her place. A young man, hardly more than a boy, heaves himself onto me, hoisting up chain mail that cuts into my flesh. For a moment our eyes meet, and he knows and I know that he's scared. And he hates me for seeing his fear. He spits in my face, and then it happens, I am torn open and pain rips through me, brutal, red, endless. Until everything goes black.

When I can see again, Gwen is crouching over Lithben, who is still unconscious. Gwen's tunic has been torn from her and she is naked and streaked with blood. Boudica's sword still clangs; six men lie dead on the ground. But there are more surrounding her, and finally, one man aims a kick that sends her sword flying, two more jump her from behind, and another comes with rope to bind her.

Then Boudica sees her daughters.

There is no word in any language for the sound she makes.

When it stops, for a moment everything is silent. Everyone stands still.

"Set up a stake," the centurion says. "Bind her to it, bare her back, and give her thirty lashes, but be sure to leave her alive."

"Alive?" one of the men dares to question. "She has killed half a dozen of our men. Surely she should be executed or taken captive."

"Those are my orders, soldier," snaps the centurion. "And those are yours."

Let me take her place, too, I plead. Let me take her place.

But this prayer is not answered.

The sound of the lash goes on and on.

Boudica never cries out.

Lithben wakes and Gwen holds her tight, stifling Lithben's cries with her hand.

Will it never end?

At last it does. And before noon, the soldiers are done with their job and gone. Gwen and Lithben go to their mother and struggle to unbind her, but the knots are too tight. They are both shaking too badly to work them and in so much shock they can't think what else to do. And so they just lean against her, with their arms around her, and weep.

That is how Sarah finds them when she returns with the warriors just before sunset.

Dusk found me pacing the sands; I had torn my face and my breasts with my fingernails till they bled. Boudica's sound was coming out of my mouth, out of my body, stronger than the sea, wilder than the wind. Then suddenly the sky blackened with wings, and my voice was lost in the cry of crows, a murder of crows.

The priestesses of Holy Island had arrived.

CHAPTER THIRTY-TWO
THE STORY ONE LAST TIME

THE PRIESTESSES, some thirty of them, made camp with me on my isle where they proposed to wait until General Suetonius and his troops attacked. I was the hostess, but they cosseted me as if I were a baby, making me soothing potions that helped me sleep without dreams. They had brought various things for the pot—leaves, roots, and portions of meat—some of which I could not identify and did not care to. As always, the pot never became empty no matter how many people ate from it. The cask of mead, too, appeared to be developing the same magical properties, and we drank deeply of it into a run of clear, star-laden nights. Sometimes, at their request, I told stories. They particularly liked to hear about Miriam (*aka* Ma) and seemed to feel she was a long-lost priestess of their own ilk. When I was too tired or heartsick to speak, they sang songs, reminiscent of Ma's humming, that had no words or human melody, songs that wove in and out of birdsong and wind and the roll of stones in the waves.

It was not an unpleasant way to spend the last days of our lives, and I might have been quite content if it hadn't been for the pain, constant yet also stabbing and sudden, when I thought of my daughters and granddaughters. Their names became a ceaseless litany in my mind. Lithben, Gwen, Boudica, Sarah. Lithben, Gwen, Boudica, Sarah. It was all I could do for them, however useless. Though I gazed and gazed into the well till my eyes ached, the fickle water would not reveal how they were faring in the aftermath of the Roman attack.

But then, I did not have need of visions to know there would be more trouble. I did not know if I was sorry or glad that I would not live to see what would happen on the other side of the Holy Isles.

It was on Beltane when we first saw the Roman troops. Our warriors and the remaining farmers had lit the Beltane fires and were keeping the rites with as much spirit as they could muster. It was a beautiful full moon night, perfect for bedding down and making love in the fields, lovemaking all the more poignant with the rites of fertility shadowed by pending battle. We old priestesses left the others to it and kept vigil on Dwynwyn's Isle. By the full moonlight we saw the warriors descending the mountain, crawling like some infestation over the moon-soaked rocks. The Romans moved without torches, perhaps hoping we would not see them as clearly as we might by day. But we did; we watched all night as they kept coming and coming. We imagined we could hear their footfalls, and the squeak of their wagon wheels even over the sound of the sea and the wind, our silence was so intent. At last we turned to each other and spoke among ourselves. Some went to warn the warriors and farmers. The rest of us laid our battle plans.

Given my lineage (daughter of the eight weather witches) and the tales I had told of my travels as a wind whistler, it is no wonder that my fellow priestesses urged me to confound the enemy with foul atmospheric conditions. So the next morning dense fog, the kind that is indistinguishable from rain and terrible for armor, settled on the Roman camp while the remaining *combrogos*, now making their own camp on the beach, enjoyed a perfect Spring morning.

Then something disconcerting happened. The fog moved to our side as if it was being pushed by something—or someone. I whistled for the wind and sent it back, and the same thing happened again. Only once had I experienced anything like this push-pull. Then it had been a tug of war with the wind. Ma and I were traveling on a merchant vessel to Ephesus when our ship was pursued by pirates. The captain ordered me to call a wind to help us outrun the other boat, but the wind kept shifting in the pirate's favor. I soon realized that there was a weather witch among the pirates—who turned out to be my long-lost daughter.

But this time it was not Sarah who drove the fog, laced with hail, back to our side of the straits.

I looked up into the swirling, stinging grey sky, and then I saw fleetingly the snowy flash of a hawk's wing. If I had any doubt of what I had seen, the sight was followed by the hawk's scream. I pulled my grey cloak over my head and huddled in the shelter of a rock, as if I were a small creature of prey.

I didn't want him to see me.

"What is it, Maeve Rhuad?" asked Moira.

"They have someone on their side who knows weather magic," I told her. "Someone who knows what I am doing."

I did not tell her that I thought I knew who it was.

"Ah," was all she said.

"It may be best if we can see them," I reconsidered. "We can't delay them forever."

I stood up, listening intently. The hawk was gone. I made a chalice of my arms and called the sun to burn away the fog.

By noon the remaining population of Mona had made camp on the beach, while the Romans constructed their camp on the opposing shore, an efficient but laborious process. They would not do anything hastily; every nut and bolt of every machine and weapon would be in place. All armor would be oiled and ready. Our side had fewer weapons, no armor to polish, so we busied ourselves with making our appearance terrifying, painting the warriors with woad in patterns both intricate and bold, sculpting their hair with lime, so that it stuck out from their heads like branches, lightning bolts, horns. Everyone sharpened daggers and swords, readied the tips of spears, oiled the wheels of chariots.

At dusk of that long day, the druids who had been allowed or chosen to remain came down from their own rites in the ancient groves. To my surprise, Ciaran was among them. I caught his eye and he approached me, somewhat sheepishly, but also clearly pleased with himself.

"What are you doing here?" I demanded, as we fell into step together, walking towards Abermenai Point. "Viviane told me that you, she and Branwen were all shipping out to different places. Viviane would have your head on a platter if she knew you had snuck back."

He grinned at the thought and looked for a moment not like a venerable archdruid but like the young Ciaran of the blue-black hair, ridiculously handsome and well aware of it.

"Well, of course I deceived her, or she wouldn't have gone. As for my head on a platter, perhaps that can be arranged," he said. "If anyone survives, they could send her my skull, gold-plated, of course. A lovely gift for the new archdruid."

"Oh, yes," I agreed. "Lovely. A chalice made of your dead lover's head. What every woman wants."

"Viviane is made of stern stuff," said Ciaran. "She's a druid, and don't forget we were rivals, too. If she had my skull, she'd get to imbibe all my power, all my wisdom."

"Such as it is," I added.

"Such as it is," he said agreeably.

When we reached the point, we turned away from the sight of the new-sprung Roman camp and looked west towards the Hibernian Sea. Our silence was sweet, companionable, two old friends watching the sun go down as if it were not the eve of our almost certain doom.

"We will be telling stories tonight," said Ciaran. "To give courage to the *combrogos*. Will you tell one?"

"I got kicked out of druid school after only a year," I reminded him. "I hardly know the canon. I don't know any battle stories at all except Queen-Maeve-Takes-a-Leak."

"Tell your story," Ciaran said, his voice suddenly serious. "Your story and Esus's."

* * *

It was a strange and wonderful thing to be telling our story for the last time on the island where we first met in the flesh, where we became lovers, where we parted on the very shore where the *combrogos* would make their stand tomorrow. A few of the remaining bards had told rousing stories before mine, encouraging the *combrogos* to bravery in battle. Mine did not fit any of the traditional categories—invasions, conceptions, cattle raids—though perhaps it could be considered a wonder voyage. I took up the tale with Esus escaping with his life across the straits and myself exiled beyond the ninth wave to faraway, exotic lands.

My story served one purpose at least, distraction from our current plight. That is, until the feeding of the five thousand, the exact same place the general had interrupted with the exact same objection.

"But why did Esus not let them make him king?" one warrior demanded, incensed enough to get to his feet. "Surely they would have fought for him against the plaguing Romans, and the more stings to the beast in the more parts of its hide, the better."

I did not have a chance to answer before an old, cantankerous druid jumped in.

"He was under a *geis*, same as all druids, and he could not bear arms."

"But he wasn't a druid," another warrior objected. "You druids planned to murder him. He never finished his studies."

"He was an initiated dedicate," another druid insisted. "It comes to the same thing."

"Well, even if he was a druid, and couldn't bloody his precious, useless hands, he could have directed the army. Look at Lovernios. He was a druid, and the best strategist we ever had."

None of the druids answered him, out of embarrassment or tact. For all the druids who remained were old enough to remember that Lovernios had lobbied for the Stranger's sacrifice. They also knew that he was my father—and Boudica's father—and that the tidal bore I called had been his death. An awkward bit of back story.

"Maeve Rhuad," Ciaran took charge. "Please continue. Perhaps Esus's reasoning will become clear to us as the story unfolds."

And perhaps not, I thought. It had not made sense to the general, who even now was probably walking through his camp, rallying his troops. I suddenly wished I had not agreed to tell our story, a story that could be interpreted as defeat. How could I tell it so that they would understand it? Had I ever understood it myself?

I had to trust the story. I had told it so many times, or rather it had told itself through me. It was alive, not a set piece. I never knew what the story would reveal or how each listener would hear it. When I got to Esus's crucifixion, some people wept openly, others became very still, and some declared that his death would be avenged. I waited until everyone had had his say, or his silence, and then I told them about the tomb. I sang for them the song I sang to my beloved, chanting over and over, *love is as strong as death, love is as strong as death.*

At last I came to the part I hoped would speak to all of them—the dawn garden, the leaves that shone with their own light, his beautiful healed and wounded body, our eternity together under the tree.

"And then I said to him, *cariad*, what is this place? Do you know what he answered?" I asked my listeners.

There was a pause; I thought I could hear everyone's heartbeat, scattered bits of life, bright as the stars. Then all at once, the *combrogos* cried out.

"Tir nan Og! Tir nan Og!"

"Yes. We were in Tir nan Og," I said when it was quiet again. "We are in Tir nan Og. That is all we need to know. That is the end of the story, and that is the beginning. Rest now."

"Maeve Rhuad," someone called out, the man who had lauded my father. "There is one more thing I'd like to know."

"What is that?" I asked, suddenly feeling uneasy.

"Will you be calling a tidal bore tomorrow? To destroy our enemies, to avenge your Esus?"

Holy Mother, I silently called out to Isis, to Ma, to Brigid, to Anna, to Dwynwyn, to all my long-lost mothers. How do I answer that? What *is* the answer?

"I don't know," I heard myself say.

I closed my eyes and remembered that day: Esus escaping across the straits with the Hibernian women, the druids hard on their heels.

"Call the wind," Dwynwyn had ordered me. "Call the tide."

And I did. I don't know how I knew what to do. I don't even know what I did. Somehow I opened: my mouth, my arms, my heart, every orifice and pore, every cell. Standing there howling on the dune, I met and mated with the elements. They took on my passion; I took on their power.

I called the wave to save Esus's life, not to drown the druids, even though they were my enemies, the ones who wanted to kill my beloved three times over. The druids had all wheeled around and ridden to safety, except for one. Except for one.

Dismounting, he sent his horse after the others. For one moment, he stood still. Then with his arms open, he walked straight towards the bore. As if his eyes were mine, I saw the black water blot out the sky.

Later the druids accused me of murdering him.

"Lovernios," I said out loud, opening my eyes and looking at the *combrogos* gathered around me. "My father. I will call on the spirit of my father, who gave himself to the wave, who died and lives in Tir fo Thuinn."

I laid claim to my paternity, which I guessed had never been fully accepted or openly acknowledged by the druids, who had turned me into a seducing silkie to avoid tarnishing their famous druid's name. That, after leaving me to the mercy of the sea as the late archdruid had so poetically expressed it.

"Why call on your father?" Ciaran asked. "I thought it was your legendary mothers who taught you weather witchery."

"My mothers, the warrior witches of Tir na mBan." I spoke the name to see if it still caused men to fall into a trance—of terror or delight.

It did. They all sighed at once. Some of them swayed. One began to sing a song without words. Another wept. For a moment I thought I could smell the blossoms of our magical orchard where the trees always bloomed and bore. All at once, I felt homesick, for Tir na mBan, for Temple Magdalen, for pleasure, for peace.

"My mothers," I said when they had come back to their ordinary senses, "have no allegiance to you, the people who exiled their daughter. It is through my father that I am one of the *combrogos*. It is his daughter Boudica who has just been grievously wronged; his granddaughters who have been raped by the Romans, as he once raped me. Yes. Raped. Me. He would have killed me, too, if he could. He tried to kill Esus."

I paused for breath. I didn't know what I would say next, but I knew there was more.

"Did you know that Esus taught his companions to love their enemies? Anyone can love their friends, he said. I say sometimes it is hard to know who your enemies are or how your friends are any different. You can love your enemy, and turn your enemy into a friend."

I thought of Paulina, who seemed so far away now and long ago, a Roman who had once abused me, and then become my follower, benefactress and finally a true friend. I remembered how she had come to warn me of the danger to Jesus from one of her compatriots, Pontius Pilate.

And there was another Roman enemy I had loved, so close now, if I whistled, the wind might carry the sound to his ear. And yet his son had ordered the atrocity inflicted upon my daughter and granddaughters.

"What does it mean?" I went on. "What does it mean to love your enemy on the eve of battle? Do you spare your enemy even though he won't spare you? Do you kill him, because he will kill you? Which is worse, death or murder?"

I fell silent again. No one jumped into the breach. I could hear the tide turn, beginning to go out. By dawn it would be near low. That's when they would cross.

"I do not know the answer to my own questions," I said at last. "I only know I will stand with you. I will call on my father Lovernios; I will call on my father Manannan Mac Lir. The son of the wave will answer for the wave." I paused for a beat, and then I added for good measure, "I have spoken."

That night we all slept on the beach near Abermenai Point where it was likely the Romans would cross. (If you are wondering, I had left Macha on the far side of Dwynwyn's Isle with a *geis* on her, if such a thing can be laid on a horse, not to leave the island until I came back or danger had passed.) The priestesses stayed together, a huddle of folded black wings, tucked heads with me gathered into their midst, though I was the only red-robed priestess, like the flash of red on a red-winged blackbird.

I didn't expect to sleep, but I must have, for I dreamed two dreams, if they were dreams.

In the first one, I am a child on Tir na mBan, alone on the cliff tops on a full moon night waiting for my father Manannan Mac Lir to come to visit me. At last I see him striding on the path the moon makes on the water. He's big enough to scoop the moon right out of the sky and drop it into the magical bag made of cranes' skins that he carries slung over his shoulder. But he doesn't need the moon; he has treasures enough, which he will spread out for me to see, bright and shining in the moonlight.

Now he is scaling the cliffs as if they are nothing more than small beach rocks, and then he is with me, not huge anymore, but old and sad and tired, his once bright hair as grey as mine has turned.

Lovernios.

Without a word to me, he opens the crane bag and lays out some dusty looking treasures. I know what they are but am shocked to see them looking so ordinary, so diminished: the king of Caledonia's shears, the king of Lochlainn's helmet, Goibne's smith hook, the bones of Assail's swine, Manannan's own shirt, and a strip from the great whale's back.

"You have saved these treasures," he says to me.

"I don't understand," I say. "How did I save them? I thought they were yours."

He doesn't answer, but as I gaze at the objects, I see them coming to life; they are ogham, letters encoded with stories, songs, histories, powers. They are the wings of the cranes inscribing their secret wisdom in the sky.

Then they are just objects again. Slowly, Lovernios puts the treasures back in the bag. Then he stands to face me. Now we are on the narrow spit of tidal sand near Dwynwyn's Isle, where we recognized each other fully for the first time, where he tried to kill me and the life I carried within, the life he had begotten.

"You are my daughter," he acknowledges me at last. "You are my daughter."

"Then, father, save me," I plead. "Save us all. Come in with the tide and save us."

Almost, but not quite, he shrugs. The sadness remains in his face, etched there, and yet he seems to have nothing to do with it.

"The hazelnut is already safe," he says. "The hazelnut of wisdom."

Then he shoulders his bag and walks over the water, following the moon across the Hibernian Sea until he disappears under a distant wave.

In the next dream, I am walking to Abermenai Point. Dawn is in its early stages, the world all shades of grey: water, sky, sand, woods, the mountains across straits, the lone figure standing there, waiting for me.

Of course it is my beloved.

As I draw nearer to him, he keeps changing.

One moment he is as old as I am, as old as he would have been if he'd lived. His resemblance to his brother is unmistakable and yet they are nothing alike.

The next moment he is the boy who stood poised on this very spit of sand, refusing to leave without me until I forced him to go.

When I reach him at last, he is as I remember him in the dawn garden. His eyes are so like Sarah's, yet nothing like.

I want to touch him, but just as on that day in the garden, there seems to be some separation between us that is at the same time no separation at all.

"Soon, *cariad*," he says. "Soon."

"Yes," I say. "Today I will be with you in Tir nan Og."

He looks at me so tenderly, amused and sorrowful at once.

"Don't count your death wounds before they're dealt," he says.

"What's that supposed to mean?" I demand. "I am going into mortal battle."

"I know," he says. "I'll be with you. I am with you always."

"You always say that," I accuse.

"Because it's true."

"It doesn't always help," I say, suddenly angry.

"I know," he admits.

And I forgive him again for leaving me here alone in my flesh for so long.

"Tell me something," I say. "I have an enemy I love. You know who he is. You know him. He intends to kill us all tomorrow. What does it mean to love an enemy in battle?"

He looks at me for a long moment, and then he smiles a small, secret smile, as if there were a joke I should understand, but don't.

"Death is as strong as love," he says. "Sometimes it is the same as love. Don't worry, Maeve, you'll know."

I woke in that same dawn light shivering, not with cold but because I knew what I intended to do.

CHAPTER THIRTY-THREE
SINGLE COMBAT

NOW. NO MORE DREAMING, no more debate, no more staring into wells and screaming at visions. Dawn and low tide were at hand. The air was unusually still, and the sound of the Romans' final preparations carried across the quarter mile or so of ebb-tide water. You could hear footfalls as the men marched the boats to the water, and the rasp of the flat hulls as they launched. You could hear armor snapping into place, cross bows being loaded, *ballistae* cocked. All of these preparations smooth and practiced. Now the infantry were loading into boats, and the cavalry were mounting their horses.

We stood waiting and watching; the black-robed priestesses (and the red one) claimed the front line, an honor no one could refuse us. Just behind us stood the last druids left on Mona in full regalia, masks of feathers and headdresses of antlers, gold torcs ready to flash blindingly when the sun cleared the mountains. Behind them waited the woad-painted warriors, *laigen* ready for the first round of assault, battle chariots at both ends of the beach ready to bear down on the first foot soldiers. Intermixed were farmers and blacksmiths, brandishing any weapons or implements they could find.

We were ready. We would never be ready.

As the first ray of sun shot over the mountains, Ciaran paced a circle and called the quarters; then one last time, he planted his staff.

"Here now is the center of the world."

In the silence that followed, even over the din of the Roman bustle, we heard the last sigh of the ebb tide, the held breath, the subtle quickening as the tide turned again.

"Call him, Maeve Rhuad," commanded the archdruid.

I turned toward the west, lifted my arms, and sang.

Father, my father, oh my father
away to the lands of the west
away to the Isles of the Blest
do not forget us here
do not forsake us here
our enemy masses on the other shore
over the water our enemy comes
Manannan Mac Lir, Lovernios

my father and the son of the wave
lift up your arm to defend us
lift up your arm to deliver us
lift up your arm, the arm of the sea
bring back the bore that bore you away
Lovernios Manannan Yahweh Sabaoth
our enemy pursues us across the straits
yea even across the Red Sea, cover them
with your mighty waters, deliver us
deliver us to our own land,
deliver us to freedom.

I sang and sang, other voices rose with me, some high, eerie, dissonant, like birds of prey, some deep and mournful, as if a sea monster sobbed.

And yet the air stayed unnaturally calm and the tide, still far away, seeped in with no urgency.

The hazelnut is already safe, I heard Lovernios say, his voice far away, a wisp of cloud on a distant horizon. "*The hazelnut of wisdom is safe.*"

"He's not coming," I turned to Ciaran. "I am so sorry. He is not coming. The wave is not coming."

"No matter, Maeve," he said with heroic kindness. "It was a bit of a long shot."

"Look!" Moira suddenly cried out, pointing across the straits. "Look, over there. Everything has stopped. They're standing frozen, some with one leg in and one out of the boats. They're scared of us, our song scared them. Come sisters, come brothers, come warriors, come my *combrogos*, lift up your voices, shriek and howl your prayers. Sing, for the love of Anu, sing!"

And we did, each in our own way, some praying, some cursing, some wailing, some raging, some lamenting, warriors beating on their shields as drums. Women, some armed and some not, took up torches and began a dance, weaving in and out among the men. The priestesses joined hands and, singing, waded into the straits towards the frozen enemy forces.

Then I saw him, a man riding out in front of his troops, a man with a general's crest on his shining helmet that the sun had just struck. I could not hear him over our din, but his men could. I knew what he was doing as he rode up and down the ranks, one hand on the reins, one hand raised and raised again and again: he was shaming them. Do not fear this rabble, this army of women and fanatics. Shamed, the soldier's fear was turning to fury. They would avenge their moment of weakness, obliterate the shame by obliterating these strange and savage people who howled and painted their faces to look like animals.

"Ya-a-a-ah!"

Their battle cry rose suddenly, thousands of voices, one voice, shooting over the straits, breaking our sound barrier.

Then it all began.

The *ballistae* let loose and stones crashed among our ranks, causing immediate disarray. Next to me, one of the priestesses went down. I turned to pull her from the water, but her skull had been crushed; she was dead. All I could do was to haul her to the beach and hope she would later be buried. When I strode again into the water, I saw the flat-bottomed boats advancing like huge water beetles over the straits, the oars for legs, the helmets of the infantry like a knobby shell. Between the boats, the cavalry churned the water as their horses struggled with cross currents treacherous even at low tide. Here and there a rider went down, or a boat capsized, but still they kept coming. Sometimes it seemed that they would never get here; it was all unreal. Each stroke of the oar or plunge of hoof seemed suspended in its own eternity. And then they were upon us.

Or their weapons were. As soon as they were within range, the infantry hurled their *pila*, spears designed to bend when they lodged in a shield, so that they could not be pulled out, forcing the warrior to abandon his shield or fight with it disabled—that is, if he hadn't already been killed. The air was thick with *pila*, as rank after rank discharged their weapons, and still they kept coming. At first I could hear the sound they made as they whizzed over my head; then I could hear only the screaming as they found their mark, or the desperate cursing as men tried in vain to right their shields. Then there was the sound of the spears our warriors cast bouncing off the superior Roman shields and armor, though now and then one found an arm or a leg.

We priestesses and the druids waded further into the straits chanting and shrieking our invocations, doing our best to unnerve and distract. Now the soldiers were disembarking, forming orderly ranks, like some ruthless mowing machine systematically cutting down our wild, disheveled horde. Their swords were out, quick thrusting swords. Ciaran planted himself in front of one soldier, who ran him through, and moved on to the next kill without a glance. I saw the blood bloom on Ciaran's white robe, just before he collapsed into the straits.

Ignoring the chaos around me, I went to him and pulled him out of water that was already red with his blood and the blood of many. Fallen druids and priestesses were everywhere. The boats and the soldiers kept coming, an infestation crawling out of the water onto the beach, stabbing and stabbing. On the sands I saw woad mixed with blood. Our warriors were fighting fiercely, without armor, many without shields, swinging their swords, sometimes succeeding in smashing a helmet or finding a soft exposed spot on a neck. But only our chariots disrupted the Roman formation at all, and the Roman cavalry had now arrived in full force. Our charioteers were under systematic assault from the second round of *pila* as well as crossbows.

It is almost impossible to describe battle, because when you are in it, nothing seems sequential. Time gets swallowed up in a horrible immediacy. It is so terrifying that you go beyond terror into some strange detachment. I kept moving bodies until there was nowhere to pile them, and the sand was so slippery with blood and guts, I could barely stand. The battle was almost all on land now. How I had survived the first onslaught I cannot tell you. But I had done enough shrieking and wailing.

It was time for me to join the battle now in full.

First, I had to find my beloved enemy.

It was so easy, I didn't even have to will it. There I was in the air, my doves' wings a small flash of white among the crows that wheeled and circled.

"Go for the eyes, my sisters."

I heard Moira speak inside my mind. So not all the Crows had been killed. Or maybe they had shifted shape at the moment of death. Maybe I was dead, too. In any case, I had nothing to lose. The best way to love my enemy in this moment would be to kill him, or failing that, be killed.

From a doves' eye view, the battle looked even more hopeless for the *combrogos*. The Romans had taken their famous saw-tooth formation now, trampling over the dead and scooping up the living to be slaughtered as they went. And there, on the sides, on a bit of raised ground, on his huge horse, was the mastermind, the director.

I flew to him and alighted on his head, just as once long ago, far away in a dream that was more than a dream, I had fluttered down on the head of my beloved. In love and flustered by my nearness to him, I had lost control of my avian bowels and shit on the poor boy's head in the Temple porticoes, unwittingly humiliating him in front of his elders. I didn't mean to do it then.

I did now. Whether I was dead or alive, real or a phantom, the shit hit the helmet. It dripped down the visor, and the general, who was directing massive slaughter, sheathed his sword for an instant to wipe it away.

When he reached for his sword again, it was gone. I stood before him with his sword in my hand.

"Your men don't need you right now," I shouted over the din. "They know what to do. Dismount and prepare to fight for your life."

Under his bespattered helmet, his face turned pale, what I could see of it. I think he actually began to shake; his armor rattled just a little.

"I don't want to kill your horse," I told him. "He's done nothing to me or my people, but if you don't get down and fight me, I will."

Still he stared at me, trying to make sense of what he was seeing.

"You're mad!" he finally said.

"Yes. Now dismount and fight."

Somewhat to my astonishment, he did what he was told.

"What am I to fight with?" he asked. "You have my sword."

"You have a dagger and a shield," I reminded him. "You're a trained warrior. You'll figure it out."

He looked at me, perplexed.

"But I could kill you!" he protested.

"Don't tell me you're afraid of a little blood!" I gestured towards the killing ground. "Draw your weapon. You will fight me."

"How did you get my sword?" he was still confused.

Another bit of guano dripped off the visor of his helmet, and light dawned, so to speak.

"Have it your way," he said. "But let's even the odds."

Shape-shifting is not something you can see happen. There are no directions, no sequential steps that you could record or teach. It happens and you make a leap into another world, another form. One moment the general stood before me, and the next my eyes tracked the flight of a hawk, rising into the air, seeking the thermal currents. Then I was in the air, too, in my dove form. Evened odds? Hardly, but I had no time to quibble. While he circled, I flew higher and higher, till I was ready to dive straight down, straight for those keen hawk eyes. (*Go for the eyes, sister.*) He was ready for me, and just the moment before my attack, he twisted on the air and raked my breast with his talons, letting me know he meant business, but not wounding me mortally. I rose and dived again, then dived and rose, as he turned on the air and held the center of the circle of attack.

Below us the battle went on, methodically, horribly, no one hearing the screaming hawk, or the throaty cries of the outraged, outranked dove. Then the fires started. The groves were being put to the torch. Heat rose and smoke billowed into the sky we had made our battlefield. I could no longer see my opponent, but I could hear him. He was calling me, calling me to follow him out of the smoke, away from the flame.

When we came to earth again, to our human selves, we were standing under the yews overlooking the straits, far away enough for now from the burning teaching groves.

"Have you had enough?" he asked.

I looked out over the straits, red with blood, wreckage and bodies floating and swirling on the tricky tides and currents. I listened to the roar of the fire, tasted the ash on the air. Bitter. Bitter. And this was only the beginning. More devastation would come unless by some fluke I managed to kill the one who commanded this huge trained beast.

"No," I said. "Let's finish this."

Somehow I still had his sword. Since I had no shield, he laid his down and unsheathed, not the standard dagger that all Roman soldiers carried as their second weapon, but a ritual blade with a fine point and an intricately carved hilt. The weapon seemed alive in his hand, live as the forms depicted on the hilt: snakes, birds, and bees, from what I could make out. It looked like the work of a Celtic metalsmith; it would be a perfect votive offering to the gods. I could almost see it, spinning through the air, splashing into Llyn Cerrig Bach. Its beauty distracted me.

"Etruscan," he told me. "Made with magic. I keep it for special occasions, when I must make ritual sacrifice."

Silently I wondered how it would be to die on that blade.

Aloud I said, "You cheat!"

And I lunged for him with his sword, so crude, so clumsy an instrument by comparison. He caught my blade and turned me with it, pricking me in the shoulder. I whirled all the way around and brought down the sword for an overhead blow. He stepped nimbly aside and caught my blade on a hilt that seemed much too delicate for this task. I fought on and did my best to use the sword in a Roman manner with quick upward thrusts. These he parried or drove downward, so that I once cut my own knee. Still I kept going, grazing him a few times when my sword bounced off his blade and caught his arm or face. Whenever he found an opening, he pricked me again, up and down my arms and legs, on the backs of my shoulders, almost as if he were making a ritual inscription for his ritual sacrifice.

"Why are you drawing this out!" I demanded.

But just then, to my surprise, I managed to find a weak spot in his armor where the shoulder plates met the torso. He sprang back before I could do more than scratch him.

"Good!" he said as if he were my fencing coach.

"Don't patronize me!" I shouted. "Kill me and have done with it!"

"There's no art in that," he answered, hardly winded.

"This is not a game!" I snarled.

"Of course it is a game," he said. "It's all a game. If you see it that way, you'll save yourself grief, and your technique will improve."

I saw an opening and went for his leg, managing to slash it before he caught and circled my sword, lifting my arm, then drawing his blade just over my breast, which he could have cut off had he chosen to.

"Next time go for an artery or a tendon," he instructed. "Now make me sweat a little."

Goaded, I managed to do just that. As we fought on and on, I didn't think anymore. I caught some kind of rhythm and just moved. I discovered I was able to feel what he was going to do before he did it, and his pricks and scratches became less frequent. I found myself falling into a trance, light-headed perhaps from the loss of blood from my minor but multiple wounds. Then out of the corner of my eye, I saw *ogham*, the blood drying in patterns, stems and cross strokes. Insanely, I looked down at my arms, trying to read the secret inscribed there. He should have killed me then. Instead, when I looked back, I found him standing out of my range, near the oldest yew tree, the one where Esus and I had always met, where we had become lovers long ago.

In one hand, he still held his blade; in the other, what I took at first for a shield, and then recognized as a mirror, a small bronze mirror as beautifully wrought as the blade, a mirror that belonged to the gods. He gazed at me steadily as the mirror pivoted in his hand, back and forth, like a leaf fluttering on a subtle breeze. A slanting ray of late sun found its way into the green world under the yews and struck the mirror, which kept turning, spiraling in and out of light, until at last he held it still.

Oh. The sword felt unbearably heavy. Somewhere fire roared; somewhere men bellowed in rage and agony. Far away in another world, the sword slipped from my hand. Oh.

The heart of the mirror shone with its own light, like the leaves on the tree of life. Hovering at the edges, smoke and blood and horror, but oh, at the heart, the heart. I started to walk towards the mirror that was no longer a mirror, but the sea, the moon, the memory I had never quite remembered. Just before I could step over the shimmering border, everything went dark and all the worlds disappeared.

When I came to myself again, I did not know where I was or how I had gotten there. I did not know why the air smelled of smoke or the sky was full of lurid red cloud. I sat up. Someone had covered me with a heavy cloak that was not mine. Someone had bandaged my arms and legs. I had been wounded. I was under the yew trees. Where was Esus? Then I remembered: he was gone. I had taken Dwynwyn's shape and untied him from the tree. I stood up slowly, my joints aching, my wounds throbbing. I ran my hand over my face, a face soft and withered as an old apple. I must still be in

Dwynwyn's shape. But where was mine? I was about to have a baby. I wanted to have my own baby. I didn't want Dwynwyn doing it for me.

"No fear of that, honey lamb, no fear," Dwynwyn's voice spoke inside me.

"Dwynwyn?" I spoke aloud. "Where are you? Give me back my shape."

"I don't have your shape, my little cabbage. I don't have any shape any more."

"But I'm an old woman!" I protested.

"Yes, sweet cakes," she agreed. "You are."

"I don't understand," I said, a wail about to rise and loose itself.

"Hush, my dove," soothed Dwynwyn in anticipation. "I told you I would come back, if you needed me. Now I'm here. Just take my hand."

"But I can't see you," I almost whimpered.

"You don't need to see me. Just take my hand."

Though I could not see her, I did as she said. Her hand felt amazingly warm and comforting. And comfort I needed. She led me from the yew grove down to the sands where Roman soldiers swarmed like ants, some piling up the dead, some pitching tents. The scene was all the more surreal for being cast in the red glow of the burning groves.

"What is happening?" I dug my nails into Dwynwyn's incorporeal hand. "What is happening here?"

Instead of Dwynwyn's voice, I heard my beloved's.

The groves will burn. The heavens will turn black with smoke, and the earth bitter with ash... and the druids will be gone forever from Mona mam Cymru.

Then the rest of the day came back to me in horrible fragmented images. It had happened; it was happening. The horror before me was no vision, no memory. It was now. I doubled over and bit my other hand to keep from howling.

Why hadn't he killed me? Why hadn't he killed me?

"Come," Dwynwyn urged. "There is more."

"No more," I pleaded.

But I let her lead me along the sands. High tide had come and now ebbed again taking with it some of the gore, but scattered over the sands there remained severed limbs, now and then a whole body. The place reeked of blood and feces. Though night had fallen, the flies were working overtime. If I'd had anything in my stomach, I would have heaved it up.

I would find him. I would accuse him.

No one challenged or even noticed my progress down the beach. Maybe I posed no threat or maybe I was a ghost, after all. If so, then I would haunt him. I followed the tug of Dwynwyn's hand as she led me through the tent city that had sprung up on the Maltreath Sands.

Outside the largest, most central tent, I saw him sitting on a low stool, writing on a piece of papyrus, no doubt an account of the battle. Neither he nor his sentries saw me where I stood just outside the pool of light cast by his torch.

"Don't speak," said Dwynwyn inside my mind. "Just pay attention."

After a while, he put down his quill, rolled up the paper, and tied it with a bit of rawhide. Then he just sat and stared, seemingly at nothing. He did not look like a general who had just triumphed in battle; he looked bone-weary, and sad. And so like my beloved, it hurt to draw a breath.

Then he turned and looked in my direction, though he still did not see me. He seemed to be straining to see beyond where I stood. Putting his writing away in the tent, he stood and stretched.

"I am going to take a turn around the camp," he told the sentinels.

Whether he intended to go look for me, I will never know. At that moment, a rider careened into the camp, his horse soaked from crossing the straits. The rider dismounted and saluted the general.

"I've come from the ninth legion. Permission to speak, Sir."

"Granted."

"We were ambushed, sir, on our way to defend Camulodunum," the soldier said, still breathless. "Had to retreat."

"Camulodunum? Who is attacking Camulodunum?"

"The Iceni queen is leading an uprising, sir. The Trinovantes have joined her. That's who ambushed us. We lost more than fifteen hundred infantry and cavalry. My commander Petilius Cerealis sent me to urge you to come at once, or the whole southeast may be lost."

"What about the procurator?" demanded the General. "What is he doing to safeguard Londinium?"

"The procurator?" the soldier made a strange barking laugh. "He's gone. He sent two hundred troops to Camulodunum and slipped away by night. It is believed he has fled to Gaul, sir."

Perhaps no one noticed the general's hands begin to tremble. No one else knew why.

"And Camulodunum?"

"Burnt to the ground. No one left alive."

It didn't seem to occur to either of them that the Romans had just done the same here.

"When I left, the rebels appeared to be heading for Londinium. They may already be there."

In a low, expressionless voice, the general began to curse. He went on cursing until he had run out of words, almost as if the cursing were a formula that must be chanted.

"An advance contingent will be ready to accompany me by daybreak," he said when he was done. "The rest will follow."

As the general rose and began to issue orders, Dwynwyn spoke in my mind one last time.

"I have called your horse. If you go now, you can catch the tide."

I would reach Boudica first. That much I could do for my daughter.

Casting my eyes one last time on my enemy, my lover, I slipped away unseen.

PART FOUR

Air
Born From The Wound

CHAPTER THIRTY-FOUR
AWAY TO THE EAST AGAIN

I CAN HEAR *the sound of a horse's hooves pounding, of someone's heart pounding. Mine. I am on that hard road. I am riding for dear life, but not just my life. I have to bring a message, I have to warn her.*

It may have been a strange mercy, all the foreseeing of events that I was helpless to prevent, for sometimes I felt as though I were still in a dream or a vision, that none of this nightmare was real. Certainly I rode in a trance state or I don't know how I could have managed to keep going without sleep, without food, stopping only to water myself and Macha, to rest for a few stunned moments while she fed on the fortunately ample wild spring grasses. She did not protest the relentless pace. Maybe it made sense to her to flee as far as she could from fire, smoke, and death. Maybe she didn't know that we were heading for the same.

I stayed on the Wyddelian Road all the way to Londinium, a place I had never been before and yet seemed so familiar to one who had frequented pretty much every Roman port in the Mediterranean. Streets of square houses laid on a grid pattern, with shops in the front. There was a market forum, wharves full of warehouses redolent with fish and spice. Walking along the streets, you could hear half a dozen languages and dialects from all over the Empire. Port towns—and Londinium, though small, was up and coming—attracted ambitious immigrants whose own lives had been disrupted by the machinations of the Empire. Everything about Londinium was unremarkable, except the mood: panic.

Business was not going on as usual. From the houses you could hear children crying, frightened by their mothers' fear or short temper. Men argued with each other in the taverns and on the corners. Some people appeared to be packing their belongings into carts. Other people held tight to makeshift weapons, blacksmiths tools, fishing spears, butchers knives. I had dismounted from Macha and was proceeding cautiously, aware that some people might find a horse useful, wishing I had a sword that I could at least brandish. I walked as if I had some purpose, listening to snatches of conversation, hoping I could find someone whose dialect I understood, someone who seemed approachable. Then someone called out to me.

"*Domina*, you with the grey mare."

The woman who hailed me spoke Latin but with a heavy native Celtic accent. She was about Boudica's age, standing in the doorway of a fairly prosperous looking house.

"*Domina,*" I answered in return, coming to stand before her, polite but wary, not wanting to give away my own origins or allegiances.

"You're not from here," she stated.

"No," I agreed, not offering more, and scrambling in my mind for a story I had forgotten I might need.

"You're wearing a soldier's cloak," she informed me.

And it suddenly dawned on me that I was. I had woken on Mona covered with this cloak and had taken it with me without thinking. Underneath was the red robe, bloodstained but still intact.

"Where did you get it?" she demanded.

"From a soldier," I answered, and then thinking more might be required, "He gave it to me to keep me from the cold. I am an old woman, you see."

But she did not see; she had no interest in me. She grabbed my cloak and held onto me, but she was looking past me.

"Are there soldiers near?" she asked. "All our soldiers are gone. The procurator sent them off to fight the rebels. Then he did a bunk. My husband was with them, with the soldiers. He hasn't come back. He's part of the home garrison. But he hasn't come back, no one has come back."

I began to get the picture. This woman was a native who had married a Roman, lived in a Roman town, enjoyed Roman luxuries. Someone Boudica would view as a collaborator, a traitor.

"He told me not to worry. He told me it was just a handful of rebels. He said the retired soldiers in the Colonia would know a thing or two about how to put down an uprising. He said they were just going as backup. But he hasn't come back. I'm here on my own with my children. We heard Camulodunum was burnt to the ground. It can't be true. Is it true?"

She was almost shaking me now, her eyes wide and wild as she teetered between denial and desperation.

"I have heard the same, *domina,*" I said, and then, abandoning caution, I went on. "I am coming from the west. The governor and his troops are a day or less behind me. They are heading for Londinium, because they believe the rebels are, too. It's anyone's guess who will arrive first."

All at once my exhaustion caught up with me; my head swam. I could hear the sound of screaming, the roar of fire. I could smell the smoke.

"*Domina, domina!*" the woman caught me under the arms. "Are you all right?"

"I'm all right," I said, as the vision—or memory—receded. "Just hungry. If you have a bit of bread or an oatcake to spare, I must be on my way."

"*Domina*, I will give you what I can. But where are you going?"

To meet up with the rebel forces, I did not say.

"Away from here," I said aloud. "*Domina*, listen to me. Don't wait for your husband, don't wait for the general. Even if he arrives first, there will be a terrible battle."

"Don't wait for my husband, don't wait for my husband!" she began to wail. "But I have no life without him. I left my tribe to marry my husband, to live among Romans. I have nowhere to go without him."

I looked at the woman and another vision rose, a place to the west riddled with waterways only the priestesses knew how to navigate.

"Go to the southwest," I spoke to her in Celtic, and saw her startle; she had not guessed I was a native. "Take as many women and children as you can. Go to the priestesses of Avalon. Tell them Maeve Rhuad sent you."

Fortified by the bread and cheese the woman gave me, I left the Wyddelian Road and followed a smaller track northeast towards Camulodunum. Before I had gone very far, I heard a sound like distant thunder behind me. Seeing a small hill off to the side of the road, I turned and rode to the top. Below me I could see Londinium sprawling along the river. Racing toward the town on the road I had so recently traveled, their helmets glinting in the sun, rode the cavalry, the advance guard with the general somewhere in the ranks. They had all but closed the lead I'd had on them. Though they'd had to cross the country, they'd arrived in Londinium before Boudica's army. It was scarcely to be credited. I wondered if Boudica had reckoned on such a swift return by the governor. There wasn't a moment to spare. I turned Macha back to the track and urged her to a gallop.

I had no idea how far from Londinium the ruins of Camulodunum lay or where Boudica and her troops would be massing. I wondered if they might have dispersed over a wider area, the better to forage or hide. I fretted that I might not be able to find them.

I need not have worried. I heard them before I saw them. That many human beings in one place, some hundred thousand, sound like surf from a distance. I had heard the sound of huge crowds in Rome, contained and amplified in Circus Maximus. But the sound of this crowd was wilder, vaster. I crested a hill and gazed down at a camp, if you could call it that, spreading out for miles in the open and under the trees. Campfires like a field of stars, pipes playing, drums tapping out a rhythm. People had erected makeshift tents and shelters. They'd brought carts and chariots, cattle and chickens. I heard children shrieking, babies wailing. This wasn't some disciplined troop of warriors. This was the *combrogos* on the move, whole villages, whole tribes, a gathering far greater than any festival crowd on Mona. No wonder they hadn't gotten to Londinium yet. What must it take to move a mass of people like that? And how in the three worlds would I find Boudica in this roiling human sea?

I soon discovered that Boudica's camp was not without organization. As I rode toward it in the dusky half light, Macha suddenly balked. She saw before I did the six men who jumped out at us, blocking our way with spears. Before I knew what was happening, I was unhorsed, bound and gagged. With a spear at my back and armed men on either side, I was led (or jerked along) by another warrior who held the rope in one hand, his shield in the other.

Thus I entered the camp of Queen Boudica.

As I lay, still trussed, against the trunk of a large tree in the company of a half dozen others who shared my accommodations, I couldn't help but contrast this reception with the one I had received at the Roman fort. Of course, there an impressive bit of shape-shifting had secured my entrée to the general's quarters. Now I was too tired to shape-shift even if it would have done any good. Maybe it wouldn't be a bad idea to get some rest before Queen Boudica's tour of inspection when she would decide whether I would be "interrogated, pounded into the pit, or offered as a sacrifice." I wondered briefly how the commander of such a massive army could have time to concern herself with the fate of a few captives, but I supposed the goddess (Andraste in this case) was in the details.

"This one." Someone nudged my bound feet, interrupting a blissful dreamless sleep. "Untie her and bring her to my tent. I will return there later."

It felt like torture to become conscious again. Every bone, every muscle, every tendon protested. I had to be half-carried, half-dragged by a warrior on either side of me.

"Where are you taking me? Where's my horse?" I demanded, remembering that I'd been forcibly parted from Macha.

"Don't worry about the old mare," said one man. "She'll be put to good use. Now you, you're the lucky one, or maybe not. The queen wants to interrogate you. Privately."

And she could have just pounded me into the pit? How many angry daughters get that chance?

I closed my eyes again and stumbled along with the men until I was roused by shrieking followed by ululation. Bele and Alyssa sprang forward and scooped me into their embrace.

"Oh, Mother of Sarah, Mother of Sarah," they laughed and wept. "We thought we'd never see you again."

"You know this woman?" asked one of the warriors.

"Of course we do!" said Alyssa. "She's the queen's—"

"Shh!" I hissed, for it wasn't clear to me that Boudica wanted the connection known.

"Well, anyway, she's the mother of our friend, Sarah."

"Sarah?" repeated the warrior. "You mean the dark-faced one, the healer woman?"

I felt a shock at hearing the title the Galatians had given me, the name I'd been called by all during Sarah's childhood. I looked in some confusion to Bele and Alyssa.

"That's right," confirmed Bele. "Our Sarah's become a famous healer. She's on her rounds now, hardly ever rests, that one."

So in the midst of war, Sarah was claiming her gift. As a little girl, she had brought home wounded animals and birds. When a man, near dead, was delivered to our door, she had helped me tend him, just before everything had gone so horribly wrong. She had been the one to restore his sight. Since then, so far as I knew, she had never acknowledged her powers as a healer.

"I'll attest to that," said the man. "She healed a break in my shield arm with her touch alone. If you are her mother, I beg your pardon for any rough handling. I'll see to it that your horse is fed and watered and I'll bring her to you here."

"Not only is she the mother of the healer woman," Bele put in. "She is a famous healer herself. But before we put her to work, she needs some healing. She's practically fainting on her feet."

"We'll leave her in your care, and if I see your daughter, I'll send her to you."

"Thank you," I managed to say to the warriors, and then I turned to Bele and Alyssa again. "Lithben? Gwen?"

"Come inside the tent, Mother of Sarah," urged Bele. "Come see for yourself."

Alyssa lifted the flap and held her torch so I could see my granddaughters spooned together under a plaid blanket, Gwen's arms wrapped around her younger sister.

"Mother of god," I whispered, meaning Isis, meaning Miriam, meaning all of us. "Mother of goddess."

I knelt beside them, my hand hovering over their cheeks, not wanting to wake them. Then I felt someone touch my cheek.

"I knew you'd come back, Grandmother," murmured Lithben. "Don't go again."

"No," I said. "I won't leave you again, *cariad*."

Alyssa came in with a cup of something warm. It felt like drinking the fire of the stars.

"It's one of Sarah's cure-alls," said Alyssa. "Don't wait up for her. Rest now."

I lay down, holding Lithben's hands in mine. When I woke again, Sarah's arms were around me, her warm breath on the back of my neck. By the pre-dawn light creeping in under the door, I saw that Boudica slept on the other side of Gwen. Near the flap, Alyssa and Bele snatched some rest. I took a moment to savor this fleeting safety, this sweetness.

The moment passed. Boudica opened her eyes, caught mine, and gestured silently: Outside.

CHAPTER THIRTY-FIVE
REPORTING

BEFORE THE SKY lightens and takes on color there is a long, seemingly endless time when the world is cold and grey, and the birds still have their heads tucked under their wings. Boudica's face was like that, too, still but cold, quiet but without peace. We sat for a while like two boulders who had tumbled to a precarious halt after some cataclysmic event.

"Are you well?" she asked, not out of politeness but as a point of necessary information.

To my surprise I realized that I was. But then I had slept in the arms of the healer woman.

"Yes," I said. "And you—"

I stopped myself. Of course she wasn't all right.

"Oh, Boudica," was all I could say.

"So you know," she said. "Who told you?"

"No one told me. I had dreams. I saw."

"You saw the rapes," she stated, her voice without affect. "You saw the whipping."

"Yes," I answered.

"Is that why you came back?" she asked after a moment.

She didn't know what had happened on Mona. Of course she didn't. No one could have reached her before me.

"I never expected to come back," I told her. "I expected to be killed in battle on Mona."

"Tell me," she said. "Tell me everything."

So I did, omitting only my visit to the fort en route. I told her of the vision in the well of eels and the plan to evacuate enough druids to preserve their knowledge. I described the battle itself, leaving out my single combat with the general. Boudica listened silently. Although her tears fell unchecked, it would be hard to say she wept. Her face didn't move; she scarcely blinked.

"The groves are gone?" she said when I paused. "The great teaching groves of Mona are gone? The druids exiled or slain?"

Her voice broke, the first sign of emotion she had showed apart from the soundless tears. Whatever happiness she had known had been in those groves among the druids. At their bidding, she had sacrificed that happiness. And now the place she had hallowed for so long was destroyed.

"They shall be avenged," she declared. "When I am done there will not be one Roman town or fort left in Pretannia. Not one Roman will remain. I will soak the land with their blood. Andraste will feast on their flesh."

An image rose of the bodies piled on the beach, the sound of the flies, the stink. I covered my mouth with my hand and forced my rising gorge back down.

"Listen, Boudica, I must tell you the rest," I said urgently. "Before I left, a messenger reached the general with news of your uprising. He left one tide behind me. He's in Londinium now."

"Why didn't you tell me last night!"

She rose to her feet so fast it was as if she dove into the sky, her hair ignited by the sun's first rays. She towered over me, even when I managed to stand.

"I was bound and gagged, if you recall."

"Never mind that," she brushed away her reproaches, my excuses. "How many men does he have with him?"

"It's an advance contingent," I said. "All cavalry. Five hundred maybe."

Boudica smiled for the first time that day. It was not a pretty sight.

"We are a hundred thousand. Londinium is doomed and your general along with it."

My general? My blood felt cold and black as sludge on a river bottom. Why would she call him that?

"By the way, where did you get that cloak?"

I decided to tell the truth.

"I tried to kill the Roman general."

"And for that he gave you his cloak," she stated rather than asked, her unspoken suspicion eloquent.

"Apparently he did. After he felled me."

She looked at me long and hard.

"And Dwynwyn gave me this garment."

I unfastened the cloak and let it fall to the ground. I stood before Boudica in the red robe streaked with the darker red of dried blood. The bloodstained necklace of skulls gleamed fiercely. I held Boudica's gaze, until she nodded almost imperceptibly.

"Sarah, Bele, Alyssa!" She turned and lifted the tent flap. "Help me gather the chieftains for a council. We march to Londinium today."

There was only time for a brief embrace before Sarah dashed off on Boudica's errand. But it was a fierce embrace, and I sensed something had changed in Sarah. Something was troubling her. Before I let her go, I searched her eyes, which still held their strange, beautiful light, but it felt as though she had withdrawn to some place darker, deeper.

"We'll talk later," she said and hurried away.

I was left with my granddaughters. Gwen savagely stirred the embers under a cook pot and Lithben came to stand next to me, slipping her hand into mine.

"Gwen's angry," she confided.

I could see that by the angle of her back, the vehemence of her movements.

"Don't speak for me, Lithben," snapped Gwen.

Then she fetched a bowl and heaped it with stirabout.

"Here," she turned and handed it to me, "Grandmother."

I sensed the title was a deliberate concession on her part. An offering. She wanted something from me.

"Thank you, Gwen," was all I said.

She would not want me to ask how she was or to offer sympathy. So I sat down cross-legged on the ground and ate silently. Lithben joined me, sitting so that our knees touched, and finally Gwen sat, too, pulling up bits of whatever vegetation was untrammeled.

"I should be at that council," Gwen finally spoke. "I am queen of the Iceni."

Despite all that happened, not much had changed between mother and daughter.

"I remember your father's will." I had been there when the disastrous document was drawn up. "And I know how the Romans have violated it."

How you have been violated, I did not say, but it was as close as I could get.

"That's why we're fighting," Lithben put in. "When the warriors came and saw what had happened to us, they wanted to fight the Romans, all the tribes together. Mother says that what happened to us was a sacrifice for the *combrogos*. A blood sacrifice," she added softly, uncertainly, as if repeating her lines without fully understanding what they meant.

"That is one of her speeches," said Gwen. "Whenever the chieftains start quarreling among themselves, she trumps them with us, the desecrated virgins, and herself the outraged mother."

I didn't have to close my eyes to remember that nightmare. The sound tearing from Boudica's body when she saw her daughters pinned to the ground.

"She loves you, Gwen," I said. "She fought for you like the goddess herself."

"The goddess," repeated Lithben. "The goddess Andraste."

"Oh yes," Gwen said bitterly. "She loves us. But she loves her cause more. She always has."

I did not argue with her. It was probably true. Anyway, Gwen needed to say it. She needed to lance her wounds.

"My father loved me, really loved me," she turned to look at me. "You could see that, couldn't you, Grandmother."

"Plain as the sun in a cloudless sky," I agreed.

And the day was shaping up to be just like that. A soft summer day, with a breeze stirring the leaves and the grasses, and yet there was something missing. I listened for a moment beyond that racket of the camp waking up. No songbirds. Too many humans here, too much human sound and strife and stench.

"But he was wrong," she said softly as if it was still hard for her to say it. "My father was wrong to trust the Romans. They dishonored him as much as they did us. More. I tried to tell her that. I tried to tell her that I want to avenge him, but she won't listen."

"Gwen wants to fight," Lithben explained. "Mother says: no, stay with the women and children, protect the women and children. You're a woman, too, Mother, says Gwen. Why don't you stay with them? I'm the queen, says mother–"

"And so am I!" Gwen cut her off. "And so are you, Lithben."

"I don't want to fight," Lithben whispered, ashamed. "I never did."

Gwen went and knelt down beside her little sister and put her arms around her. However angry she was with Boudica, towards Lithben she could be tender.

"You don't have to fight, Lithben. I will fight for both of us."

Lithben clung to her sister.

"It's all right, Lithben. You have Grandmother now."

I wasn't sure I liked where this was going.

"It's all right," Lithben repeated, brightening. "I have Grandmother now."

"Grandmother," Gwen stood. "I am going to join in the council, whether my mother wants me there or not. Lithben, you and Grandmother can take down the tent and load the cart."

She turned and strode away, her gait determined like her mother's.

"Gwen," I called after her.

She did me the courtesy of turning back.

"When you are in council, listen carefully to what is said and not said. When you speak, speak wisely, without heat or haste. Like a true queen."

She gave me a rare smile. My heart caught at the sight.

* * *

"You put her up to it!" Boudica accused.

She had yanked my arm, none too gently, and drawn me aside while the others finished breaking camp.

"You must have! She never would have dared interrupt a council meeting like that if you hadn't."

"I am afraid she would and did," I said as calmly as I could. "Gwen takes after you, far more than she takes after her father. Surely you can see that? If I had anything to do with it, it's simply that Gwen felt she could leave Lithben with me. She is very protective of her sister."

Boudica appeared to consider what I said, her feathers slowly unruffling.

"I have to protect them both," she said. "Surely you understand that."

Oh, I surely did, and I also understood better than Boudica how easy, maybe inevitable, it was to fail to protect the ones you loved best.

"Gwen thinks I am disrespecting her father's will. She thinks I want to be queen myself. She's dead wrong. I want to make sure there is a free people for her to rule, land where she can be sovereign. Unless we drive the Romans out, there won't be. Unless we drive the Romans out, we'll all be dead, or worse, slaves."

I stayed silent. It is hard to answer someone who is giving her stump speech.

"And I want her to survive. I can't let her go into battle. She has nowhere near enough experience, and even if she did, she could be killed. If anyone knew who she was, she'd be a target. Make her understand. She'll listen to you."

It was not a good idea, I knew that, not a good idea at all to be a go-between at Boudica's behest. To be her mouthpiece, her bull horn. But how could I say no? Hadn't I pleaded with Ma in a similar way when Sarah was young? And hadn't she told me repeatedly to let Sarah be, not to interfere with her fate?

"I will say whatever I can," I conceded. "But you must speak to her first. You must ask her to sacrifice her longing to fight for the sake of the *combrogos,* just as you had to sacrifice your longing to be a *brehon*. Tell her the best way for her to avenge her father is to live to fulfill his will for her to be queen. Beg her to let you sacrifice your life for her life. Go to her with your heart in your hand. Do it now."

Boudica gave me a strange look. I could not tell if she was seeing me or seeing through me to some past or future just out of her grasp.

"I will ask her to ride with me today," Boudica said. "Then we will see."

CHAPTER THIRTY-SIX
DAUGHTER OF ESUS

AN ARMY OF THAT SIZE (no one ever agreed exactly how large it was, let's say one hundred thousand warriors with families in tow) moves over the land like an unnatural disaster, a human glacier or lava flow, an infestation. The land isn't made to bear such movement. It trembles under the fall of so many feet, turns to mud or clouds of dust, depending. Streams get fouled, crops get consumed or trampled, cattle get rustled and eaten. It is a slow, inexorable business. This army was still fresh, flush from victory and laden with food and loot, so morale, so to speak, was good. Direction, target, and strategy were not in question.

Lithben and I stayed together, both of us riding and keeping pace, more or less, with Boudica's entourage. Every now and then I caught sight of Boudica and Gwen riding together in a battle chariot. Sarah, Alyssa, and Bele checked on Lithben and me now and then, but seemed busy riding up and down the ranks as if they were the herd dogs of the army. I still had not had a chance to speak with Sarah alone or at any length. I began to wonder if she were avoiding me for some reason. But an army on the move is scarcely the right time or place for an intimate talk.

My contingent arrived around sunset at the base of the hill I had climbed only yesterday. On the other side lay Londinium. While the rest of the army was arriving, small parties of scouts would go out to assess the town's defenses and the best points for a dawn attack. Sarah, Bele, and Alyssa were among the scouts, and Gwen stayed in council with her mother. Lithben and I, the too young and too old, were left to ourselves and went to bed early, worn out as much from the surrounding tension and anticipation as from the day's march.

"Mother," Sarah's voice was so soft I thought it was part of my dream. "Mother, I need you."

Sarah needing me. It must be a dream. She hadn't cried for me in the night since she was a little girl.

I felt a hand hovering over me, not quite touching, a hand full of heat and hesitance.

"Sarah." I woke up all the way. "I'm here. What is it?"

"Will you come apart with me?" she asked. "Away from the others."

Easier said than done when you are camping with an army. But we wove our way through tents, over people sleeping on the ground, past sentries who recognized Sarah, around the base of the hill to the other side where in the distance we could see the torches of the unfortified port town and the river dark beyond it.

Sarah and I sat down together in a soon-to-be trampled field, our knees just touching. I waited for a cue from her.

"Why did my father turn away?" she asked. "When the people wanted to make him king? When the people wanted to fight for him?"

Because it wasn't his way. He wasn't a warrior. He did not want a kingdom, not that kind of kingdom. All those answers might be true, but I did not give any of them. He had not given any of them. He had never explained. Just turned away, as Sarah had put it, more simply, more eloquently.

"Dear child," I said at last, for she was my child, and his child. "I don't know. You can ask him. Maybe he will tell you himself."

She shook her head.

"I already know."

"What do you know, *cariad*, Colomen Du?"

I waited again and at last she spoke.

"He did not want to do what I have done."

Again I waited.

"Camulodunum," she said. "Do you know what happened there?"

"I heard it has been burned to the ground. I heard there is no one left alive."

I spoke carefully, neutrally.

"No one left alive," she repeated. "No one left alive."

I reached for her hand, but she shook me off.

"We killed the soldiers first," she went on in a tight voice. "There weren't very many of them. There were so many of us. A few of us died, but there were so many more. We kept coming and coming and coming. It was so loud, so loud. Everyone was screaming. The people were screaming. They were stupid, so stupid. But what else could they do? The ones who weren't slaughtered on the spot ran to their big Roman temple and bolted the door. Why did they think they would be safe there? Why? Did they think we would fear their Roman gods?"

She stopped for breath, anguish and anger vying together, tearing at her throat.

"They rounded themselves up for us. It wasn't hard. It was so not hard. We destroyed the roof. We rained down on them, thousands of us. We butchered them, all of them, where they stood—men, women, children. It happened so fast, so fast. And yet it seemed like it went on forever, that there had only ever been this screaming, this fear, this grim hacking away at people as if they were nothing, brush to be cleared, corn to be scythed. We left them drowning in their own blood, any who still breathed, and any who did not die face down in the blood bath, died in the fire. We torched the temple. We torched the town."

She stopped again. I could hear her teeth grinding. I could feel the heat coming off her in waves as she sweated even in the chill night.

"There was no one left alive. I was there. I don't even know what I did, how many I killed. But I was there. I was part of it."

"Sarah," all I could do was say her name. "Sarah."

I wanted to gather her in my arms, cradle her like a baby. She was my child, no matter what she had done. Whatever she had done, I was part of it. I had done it, too. But I sensed she could not bear to be touched. She held herself stiff and apart. She did not want comfort, could not allow herself to receive it.

"You tried to tell us so many times that it wasn't simple," she spoke again, "but after what they did to Gwen and Lithben, for a while everything did seem simple, pure and simple. I wanted revenge, too. I wanted to drive every last Roman out of the Holy Isles. I thought I knew what I was doing. When I was a pirate, I fought battles. I've even killed armed men before. I thought I was a proven warrior with a chance to fight for a just cause."

At last I took her hand. She did not seem to notice. But when the fire of the stars began to flow from my hand into hers, it was met with a faint answering fire.

"The people in that temple, they were just people," she spoke more softly. "I could say that they are part of a corrupt occupation, and they are. I could say that they've benefited from oppression, and they have. That's what Boudica did say when I went to her afterwards. To her they are not innocent. To her they are not even human. In her mind every one of them raped her daughters. But when I see what we did in that temple happening over and over and over in my mind, all I know is their flesh was just flesh. Their fear was just fear, and the mothers...and the mothers shielding their children with their bodies were just...."

A gasp tore from her body as if she were being ripped open. I could feel it in my own body, and for a moment I couldn't breathe. It felt like the sickly stillness before a terrible storm. Then the storm broke, her sobs broke one after another, huge waves battering a shore. Finally she let me hold her. That much at least I could do for her, be the rocks to her wild sea of grief.

At last she quieted. For a moment it even seemed she slept, her head heavy on my breast like a baby's, her breathing soft and deep. Then she startled and drew apart from me.

"Tomorrow," she said. "It's going to happen all over again tomorrow."

"Maybe not," I ventured. "Not the way it did in Camulodunum. The Roman governor is there. The town will be defended. It will be a fight, not just slaughter."

As soon as I spoke, I realized I did not believe my own words. Nothing was tidy about this or any war. No odds were even. The Romans had slaughtered everyone in sight on Mona. And Boudica fully expected to overwhelm the general's inferior numbers and do the same in Londinium.

"But didn't you know? He's not there!" Sarah said. "I was with the scouts; there is no sign of any troops. The governor has abandoned the town."

"Are you sure?" I asked her. "Could it be a trick? Could the troops be hiding somewhere planning an ambush?"

"I don't think so. Ambush isn't a Roman strong suit. We covered a pretty wide area to make sure. My job was to infiltrate the town, because I'm dark and don't look or speak like a native. From what I heard, the general tried to evacuate. He knew he couldn't defend the town. The only people left are too infirm to escape or else they are wealthy or stubborn, determined not to lose all they've invested in the port. They were outraged that the general beat a retreat. They have some crazy idea that they will be able to mount a civilian defense."

She hesitated. I sensed there was more.

"I tried to warn them, Mother. Some of them listened. Some didn't. If Boudica knew I had tried to help her enemies, she would believe I had betrayed her. She might even execute me."

I took her hand again.

"If you are a traitor, then I am, too," I told her. "I did the same thing when I stopped in Londinium on the way to find Boudica's camp."

"Perhaps we should confess," Sarah laughed. "Maybe she would execute us together."

Her laughter was bitter and short-lived. Part of her meant it. Part of her wanted any out she could find.

"And Boudica is determined to attack, even though the town is almost deserted?"

"We argued about it in council," Sarah answered. "I said we should pursue the general, ambush his troops the way the Trinovantes did the Ninth Legion. That's the way the *combrogos* have always fought best. Boudica insists we've grown too big to fight that way. She says we've never had the advantage of superior numbers before. We've got to make a clean sweep, she says, wipe out all their centers of power. She says we are unbeatable now. No one and nothing can stand against us."

She paused again. Half a dozen reasonable and unreasonable questions rose in me and died. I did not want to suggest that Sarah could have done more, said more, that she could have turned this tide. As if she had heard me anyway, she went on.

"When she speaks, Mother, everyone comes under her sway. It's like listening to some huge force, a wind, an avalanche. Or maybe it's more that the *combrogos* have become that force, and she's the one who knows how to ride it. She's got the reins and it doesn't matter who or what gets trampled. Or maybe it's all out of control and she's simply holding on for dear life. She's got to go. She can't stop now. It can't stop now. Oh, Mother. Oh, Mother, what am I to do? What can I do?"

She put her head in my lap and curled into a tight ball, as if she wished she could go back into the womb, unmake this life that had taken such a devastating turn. As I held her, I felt the fire of the stars, not just in my hands but all around us, rocking us on a sea, golden as her eyes. What did it matter if we were two exiles without sail or oar?

"Esus's daughter, healer woman," I spoke at last. "You will know what to do. For this you were born. For this you came into the world."

She sat up and looked at me. I could not see her eyes in the darkness, but I could feel them.

"I am your daughter, too," she said. "You are the one who gave up your life to protect me, you are the one who searched for me without ceasing when I ran away, who came to my rescue. Look how I have repaid you. You could be living peacefully in your cave. I could be living peacefully by the sea, maybe giving you grandchildren to come and visit. Instead here we are in the midst of this horror that I am part of. How can you love me? How can you forgive me? How can you call me my father's daughter?"

She sounded almost angry now. And I wondered if I was failing her again. Did she want me to judge her, condemn her? I couldn't. I couldn't. I thought of reasoning with her, of reassuring her that she'd been right. I needed to find Boudica. She had given me Lithben and Gwen, grandchildren I never would have known. Then in this dark night, in the roiling uncertainty, a memory rose of Sarah's father in the harsh light of the Temple courtyard, scrawling with his finger in the dust, writing our names in *ogham*. Then he spoke:

"Let the one among you who is guiltless cast the first stone."

"Who among us is guiltless?" I said out loud.

Sarah didn't answer. I went on speaking the words her father had spoken to me, so long ago.

"Be free from sin. Be free."

CHAPTER THIRTY-SEVEN
ANDRASTE

WHAT HAPPENED in Londinium cannot be described as a battle. The town was even less defended than Camulodunum. Boudica unleashed her army and before noon there was little left but rubble and corpses burning in the town where they once lived. The sky was black with smoke, and a hot, foul wind blew it all the way to where we noncombatants waited in our moveable camp. The mood among the women, children, and old people had shifted. The novelty of being on the march was wearing off. Children fretted, mothers spoke sharply to them. Even though victory was assured, waiting was hard. Gwen paced incessantly, and Lithben sat listlessly, looking down into her lap.

"She should have let me fight," Gwen declared again, as she had about a hundred times that morning. "There was no real danger, no danger to us."

"There is always danger in battle, Gwen," I said wearily.

"Both *your* daughters are fighting," she said. "Sarah is not all that much older than me."

At Sarah's name, sudden tears welled. She had gone into the town with only her dagger. I had pleaded with her to stay with us. But she refused. She said she knew now what she had to do, what she was born to do. She would heal whomever she could heal. She would ease the death of anyone mortally wounded. *Cariad*, I prayed silently to her father, be with your daughter.

"Stop it, Gwen," Lithben looked up. "You're making Grandmother cry."

Gwen stopped her pacing and came to sit next to me.

"I'm sorry, Grandmother," she said stiffly.

"I know it's hard to wait."

"I should be good at it by now," said Gwen. "It's all I've ever done."

I took Gwen's hand, remembering how patiently she had cared for her father.

"You will make a good queen, Gwen." I said.

"I don't want to be queen," announced Lithben. "I just want to go home."

So do I, I thought, but I had no idea where home might be.

The warriors began to return, laden with loot, ready to drink and feast and brag into the night. Sarah must still be tending to the wounded. I wished I could go find her and help her, but I didn't want to leave Lithben or drag her into the midst of the carnage. Then Bele came rushing toward us.

"Sarah needs you to come right away," she called out to me.

I was already on my feet, Lithben holding tightly to my hand.

"No," Bele shook her head vehemently. "You must come alone."

"You said you wouldn't leave me, Grandmother, you *said*."

I looked at Bele questioningly. She wrung her hands.

"I can't explain," she said. "Just come."

"Lithben," I turned to the girl and held her close. "I am just going to see what Sarah wants. I will come back as soon as I can. Stay with Gwen. You'll be all right."

"I don't see why either of us should stay," objected Gwen, angrily. "There is no danger now. The battle is over. I am not a child. What's going on, Bele? Has something happened to my mother? Is she wounded? I need to know."

Again Bele seemed at a loss for words.

"Mother of Sarah, please just come. I am sorry, Gwen. I can't explain."

"I am sorry, too, Gwen," I said. "Sarah must have a reason. Please stay with Lithben."

Without waiting to hear whether Gwen conceded, I went off with the increasingly agitated Bele.

"It's Boudica. She's about to do something terrible," Bele told me in a low voice as soon as we were out of earshot of Gwen and Lithben. "Sarah can't get through to her. Maybe you can."

A cold, heavy doubt I'd carried for so long that I had forgotten its existence rose from the pit of my stomach into my throat. It tasted of terror. My legs began to shake as I followed Bele out of the camp, skirting the smoldering town and heading into a wood so thick that twilight had already come. At length we came to a small clearing where Boudica, spear in hand, and a dozen or so chieftains stood around a beam balanced between two oak trees. From this beam, suspended by their wrists, nine women hung, stripped naked.

At first I thought they were dead, but then one of the women moaned. I grabbed hold of Bele to keep my knees from buckling under me. Sarah, standing on the edge of the circle, caught sight of me and came to take my other arm. Between them, I managed to walk forward until I was face to face with Boudica.

Her face was empty as a stone, emptier. The face of a stone would have more expression. Empty as a cloudless sky at dawn but without hope. Empty as a pool of still water, but without any light or reflection. Her silence seemed as though it had begun before time and would go on forever, as though it could swallow whole worlds. I felt helpless before her, helpless to reach her, helpless to know her.

"Have you come to witness the sacrifice?" she asked blandly, as if she were saying something as perfunctory as will you be joining us for dinner?

"Sacrifice?" I managed to croak. My mouth and throat felt parched as the Judean hills at noon.

"Sacrifice," she repeated. "To our goddess, Andraste. Did I not promise she would feast on Roman flesh? Drink Roman blood? She has fought hard for her children, for the *combrogos*. She is hungry. She must be fed. And revenge is the sweetest food, her favorite food."

I was distantly aware of the warriors murmuring among themselves and Sarah and Bele standing near me. The creak of tree branches echoed the groans and sobs of the hanging women. But my focus on Boudica and hers on me was so intense it was as if someone had drawn an invisible circle around us. Inside it we were alone.

"I don't know Andraste," I stated. "I am a priestess of Isis. She prefers honey, wine, songs, beautiful robes."

"Isis," Boudica said, the first note of expression sounding in her voice: contempt. "She is a whore. She has no people of her own. Even Romans worship her. We burned her temple in Londinium today. She has no power here. You must put aside your foreign past, daughter of Lovernios."

She identified me for the first time. Why had she chosen to call me daughter instead of mother, daughter of the man who had begotten us both?

"You have seen the burning groves of Mona," Boudica went on. "You have waded through the corpses of the druids. If you do not know Andraste, surely you know the Morrigan."

The triple goddess of war, death, and slaughter who sometimes took the form of a carrion crow.

"I know the Morrigan. She feeds on the flesh of warriors slain in honorable battle, not on helpless captives," I asserted, though I did not in fact know that her taste was so discriminating. "Andraste has been well served already. She does not need the blood of these women. Hold them hostage. But do not torture them."

Boudica stared at me, and the hairs stood up on the back of my neck. She looked so like her father, our father.

"Do not dare to speak for Andraste. By your own confession, you do not know her. Your time among the Romans has made you soft, decadent, like that Roman dog Catus Decianus who fled with his tail between his legs. But the Roman wolf is not soft when it comes to what it wants, our land, our wealth, our children, our very *lives*. The Roman wolf showed no mercy when my daughters cried out. I will show no mercy now."

How could I hope to sway an outraged mother? How could any revenge ever be enough for her? Two leveled towns, thousands dead hadn't appeased her.

"It is true," I said. "The Romans show no mercy to their enemies. I know that as well as you, as well as anyone. They tortured and killed Sarah's father before my eyes, before his mother's eyes. I say to you now what he said to the *combrogos* long ago when he warned that one day Mona would burn: "*Rome is not a place. Rome is not an army. Rome is cruelty and idolatry and slavery. Wherever these flourish, Rome is in your midst.*"

I paused, praying for Esus's words to find their mark at last, here in this dark grove on the other side of the Holy Isles, here in Boudica's wounded heart.

"Let's banish Rome from our midst, not just Romans," I went on. "We are the *combrogos*. We are the victorious today, strong enough to show mercy."

"Mercy," she repeated, as if she were tasting the word, not sure it was fit to swallow. "Mercy. You preach to me about mercy, Lovernios' daughter? The mercy of stealing a sacrifice meant for the gods, the mercy of drowning your own father in a tidal bore. The mercy of leaving your child to be raised by strangers and only returning when it suited you."

I wanted to protest again that I hadn't left her willingly, but I could not deny the second half of the charge, so I let it stand.

"And tell me," she took a step closer to me, and I had all I could do not to back away from her, "when you visited the Roman governor on the way to Mona was that an act of mercy, too?"

I felt hot all over, and then cold. My heart beat like the wings of a wounded bird. It did not help that I could hear Sarah's sharp indrawn breath.

"I had you followed," she said bluntly. "Did you think I wouldn't?"

"I thought it was the Romans who set a tail on me."

"Oh, they had you followed, too, no doubt. The *combrogos* are just better at not being seen. No one trusts a whore."

I felt Sarah stiffen at the epithet, even though she had used it once herself. Neither of them understood that instead of shaming me, the word restored me to myself—the self who had survived slavery to become a priestess and healer, the self who welcomed the god-bearing stranger at Temple Magdalen. The self who embodied the goddess.

"I went to the governor to tell him of the procurator's outrages against the *combrogos*." I had nothing to lose by telling the truth and no power to make her believe it. "I begged the governor to pull rank and restrain him."

"Why would the governor even have agreed to see you, let alone listen to you?" Boudica asked shrewdly. "Who are you to him?"

I took a deep breath. "I was his lover."

"Was." The word wavered between a question and a statement.

"Was," I repeated, feeling that I was on trial for the crime of being myself. The outcome would determine not my fate alone, but the fate of the women who swayed in the still air. "On Mona I tried to kill him."

"So you told me. But you failed. And your lover showed you mercy. Mercy." She spat the word at my feet. "His mistake. It will not be mine."

The look she gave me I had seen on only one other person's face. For a moment I thought she intended to kill me herself. It didn't matter why. I almost didn't care. I almost wished she would, if it would ease the pain, quench the rage that drove her. I searched her face, and one last time I tried to see the child I'd held so briefly to my breast.

"Boudica," I whispered now as I had whispered then. Victorious one, I had named her, but this was not victory; this was the beginning of some bitter end. "Boudica, not this way. Not this way, Boudica."

Then without warning Boudica pushed me so forcefully that I fell. Sarah was instantly at my side, helping me up, while Boudica turned to her victims.

"Andraste!" her voice erupted from her body into the deepening twilight. "Andraste! Andraste!"

The warriors took up the chant. At a signal from Boudica, two men sprang forward and held apart the legs of the first woman. Boudica carefully, almost lovingly, positioned her spear in the lips of the woman's vulva.

"To you, Andraste, I dedicate this revenge for the rape of my daughters, for the rape of the land, for the rape of the *combrogos*."

And she thrust her spear straight up and into the woman until it all but disappeared, like the woman's death cry into a sudden awful stillness broken only by the sound of someone screaming at the edge of the clearing.

Lithben. Oh my goddess. Lithben.

Gwen must have followed us and dragged her sister with her. I launched myself at Boudica, only to be restrained by two warriors.

"You will watch," Boudica rounded on me. "You will witness. You will learn what it means to be a real mother. You will learn what it means to sacrifice for the *combrogos*."

While Boudica's back was turned, Sarah seized her moment. Before anyone could stop her, she slit the rest of the women's throats quickly, painlessly. When Boudica returned to her work, she did not seem to notice the blood or did not care if she did. Her victims were still warm. Over and over she thrust her spear into the now silent bodies.

When she was done, she turned toward us again, her face in the waning light as drained of color as the sky, her hands dark with blood. She did not look triumphant, only tired, so tired. I thought of my last glimpse of the general as he sat alone outside his tent, recording the day's carnage.

"Before you throw the bodies into the pit," she addressed her warriors. "Cut off their left breasts. Stuff them into their mouths and sew them fast. Thus will Rome choke even as it feeds on itself. Our victory is ensured! We will hold council again in the morning. I must see to my daughters now."

But before Boudica could reach them, Lithben slipped Gwen's grasp and fled.

CHAPTER THIRTY-EIGHT
LOAVES AND FISHES

THIS STORY IS not the one I wanted to be telling.

There's an understatement, you say. But understand. It is not that I have never known suffering. My story, like everyone's, is shot through with sorrow—arrows of it, streams of it, a dark defining pattern in this unfinished, unraveling weaving. But I was married to the meaning-maker, the redeemer. I raised him, however briefly and poignantly, from the dead. I triumphed with him. I stood with him under the tree of life. Perhaps I stand there still.

Yet I am also here with my daughter by incest and rape, who has just raped and killed nine women with her spear in front of her own daughters, a daughter who hates me as much as our father did, a daughter I have failed to reach, a daughter who will destroy whatever is in her path. Meanwhile my other daughter atones in whatever way she can for evil she never meant to do, and my granddaughters suffer helplessly, at the mercy of their mother's fate. Where is redemption here, for her, for me, for any of us? Without it, how can I bear to tell this story?

When we arrived back at our tent, Lithben was nowhere to be found. It was night now, and the drunken victory party of thousands was in full swing. A warrior camp that stretched over more than a mile of countryside was no place for a young girl to wonder alone, dazed and terrified. We had to find her. Sarah, Alyssa, Bele, Gwen and I conferred about how best to comb the territory, but Boudica was eerily calm.

"Why are you all making such a fuss?" she wondered. "She can't have gone far. She'll find her way back."

The rest of us exchanged glances, silently casting lots for who would speak. When it came to confronting Boudica, I always seemed to win, perhaps because I had nothing to lose.

"She's had a terrible shock," I said bluntly. "We can't be sure what she'll do. The sooner we find her the better."

"A shock?" Boudica frowned. "I don't know what you mean."

"Mother," Gwen stepped up. "It is my fault. Grandmother told me to stay with Lithben here, but I didn't want to be left behind again. I took Lithben and followed Grandmother to the grove. We were both there. We saw."

"Saw what?" Boudica's voice was not cold exactly, but closed, stiff, like a door rusted on its hinges.

"We saw what you did to those women. We saw you kill them."

By the firelight, I could see that Gwen was trembling, but she stood her ground. She had become a queen in her own right.

"Those were not women, Gwen. They were Roman whores," Boudica said, her voice bizarrely mild. "And I did not kill them. I sacrificed them, to Andraste. I avenged you, you and Lithben. Now you are virgins again. Now you will be queens. Don't you see? Everything is all right now."

"But Lithben is too young to understand, Mother. She was frightened."

Boudica seemed to consider for a moment

"She always was more timid than you," she said at length. "But she's a good girl. She's always stayed close to me. She's here now. We just can't see her. I never had to worry about where she was. She never went away from me, not like you, Gwen. You always hated me. You only wanted your father. But now you see that he was wrong, now you've come back to me. You won't leave me again. Now you know, everything I've ever done I did for you, for you and for Lithben."

Boudica spoke in a childlike voice that contrasted oddly with her deep pitch. She did not look at any of us but gazed intently into her lap as she sat cross-legged on the ground. It was hard to imagine that she was the same woman who had just split nine women end to end—except for the blood staining her hands and arms up to her elbows.

"You can come out now, Lithben," coaxed Boudica. "Come out, come out wherever you are. I'll sing you to sleep."

And she began to croon, a tuneless tune with words I could not catch.

Gwen turned to me, clearly shaken by her mother's strange behavior.

"I think I should stay with her," she said in a low voice. "The rest of you, go."

"But she's gone round the bend," Alyssa whispered what we were all thinking. "One of us should stay and help you."

"I'll stay," said Sarah, and I knew what she was thinking. Maybe she could find a way to drive out Boudica's demons.

"No!" Gwen was proud, vehement. "I can manage. I'll clean her up and put her to bed. Just please, *please* find my sister."

Sarah and I exchanged a glance. Gwen was no stranger to caretaking, and Sarah knew better than anyone how fast and far a young girl could run.

"All right," agreed Sarah. "Everyone meet back here by dawn, no matter what."

All night we walked from fire to fire in the vast camp. We had agreed to describe her but not to identify her as Boudica's daughter for fear of creating alarm or motivating someone to hold her for ransom. The old tribal feuds were in temporary abeyance only. I also looked in every tree and behind every rock outcropping, every dip and fold in the land. By dawn a cold summer drizzle had begun to fall. I headed back, exhausted and chilled, hoping against hope that one of the others had found her.

When I reached Boudica's camp, it was crowded with warriors and chieftains in council with Boudica, all seated cross-legged on the ground. Gwen sat beside her mother, and she had indeed cleaned her up. Boudica wore a fresh plaid tunic; in the dismal light her hair glowed brighter than ever, so did her eyes, almost feverishly. She looked strangely young, more like a bride than a battle-weary war leader. There was not a trace of the frantic mother about her. Lithben must be back safe and sound. Then Gwen caught sight of me, and sent her silent question over the lime-spiked hair of the warriors.

No, I answered silently. One by one, Sarah, Bele, and Alyssa returned. No, no, and no.

"Verulamium is next," Boudica was saying. "We can get there in two day's march."

"By then it will be deserted," objected one of the warriors. "After Londinium, no one will stay around for a massacre. Why waste our time? It's the Roman army we have to destroy. Some people—not mine, mind you—are getting restless. There are crops back home to be taken care of. How long do you think you can hold all these tribes together?"

"The Roman army is on the run," declared Boudica. "And Verulamium is right in our path. It is a vile city, viler than Camulodunum and Londinium, cities built by Romans and foreigners. The people of Verulamium were once our *combrogos*; now they curry favor with the Romans, flattering them with imitation, looking down at the rest of us, flaunting their baths, their theatres, their toilets. Collaborators, traitors. Their city and any like it we will turn to rubble and ash."

"After we've picked it clean!" put in another warrior.

"I'll lay odds they've taken everything they can carry," the first man said. "I tell you again it's a waste of time."

"It won't take much time to put it to the torch," another spoke up.

As the debate went on, I caught Gwen's eye again and signaled to her. No one seemed to notice when she stood up, not even her mother. Gwen was beautiful in her own right, strong, and I would never have called her self-effacing, but she knew how not to be noticed. Or maybe it was just that Boudica took up any space that Gwen might have filled on her own. I beckoned to the others as well and we went apart to a cluster of yew trees that gave us shelter against the rain and some privacy.

"No word from her, no sign?" we all asked at once, all of us already knowing the answer.

"Gwen, your mother must be worried now," said Bele. "How can she march until Lithben is found?"

Gwen's composure suddenly gave way and she covered her face with her hands and wept. She stiffened at first when Sarah and Alyssa put their arms around her, and then she let go and finally turned to Sarah and wept onto her shoulder. My heart broke for her. She was so young, so young to have lost and suffered so much. After a moment she pulled away and stood up straight again.

"Mother insists Lithben is not lost," Gwen told us. "One moment I think she's mad, and another I think she might be right. Lithben could be hiding close by. She used to do that when we were little. Just hide, almost in plain sight. After a while, Mother stopped worrying when she disappeared. So her saying Lithben is hiding may not be as crazy as it sounds."

That was some reassurance, but not much.

"And if she's not hiding," I said after a moment, "do you think she would try to go home? And if she did, would she know which way to go?"

I don't want to be a queen. I want to go home, she'd said only yesterday.

"She might know," said Gwen. "And if she took her pony, her pony might know."

"We should have thought of that last night!" exclaimed Alyssa, smacking her forehead. "Well, it's easy enough to find out now. All our horses are pastured together."

"And if she did take her horse that would explain why we couldn't find her in camp," added Sarah.

"If we can't find her soon, one of us should ride north to look for her, even if her pony is here," said Bele, and then she added. "Maybe all of us should go."

No one spoke, each of us pondering Bele's implication. Leave Boudica, abandon her cause.

"I can't," Gwen spoke first. "Whether my mother is right or wrong in what she's done, what she did last night, I can't leave her now. And whether the *combrogos* are fighting for my sister and me, or are just out for themselves, I am still the queen of the Iceni. If my mother really is mad, I must be the one to lead."

I crossed our small circle and took Gwen's face in my hands, kissing first one cheek, then the other before gathering her into an embrace, the first one she'd ever fully returned.

"I'll go," I told her. "I'll go alone."

"Mother!" Sarah's voice held all the anguish of all our partings.

"I know," I said. "I know."

Though it was hard to put into words what I knew: that Sarah had to see it through, that she had to go on doing her work as a healer, as a mercy killer.

"Mother of Sarah!" Bele and Alyssa both cried out, also not saying what I knew, that they would never leave Sarah.

"It's best this way," I assured them. "I made a promise to Lithben not to leave her. Now I promise I will find her. I am used to looking for runaway daughters."

I smiled at Sarah, hoping she knew, hoping she could see and, if we never met again, always remember how much I loved her. She smiled back, and I realized I had not seen her smile since I left for Mona. In the light of her smile, in the light of her eyes, for a moment there was no rain, no war, no horror. We stood in the shelter of the great golden tree.

"What will you do when you find her?" asked Gwen, calling me back from eternity to the present.

And I knew she was asking, will I see ever see my sister again?

"I will do all I can to protect her," I said. "When this war is over, we will all be together."

I spoke as if it were a simple statement of fact. We all chose to believe my words would come true.

It was strange to travel through land trampled by an army. The earth itself is also a victim of war, and in the rain it seemed the ground bled mud in deep grooves left by wheels, and the countless hooves and feet. Birds and animals that lived in meadow, swamp, or thicket had fled before the army, and so the countryside was eerily silent. Farmsteads were mostly deserted, storehouses emptied to feed a whole people on the move. Macha and I slogged north, my eyes always peeled for some sign of a pony's hooves heading in the opposite direction from the horde. But the muddy ground was hard to read. I could only hope that Gwen was right and that the pony, which had indeed disappeared with Lithben, would lead her home.

By afternoon, the clouds thinned, and then a fresh wind blew them away, leaving the sky a soft, delicate blue. The sun slanted from the west, each clod of disturbed earth casting a shadow over the ground. Yet despite the devastation all around me, I could not help feeling cheered by the sun, which shone, as always, on good and evil alike, just as the rain fell on the righteous and the unrighteous. How could you even tell one from the other? I couldn't any more. Love your neighbor, love your enemies, pray for those who persecute you, my beloved had said. Why all the words, why all the distinctions? Love. Pray. That was all, no matter what good it did or didn't do. I did not pray with words, but simply let people come to my mind, brought them here with me to this benign light where I could just see them, without any pressure to judge them or myself.

At dusk, I found Lithben, standing with her pony under an oak tree at a fork in the road. I slipped from Macha's back and rushed to embrace her. She let me hold her, but did not cling to me. In fact she was strangely calm, and I wondered for a moment if she had gone mad, like her mother.

"I knew you would come," she said, as if sensing my fear. "He told me to wait for you here."

"Who did?"

"The man," she answered simply. "And he said if we take this path we'll come to a hut and a well with good water."

"Who is this man?" I asked. "How did he know I was coming?"

She shrugged, as if it were a stupid question and she had expected more sense from me.

"He's still here," she said. "You just can't see him. He says he's always here. I just never needed him before."

"Oh," I said, light, so to speak, dawning. "Him. Well, let's find this hut then."

We walked on, leading our horses and holding hands, neither of us feeling a need to speak. We soon found the hut, so welcoming that it seemed whoever lived there had just stepped out. The water in the well was indeed good, so sweet and refreshing that we hardly needed the loaf of bread and the dried fishes we found waiting for us inside.

CHAPTER THIRTY-NINE
MATRILINEAGE

I THOUGHT I might dream of my beloved that night. He seemed so close, so tangible, as Lithben and I bedded down in the hut that was fleetingly ours. I felt his warmth enfold me, and I settled into the first deep sleep I'd had since I slept in Sarah's arms the night of my return. I was too tired to dream. So was Lithben. We slept round the clock, woke briefly to eat and drink and relieve ourselves, and, discovering it was night again, went back to bed. Perhaps we could just sleep through all the horror, wake up when it was over, wake up and find it had all been a bad dream. Then, the next morning, I opened my eyes to find Lithben sitting watching me, waiting for me.

"My mother wants me," she stated.

I was struck by her phrasing.

"Do you want your mother?"

She stared at me for a moment as if she couldn't comprehend the question. Then her eyes filled and her lip trembled. Part of me wanted to gather her into my arms and rock her, but I heeded an instinct to wait.

"Yes," she whispered, and then the tears started to fall, the silent tears that always seem to have their own life and will. "I want her the way she was."

"Tell me," I asked her, sensing that she needed to talk but also wanting to know, to know my strange, estranged daughter in another way. From what I had seen, Lithben had always been afraid of her mother. Yet when I thought back to my first sight of both, I remembered that Lithben had leaned against her mother as if she were a great sheltering tree.

"She wasn't always angry, not with us," Lithben began. "When we were little she used to play with us, games like hide and seek. She would take us out on rides and walks and teach us the names of birds and animals, how to recognize their calls, how to follow their tracks. We would pick berries and gather nuts together. And in the winter, she told us stories, all the stories she learned at school.

"When she left Father, she would not go without me. I saw that Father was sad. He didn't want anyone to go, but he would never fight with Mother. He tried to get Gwen to go with Mother, too, but she refused, and Mother was so hurt, she wouldn't even speak to Gwen. I had to go with her."

Lithben paused for a moment, a child looking back on what was now her childhood, for better or worse, a childhood utterly lost to her.

"Did you want to stay with your father?"

Lithben shook her head, "I wanted *her* to stay with him. But I wanted her even more. I always slept in her arms at night. For a while after she left Father, she would cry. She would tell me I was her baby. She said I was all she had. She told me she would teach me everything she knew. She said she would make me a strong, beautiful queen."

"And what did you say?" I asked.

Her silence answered. Nothing. Nothing.

"I didn't mean to run away," she said at length.

"But you ran away for a reason," I ventured. "Because of what you saw your mother do."

She nodded.

"I am sorry I couldn't shield you from that," I told her. "I am sorry you had to see. I am sorry for all you've been through. Your mother is, too. She hated that you were hurt, so she wanted to hurt someone back."

"You tried to stop her," Lithben observed. "But you couldn't. Why does she hate you, Grandmother?"

Lithben, the baby of the family, didn't miss anything.

"I think because I never played hide and seek with her, never picked berries with her, never told her stories, never got to tell her she was my baby."

Lithben nodded again.

"Sarah is your baby," she stated.

"Yes," I admitted. "And I am sorrier than anyone will ever know that your mother couldn't be."

We sat silently for a time, grandmother and granddaughter, two links in a troubled lineage.

"Lithben," I said at last. "What do you want to do now? Do you want to go home?"

Lithben looked at me as if I were speaking a language she was struggling to learn. Of course, no one had ever consulted this child about her wishes. Maybe I shouldn't now. Maybe it would be easier for me to decide for her, but how could I? What was home? An abandoned village where she and her sister had been raped?

"I want my mother."

I waited a moment, to see if there was more.

"Are you sure, Lithben? Your mother as she is now in the midst of this war? Your mother as you last saw her?"

“I want my mother,” she stated firmly. “I know what war is now. Come on, Grandmother. Let’s go.”

It was not hard to pick up the trail of Boudica’s massive army. We took the fork that led southwest, and I soon realized it was the road Sarah, Bele, Alyssa and I had followed in reverse when we first headed for Iceni country. By the end of the day, we had arrived at the Wyddelian near what had been Verulamium, the town where I’d wanted to stop and treat myself to baths and other decadent luxuries. Now, as Boudica had vowed, it was nothing but rubble and very soon only ash, for some of the fires still burned. It was clear from the condition of the countryside that the army had continued west along the main road. Judging from the rawness of the ruin, I did not think we were far behind. Neither of us wanted to camp near the smoke and desolation of the town. Having stocked up on sleep and with some bread and fish still left, and plenty of water, we decided to ride on through the evening and into the night. The moon, just a few days shy of full, rose behind us and cast our shadows before us on the hard road I had already traveled so many times: east, then west to Mona, then east to Londinium, and now west again...to what?

The moon traveled with us, then overtook us, leading us on and on to the west until we came to the crest of a hill and saw the army spread out in a valley on either side of the road, campfires a crude echo of the stars, and the stench of so many humans together evident but not as overwhelming in the night’s chill.

“My mother will be camped near the front,” said Lithben as we paused for a moment to consider our course.

“Maybe we can skirt around on one side,” I suggested. “Then wait till daylight to find her.”

We turned from the road and began to ride around the sprawling encampment. We hadn’t gone far when we were challenged by a sentinel.

“Who are you and where are you going?” the warrior demanded, backing up his words with a poised spear. “I see you wear a Roman cloak. Give an accounting of yourselves or prepare to breathe your last.”

Damn the cloak, I thought, as I pondered how best to respond.

“I am Lithben, Queen of the Iceni, daughter of Queen Boudica, who is the daughter of my grandmother Maeve Rhuad, who has no other cloak to wear, who is the daughter of the warrior witches of Tir na mBan, who are the daughters of the Cailleach, who is the daughter of Bride herself!” Lithben astonished me by reciting her matrilineage. “Take us to my mother.”

The man did not go into trance or swoon as men from the west were wont to do at the name Tir na mBan, but he seemed properly impressed and asked no further questions.

"Follow me," he said.

We dismounted and led our horses through the maze of the tent city. Just before dawn broke, the sentinel ushered us into Boudica's camp where he tethered our horses for us.

"There's the queen's tent," he gestured, but of course we already knew.

Silently Lithben lifted the flap and went in first, with me following.

Boudica was awake, sitting over the embers of a dying fire at the center of the tent where the smoke rose and spiraled through a hole. She no longer looked young and feverish as she had when I last saw her. Staring down into the fire, she looked haggard and gaunt, as if she had lost ten pounds and gained ten years in our absence. Then she caught sight of Lithben. When she smiled I realized I had almost never seen her smile; it changed her face entirely and made it beautiful the way sun on a black cloud is beautiful, even though you know it could still storm.

"I knew you were only hiding," she said. "I told them you were only hiding."

But her voice broke, and when she rose to hold her daughter I could tell she was trembling. Over Lithben's shoulder, she caught my eye, and nodded so subtly I almost couldn't be sure she had. But it didn't matter. This mother had her daughter back. This daughter had her mother. I turned and looked in the dark tent for my own younger daughter.

Considering we were in the midst of war with rations running short, it was a very jolly breakfast. Gwen shared a bowl of stirabout with Lithben and ate with her arm around her, as if she would never let go of her again. Boudica looked on, her expression uncharacteristically serene. Bele and Alyssa kept up a lively banter. Best of all for me, Sarah seemed herself again. After breakfast, we walked apart from the others beyond the encampment into a sunny glade just off the road.

"I am so glad you found her so quickly," Sarah said again.

"Your father had a hand in it," I answered, and I told her the story.

"I wonder why you had to search so long for me," Sarah said, almost neutrally. "Why didn't he help then?"

I had often wondered the same thing.

"Perhaps he did," I paused, remembering the dreams that would come to me during our long separation, and the unexpected way we had found each other again—through the agency of my nemesis Paul of Tarsus. "And we had time on our side."

Then I stopped, realizing the implication of my words: Boudica does not. I did not want to predict disaster.

"We saw Verulamium," I ventured, wanting to give Sarah a chance to speak if she needed to. "I hope there was no...aftermath."

"You mean torture and sacrifice," she said bluntly. "No, I am happy to report. There was no one there at all. Not only that, they took everything of value with them. The people in Londinium were foreigners. I think they kept expecting the cavalry to come charging to their rescue. They didn't believe a bunch of uppity natives could wipe them out. The people of Verulamium are natives themselves. They know better."

We came to an oak tree and sat down among the roots, resting our backs against the trunk. Unbidden, the teaching groves of Mona came into my mind. I hadn't had time to mourn yet. I had a backwash of grief to release, if I lived so long.

"What next?" I asked.

"No more burning empty towns," said Sarah. "Some people are disgruntled and falling away. Boudica's got to keep the *combrogos* fired up. She's got to make them believe victory is within reach."

I closed my eyes. Never far away from my mind were the sounds of metal meeting metal, humans and horses screaming, the stench of blood and shit.

"Is it?" I asked quietly.

Sarah didn't answer right away.

"I hate what has happened," she said at last. "I hate what Boudica has done. What I have done. But she might, we might just win this war. The Roman procurator has fled, and the Roman governor has only a legion and a half left, we figure maybe ten thousand men. Even with the losses to our ranks, we outnumber them almost ten to one. Unless they flee the island altogether, they'll have to face us in battle. If we defeat the governor's troops, Rome will have no real presence here. They would have to conquer all over again. They might decide it's not worth the trouble."

I waited for a moment.

"Sarah, you are saying 'we.' Are you going to fight? Is this your cause?"

"Isn't it yours, Mother? After what you saw on Mona, isn't it yours? After what they did to Lithben and Gwen, isn't it your cause, too? Don't you want the Romans to leave the Holy Isles forever?"

I did not know how to answer. I could not think. The noise of battle was so loud in my head.

"I don't know, Sarah," I said. "I don't know if I believe in causes. It is hard for me to know a cause, to love a cause, the way I love a person."

That had been my original crime, loving Esus more than the idea of the *combrogos*. And so I meddled, as the old archdruid put it, in high mysteries.

"I'm not claiming it as a virtue," I added. "It's just my nature."

There was another silence. High above us, a faint breeze stirred in the canopy.

"And it is my nature to fight," Sarah said. "To do that, I have to take a stand. I have to choose a side."

"You are also a healer, Sarah," I put in, aware that I was on tricky ground. "Can you reconcile the two?"

"I may be wrong," she acknowledged. "It may be that you have to choose, like the druids, like my father. It may be that a healer shouldn't hold a weapon. But I believe the power to heal and the power to kill come from the same place."

Who else had said that? With a shock, I realized it was the general.

"I have thought hard about it. I have prayed. I will never again attack or kill an unarmed, unprepared person. But I will fight against the Roman army. I will fight this battle."

"Wars are never just between armies," I said carefully. "The innocent always get hurt."

"Yes," she agreed. "The innocent always get hurt. War or no war, the innocent always get hurt. Someone has to fight for the innocent. I have to fight, even if I am no longer innocent myself—*because* I am not innocent. Do you judge me for my nature, Mother?"

She looked at me, turning the full force of her golden gaze on me.

"Oh, *cariad*," I reached for her hand. "I don't judge you. I only love you."

And I don't want to lose you, I added silently.

"You can't lose me," she spoke to my thought. "Didn't you learn anything from my father?"

I pondered which lesson she meant. Love is as strong as death? I am with you always? But before I could answer, she got to her feet and helped me to mine.

"We'd better be getting back," she said. "It will be a long march today."

CHAPTER FORTY
FOR THIS SHE WAS BORN

AND IT WAS a long march. That day and the next and the next, along that hard road. Each evening, Boudica toured our whole camp, and by the end of each night, she was hoarse from exhorting the multitudes, firing them up, as Sarah had said she must. She was persuasive. Sometimes she almost persuaded me.

Late in the afternoon of the third day, we made camp on the plain near the fort where I had twice spent the night with the general, the plain that Sarah, Bele, Alyssa and I had galloped across so that the general would not know we were heading east. Our camp spread out across the plain almost all the way to the trees where we had rested our horses while Sarah and I had had it out. From the watch towers of the fort, our army would be a daunting, dismaying sight.

Except, as it turned out, the fort was deserted, or, more accurately, had been abandoned.

"It looks as though they might have left as recently as this morning," Alyssa said to Boudica when she, Bele and Sarah returned to our camp from reconnaissance.

"The cook fires are still smoldering," added Bele. "The latrines are full of fresh shit."

Boudica nodded, listening intently. An important detail.

"Fresh horseshit in the stables, too, and mud around the troughs and wells," put in Sarah. "It almost seems too obvious. Why didn't they take more trouble to cover their tracks?"

Boudica shrugged. "They probably sent out a scout and saw how close we were. They panicked. They know they can't hold that fort against our numbers. We'd kill them like rats in their own hole, just as we did at Camulodunum. Did they leave any supplies worth looting?"

Sarah didn't answer; she had turned her face away so none of us could see her struggle at the mention of slaughter at the temple.

"Not so much as a grain or a straw," said Alyssa. "Should we torch the place?"

Boudica considered for a moment.

"Not yet," she decided. "There's a good water supply there, shelter, and towers to keep a lookout. We may want to use the fort for tending our wounded or sick—or for holding prisoners. The Roman army can't be far away now. They are not few enough or skilled enough to disappear into the landscape. You three, gather all the scouts and send them out. Find their trail. We'll hunt them down and overwhelm them—perhaps as soon as tomorrow. I will gather the chieftains. Gwen, come with me. They need to see their queen."

All the weariness had fallen away from Boudica, like a cloak discarded and forgotten in the heat of the day. Her face was naked with excitement. Gwen could not hide her own excitement or her pride. So much slighter and darker than her mother, she seemed shinier than I'd ever seen her. Lithben watched them silently. Boudica, feeling her glance, came over to where her younger daughter was sitting and bent to caress her cheek.

"I won't be long, *cariad*," she said.

"Mother, Lithben should come with us," insisted Gwen. "She is queen, too."

"It's all right," said Lithben quickly. "I would rather stay with Grandmother."

While Boudica and Gwen made the rounds, visiting various important contingents in the camp, Lithben and I tended the fire, adding what we had to an increasingly watery soup. Ever since her encounter with "the man," as she called my beloved, Lithben had been much calmer, even peaceful. I found it restful to be with her, like sitting beside a still lake. Neither of us felt much need to speak. In our relative quiet, with the noise of the camp all around us, I could not shake the sense that we were being watched. Of course an army the size of ours can never be a secret. The Romans were no doubt aware of our presence, probably had their scouts watching our scouts. Now and then, I looked up from the cauldron to the ridge in the distance. As dusk fell, I could see no signs of life there, no smoke, no fire. Just a heavy darkness, a suspended wave, the spine of a sleeping serpent.

"We know where they are," announced Bele when the three of them rejoined us for our meager meal.

"Such as they are," added Alyssa. "It looks as though the troops that were supposed to join the general from Mona never made it. Are you sure that was their order, Mother of Sarah? Maybe they had to stay to hold the island."

All eyes turned to me. The look in Boudica's was hard to read. Wariness at this strange role I had turned up so unexpectedly to play? Sadness at the loss of the place that held our most intimate and broken connection?

"I'm sure," I answered. "There was no one left on Mona to subdue. All but a small contingent was supposed to follow the cavalry."

"The infantry could have been ambushed in the mountains," said Boudica. "After the sacrilege the Romans committed on Mona, the western resistance would have rallied, despite their losses. Our victory here will bring them more balm. Where is this raggle taggle remnant of the imperial Roman army?"

"Less than an hour's ride just off the road to the southwest," said Alyssa. "They may be intending to make a run for the nearest coast."

How long would Boudica pursue them? How long could she hold together so massive an army? Maybe the general was betting that she couldn't, that with their smaller numbers, his remaining forces would escape. For a moment, I let myself hope against hope: the Romans gone from the land without more bloodshed. But General Gaius Suetonius Paulinus, governor of Pretannia, would not see it that way. For him, escape would be utter, impossible humiliation. How could he return to Rome having lost Pretannia to a barbarian queen?

"Do you think they intend to move by night?" Boudica was asking.

"They seem to have pitched camp. They've got fires going," said Sarah. "We posted a watch in case they make any sudden moves. But...there's something wrong about this whole thing."

"What is that?" Boudica demanded.

Sarah pondered for a moment, searching for words to express the uneasiness I felt in my own gut.

"It was too easy to find them," she finally spoke. "They kept dropping clues, a sandal here, a loose arrow there."

"That just shows they are getting desperate," said Boudica. "They know they have failed. They know they are doomed."

"No, Boudica, listen!" I decided I had to speak whether I angered her or not. "I think Sarah's right. Something is wrong. I know the general," I paused feeling disapproval and distaste rise up all around me like a chill ground mist. "He would rather die than run away."

"We all like to think that about the men we love." Boudica's tone froze all my internal organs. "Don't we, daughter of Lovernios? But you forget, your general has already run away once, from Londinium."

"That might have been purely strategic," Sarah pointed out. "He knew he couldn't defend the town."

"Exactly," said Boudica. "And it's strategic for him to retreat now, strategic as in preserving his own murderous, cowardly hide. There is nothing brave about what he did on Mona. His troops outnumbered our remnant. Now the odds are reversed one hundredfold. He is running, tail between his legs, just as the foul treacherous procurator did, just as all Romans do when they can't beat the odds. The general's troops are hirelings. They fight because they are paid to fight. They are not warriors. I doubt most of them care anything about Rome or its Empire. The *combrogos* are fighting for our lives, our families, for this holy ground that is our mother. Even if the general's numbers equaled ours, that Roman cur could not prevail against us. And he will not escape. Andraste will not allow it. Even now, she has him in her sights; she is snaring him in her traps."

She had gone into full blown oration, and though her audience now was small, we were captivated; we were captive.

"Tonight we will augur," Boudica declared. "I have asked the chiefs to gather the people at moonrise. If the signs are auspicious, we will mass on them tomorrow. We will force them to fight. We will finish them once and for all."

As the moon rose over the plain, glinting off swords and spears, whitening limed hair, Boudica stood in the center of her vast army, her silence spreading out in ripples, so that you could actually hear the sound of the river.

I stood next to Lithben in the inner circle, Gwen and Sarah to our left. Boudica signaled Sarah, who went to our tent and returned with something wrapped in a plaid, something that appeared to be alive, for it squirmed and kicked as Sarah handed it to Boudica. Not another sacrifice. Please, no. Lithben must have been had the same thought, for she reached for my hand and held it tightly.

"My *combrogos*!" Boudica's voice boomed out, as if it was the voice of the plain itself. "In my arms I hold a sacred hare, a messenger from Andraste herself. If the hare runs to my right when I release her, victory is assured!"

Thank Bride, no slit throats, no casting of entrails. I felt Lithben's hand relax. It could have been much worse.

Boudica knelt down, clasping the hare between her knees as she unwound the plaid. The poor creature hesitated for a moment, no doubt terrified, then it shot away to Boudica's right and wild cheering rolled through the crowd just as the silence had, and then a chant began.

"Boudica! Boudica! Boudica!"

Boudica stood again, her arms uplifted, gathering the power of the sound, the power of the moon.

"Andraste!" Boudica spoke when the chant finally receded. "Andraste, I call on you tonight, not just as a priestess to her goddess but as a woman to a woman, a mother to a mother."

I don't know how she managed it. For though she was speaking to a multitude in a voice that easily carried half a mile, it felt as though we were sharing an intimate moment, catching a glimpse of her naked soul.

"The *combrogos* are your children, even as my daughters are mine. They have been raped by these invaders, they have been wronged! Even as my body was lashed, so has your body, the sacred ground of the Holy Isles, been desecrated, violated, trampled under vile Roman feet. Andraste, my goddess, my mother, my sister, my *combrogo*. To you we have offered the sacrifice of our enemies' blood. To you we offer the sacrifice of our own peril. Some of us will die in battle for your honor, for our honor. These brave ones we know you will receive with open arms. These brave ones will feast with you tomorrow in the Isles of the Blest, knowing that with their blood they will have restored our freedom and our sovereignty–your sovereignty!"

Sound rose from the crowd again, not cheering; it was more like the sound of storm wind, wild, mournful, angry, and ecstatic all at once. Boudica was the still point of that storm, its source, its ending, her face austere as the moon, her hair gleaming in the firelight.

This is how I will remember her, I thought. This is how I will always remember her. For this she was born, for better or for worse, for this she was born.

"My *combrogos*," she said when silence fell again. "I am proud to be one of you. I am proud to fight beside you, I will be proud to die, if that is my fate, and proud to live and rejoice with you in our sure victory! Rest now, my beloved *combrogos*, rest well. Tomorrow we fight as one people, we will prevail against our enemy, we will restore our goddess to her sovereignty, and our great deeds will live forever in the memory of all who come after us."

CHAPTER FORTY-ONE
HAWK AND DOVE

I DID NOT expect to sleep. The sense that something was wrong would not leave me. Boudica, despite her admonition to rest, was nowhere in sight. Sarah, too, was on the prowl. I feared she might be following up on her own suspicions.

"Don't worry about your girl, Mother of Sarah," Alyssa tried to reassure me, as I sat with her and Bele around our fire. "If she doesn't want to be seen, she won't be."

"She is like a walking piece of night," agreed Bele. "She can turn herself into the shadow of a tree branch. A stalking wild cat makes more noise than she does."

"And if she finds out something," added Alyssa, "she's about the only one who stands any chance of influencing Boudica."

"Why is that?" I wondered.

"Everyone respects Sarah," Alyssa stated the obvious. "Some people are a little afraid of her, but in a good way, because she always says what's true, not what people want to hear."

"She can't help herself," I laughed. "She's her father's daughter."

"And her mother's," said Bele quietly. "Don't you see, Mother of Sarah? Boudica and Sarah are both your daughters. Letting Sarah close to her (as close as she lets anyone) is the only way Boudica can let herself love you."

With Bele's astute observation fresh in my mind, I finally went into the tent and curled up next to Lithben and Gwen.

Screams of horses and humans, metal striking metal, the sickening sound of a blade finding flesh, a skull splitting, the stench of blood and piss, guts sliced open, the merciful, merciless sunlight pouring down as if this were just any other day, the shadows of carrion crows and vultures circling, circling, waiting for their feast.

I woke abruptly, my teeth sunk in my own hand to stifle my screams. I had not dreamed of the horrors I'd witnessed on Mona. The nightmare was the same one that had invaded my waking moments ever since I had met the general in that valley in the folds of the ridge—the dark ridge less than a mile from this camp.

It doesn't have to be this way, I spoke to him in my mind. *It doesn't have to happen.*

I slipped out from under my blanket, not yet knowing what I intended to do, only that I had to do something.

"Grandmother," Lithben woke. "Grandmother, where are you going?"

I knelt beside her and took her hand. I could not lie to her.

"There is something I have to do," I said. "I don't know quite what it is yet."

All at once, I realized: that was not true. I did know. I was going to that ridge.

"There is somewhere I have to go. Alone," I added before she could ask to come with me.

She was so quiet for a moment, her hand in mine so soft, I almost thought she had fallen back to sleep.

"You will not be alone, Grandmother," she pronounced. "He will be with you."

Now I was the one who clung to her. I had promised not to leave her again, but I was, and there was no certainty that I would come back.

"He'll be with me, too. It's all right, Grandmother. You can go."

With the blessing of the youngest of my line, I went forth into an ageing night.

Sarah was not the only one who knew how to move silently. My feet remembered how to sense the ground before falling, never breaking a twig, hardly stirring a leaf. My hands fluttered out delicate and sensitive as antennae, moving branches that might have snapped. My eyes knew the dazzle and dapple of moonlight, how what appeared solid was not and how what seemed to be shadow might be rock. For a time, I was only my senses and sensations. It was a relief to forget everything else.

Then I arrived at the top of the ridge, and of course he was there, just as he had been there so inevitably and inexplicably that night on the cliffs. A sliver of moonlight fell across his face, though his armored body was carefully concealed in shadow.

You won't be alone, grandmother. He'll be with you.

Jesus, I felt for him, are you with me? What do I do now? Am I your brother's keeper?

He didn't answer, but I felt his presence as a calm that came over me, like the sorrowful calm I had felt when we washed his body in the tomb. I was in the only place I could be, doing the only thing I could do, which at this moment was to watch, wait.

The general was gazing out across the plain. I knew what he was seeing: his enemy massed almost to the horizon.

A breeze sprang up and lifted the branches of the tree that sheltered me. He must have caught sight of me out of the corner of his eye. He turned his head and looked straight at me. I don't know whether he thought I was real or an apparition, whether he would have followed me if I had fled, because I didn't. I took a step closer to him, then another to match the step he took until we stood face to face.

"Who are you?" he said, so softly I don't know if he spoke aloud or in my mind.

I couldn't answer. I shook my head, as if the barest wind touched my leaves.

"Why do you hunt me? Why do you haunt me?" he demanded. "I only did what I had to do. I only do what I must."

His words took me by surprise. Did he want me to forgive him? Exonerate him?

Before I could answer, I heard the whinny of a horse in the valley, followed by a man's curse. I turned and looked to the valley floor. No campfires burned there, but something caught the moon's light and gave it back: helmets, spears, armor. Suddenly dizzy, I reached out and caught the general's arm to steady myself. Massed below me were the troops that had followed from Mona. The cavalry camped down the road were only a decoy.

I had to warn Boudica.

I let go of his arm, but before I could even turn, he grasped both my arms and whirled me around so that my back was to him, my wrists crossed and held fast.

"I can't let you go," he said, his mouth so close to my ear, he sounded more like a lover than a captor. "You must understand that. It is nothing personal. I have a job to do."

I searched my mind for Sarah's instructions on how to break a hold, but I decided I did not want to writhe ineffectually and further his suspicions of me. My tongue had always been my best defense—and offense.

"If it's not personal, then why do you care so much about whether I understand? If it's not personal, why didn't you kill me when you had the chance on Mona? Why not kill me now?"

"Don't tempt me."

I wished I could tempt him in another way, tempt him to forget that we were enemies.

"Do you really think I care if I live or die?" I demanded. "I've lived long enough, and I've seen too much."

"I think you care if other people live or die," he answered. "You proved that on Mona. You tried to kill me, remember?"

"I hope you didn't take it personally," I said. "I was just doing a job."

"I was flattered."

"Don't be," I said sharply. "You're the general. I simply thought of killing you as lopping the head off a beast. Too bad I botched the job."

"Were you planning to finish the job tonight?" he inquired. "Or were you just spying?"

"Neither," I said. "I was—"

Here is your chance, my beloved spoke in my mind. *Here is your chance to speak the truth.*

"Do you remember?" I changed my course. "Do you remember when we came across each other in that valley down there? Do you remember what we both saw then?"

"Yes." His grip tightened, but it felt more desperate than restrictive.

"That's why I came here tonight," I told him, "because I dreamed of that horror again."

He did not answer, but I could tell he believed me, whether or not it made sense to him. His grip relaxed a little, but I did not try to loose myself. We just stood together, listening to the night sounds around us, the wind riffling through trees on the ridge, the men and horses below, stirring in their sleep or wakefulness.

"Do you remember?" I spoke again. "Do you remember the night we spent together on the watchtower?"

"What is the point? What is the point in remembering that?" he asked, his voice low, equal parts angry and sad.

"This battle doesn't have to happen." I turned so that I could feel the pulse of his throat next to my mouth. "I told you then. I am telling you now. It doesn't have to happen."

His whole body tightened again. I could almost hear it creaking as he braced himself—but against what? The truth? His own longing?

"I told you then, and I am telling you now, you are wrong," he said. "It does have to happen. You can't stop it. I can't stop it. Why do you think you dreamed it? You only dreamed what must be."

I did not know how to argue with him. Below us were two armies ready to fight to the death. I did not know how to argue with that. Yet we were not done, not done with each other.

"Why do you think we met on the cliffs and saw each other the way we did?" I asked.

"Madness, moonlight." He said the words as if they were curses. "Who knows why the gods taunt us."

"Or haunt us, hunt us," I repeated his earlier words. "Listen, my beloved enemy. We have the same wounds, you and I. You came here to find your son. I came here to find my daughter."

"My son," he said bitterly. "My son is a coward."

I wonder still if I should have told him in that moment what his son had done to my daughter, how this nightmare about to play out was authored by our own lost children. And we, we had failed to stop them.

"My daughter," I began. "My *daughter*–"

I could not finish the sentence, but in that moment he heard, he knew.

He loosed my wrists and turned me to face him, holding me by the shoulders as he looked into my face, confirming everything.

Fly, a voice inside me spoke, Dwynwyn's, my own. Fly.

If you had been watching the sky that night, you would have seen a dove flying out toward the plain, catching the moon on her wings, casting a fleeting shadow, while a hawk higher and faster circled around and back, diving, catching the dove in his talons, bearing her away back to the dark ridge.

CHAPTER FORTY-TWO
BATTLE

When I come to myself, I am surrounded by the sound of water flowing through reeds, washing over small bright pebbles. At least I think they are bright, for the light behind my eyelids is so golden, I think everything in the world must shine. When I open my eyes, I see that it is so. I am on a shoals in the middle of a great golden river. To one side is a country so bright I can hardly look at it. To the other...I find I don't want to look to the other side. My heart hurts when I do, as if it has been pierced by sharp talons.

"It has been, my dear."

I look towards the voice that is slow and gentle as water stilled when a river widens.

"Lazarus!" I reach for him and we embrace without embracing; the way sunlight touches skin.

"Am I dead?" I ask after a moment.

"You are in the place between," he answers. "Don't you recognize it? You once waited here with me. This time he has asked me to wait here with you."

Lazarus did not have to tell me who *he* was.

"Why do I have to wait?" I want to know.

"Why did I?" he counters.

"He called you back," I answer. "Is he going to call me back?"

"Do you want to go?"

The other side of the river is waking. The light there is not golden, it is harsh. There you can see every blade of grass and its shadow. *The country of life is hard*, I remember. *The stones there are so sharp*.

My daughters are there; my granddaughters. Sarah, Lithben, Boudica, Gwen.

"I must go back," I whisper to Lazarus. "I have to go back."

"Fly then, Shekinah. Dove of Asherah, fly."

I am back in the country of life, in our dismantled camp. The field has been cleared, all the carts to the far end, and the warriors are massing, with charioteers racing up and down the loose ranks to create a semblance of order. Along the front lines rides Boudica, with Gwen and Lithben beside her. Like all the warriors, Boudica is swirling with woad, her arm torcs gleaming in the sun. I know she is speaking. Her *laigen*, in her raised arm, pierces the sky over and over, but I can't hear what she says. There is a roaring sound of wind or water, but the air is calm, the river at a late summer low. The people's voices wash over the plain, pour into the empty bowl of sky. I am the sound; I am exhilaration and release, readiness to charge, to hurl, to slash and stab. I am the excitement surging through blood, bone, and muscle. No more waiting. No more waiting. Today is the day.

I have no form here, not even my dove form. For a moment I am giddy with terror. Then I discover I can move at will, widen or narrow this awareness. I follow Boudica as she circles the entire field all the way to the back where the women and children throng around the carts. Now she steps out of the chariot and embraces Gwen and Lithben.

For a moment I am in her heart. She doesn't want to let them go. She doesn't ever want to let them go. For a moment, she is just a mother, like any other mother.

Gwen is biting her lip, fighting tears, fighting rage. Fighting wanting to fight.

Lithben is weeping silently. She is losing her mother, losing her mother again.

Then abruptly Boudica lets go, mounts her chariot and drives back to the front, followed always by wild cheering.

Where is Sarah? Where is Sarah?

As soon as I think her name, I see Sarah riding along the opposite flank of the army, leading Macha with her, ignoring the din, searching for Lithben and Gwen. When she finds them, she dismounts.

"Where is my mother?" she asks, startled not to see me at Lithben's side.

"She's gone," answers Gwen, anger covering her fear. "She disappeared in the night. She said she wouldn't leave Lithben. She broke her word."

"Disappeared?" Now Sarah is panicking.

"She didn't disappear," says Lithben patiently, as if she were the grownup, having to soothe an unreasonable child. "She told me she had something to do. And she isn't gone. She's here with us now."

Gwen and Sarah exchange worried glances.

"She'd better not be dead," Sarah mutters. "Or I'll kill her!"

"She's not dead, Sarah," Lithben insists. "She's here."

I am here, I think to them with all my might, I am here.

"Well, if she's not dead, she's bloody well invisible," says Gwen exasperated. "And I wish she wouldn't be. Oh, Sarah, please, please let me take her horse and ride with you! I know how to fight. My mother trained me herself."

"She trained me, too," puts in Lithben more as a point of fact than anything else.

"You are not to go into battle!" says Sarah sharply. "You know perfectly well why. If you're going to be the queens of the Iceni, you have to stay alive. If I let you disobey your mother's orders, she'd kill us both. Listen to me. You keep Macha here with you. If you sense any danger, any at all, don't wait. Both of you get on Macha and ride away from here as fast as you can. That's an order. Do you hear me!"

Gwen's silence is her answer.

"I hear you, Sarah," says Lithben. "Don't worry. Grandmother will tell us what to do."

Sarah throws up her hands and then gathers both her nieces into a swift embrace.

"Now," says Sarah, "I've got to find your mother."

Before it's too late, Sarah does not say aloud.

"She's heading back to the front," Gwen relents. "That way."

It's a trap. It's a trap. It's a trap. The words sound over and over in Sarah's mind as she gallops after Boudica.

Whatever I am becomes a prayer. Let Sarah reach her in time. Let Sarah reach her.

Let me reach her.

Boudica, Boudica, Boudica!

Inside Boudica's mind there is deadly quiet while behind her the roar rises and rises. Then she sees them, the Roman cavalry in the distance riding straight toward her army.

The fools, the fools, she exults, as she raises her *laigen* high above her head.

And then in the next moment, Boudica understands:

It's a trap.

She lets out a sound so huge, so desolate. If anyone heard it, they would weep. But no one does hear it. Boudica has no choice now. She must ride the wave to its end.

I cannot bear it. I cannot bear it.

Lazarus's hands hold mine without holding them. The river flows around us, joyous, soothing. I can't stay here.

I am in the valley now between the ridges. I am hearing the fury of Boudica's army rushing towards the Roman soldiers as if I am one of their rank. It doesn't feel like an enemy army; it feels like a natural disaster. Every fiber in their bodies wants to run. It takes all their years of training and discipline to stand still. Some of them can't help shaking. Their armor rattles, and shame underscores their terror.

Then I find myself looking out at them, the infantry in their perfect formations, red and gold shields polished bright, *pila* at the ready. The archers are in place, and the cavalry will soon arrive with the enemy behind them. Strangely I find my heart welling with love for these men. Then I understand; I am seeing them through the general's eyes. They are his; he has trained them; he has made them what they are. He has been with some of them for years. He knows they will not fail him. They are what matters. Not Rome, not Pretannia. These men.

"Have no fear," he is saying, even though he knows they do, and he does not blame them. "We fight against an enemy who has no plan, no discipline. An enemy drunk on easy victories against civilians, an enemy overconfident because of its size. They will hurl themselves against us and shatter. For we are solid as rock, as a mountain. We will withstand them; we will make a mountain of their dead. Keep your ranks tight, keep your eye on the standards, and you will know exactly what to do at each moment. There will be no uncertainty, no chaos. We have made a good trap. The enemy is doomed, and before this day is out, we will win not only victory but lasting fame."

No more words. The cavalry thunder into the valley and take their places guarding the flanks. Boudica's army is only seconds away. Now they are close enough for the men to see the painted faces, the wild eyes of the enemy. They wait, they wait. The trumpet blasts, the standard is raised half way; the men ready the *pila*. Then the next blast, the eagle atop the standard plunges into the sky.

And now I am with the *combrogos*, the first ones, the brave ones who will not stop, who cannot stop. The Roman spears sing in the air; the sky is black with them. There is no time for fear. Some drop without a sound. Then the screams begin. The ones who have not fallen must rush on, over the dead, over the wounded. Another round of *pila* and another and another. There is no time to stop to pull the spear out of your shield if you have a shield. Drop it, keep going. Thousands are behind you, pressing you forward. Climb, climb over your friend, climb over your brother, your father, your sister. Don't stop. There is a Roman there, waiting for you behind his immense, heavy shield, fending you off till he finds your soft belly and thrusts the sword swift up into your heart.

Now I am in two worlds at once: in the thick of battle, in the place between sword and flesh; in the straining heart, in the pierced heart. Each death wound is a doorway, a birth canal to the Otherworld, where the river flows, the golden river, the merciful river. Hundreds are arriving, thousands are arriving. They come coated with dirt and blood, fear and horror. They don't know yet that it's over. There are many here to welcome them, to take their hands the way Lazarus took mine. They are guiding the newborn dead into the river. They are washing them in the cool golden waters. I recognize Ciaran and Moira and many of the fallen from Mona. I can still hear the screams from the country of life, but here someone is singing. I am singing. We are singing. The river is singing, a song without words, a mother song that washes away the pain. Among the river reeds, the birds sing, too, then rise, flock after flock, to bathe their wings in light.

I long to stay here, singing with the river. But something is drawing me back, away from this light into the stench and dust and din of the battle beneath a sky where vultures gather, patient and certain as they circle and circle.

The trumpet blares again, three blasts. The standard is raised and thrust forward, and the ranks obey instantly, reconfiguring as a monster with huge teeth. Lockstep by lockstep, the soldiers advance in saw tooth formation, the nails in the sandals holding firm in the slick mess of blood, guts, lost limbs. On and on they march, killing as they go, pushing the dead and living before them in one tangled mass.

"Hold!" screams Boudica from her chariot. "Hold your ground!"

But they can't hear her any more; they can't heed her. She feels it before she sees it: her army is turning, her people are running for their lives. She aims her chariot directly towards the Roman ranks. Roman arrows fly. Her horses sink to their knees and fall. She is hurtled from her chariot. On the ground, she struggles against the tide of retreat, reaching the front ranks of the Roman army, her sword swinging, whirling so swiftly no can touch her, and in all its wildness, deadly, accurate. She fights on and on, all the way back down the field.

Still on her horse, Sarah breaks free of the stampede. She is racing to reach the women and children, to warn them.

I can be there faster. I can be there now.

"Lithben," I speak to her mind. "You and Gwen get on Macha. Ride away as far as you can, ride away now."

I watch as they gallop away to the shelter of the trees in the distance, just as the first wave of fleeing warriors crashes into the barrier of carts and wagons. The Roman cavalry closes in, and the final slaughter begins. No one is spared. When the last of Boudica's army is forced back to the edge of the plain, she turns at last and looks: men, women, children piled in heaps around their carts.

It is finished.

There is nothing I can do for her, this child I carried under my heart. This child I held in my arms so fleetingly. There is no mending of the tear in her heart or mine when they tore her from me. And yet I will be with her in this last bitterness. I will *be* her. I will be in her heart when she drives the blade home.

CHAPTER FORTY-THREE
CALLED BACK

THE RIVER IS SINGING all around me. I am lying on the shoals, watching currents of air swirl in golden light. Lazarus is with me, holding my hand without holding it.

I am so tired, so tired.

"Rest now," says Lazarus. "I will wait with you."

"Why do I have to wait?" I ask.

"Rest now," he says again. "Wait."

And I do. I rest for what seems like a long time. The river flows. The birds sing. The pebbles shine. And then something changes.

Why is the river so sad? I wonder. Why is the river weeping so bitterly?

"Mother," someone is saying. "Mama, don't be dead. Please don't be dead."

Sarah. It's Sarah. I wish I could go to her, but I don't think I can.

"Mama," she weeps. "Mama."

"Beloved daughter."

Someone else is speaking, but not to me.

"Call her back, call her back, as I once called Lazarus, as she once called me."

"Father, I don't know how. Help me."

I hear no more words, but someone is holding my heart in her hands, as if it were a wounded bird. My heart is alive. Its wings stir and flutter.

"Maeve," says a voice that shines with its own light, golden as the leaves on the tree of life. "Maeve Rhuad, come back to us, come back to me."

When I open my eyes, I am looking into Sarah's. She is bending over me, her hands over my heart.

I stood with Sarah on the ridge, overlooking the plain, the setting sun casting in gold the devastation below, as if its light had borrowed a little mercy from the Otherworld. It was hard to believe it was the same day that had dawned that morning.

"The general told me where to find you," Sarah said. "He let me go to look for you, because he knew I would come back."

"How could he be sure of that?" I wondered, still feeling shaky and disoriented. It was strange to be back in a body, even one miraculously restored by Sarah's touch.

"He has taken Gwen and Lithben captive."

"But they got away! I saw them. They rode away!"

I did not have to explain to Sarah how I knew that. She seemed to understand that I had been there at the battle, even as I lay dead or near dead on the ridge.

"They came back when it was over. They came looking for their mother."

Of course they did.

"Boudica is dead," said Sarah. "She died by her own sword."

"I know," I answered. "I know."

We stood silent for a time.

"Alyssa, Bele?" I finally asked.

She shook her head.

"They were killed in the final onslaught. I would have been, too, no doubt, but I went to look for Lithben and Gwen."

I listened for anguish and self-reproach but she seemed to have passed beyond that into some stark, empty place.

"The general is holding anyone connected to Boudica's family. You know what that means, don't you?"

He would execute us publicly and display our remains in some gruesome way. Or he would take us to Rome where we would be publicly paraded and humiliated.

"Yes, I know what that means. And you know what, Sarah?" I paused, feeling giddy and certain at once. "That is not happening. Let's go."

You can imagine—or maybe you cannot—what it was like to cross that killing plain at dusk, where preparations for mass burning for the enemy and burial for the troops were only just underway. Someone was no doubt in charge of the body count. Eighty thousand of the *combrogos*, four hundred Romans. Not an inch of earth unstained.

At last we arrived at the fort Boudica had intended to occupy. The fallen queen's mother and sister did not have to wait to be escorted to the prison cell where Lithben and Gwen kept a huddled vigil over their mother's body.

Lithben jumped up and ran into my arms. Gwen barely lifted her head. She kept holding her mother's hand and stroking it, as if she could rub life back into her. Sarah sat down next to Gwen and put a hand gently on her back. In the dim light, I could see the fire of the stars pulsing there.

None of us spoke.

After a moment, Lithben took my hand and led me to her mother's body and placed Boudica's other hand in mine, her sword hand. Boudica still wore her bloody battle clothes. No one had brought water for washing her. I put down her hand, touched her bruised cheek, and then lifted a lock of bright red hair to my face and breathed the scent, dust, blood, but some faint lingering sweetness, the scent of a newborn's head.

Then I got to my feet.

"Guard," I called to the man posted outside our cell. "Tell General Gaius Suetonius Paulinus that I will see him now."

I unfastened my Roman cloak and let it fall, and I stood in my blood red tunic and necklace of skulls.

"Tell him Maeve Rhuad, mother of Queen Boudica, will see him now."

I don't know what it was about my aspect that persuaded the man he should obey, but he went.

I stood waiting, sending roots into the blood-drenched plain, sending my branches to the moon and stars wheeling over it. At last I heard two sets of footsteps approaching. The guard went back to his place, and the general stood before me: this man who had faced and defeated a vast army, looking pale and shaken.

"I thought you were dead," he said in a low voice. "I thought I had killed you."

"Then why did you send my daughter to find me?"

"I had to know," he said simply.

He had killed tens of thousands today. Hundreds of his own men had fallen. Why should my life or death matter so much to him? Unless he feared me. Unless he loved me.

"I was dead," I told him, "and it would have been a lot more pleasant to stay that way. But I came back from death. I came back to tell you something you need to know."

Now he would have to listen to me.

"Yes?" he asked, wary, resigned.

"Your son ordered the rape of my two granddaughters, the same ones you have now imprisoned. Your son had their mother beaten in front of them. Your son started the war that you had to finish, the war you have just won."

For what it is worth, he did not look away from me; for what it is worth, he made no defense. He waited. Behind me, Lithben, Gwen, and Sarah were as still as Boudica.

"Now," I said. "You will give us water to wash my daughter's body and oil to anoint her and a shroud to wrap her in. You will give us five days' provisions, a cart and our horses. At dawn we will leave this fort, and you will see to it that none of your men harms us or follows us."

It was so quiet in the prison cell, I could hear the moans of the wounded in the courtyard outside; I could hear the rats scuttling in the walls.

"Why would I release the heirs of Boudica and Prasutagus? I have just put down one rebellion. Why would I sow the seeds for another?"

Reasonable questions, inevitable questions. While I waited for answers, I closed my eyes and saw us on the cliffs before either of us knew who the other was, when we were only a boy and a girl, stripped of our age by some inexplicable magic. A boy and a girl wounded and lost like everyone else.

"There are three reasons," I said at last. "First, honor demands that you make amends for the harm the son of your bloodline has done to the daughters of my bloodline."

I paused, feeling him tighten, ready to resist.

"And the other reasons?"

"The love you bear me. The love I bear you."

He was silent for a moment, his face still. I could see him swallow once, twice. Then he took a breath, as if he had just surfaced from some airless place.

"It shall be as you will."

And he turned on his heel and walked away.

History records the general's ruthlessness in the aftermath of the rebellion. He hunted out the remnants with dogged thoroughness. Some may not believe he would have been capable of such an act of mercy—even of folly. Perhaps he regretted it; perhaps he was called to account for it, and believed he had to prove his loyalty to Rome and his efficiency as the Empire's lone representative in an unruly outpost. I will never know. I never saw him again. I only know he honored his word to me.

We walked southwest. We walked in a daze, so numb we could hardly feel the ground under our feet or notice our own hunger and thirst. The weather cooled and the sun covered itself in cloud, so the smell of Boudica's body did not overwhelm us. On the fourth day, we saw the Tor in the distance. On the fifth day we entered the mists shrouding the isles and waterways of Avalon. Aoife was waiting for us in a boat. Priestesses came to take Macha and Sarah's Blackfire to the stables. The four of us, Sarah, Lithben, Gwen, and I, lifted Boudica's body into the boat. Aoife rowed us over the dark waters to the healers' island.

There in the hut, where Sarah and I had kept vigil with Joseph, the priestesses gave us wine mulled with herbs, bitter and sweet. We lay down on mats woven of river reeds and slept at last without fear, without dreams.

The next day, with all the priestesses attending, we buried Boudica on Beekeeper's Island, a place that Saint Brigid later visited on pilgrimage to honor a shrine there dedicated to me. No historical accounts will tell you of this burial. You can believe my story or not as you will. This you cannot doubt: Boudica was as great and flawed a hero as any who ever lived. She knew very little happiness in her life. It comforts me to think of her body turning into the earth of a place that has a different kind of power than the powers she fought against so fiercely.

CHAPTER FORTY-FOUR
THE END IS IN THE BEGINNING

WITH MANY OTHER homeless refugees from the war, we spent the winter in Avalon. I watched as numbness gave way to grief, Lithben and Gwen grieving for their mother each in her own way, Sarah grieving for companions she'd lived with for longer than she'd lived with me. I just grieved. Grief cut deep channels around islands of respite. I traveled on these channels, visiting different times and places, different loves, different losses. It was winter, time to pull in, to gather wool and spin, spin a cocoon, a shroud, a dream within a dream.

Then spring came. The quiet refuge went wild with the sound of birds migrating, mating, nesting. Willows burst into gold and the alders flamed red. The waters surged with rain and snow melt. Joseph of Arimathea's thorn tree bloomed and bloomed. Lambs were born, herds of white clouds in the green grass. Beautiful as it was, I wasn't sure how I felt about all this burgeoning life. Begin again? I thought. Begin all over again? Resurrection can feel relentless. I wandered about grousing a bit to my beloved about his part in it—and mine.

One day Aoife came looking for me and found me helping Gwen and Lithben gather swamp marigold.

"Maeve Rhuad, I would speak with you."

Eventually, I thought, knowing Aoife's long silent preambles. This was no exception. We walked to a boat and she rowed me silently through the loud marsh till we came to the isle of the Tor. We disembarked and sat on greensward at the foot of the Tor where Aoife set forth a small feast of honey cakes and mead.

We ate and drank in silence, the spring sun strong, the air still cool and fresh, two old women enjoying their creature comforts.

"Maeve Rhuad," she finally spoke, "we have been observing your granddaughters. Your daughter Sarah we already know has the gift of healing in her hands, and we see now she has claimed her gift, though I will also say she seems restless, as if part of her is not here."

I had noticed that, too, and wondered what to do. Ever since she ran away from the mountain, Sarah had been a wanderer. Even when she lived in the Camargue with the other sometime pirates, she had lived in a wheeled tent.

"Gwen has a different gift," Aoife continued. "She has patience. She has discipline. We'd like to train her to be a priestess of Avalon."

"And Lithben?" I asked, though I hardly needed to ask.

"There has not been a seer of her skill in my lifetime."

"Not since Miriam," I said aloud, forgetting that Miriam was Sarah's foremother, not Lithben's.

Aoife was quiet again and did not seem to need to ask who Miriam was.

"Lithben needs no training that we could give her, but she is welcome to stay with us, as you are, Maeve Rhuad. We would be honored."

Now I was quiet. Aoife wasn't finished. There was a *but* somewhere.

"What are you saying, Aoife, what are you asking?"

"I am asking you what you want, Maeve Rhuad."

Want. Did I want anything? Must I want anything?

"Maeve Rhuad, I will leave you to walk the spiral path of the Tor."

And that's an order, she might as well have added, as she packed up our picnic and hotfooted it to the boat.

"Aoife," I protested. "Have mercy. Climb that thing! Again? There are plenty of ways to divine that don't involve sore feet and sweat."

Aoife's only answer was her laughter as she rowed away.

So I climbed, or rather I wound around and around, I spiraled, I wove. Each step got lighter and lighter, and so did my heart as I rose and rose. Finally I stood at the top, the water and land spread below me reaching the round horizon of the whole world.

I turned slowly in a circle, then faster, till I spun. When I stopped spinning and the world stopped spinning, I saw in the far blue distance the shape of a woman's body, reclining in the sea, rising from the sea.

Sarah is at the helm; all her old pirate skills have revived. We have a boat, a brave little boat with oars and sail. We sail west northwest past Mona, past Man, past the shore of Caledonia.

"Is Tir na mBan in this world or the Otherworld, Grandmother?" asks Lithben.

"It is between the worlds," I say.

"When will we get there?" she asks, more to hear my voice than because she needs to know.

"When the moon is right," I tell her.

At last one evening, we see the island, rising dark from a red sea, the daughter moon hanging low between her breasts. From her thighs, the breeze carries the scent of apples towards us over the water.

Sarah starts the song, and we all sing with her.

Hail to thee, thou new moon
Jewel of Guidance in the night
Hail to thee, thou new moon
Jewel of Guidance on the billows
Hail to thee, thou new moon
Jewel of Guidance on the Ocean
Hail to thee, thou new moon.
Jewel of Guidance of my love.

Then we are home.

Between Bride's Breasts is a green valley. The light there is gold. People have spent lifetimes trying to paint that light. They'd fill skies with it and place the earth-colored robes of saints before it. Or birds would fly there, delicate specks of darkness. Painters would take that gold and put it around his head and his mother's. But to me the light in the paintings looks too heavy and dead, gold cooled to metal, something you can take off and put on.

This light isn't like that, though I won't say it isn't heavy. Its heaviness is warmth and sweetness and languor. Living gold. It lives in that valley. You can taste this light. It's food, you see, and drink. You can feel it flow through the rivers of your arteries and veins. In the heart of the valley wells a pool. Nine hazelnut trees grow around it, bending their branches over it, dropping their wisdom-ripe nuts to the salmon swimming there. Five streams flow out from the pool into all the holy rivers of the world.

That is where I live now. I listen to the song of the stones—and the wind and the water and the stars. Years pass, if time passes at all in this place. I sit and gaze into the well of wisdom where I first saw my beloved across the worlds. Sometimes I catch glimpses of him still; sometimes I just look at the sky reflected in the water that leads the way into some unknown depth of earth.

One day I see the Temple of Jerusalem as if I am looking at it from the Mount of Olives. The Temple is burning. Soldiers swarm in the Kedron Valley and the air is full of wailing and smoke. At the same time, I see the soldiers storming the beach on Mona, the burning groves blackening the sky. And then I see Boudica standing alone, gazing at the end of her world.

"All temples fall, Maeve," my beloved says.

Wild roses overrunning Temple Magdalen, a stork taking flight from the last pillar of the Temple of Artemis.

Then I see him, walking through a field, flinging seeds into the sky, letting them fall where they will, among stones and thorns, onto soft earth, into cracks of the sky, the cracks of parched lips.

Slowly I get to my feet, bare feet, the most beautiful feet I have ever seen, surely the feet of a goddess. I admire them for a moment.

Then I look into the well again; it gives back the gold of the sky, the gold of the tree whose leaves shine with their own light, the gold of our daughter's eyes. He is waiting for me there. His hand is open. The way is open.

With my beautiful feet, I step into the water.

EPILOGUE

All temples fall, all temples fall.

It's all in the hazelnut
the fire in your head

it's all in the mustard seed
flying from your hand.

All temples fall, children, all temples fall.

Seeds grow in the night
no one knows how

the trees fill the heavens
the birds crowd the bough.

All temples fall, sisters, all temples fall.

The dead take the field
at the end of every fight

from the last ruined column
a stork takes flight.

All temples fall, brothers, all temples fall.

The roses grow wild
where lovers lingered late

and black smoke billows
from the beautiful gate.

All temples fall, beloved, all temples fall.

Deep in the hazelnut
the fire still burns

and the mustard seeds rise
on the wings of the birds.

All temples fall, all temples fall.

ACKNOWLEDGMENTS

I WOULD LIKE to thank my martial arts teacher, Hawksbrother, for his keen insight into the character of Gaius Suetonius Paulinus. I also have Hawksbrother to thank for Maeve and Suetonius's love affair, their penchant for shape-shifting, and their parallel quests for long-lost children. Without these key plot elements, the story would have been much less complex.

Thanks to my dear friend and fellow writer, Cait Johnson, for her suggestion that Jesus and Suetonius could have been brethren in a literal, not just theological, sense. Thanks also for her steadfast encouragement.

I send gratitude and appreciation to Hilary Belden, my gracious hostess in England when I researched Boudica's story.

Jhenah Telyndru, author of *Avalon Within, a Sacred Journey of Myth, Mystery, and Inner Wisdom,* augmented her splendid book with additional consultations about where in Avalon events in the novel might have taken place. My thanks to this generous author.

Thanks to my sister-out-law, Debbie Stone, first reader and tireless proofreader of all my books. I can't imagine bringing a book to birth without her.

Thanks also to my *combrogo,* Tim Dillinger, whose journey with Maeve brought him to late-night proofing with Debbie and me as well as to the magnificent team at Monkfish. Thanks always to Paul Cohen, and to Georgia Dent, whose brilliant design illumines this book. And thanks to my steadfast agent, Deirdre Mullane.

And finally gratitude and love to my husband Douglas who is my ground.

SOURCE ACKNOWLEDGMENTS

Much of my research for the parts of the novel that take place on Mona dates to my writing of *Magdalen Rising*. My exploration of Celtic lore and literature began then.

Jhenah Telyndru's *Avalon Within* (aforementioned) was an excellent guide to the Glastonbury Tor and the surrounding sacred sites.

Boudica's story is well known, and there are several re-enactments of her final battle available on YouTube. The book I relied on most was *Boudica, The Life of Britain's Legendary Queen* by Vanessa Collingridge.

Like anyone writing about Boudica, I also read the accounts of the Roman historians Tacitus and Dio Cassius.

The hymn "Hail to thou new moon" and the blessing "Bride be taking charge of you in every strait" come from *Carmina Gadelica: Hymns and Incantations collected in the Highlands and Islands of Scotland in the Last Century* (really the 19th) by Alexander Carmichael. This work is now in the public domain.

ONSITE RESEARCH

During the writing of each of The Maeve Chronicles, I have been fortunate to be able to travel. For *Red-Robed Priestess*, I visited Iceni country in Norfolk as well as Colchester, London, and St Albans (Camulodunum, Londinium, and Verulamium), the sites her army razed. I also went to southern Britain and saw the ruins of the port town where Maeve and Suetonius would have come ashore. No one knows for certain where Boudica fought her last disastrous battle. Following the story line of a BBC program, I traveled to Mancetter, a small village near Atherstone in Warwickshire, where I wandered the countryside until I found a valley that matched Tacitus's description. Having walked there from the broad plain where Boudica's army might have assembled, I realized that she would not have been able to see the trap Suetonius had laid for her until it was too late. For a fuller account, please see "Boudica's Last Battlefield" on my website.

In addition to Hilary Belden, who provided me my home base in London, I would like to thank the following:

Bernard Penny of the Verulamium Museum for detailed information on items in the museum and for many entertaining stories about Roman times.

The Re-Enactor at Verulamium Museum for his dramatic presentation about the life of a Roman Soldier in the Fourteenth Legion.

Gerry and Angela Evans of Quarry Farm who pointed me the way to the footpath and on whose farm I found what I believe is Boudica's last battlefield.

The Reverend Canon Adrian Mairs who told me how to find the site of the fort where some of the Fourteenth Legion were stationed.

Donna Davis and Martin Silcock of the Blue Boar in Mancetter for helpful information, directions and the best breakfast ever.

John Grigsby of the Roman fort at Richborough who told me where Suetonius would have departed from and landed en route to his governorship in Britain.

In closing, I want to thank all my sources, literary and personal, on both sides of the Atlantic. Any historical, military, or geographical inaccuracies in *Red-Robed Priestess* are mine.

MAEVE

Who can say what we are to each other?
Who imagined whom?

You have called me forth
as much as, more than, I have you.

Your folly and bravery
are all I aspire to.

Do not forsake me
in the hard or beautiful time to come

though our daily work is done.